THE RED MEN

THE
RED MEN
Patrick McGinley

A
Joan
Kahn
BOOK
St. Martin's Press
New York

THE RED MEN. Copyright © 1987 by Patrick McGinley. All rights reserved. Printed
in the United States of America. No part of this book may be used or reproduced
in any manner whatsoever without written permission except in the case of brief
quotations embodied in critical articles or reviews. For information, address
St. Martin's Press, 175 Fifth Avenue, New York, N.Y. 10010.

Library of Congress Cataloging-in-Publication Data

McGinley, Patrick, 1937—
      The Red Men.
"A Joan Kahn book "
      I. Title.
PR6063.A21787R4   1987   823'.914   86-26293
ISBN 0-312-00180-0

First published in Great Britain by Jonathan Cape Ltd.

First U.S. Edition

10   9   8   7   6   5   4   3   2   1

To
Mary Kate

1

On the eve of his seventy-seventh birthday Gulban told his four sons that he wished to see them in his room at eleven the following morning.

'He's made a will at last, that's what it is,' said Joey, the youngest, as they waited outside his office. 'That sickly runt of a solicitor has been coming and going like a wasp after jam for the last fortnight.'

'Maybe he's throwing a surprise party,' said Cookie. 'And not one of us has bought a present.'

'He was never one for style and appearance,' said Father Bosco, the eldest son, who was curate in a seaside town forty miles away.

Jack, the second eldest and their father's favourite, said nothing.

'I hope he's made a will,' Joey went on. 'We've been waiting long enough, haven't we, Jack? The question is: will he leave the hotel, shop and farm to just one of us or will he divide the estate? The hotel to Jack, the farm to Cookie and the shop to me. I'd certainly settle for that. Father Bosco has given up his claim to the things that are Caesar's. All he can reasonably expect is the old man's blessing. What do you think, Jack?'

'I think you're a loud-mouth.'

'Jack's the favourite,' Joey said to Cookie. 'He can afford to play it cool. The youngest son has nothing to lose. By tradition he's reckless, radical and irresponsible. Is it possible that Gulban in his old age might prefer the spark of rebellion to the po-face of responsibility? Though he doesn't despise money, he's a despiser of bourgeois values.'

Gravelly voices raised in mutual congratulation made them turn to the affronting wood of the door. Mr Looby, the solicitor, emerged with a mahogany-coloured brief-case which bore the initials 'LJL' in italic on its side. He smiled at each of them in turn and glided smoothly but creakingly towards the lobby.

'That's a good sign,' said Cookie. 'We're all in business. If the estate were going to only one of us, he wouldn't have wasted a smile on the disinherited three.'

'It's possible that he's simply amiable and good-natured,' said Father Bosco.

'We know you're not allowed to think evil, Padre, but Cookie can and so can I. Jack never thinks evil. He prefers the half-way house of cynicism — second-hand wisdom heard at its loudest in the flea market.'

Gulban pulled open the heavy door.

'All present and correct?'

'All present and weak from waiting,' Joey replied.

They filed into their father's office and made for the four straight-backed chairs that had been placed in a row before his desk. Jack, like Gulban, was dark-haired and solid-looking. The other three were red-haired, light-boned and somewhat boyish, as if they belonged to a younger generation than Jack. Father Bosco sat upright, tall, spare and stiffly remote; Cookie sat sideways with a hint of unease and uncertainty; and Joey, looking fiery and fiercely critical, perched on the edge of the chair in a state of readiness for any battle of wits that might ensue.

Gulban went round behind the desk on which lay a ledger, a calculator and two ragged piles of invoices and statements. He turned and looked at his sons, then eased himself slowly into the leather-covered armchair. He was stocky and broad with a subsiding pot-belly that nestled beneath the high waistband of his trousers. Bristly, black hair darkened his ruddy face and sprouted in tufts from his ears and nostrils and from under his open shirt collar.

'If hair makes a man,' thought Joey, 'Gulban is super-man.'

'Today is the longest day of the year,' their father began. 'Today I'm seventy-seven, and though I'm still in good nick, a long day's work takes more out of me now than it used to. The truth must be faced: I won't be around for ever. One of you must take over from me, and must do not just well but better. I've thought of a plan which Looby describes as "irregular". He overstayed his time trying to persuade me to make it "regular". He has known me for years. He should have known better than to try to make me change my mind.'

The four sons listened with arms folded. Joey's eye was fixed on a little tuft of black hair on the tip of his father's nose. Cookie was concentrating on the toecaps of his shoes beneath the desk. Jack was staring at the pile of invoices and Father Bosco was gazing upwards at the white cornice of the ceiling. Though the windows were open, the air in the room was still.

'We Herons have a proud and courageous history. Your great-grandfather had four sons: Owen, Andy, Conall and Den. Times were hard on this headland then. When the old man died, they sold the place and took the boat to America to set up as pedlars in the Midwest. They were strong, good-looking men. Soon their fame spread before them, not just in their wake. They lived by their cunning, they never carried a gun. They were known as the Red Men because of their ginger hair.'

Joey stifled a yawn and glanced at Jack who was listening as though he'd never heard a word of this tired old litany before.

'Owen and Andy were killed in a train crash, and when Den died of consumption, Conall packed his bags and came home. He bought a little shop below in the village. It was only a huckster's, but with skill and graft he made it into a paying concern. Like me he got married late. I was the only son, I inherited before I had turned eighteen. As you know, I didn't rest on the family laurels. I made the shop into the best store in the barony. When I was forty-two, the worst was over. I found time to get married and the four of you were born.'

'Tell us more about the Red Men, Father.' Cookie mimicked the smile of a child demanding a favourite bedtime story. His father continued as if he had not heard.

'While you were only youngsters, I bought this hotel. It was then called Matlock House. I could have called it Heron House. Instead I renamed it House of Heron, because I wanted people to see not just stone and mortar but the family and its head as well.'

'Were you thinking of the House of Atreus, Father?' Cookie gave a side-glance at Joey.

'Never heard of it. My education was less expensive than yours.'

'He was thinking of the House of Rothschild,' Joey suggested.

The other two brothers kept silent. Father Bosco seemed to be praying for patience, while Jack looked as serene as if the Lord, in answering the priest's prayer, had confused one of them with the other.

'The hotel is what gives us Herons our position and reputation. Without it we'd be village shopkeepers. Yet the shop, as your grandfather might say, is our pork barrel. What we make there, we spend here. And that, my sons, is not what I call business.'

'It's what the preacher calls *vanitas vanitatum*,' Cookie smiled. 'Don't you agree, Father Bosco?'

'Intellectual vanity is worst of all,' said the priest.

'It costs less,' said Joey.

'It costs nothing,' Cookie emphasised.

'The foundations I've laid are solid,' Gulban continued. 'They'll bear a lot of extra weight. The business must grow. The hotel must be made to pay its way. Whoever inherits will have his work cut out. What we need is imagination and the courage of the Red Men.'

'The Red Men are dead,' said Joey.

'Now you four are the Red Men. What I seek from each of you is proof that you are worthy of the name. Jack, like me, is dark-haired, but he is more industrious than all the Red Men put together. Has he got their business brains? We must find out. The rest of you have the hair of the Red Men, but have you got their practical intelligence? That's something else I must find out, and until I do I shall continue to keep an open mind.'

In the vastness of the outside day a cuckoo called twice and stopped abruptly. Silence smote the immobile air. Joey and Cookie turned to the open window. Jack and Father Bosco looked frozen in their separate responsibilities. The cuckoo called again, unwinding the stricture of tension in the room.

'Looby wanted me to appoint one of you as my heir today, but I've decided that each of you must feel that he's had a sporting chance. The lucky man will take over from me on my next birthday.'

'I don't know why you wanted me here,' Father Bosco said.

'You may have left us for what you say are higher things. You're still my son, though. You must be in with a chance like the others. Whether you take it or leave it is up to you.'

He lifted his blotter and uncovered four brown envelopes with a name in pencil on each of them. Then he handed them out across the desk, the first to Father Bosco, the second to Jack, the third to Cookie and the last to Joey.

'No need to open them now. Each contains a cheque drawn on my account. Each of you has got the sum I think he deserves. You can do with it what you like. You can squander it or invest it, you can even put it away in a stocking. We'll meet again in this room on my next birthday. You'll present your accounts and I'll declare the winner.'

'It's a foolish and wayward thing to do,' said Father Bosco. 'It will only lead to rivalry and disappointment. It may even lead to dishonesty.'

'It's meant to bring out the best in you,' said his father.

'Will we have to return the money and what it's earned?' Jack spoke for the first time.

'No, the principal and the interest, if that's how you look at it, will be yours.'

'Will the man who shows the biggest increase win?' Jack pursued.

'No, that would be taking too narrow a view.'

'Will the man who shows the smallest increase win?' Cookie asked.

'That might favour you, I know. It would nevertheless be irresponsible.'

'How are we to know what to do?' Jack asked.

'It would be easy if I said, "Turn each pound into three." You must think for yourselves, as if I were dead. One man will invest with caution and earn a modest dividend. Another will invest boldly and perhaps make a killing. A third may use the money for self-indulgence. The fourth may use it to create something new.'

'Give us an example,' said Joey.

'You're interested in science. You might invent a new valve for lavatory cisterns to replace the ballcock, which is even older than me and a great deal rustier.'

Cookie gave a nervous laugh and Jack looked genuinely puzzled.

'Do something daring, something only you would think of. Ask yourselves, "If one of the Red Men got his horny hand on this cheque, what would be his first thought?" All I'm trying to discover is which of you has the true genius of the Herons.'

'I can't accept money for such a purpose,' Father Bosco said. 'I don't believe that money is the measure of all things.'

'Then give it to the poor,' said his father. 'If they

haven't changed, they won't be too squeamish to accept.'

'Supposing Father Bosco gives his share to a tramp, will he still be in the running?' Jack asked.

'Of course he will. Isn't that the beauty of it?'

'It's not possible to weigh such different uses one against the other,' Joey told him.

'It is for me. At my age the mind is no longer cluttered. Everything is crystal clear. Any further questions?'

When no one replied, Gulban got up from his chair and said, 'Cookie, you're our Tennyson and our Gibbon rolled into one. When you come to write the history of the Red Men, I want my seventy-seventh birthday to be known as the Day of the Talents.'

Cookie guffawed with reckless incredulity. Joey touched Father Bosco's sleeve and whispered, 'Now you know where you are. With your knowledge of scripture, you're bound to have a head start on Jack.'

They trooped out of the room looking sheepishly at one another, as the oak door closed behind them.

'Day of the Talents, my foot,' spat Jack. 'It's the Year of the Talents — all three hundred and sixty-six days of it.'

He stuffed the brown envelope in his hip-pocket and made straight for the stairs and his bedroom.

'Are you staying to lunch?' Cookie asked Father Bosco.

'I never eat lunch except at weekends, only breakfast and a light dinner.'

'I hope they're hot dinners,' said Joey.

'Hot in winter, cold in summer.'

'How you must hate the summer, the cuckoo, house martins and bikinis on beaches. How you must look forward to the arrival of the barnacle goose.' Joey looked up at his brother's high, bald forehead.

'Come on, Bosco, let's have a drink at least,' Cookie smiled.

'I've got to get back. He brought me here under false pretences.'

Cookie and Joey walked with him to the car park by the

side entrance. He was straight in the back and thin about the shoulders. If he were even one inch shorter, he wouldn't look so utterly alone in the world, Cookie told himself.

'Do you think he's sane?' He turned to the priest.

'I don't think he's wise. For a start he's being unfair to Jack. He's the only businessman among us. He could run a chain of hotels and still find time — '

'For women?' Joey suggested.

Ignoring him, Father Bosco got into his Fiat, a possession of which he was inordinately proud. He loved the dry sound of the engine starting on frosty mornings. He would tell his parishioners that there was no better car on hills, and when driving alone, he would often say aloud, 'Come on now, Sally, that's the girl.'

'You mustn't over-indulge in humility, Father Bosco,' Joey smiled. 'You have as much right as Jack to call yourself a Red Man. You run a red car and you're closer to a red hat than Jack will ever be, even allowing for disappointment in love and a late, late vocation.'

'Some things are sacred, Joey, which is just as well. If there was nothing sacred, there would be no sacrilege and you would lack an occupation.'

He turned the key in the ignition. The engine fired at once, and with a formal wave he shot through the gate, narrowly missing a stray ram.

'He almost made soup,' Joey laughed.

'Even if he had, he's in too much of a hurry to eat it. I'm surprised he doesn't get ulcers.'

'Our Father Chrome-Dome is almost as serious as Brother Jack.'

'You shouldn't make fun of him. As a priest, he's got to turn the other cheek.'

'I wasn't making fun. I'll bet any money he'll be a cardinal before you're a professor. He's only thirty-three and he looks like a Prince of the Church already. He's even going bald in precisely the right place, and he combs back what's left in case you should miss the apostolic forehead. If it had a lantern and a cross on top, it might have been designed by Michelangelo.'

'He's a man of simple pleasures, is our brother. What he likes best is tearing from here to town in forty-five minutes. He's right about Jack, though. He's been slaving here since he was sixteen. If industry is to be rewarded, he should get it.'

'He will get it,' said Joey. 'All this talk about talents is a cod, Gulban taking the mickey and keeping Jack on tenterhooks for another twelvemonth.'

He pulled the envelope from his pocket and shook it.

'You don't seem to be in any hurry to open yours,' he said to Cookie. 'Perhaps we should open them in secret.'

'Jack went to his room to open his.'

'He's so serious about everything: the hotel, the shop, the farm and his middle-aged women. He can't get enough work and he can't get enough sex. What's to become of him?'

'Is he serious about Pauline?' Cookie glanced quickly at Joey. The scar on the left side of his brother's face screamed at the easeful day. Cookie looked down at the loose gravel of the driveway and prodded a pebble with his shoe.

They stood on the steps of the front entrance facing the torque-shaped village among the flat fields below. The hotel was built on a rise overlooking the sea to the north and west. In front was a straight, blue-metalled road, beyond which rose a long hill that sagged in the middle with one white cottage at its foot. The road ran westwards down to the village, and after a U-turn back eastwards round the other side of the hill.

South of the village stood a white, flat-roofed house set in an acre of ground surrounded by a high red brick wall. From the village you could not see the house because of the wall, but you could see both house and grounds from the hotel, dainty and symmetrical and somehow pathetic in their isolation. The house had been built by a landscape painter called Bugler and was now the home of his middle-aged widow and only daughter Alicia. A school-master who was in the habit of visiting Mrs Bugler christened it Fort Knox, and the name stuck. Like the hotel itself, it was an alien object in an austere landscape of fenced fields and open sheep pasture where winter gales ensured that only the hardiest trees survived. Today, however, there was hardly a breath of air. The whole headland lay serenely in a kind of sensual contemplation of the sky, the sea and the haze on the horizon in between.

Joey said that he was going down to the shop. Cookie entered the hotel's glass-roofed porch which Pauline had turned into a greenhouse of exotic-looking plants in earthenware pots. A Frenchman and his wife were asking the receptionist why there was no mutton on the menu though the hills around were white with sheep. Cookie smiled and escaped upstairs to his narrow bedroom at the back.

He slit open the brown envelope with his penknife and sat on the edge of the single bed. The cheque, made out in his father's hand and carefully crossed 'Account payee only', was for £10,000. It was more than he'd expected; large enough to be taken seriously, yet not so large as to demand to be taken solemnly. It would be foolish to compete with Jack, though. Better to treat the money as a windfall, use it only for convenience and pleasure. He could buy a sports car like Jack's and still have enough left over to cut a dash at weekends till he landed a job. With a car he would be able to enjoy the summer and perhaps find a summery girl to share his enjoyment.

He raised the lower sash and placed *Clarissa, Or the History of a Young Lady* underneath for support. The room was lined with books, and on a little table in one corner lay his Ph.D. thesis on the idea of seduction as extended metaphor in the works of Samuel Richardson. The window faced north. He looked down on a bumpy stretch of brown moorland with a black coastline and a lazy green sea beyond. There was not a house, road or tree to alleviate the inhospitable bleakness of the scene. Gulban and Pauline had their rooms in the front. Pauline's was the best. She had the large corner room with a south window facing the river and the mountain, and a west window looking out on the island, the lighthouse and the widening bay.

2

She glided silently from the mirror to the window, as if reluctant to end a protracted dream. A man with a dog was gathering sheep on the hill. The dog herded the sheep into a corner between two dry-stone walls, then waited till the man came up. One of the sheep broke loose and the dog pursued, going wide in a semicircle at full stretch, while the man kept the rest together with a wave of his stick. The sheep slithered to a stop when it saw the dog in front, and the man watched without a movement as the dog brought back the straggler to the flock.

She returned to the mirror and tied a lavender ribbon in her hair. After a warm day in the stuffy back office poring over accounts, checking invoices and statements, and making out the cheques which Gulban would sign before bedtime, her mind was a whirligig, unable to think. Now the cool, leisurely evening lay ahead. Already it had taken possession of both land and sea. The whole promontory and the wider bay were suffused with a golden brightness that had invaded her bedroom, flinging a thousand stippled reflections on the cream-coloured walls.

A double knock made her turn to the door. 'Pauline!'

'Just give me five minutes, Jack. I'm almost ready.'

'I'll wait for you in the car.'

That morning Gulban had spoken. At last he had admitted that he did not expect to go on for ever.

'This calls for a celebration,' Jack told her afterwards. 'This evening we'll go to town and have dinner in the Atlantic Grill.'

She had watched the brothers waiting like schoolboys outside Gulban's office. He loved to keep them dangling, and Cookie and Joey made jokes to conceal from themselves the knowledge that they depended on him. Surely, it was all a sham, the pretence that Bosco, Cookie and Joey had a chance. On their own they seemed sound enough, but in Jack's company they looked alien and unassimilated, as if they dyed their hair red. They lived on the periphery. They would never change a particle of the world because they did not believe in the world. Yet, they considered themselves a cut above Jack who had slaved for his father since he was sixteen, while the pampered three had been sent to boarding school 'to have the corners knocked off them', as Gulban had put it.

Jack was thirty, nearly four years older than her. Unlike the others, he was serious, strong-minded and self-reliant. Everyone said that he was the only one of them who had inherited Gulban's doggedness and drive. If he had a fault, it was his uncritical response to Gulban, which had kept him treading water at the hotel while other men of his age had already settled down with a clear goal to pursue.

From the window she watched a red Mini leave the village for Fort Knox. It skimmed the surface of the narrow road, a light aircraft gathering speed for take-off, then vanished through the gate, only to reappear between the low bushes on either side of the driveway beyond. The house, the grounds and the high surrounding wall were the dream of a man who could not bear to live in the glasshouse his wife inhabited. As the car pulled up and the driver got out, Pauline herself lived for a moment on the edge of a dream that threatened to curdle into nightmare. She saw Mrs Bugler in the hotel lounge rising from her chair and turning to inspect the empty seat. The memory was sharp and unsettling: the impulsiveness of the getting up, the condescending backward glance, and then the affectation of the turning away, conveying to the irreverent observer that life was altogether predictable, that, at least for her, there was never any real need to glance backwards.

Mr Bugler had been a quiet, civilised man who found life and Mrs Bugler more than he could cope with. The Sunday before his final breakdown he went to church in his pyjamas. Few thought it strange. Some concluded that it must be the new fashion. Flanagan, the schoolmaster, had said that 'Knox' should be spelt 'Nox' because the fame of the house had little to do with anything that happened there during the day.

Jack was waiting for her in the lobby, having parked his gleaming sports car at the front entrance. They nosed out between the white piers of the concealed gateway. As they picked up speed on the straight road, she visualised a sea bird flying over a smooth expanse of water.

'What did he really say?' she asked.

'Just what I told you.'

'You're no good at reporting. Tell me everything. I want to hear his exact words.'

He recounted what his father had said that morning, without mentioning Father Bosco, Cookie or Joey.

'And you say that's cause for celebration! It's a bit thick if you ask me. After keeping you dangling for ten years without even paying you a proper salary. He treats me better than he does you.'

'What he said this morning was a declaration of intent.'

'It's hardly a declaration, only a suggestion.'

'Everything will be resolved. Within a year all the uncertainty will come to an end.'

'You should have demanded to know what he's up to.'

'I had a word with him in private after the others left. He's nobody's fool. Everything he does is for a sound business reason. He takes the view that nothing should come to a man either too early or too easily. He said that he did not expect me to understand, that all would become clear only a twelvemonth from today.'

'You read that to mean that you'll inherit.'

'There's no one else. Any other reading is out of the question.'

'I don't understand you. You're hard as rock with everyone else, but when it comes to Gulban — '

'The day was long enough. Let's put it behind us and enjoy the evening.'

She sensed a note of annoyance in his voice. Though forthright himself, from her he preferred obliquity.

The road ahead ran through a cutting with a narrow drain on either side, the smooth-worn surface concealing little undulations that kept them jouncing ever so slightly as they sped along. She stared out over the bonnet, bound by the cutting and his deliberate silence. The warm day was somewhere behind, the best of the evening was yet to come. She should have been serenely happy, relaxing in the release from paperwork. Instead she had an uneasy sense of diminishment, as if the choices made for her far outnumbered those she had made herself. They emerged from the cutting into a basin of greenish-brown moorland with a glinting lough and an angler in grey waders knee-deep among reeds.

'It's too early to eat,' he said. 'We might stop at the Spoke and Felly for a drink. I like the landlord. He's a Dubliner called Forker, and the best bridge-player in the county.'

'Does Mrs Bugler go there?'

'Now and again.'

'Tell me something, Jack. Do you go to Fort Knox for Mrs Bugler's company or Alicia's?'

'I go for the bridge. There's Forker, Flanagan, Mrs Bugler and myself.'

'Lucky Mrs Bugler.'

'As a player, she's less than brilliant.'

'I want you to promise me something. If she comes into Forker's, say we're in a hurry. Don't mention the Atlantic Grill in case we end up in a threesome — or worse.'

'I can tell you don't like her.'

'I'm too young to remember her as a woman. What I see now is a monster.'

'Forker says that in her middle age she's midway to being a man.'

The Spoke and Felly was set on a slope among trees overlooking a glen with a stony river. The low sunlight struck through the open door, sharpening the tiles of the hallway and the faded green of the skirting beyond. There was no one in the bar, so they waited on high stools before an altar of old-fashioned shelves, empty except for a row of upturned glasses. On one wall was a cream-coloured tray with the likeness of a mallard so perfect in its plumage that you could not imagine it alive and quacking, and on the opposite wall was a handwritten notice which said, 'Please don't ask for champagne. We don't stock it.'

The sense of time passing in a motionless world made her slightly dizzy. Jack placed his watch on the counter and counted the revolutions of the wheel inside the black meter above the window.

'Twelve to the minute,' he said. 'He's using electricity, but not a lot.'

A short, fat man waddled in from the back and shook hands with them both. As he joked with Jack, his breath exploded in little puffs from between tight lips and fine perspiration laminated his pale forehead. He looked distinctly vulnerable, the picture of mortal humanity faint from overeating and overexertion, and he quickly filled the small bar with a damp, sharp smell more appropriate to a rainy day.

Jack ordered sherry for Pauline and whiskey for himself. Forker coughed and seemed to lose his breath, then ran his hand across his forehead to arrest a trickle of sweat before it had time to enter his left eyebrow.

'Would you believe it?' he smiled. 'There isn't a drink on the premises. I've been waiting for a delivery for the past month; but don't worry, I'll nip down to the village for a bottle this minute. It would be simpler if we could all settle for the same drink. I shall be having a drop myself, of course. There's tenpence off Bell's in the supermarket till Saturday.'

He looked at Pauline who didn't seem in the least impressed with his show of initiative.

'I've got a bottle of Scotch in the car,' said Jack. 'We'll all drink that. I'm sure Pauline won't mind.'

While Jack went to the car, Forker laid out three glasses, a jug of water, and a bottle of milk on the counter. He poured two large measures of the Scotch for Pauline and Jack and an even larger one for himself, which he whitened with a splash of milk from the bottle.

'The Scotch is for my nerves, the milk for my ulcer,' he explained.

The two men discussed bridge while Pauline stood by the window gazing down the slope to the stony river below the trees. Jack looked flushed and elated when at last he said goodbye to Forker. He drove quickly and aggressively, telling stories about Forker's drunkenness and fecklessness, while she studied the swarthy hills to the right and left. They turned a corner above a wide bay with a rocky island close to the shore and a row of seagulls perched on its jagged crest.

'There isn't a soul on the beach,' she said. 'Let's stop and go down for a walk.' The urgency of the words surprised her. It was her way of saying, 'Let's stop the evening and start again from a new and better place.'

The sand at the upper end of the beach was coarse, silvery and soft. Along the water's edge it was finer and firmer, and darker too. A single seagull rose ahead of them screaming at the sun. They skirted clumps of strong-smelling wrack, thick with sandhoppers, and a complex network of canals which could only have been dug by a boy who was already an engineer. They came to a rocky spit with a high stone wall running down to the edge of the beach. They climbed up the slope in its shadow, which reminded her of the lengthening shadow of Fort Knox as the sun went down behind the sea cliffs. Round the corner was another wall and a rusty gate with a stile of jutting stones beside it.

'I never knew there was a graveyard here,' she said.

'It's no longer in use, except by courting couples in search of sanctuary. You can see it's old. There are no crosses, only plain rectangular headstones.'

They walked between the graves, reading lapidary inscriptions: *Edith Ann Hudson, died 1761*; *David Rammage, died 1902*; *William Tremayne, died 1779*. The mossy headstones leant this way and that: some forwards, some backwards, and one or two sideways in the attitude of a headless man with one high shoulder. In the corner at the far end, blown sand had partly covered a limestone slab, obscuring the worn inscription. As she removed the sand with her hand, he leant against the wall and lit a cigarette.

'It's a foreign name,' she told him. ' "Giacomo" is all I can make out.'

'Foreigner or native, he's a sitting tenant. I don't think he need have any fear of eviction.'

'Do you ever feel that you'd like to be away?' she asked.

'We are away. Gulban and the hotel are in a different parish.'

'I meant away, away.'

'No, I've never wanted to be away, away. This is far enough away for me.'

A cuckoo called behind them. They both looked over the wall and listened. She called four times in succession, pausing between calls to imprison the air in a cupola of mysterious clarity. They looked all round, she sounded so tantalisingly near.

'The best of a summer day, I always think, is hearing the cuckoo in late evening,' Pauline said.

'Seeing is better than hearing. I should have brought my new binoculars.'

'I want to hear her one more time. If she calls again, I shall never forget this evening.'

'We'll walk back now,' he said after a silence.

'I'd like to come again some time.'

'We could bring a packed lunch and make a day of it.'

'I often think men are brutes.'

'Not all men,' he smiled. 'Only those that are brutal.'

With a laugh he helped her down from the stile, then kissed her precisely on the mouth, as if to prove a theorem. *Quod erat demonstrandum.* Q.E.D. Quite Easily Done, as Cookie would have it. She paused to look at three seagulls on a rock, two white-breasted adults with their greyish-brown offspring crouching between them. The adults rose effortlessly into the breeze, wheeling out wide over the flat water. The youngster screamed for them, lowering its head and raising its beak to the sky with an ugly swelling of the neck. Its thin, reedy shriek split the air, piercing her through and through with intimations of loss and discord. The parents returned and the young one approached them gingerly on tender feet.

'It's the youngster that looks old,' she said. 'It's walking like Gulban, with just that hint of care.'

'You must have keen sight to notice that. I should have brought my binoculars. In future I must keep them in the car.'

He was silent for the remainder of the journey. She turned her head so that the breeze brushed back her hair, and she thought of summer twilight in a cool room with a pendulum clock ticking precisely and time passing imperceptibly.

'She'll never get anywhere with Jack, he's too fond of women,' one of the waitresses had said last week when she wasn't meant to be listening. She herself knew that she wouldn't get anywhere with Jack, and she also knew that somehow it didn't matter.

The Atlantic Grill was a circus of clattering plates, bustling waitresses and noisy conversation. They waited half an hour for the hors-d'oeuvre, and they had finished a bottle of wine before the main course arrived — the meat first, followed five minutes later by the vegetables. Jack, relaxed and happy after the Scotch and the wine, began telling her about his plans for the hotel.

'It's a stuffy old crypt,' he said. 'On my first day I shall open one window and let in a little eddy of fresh air.'

'Gulban may close it again.'

'Not if he sees profit in fresh air.'

'Your brothers may have something to say as well.'

' "Say" is the word. They're only talkers, less interested in profit than in an audience. Joey lectures us on science, Cookie on literature, and Father Bosco on God. Of the three, Bosco makes most sense. Now, he could run a business if only he wasn't so obsessed with things that money can't buy.'

'Have you ever thought about why he became a priest? Growing up, he was more devilish than any of you.'

'He grew up too quickly. He had exhausted us all before he was fourteen.'

'It's a lonely life being a priest. Maybe it was the extra loneliness that attracted him.'

'Marriage is the only certain cure for loneliness. Pauline, we'll get married. We've been courting long enough.'

He reached across the table and locked her fine-boned wrist in the vice of his forefinger and thumb.

'It isn't a good enough reason to get married,' she smiled.

'I'm serious. I've thought of nothing else since Gulban showed his hand this morning. We've been wasting valuable time. I'll say it again, and I'll say it properly. Pauline, will you marry me?'

'It's all a bit sudden. I'd like time to think.'

'How much time?'

'A week.'

'I know what you're up to. You're going to do a novena, God preserve me.'

'A novena takes nine days, not seven. No, I'm just going to think it over, and I want you to be sober when I give my answer.'

Jack responded by ordering another bottle of wine.

'Why are you intent on getting drunk this evening? It's not like you,' she said.

'I feel like letting rip. Ah, Pauline, we'll shake the old lodge into rambunctious life. A wind will tear through the door and blow the cobwebs out the windows.'

'Don't count your chickens. Remember Joey, Cookie and Father Bosco. They may be celebrating too.'

He was gazing down into his wine glass, his high, heavy head bent in an attitude of butting. It was a powerful head with little flesh to cover the jagged bone structure. It made her think of flint-stone beneath a coat of moss, hard to the touch and deceptively soft to look at.

'They're all knots to be undone, and the tightest knot, the closest to my throat, is Gulban. He's holding me back, he knows it himself. Nothing has changed in our family since Mother died twenty years ago. Even Sunday lunch is always shoulder of mutton. We never have fish, because he doesn't like fish. And when he says that he wouldn't eat salmon or lobster if his life depended on it, he gives the impression that anyone who would is morally deficient. He knows only one way of life — his own. It's as well that I'm not dependent on him. You and I could make a go of it anywhere. In many ways the best thing we could do is start a new life away from his curmudgeonly niggling.'

'I said I'd give you my answer within a week. You'd be foolish to leave now, though. Another year won't kill you.'

'If you do say "yes", I'd like to take you to America for our honeymoon.'

'It isn't as romantic as Italy.' She tried to tease him.

'We won't go to New York or Hollywood. We'll take a train to Chicago, Peoria, Kansas City and Des Moines.'

'They don't attract me.'

'They're the cities of the Red Men. Gulban made them live in the bedtime stories he told us when we were small. For that at least he deserves my thanks. So let's drink to the Red Men. For me they weren't just ancestors, they were heroes.'

3

With drums and guns, and guns and drums,
The enemy nearly slew ye,
My darling dear, you look so queer,
Och, Johnny, I hardly knew ye.

His dark baritone rose above the purr of the engine on
the level road, her father's song but not her father's voice.
He was only forty when he died, and she was then only
nine. The loss was the first touch of an icy tide that had not
ceased to flow, and it denied her the university education
that would have been hers had he lived. She was left with
her mother in genteel poverty, outside life, looking in
through the windows of the House of Heron. For the past
eight years she had slaved for Gulban, inside at last but
not an insider. Now everything would change. It was a
dream she could hardly admit to having dreamt.

A drooping branch scraped the wing of the car.

'Jack,' she shouted. 'Keep out of the ditch.'

'It's not the wine. I'm tired after the work and the day.'

'Pull in here. You can have a nap while I drive.'

'What I need is a walk to wake me up. We'll go down to
the beach again. We should be there inside five minutes.'

The tide had come in since they left. Under the half-
moon the beach was a narrow strip of grey with shaggy
clumps of bent-grass at the upper end. Ahead, the rocky
spit and the dark graveyard wall ran down into the water,
which looked shallow, flat and pale.

He led her into the shadow of the graveyard wall and

kissed her on the mouth and neck, then on the mouth again. His kissing was quiet and insistent, pulling slowly at the tides of memory within her, awakening associations, in a landscape of dream. She was caught between the rough stonework of the wall and the jagged bone of his body. For reassurance she sought the flesh inside his shirt, kneading with her fingers the unyielding muscle along his spine. She was standing, not in the shadow of a wall, but in the lee of an erratic tor that rose solitary and unreconciled out of a flat, unknowable terrain.

They made love where they stood, and all the time her mind was a windhover scanning an ebbing tide that sighed as it retreated and moaned among rocks as it sought unavailingly to return. She was not free; like the tide she moved within constraints that seemed alien, mechanical and inexorable. She felt entrapped by a grapple of arbitrary memories: the discordant scream of the seagull, Mrs Bugler turning to inspect her empty seat, the cuckoo that failed to call again. She told herself that it was not his fault that the evening had been, for her, a barefoot walk over sharp stones.

'We should have done that before. It was a lovely end to a special evening.' He hugged her again.

'It was my answer to your question.'

'Then I should have asked it long ago.' With his arms round her waist, he lifted her clean off the ground. 'It's only the beginning,' he said. 'We'll go from strength to strength, the two of us. We'll have a swim now to wake us up for the road.'

'The water will be icy.'

'That's just it.' He pulled off his unbuttoned shirt.

'You go in. I'll sit here on a rock and wait.'

First she listened to his splashing. Then he passed the sandy shelf where the waves curled and broke, and he waded out into the smooth water beyond, with faint moonlight on one shoulder. The night was full of sea sounds and wafted perfumes that came and went between the irregular slapping and gurgling. Now he was swimming away from the shore, a black head turning between glinting arms and elbows. He seemed determined to leave land and life behind. She began to feel the edge of the breeze on her neck. Then he turned and propelled himself backwards to the shore with splashing feet. He rose out of the sea, a dark animal between two elements, neither of which was his own. She turned towards the eastern sky. She wanted the sun to come up that minute and the dawn light to dance on his dripping skin. She wanted morning to be hard and clear, without muted edges or colours that merged in deceptive ambiguity. She wished for clarity and definition, because clarity and definition was what a life with Jack would mean.

He dried himself with his underpants and put on his shirt and trousers.

'It was like ice. Better than the coldest of cold showers. 'I'll be all right now, wait and see.'

'What will Gulban say when he hears we're to be married?' she asked.

'He'll be pleased. He has a high opinion of you, though it would choke him to admit it. Gulban wouldn't admit to having a high opinion of anyone.'

When they got back to the car, he put his wet underpants in the glove compartment, and she sat beside him with her cardigan round her shoulders. A rain forest of cloud had sprung up before them in the west, and in the south a yellowy haze had melted the rim of the moon.

He drove slowly and in silence, while she thought of Gulban whom her mother used to call Gull, but only when they were alone. Gull was not an abbreviation of Gulban, the name Joey gave him as a baby after he'd heard Bosco jokingly refer to his father as Gulbenkian. Neither was it meant to denote a man who is easily deceived. Her mother called him Gull because she saw him as the living embodiment of greed. 'Nothing will satisfy him,' she would say. 'He hasn't one appetite that isn't insatiable.'

After Pauline's father died, Gulban began visiting her mother in the evenings. Her mother was still good-looking then, and Gulban may have seen her as the residue of a talented man's estate, what her mother once called 'an acquisition to flaunt before the congregation on Sundays'. Her husband had been dead only two months when Gulban proposed to her. She was a far-sighted woman who didn't say yes and didn't say no, but many years later she told Pauline that even if her eternal salvation depended on it, she'd never forgive him for being so insensitive. Pauline suspected that she must have feared him. For all Pauline knew, she may have given him oblique encouragement, because his visits continued for another five years.

He would drop in after supper and sit in her father's low armchair while her mother played the piano, or he would take Pauline on his knee and give her mental arithmetic, because, he said, 'a girl who can add and subtract quickly will never put a foot wrong that she can't put right again'. When she was fourteen, he told her mother that he would pay for her education.

'She's so bright that she should be given a chance,' he said. 'She's so bright that half a chance will be enough.'

His ploy may have been transparent, but her mother expressed her pleasure with a smile, and she told Pauline to give him a big hug which she dutifully did. The boarding school he chose was the cheapest he could find after a search that took so long that the Michaelmas term was already three weeks old when she started. The older girls giggled when they saw her uniform which had been bought second-hand by Gulban and was two sizes too big for her.

'She's about to make her growth,' he had told her mother. 'She'll grow into it before Christmas.'

When he'd gone, her mother remarked that it was a pity

his generosity had been compromised by parsimony, and that they must not hold it against him because counting pennies was second nature to him. Such generosity had been a great sacrifice for so careful a man, not least because it was to remain a secret between the three of them.

Uncertainty pursued her throughout her schooldays. Her mother would remind her to smile whenever he spoke to her, though Pauline was by then old enough to sense that it was her mother's smiles that mattered. When she was in her fourth year, his visits stopped, and the following summer he told her mother that he could not see his way to pay for her final year. Pauline was heart-broken. She was a keen pupil with academic ambitions. Overnight the future she had confidently imagined for herself had become a pipe-dream. By then her mother's health had begun to fail. Pauline stayed at home to look after her, and was soon to discover that whatever money her father had left had gone. When Gulban offered her a job as a receptionist at the hotel, she was only too pleased to accept. She worked hard, and she tried not to bear him a grudge. When he —

'Christ!' Jack cried, as they turned a corner.

He braked sharply, and they skidded towards a sleepy-looking sheep that had been lying in the middle of the road. He steered this way and that. There was a sickening thump.

'Stupid animal,' he said, reversing.

They were in the cutting with a high bank on each side. He got out and dragged the sheep by the hind legs to the grass verge, before pushing it over the edge into the drain. The broken streak of blood glinting in the headlights made her feel slightly sick.

'Damn,' he said, 'the wing is dented.'

'And the sheep is dead,' she reminded him.

'Are you all right?' He climbed back into the car without opening the door.

'I think you'd better let me drive.'

'It wasn't my fault.'

'You came into the bend too quickly.'

'There was nothing I could do. She was lying right in my path. Only quick thinking kept us out of the drain.'

'Be reasonable, Jack. You've had too much to drink. You're tired. We've had a narrow escape, so don't let's tempt providence again.'

'Look who's talking! You've had as much wine as I've had.'

'I had only half a glass from the second bottle.'

'Are you sure?'

'Yes.'

'Perhaps you'd better drive, then. If we're stopped, you'll have a better chance of cheating the breathalyser. But be careful. We mustn't kill any more sheep. Sheep are harmless, even if they are stupid. They shouldn't be killed except for gigot, rib or loin chops.'

'Jack!'

They changed places and she put on her cardigan because she had become aware of a dampness in the air. She liked driving his new sports car. It was low on the road. It cleared hills like a bird and held well on corners. It was solid and reliable, and perhaps a bit predictable, like Jack himself. In the lower end of a valley they ran into a patch of fog which was gone in a minute. The icy indifference of its touch made her shiver, and she remembered Jack dragging the dead sheep with one hand.

'We won't bother getting engaged,' he said. 'We'll surprise everyone and get married before Christmas.'

'October is my favourite month. I'd like to get married in October.'

'What about the last day of October? The tourists will have gone, we can go off on our honeymoon with a clear conscience, and we'll have a whole hotel for the reception. It will be a family affair: Gulban will give the bride away, Cookie will be best man, and Father Bosco will bless the lucky couple. All that remains is to find a suitable job for Joey.'

'Jack,' she said, 'I want you to promise me something.'

'Is it a condition?'

'No, I'd just like you to give up going to Fort Knox.'

'I'm fond of bridge. Apart from driving, it's my only relaxation.'

'I don't mind bridge, but I don't like Mrs Bugler. People talk about her, she's got a reputation.'

'She's a formidable lady.'

'You know what I mean.'

'Only people who've never been inside Fort Knox say these things. If she lived in a glasshouse, they wouldn't find her half as interesting.'

'She's ruined several young boys from around. I over-heard one of the waitresses say yesterday that she isn't the village bicycle but the village tandem.'

'I'm trying to imagine it. The mind just boggles and boggles.'

'Jack, will you promise?'

'I'll sleep on it and tell you when I wake up.' He gave her a playful peck on the cheek.

It was half-past three and dawn was creeping up the sky. A house at the end of a lane was still a dark, unknowable form, and two shadowy bullocks rising for an early bite in a field of tussocks moved slowly with eerie unfamiliarity. She came over the crest of a hill to find two floating bars of mist below and three lumps of cloud on the western horizon, three black sheep grazing with their backs to the wind. She drove slowly down into the mist, her fingers tight on the wheel. It was blowing across the road from the right, yet when she reached the spot, it had vanished. She felt lonely and uneasy for no identifiable reason; she would have preferred it if Jack were awake. Then she realised that though she'd driven along this road many times before, she had no idea where she was. Nothing looked familiar. The road and the green verge on her left flowing towards her into the beam of the head-lights were endless and featureless. In vain she sought a landmark that might set her mind at rest.

As she went into a corner between steep hills, the flowing road vanished. Without warning, she was sur-rounded by thick, grey mist. She knew that she must stop at once. She braked, and the nose of the car went up. She was airborne, the steering-wheel loose in her hands. With a sickening thrill she knew that she was going to die. The nosedive came abruptly. She saw a clutter of intestines, and a cargo of herring being unloaded, slithering into boxes in a cascade of quicksilver. There was a metallic scratching and birdlike wail, a loud kra-a-ah of pain followed by a thud and a headlong scrunch against up-rushing, irresistible dark.

She woke and knew that Jack had gone from her side. It was light. The mist had dissolved. The car was up-ended in a narrow river with its rear resting on the bank. The windscreen was shattered. Her arm and cheek were bleed-ing, and her left side was a flight of arrows shooting pain all the way down her leg. The musical gurgle of water falling among rocks accentuated the terrible silence. Jack had been thrown clear. He was lying face down in the shallow river with his head between two stones.

'Jack, Jack!' she called. 'Oh, no!'

When she tried to move, the car rocked on its pedestal. Slowly she dragged herself out of the seat, over the boot on to the heathery bank, the pain in her arm and leg no longer hers alone. She allowed herself to slide down into the water near the spot where he was lying prone. She lifted his head and turned him over. The open gash above his right temple had been washed clean by the flowing water. Thin blood trickled afresh. She sought his pulse. She tore open his shirt to feel his heartbeat, and with both hands slapped his cheeks. Her head seemed to roll on her shoulders. He made neither murmur nor movement.

She leant against the peaty river bank, her feet in the

running water. The slimy stones were reddish-brown, as was the shoal of fine gravel, upstream from which rose a bleached stump of bog-oak, a gigantic molar with a two-pronged root that penetrated her skull and brain in a gratuitous act of violence. Within her was a stranger who saw nothing but fragments — pointed rock, torn flesh, splintered bone — washed by water that sluiced and trickled. A wagtail balanced on the opposite bank. The river was an ocean she must cross to reach what people called the world. Now the hotel would empty, the bustle of guests would give way to silence. All evening he had seemed driven by demons, set on a course of self-destruction. He drank wine like water. He talked and talked, the words obscuring an overwhelming compulsion. He'd been pitched from his seat. The impact had stunned him. Water had got into his lungs. Death from asphyxiation. Her mind rejected the flashy lure of inevitability. His death was senseless, absurd, incomprehensible. She kissed him on the mouth. She could not understand why she was not moved to tears, why the thing she felt was rage and a cold, inhuman urge for revenge.

It was five o'clock. Almost two hours had gone since she'd left the road. She dragged him downstream past the car, on to a low part of the river bank. He was cold and limp. His right arm swung as if broken. He looked unshaven, which was strange because when he kissed her by the graveyard wall his chin felt smooth. A green streak of algae hung from the corner of his mouth. She went back to the rocks and with cupped hands poured water over them to wash the bloodstains away. The car was a tin toy broken by an impatient child. She examined the padded steering-wheel and took her handbag from under the driver's seat. As she climbed the stony slope to the road above, she rested several times to breathe. Her side ached and her left eye kept closing. There were no skid marks where she'd gone off the road. The car had shot up over the sod dyke, there hadn't even been time to brake. Now she knew where she was, but the knowledge had come too late. There was a village about a mile further on. She sat on the roadside wondering if that was where she should go.

Brown hills rose round her with a blue road winding. The sky was clear and sheep were grazing between rocks where grass was kindly and green. Below was a stone bridge with a little hump. No car passed. She remembered that it was Sunday. She walked down the incline, keeping off the grass selvage which was peppered black with sheep shairn. A dog came running with his nose to the ground. He jumped the river and stood still when he saw her. She sat on the wall of the bridge, reluctant to move out of sight of the body. A grey van roared on the hill below. She waved her arms, willing it to stop. The effort was inhuman; now all depended on her alone. She was standing in the centre of the road. The driver caught her arm and she sank to her knees.

They put her to bed in her own room at the hotel. The doctor came and gave her a warm drink and two tablets. Then he pulled the curtains and told her that she would sleep.

4

When she opened her eyes, she saw Gulban in a chair at the end of the room. The curtains of the west window were half-drawn. He was sitting in the light and the bed on which she lay was in shadow. Spiky tufts of unruly hair sprouted from the sides of his head, black clusters of blighted tops that obscured the outline of the tuberose skull. He looked hunched and rigid, his body alert for the unexpected. She had seen him as a sour dandelion of a man whose weapon was his genius for dispassionate belittlement. Now her heart went out to him. In less than twenty-four hours he had shrunk into the set of a tired old man.

'Gulban,' she whispered, 'I'm sorry.'

He dragged his chair to the bed and took her hand.

'Are you feeling better now?'

'My side's still sore but I'm not as weak as I was.'

'The doctor said you were suffering from shock. You must try to remember what happened.'

She looked up at him, suddenly aware that she was the only witness.

'We went to town for a meal. We were driving back. Jack felt sleepy, so we stopped at Undercliff for a swim. After that he seemed his usual chirpy self. There was a half-moon with patches of mist near the ground. I must have been tired because I nodded off. When I came round, the car was in the river and Jack was lying face down in the water. It was only the safety belt that kept me from being thrown.'

'Wasn't he wearing his?'

'No.'

'Did he have much to drink?'

'We had a bottle of wine with dinner and a Scotch or two before. We were celebrating, you see. We had decided to get married in October.'

She turned to the wall as tears welled in her eyes.

'It was my wish.' Gulban took her hand. 'I couldn't understand why he waited so long.'

'He was cautious in some things. He wanted us both to be sure.'

'It was an odd thing to do, going swimming in the middle of the night.'

'It was a special evening. We wanted to do things we'd always remember.'

She felt bound by circumstance. Half-heartedly, she raised a hand, but the truth was not within her grasp.

'It's a senseless death. He was the only man among them with the gift of common sense. Now I'm left with specialists who enjoy the sound of their own tongues wagging. Jack was not a talker, he just got on with it. If he had genius, he kept it under a bushel. I often think that the other three are only splinters of one fully rounded man. Why did he have to die, Pauline?'

'I don't know.'

'It's wrecked your happiness and it will shorten what's left of my life. I hope it was for his own sins he was taken.'

'It was an accident. He ran into fog. It could have happened to any man.'

'You'd better get some sleep now. The sergeant will be after you for a statement. There will be an inquest. You'll have to give evidence to satisfy the manufacturers of red tape. No one knew him except you and me.'

After he'd gone, she lay on her back fighting tears. She had wanted to tell the truth, and now the truth was in abeyance. Jack was dead; no amount of truth-telling would bring him back. What she sought was peace of mind and an escape from useless recrimination. She wondered if in the act of deceiving she had taken on a burden too heavy to be borne. The coroner's inquest was now irrelevant. The real inquest — the dispassionate examination of motive and behaviour — would be carried out by her alone. She herself would be defendant and prosecutor, judge and jury. It was a prospect she did not relish; she had never been given to self-indulgence or self-deception.

She stayed in bed throughout the evening and the following morning, enshrouded in a paralysing mist that seeped into her lungs, heart and stomach. Father Bosco, Cookie and Joey came up to see her. She elaborated on the story she had told their father, and as she repeated it to the Sergeant she noted that it had become more real with retelling. When he left, she dressed and crawled down the stairs with one shaky hand on the banisters. Father Bosco, Cookie and Joey were waiting in the corridor outside Gulban's office, and Gulban spotted her as he opened the door.

'You'd better come in, too, Pauline,' he said. 'It may be painful to talk but nothing is worse than solitary sorrowing.'

He sank into the chair behind his desk and the four of them sat on the high-backed chairs facing him. For a moment they all heard the dry ticking of the clock above the mantelpiece.

'I've had word that the autopsy is over,' he said. 'We'll get him back this evening. Now we must talk about the funeral. You'll all agree that we owe him a good one.'

'I'll say the funeral Mass, of course,' said Father Bosco.

'It must be a High Mass with four priests concelebrating to represent my four sons and the four Red Men. The concelebrants will stretch out their hands at the Consecration. Nothing gives a greater sense of power, dignity and ceremonial.'

'It gives me a sense of divine power being multiplied

exponentially.' Joey looked at Father Bosco who showed no awareness of the hint of blasphemy.

'Can you lay on three other priests?' Gulban asked.

'I'm sure I can,' Father Bosco replied.

'They'll expect payment, of course,' said Gulban. 'I'm aware of that.'

'No, they won't. Jack was my brother and they're my brothers too.'

'I'm not going to spare any expense. We want the largest turn-out ever.'

'We can't coerce people into coming,' Joey reminded his father.

'We can encourage them. We'll have a proper organist and an undertaker from town with a big hearse, and we'll have shiny black limousines for the family. People are curious. If they don't come to pray, they'll come to gawk. No one has ever seen an undertaker or a hearse on this headland before.'

'I'd prefer a quiet funeral,' said Father Bosco. 'Just the family, a few neighbours and friends of Jack. It's more becoming than a vulgar spectacle.'

'Don't think I don't feel grief,' said Gulban. 'Jack was dear to me. He worked like a demon and never asked me for a penny. The debt I owe him must be repaid. It must be seen to be repaid.'

'The best way to repay him is to have Requiem Masses said for his soul.' Father Bosco blushed with the effort of speaking firmly.

'An elaborate funeral will serve a real purpose. It will externalise our grief, it will give it a visible form and motion,' said Joey with an ambiguous glance at his eldest brother.

'What do you think?' Gulban turned to Cookie.

'Jack wasn't religious. He'd vote for a quiet funeral with a Low Mass said by Father Bosco on his own.'

'We'll let Pauline decide,' said Gulban.

For a moment she hesitated. She stared at the carpet

beneath his desk, waiting for words to form a recognisable shape in her mind, aware of a transparent blankness, a square of thin glass held up against nothingness. She struggled for purchase, then breathed with relief as the gift of a sentence gave her a foothold on firm ground.

'Jack was a straightforward man,' she said slowly. 'He had a strong sense of family history. When he spoke of the Red Men, you could see that they were real to him. For our honeymoon he'd promised to take me to see their cities: Chicago, Peoria and Des Moines — I forget the fourth. He had a sense of occasion, too. He deserves the best send-off we can give him. We can only do it once, so we should do it well.'

She broke down and wept. Gulban and the others waited till she'd dried her eyes.

'We'll have all the trimmings, then,' said Gulban, bringing the meeting to a close.

He was as good as his word. Jack was buried the following Wednesday with more solemn ceremonial than had ever been seen on the headland. The coffin was taken by hearse for two winding miles along the shore road to the church, and the family followed in two black chauffeur-driven limousines — Gulban and Pauline in the first and Cookie and Joey in the second. A red-nosed undertaker with a black moustache conducted Gulban and Pauline up the aisle to the front pew, where they sat alone. She was dressed in black from head to toe, and in her right hand she carried a single white lough-lily which Slash Gildea, who ran the hotel farm, had plucked for her that morning. Pale and drawn beneath her veil, she moved silently and mechanically with short steps, hardly aware of the already assembled congregation. All she knew was that Gulban was supporting her and that Jack lay on his back in the heavy, varnished coffin on wooden trestles before the altar. She felt unsteady on her feet; she had tasted nothing but orange juice and white grapes for three days. Glorious sunlight poured through the high window of the east transept, yet she felt no ray of heat or hope, only a sickening gripe of cold in the pit of her stomach.

Cookie and Joey occupied the seat behind her. The nave was crowded. The Mass servers were lighting candles. The postmistress, who normally took charge of the organ, sat censoriously in the west transept, her prim face raised to the choir where the organist from town rocked audaciously on her stool.

Mass began. Organ music tumbled in the empty spaces between the exposed couples of the roof. In the sanctuary the four concelebrating priests glided back and forth over the thick, red carpet, as she sought some kind of purchase on the smoothly worn words.

After the readings Father Bosco gave the address, looking down on the long, narrow coffin, speaking each word as if no other word mattered. He recalled Jack as man and boy, lifting him out of her reach into a far-off world of measureless time and imperturbability. Only at the end did he allow himself a little emotional flourish. With both hands stretched out towards the coffin below, he whispered in a voice that all could not but hear, 'Dear brother and friend, dear Jack, farewell!'

The words had such an effect on her that she lost all awareness of the service. When the Communion bell recalled her, she realised that she'd missed the prayers for the living, the Consecration and the prayers for the dead. She went to the altar rails with Gulban, and Father Bosco gave them both the Eucharist with immaculate hands. After Communion the four priests sat side by side with their hands on their knees and their chasubles draped over the backs of their chairs. The organist played 'Jesu, Joy of Man's Desiring', invoking harmony and peace on earth and grace falling with summer sunlight through high clerestory windows. On and on it flowed without an interrupting wave or ripple, yet all she could feel was rebellion and antagonism. Every cell in her body shook with a sense of wrongness and divine injustice. Her grief was not in her mind but in the infolding depths of her womb which was being tugged from her by every living thing that moved.

At the graveside she stood between Gulban and his sons, still holding the white lough-lily. On the far side of the cemetery wall was a slender ash tree with greenish sunlight dancing between its upreaching branches. Its shadow fell on the varnished wood of the coffin. She peered over the edge as it was lowered on ropes, leaning forward to catch the last glint of the plate. Above were pure, blue sky and living, dancing leaves. She threw the lough-lily into the open grave, then Gulban whisked her towards the waiting limousine. He hardly spoke on the way home. She sat upright in frozen rigidity, looking down on her black gloves with vacant incomprehension.

'You ought to wear black,' he had said the day before. 'In black it's easier to behave with dignity.' Now he took her hand and said, 'We're closer than ever, Pauline. No one understood him except us.'

When they got back to the hotel, there were drinks and sandwiches in Gulban's office for a few close neighbours and friends. Conversation was hushed and strained. There was plenty of whiskey, but no one had either the will or the wish to drink it. The rigor of death held them spellbound, until at last two strong-minded men got up and said that they were sorry to have to go so soon. Gradually, the other mourners took their leave. Then Gulban, Father Bosco, Cookie, Joey and herself were alone in the room.

'We'll have a bite to eat now,' said Gulban. 'And since we're all together, I have something to say.'

They started with leek and potato soup which was smooth and creamy except for spiky bits of parsley floating greenly on the surface. Gulban stood up to carve the saddle of mutton and paused half-way through to re-sharpen. Silence was observed as the gravy-boat went round the table. Then, with a welcome clattering of spoons, they helped themselves to cauliflower, peas and roast potatoes.

'I was right,' Gulban said after the first mouthful. 'People came to stare, not to pay offerings. For such a large funeral they hardly broke the record. If I hadn't paid a hundred and fifty pounds for the family, the sum collected would have shamed us. Jack, I'm afraid, was too serious to be popular. Nevertheless, if he's looking down, he has a right to be proud. The four priests filled the sanctuary; your sermon, Bosco, had just the right amount of feeling; and the organist got notes out of the old organ that must have surprised the postmistress. The whole service spelt one word: DIGNITY. What do you think, Bosco? Are you satisfied?'

Father Bosco considered for a moment.

'Jack is dead. I trust he's in heaven, but none of us must presume. He was taken while his capacity for sin was still unimpaired, so he may be suffering. We should pray for him, because prayer, not pomp, may be what he'd most appreciate.'

'I know all that,' said Gulban. 'But we have the living to think about as well.'

He paused to look across at Pauline.

'The living must somehow continue to live. A dignified funeral may be costly, but it's a fitting end. It rounds things off. It closes a chapter for the deceased and helps those of us who are left to start another.'

Pauline clasped her hands and stared at the white knuckles.

'You haven't eaten one solid mouthful,' Gulban reproved her. 'All you've touched is the soup. Try the mint sauce, it might tempt you to eat a little of the meat.'

'I'll be all right,' she said. 'I'll be able to eat tomorrow.'

She longed for the solitude of her bedroom, away from words and gestures that only sharpened her sense of wrongness, of nakedness, of a life that had been smashed and mangled. She had lost her perception of order; all was chaos and disjunction. Words were treacherous, their truth leached away by over-long service in the causes of self-love and self-deception. The cooling gravy on her plate bound the mutton into paving slabs laid in concrete. She looked at Gulban, Bosco, Cookie and Joey with a sense of defilement and violation.

'Today we're grieving,' Gulban resumed over the coffee. 'We shall continue to grieve for a long time to come, especially when we're alone or wake up in the middle of the night. Life, we know, must go on, and work is a cure for anguish. Tomorrow we must start again, if we want to escape suffocation. Work is external. You can see it being done, and you can measure it when it is done. It's the bridge to sanity, to the world outside our thoughts. There must be no self-pity, no standing back to take stock. The best action is gut reaction, so tomorrow we won't stop to think. You, Cookie, will take Jack's place at the hotel. Joey will remain in the shop, and Bosco will pray for us all. Remember, Bosco, you too are in the running — provided your prayers get answered. You're all in the running — you've nothing to lose but your shirts.'

'I pray to be left out of the reckoning,' Father Bosco smiled.

'That's a prayer that only I can answer. Pray a real prayer and see what happens.'

He looked round the table, seeking an eye that might dare to meet his own.

'I want all of you to realize that I'm your judge, so don't forget the Day of the Talents, because life itself is only the deployment of talents. Don't bury them and don't squander them. Sadly, Jack didn't have his long enough to do either.'

He rose from his place at the head of the table and laid a hand on Pauline's shoulder.

'It's been a testing day for you,' he said. 'You should try

to rest now. We all need to be alone with ourselves on occasion.'

She rose slowly and stiffly and followed him out of the room.

5

With Gulban's departure, the quality of the light seemed to change. It became gentler and at the same time livelier, causing the brothers to subside in their chairs. Suddenly, a light-hearted witticism seemed a distinct possibility. Cookie lit a cigarette and Father Bosco a small cigar.

'I wouldn't have minded a glass of wine with my meal,' Joey said.

'Today a glass would hardly have registered,' Cookie observed.

'It wasn't an occasion for self-indulgence,' Father Bosco reminded them.

'Let's go up to my room,' said Joey. 'I've got half a bottle of brandy.'

'I'm hearing confessions at six. I must get back.' Father Bosco rose from the table.

'Stay for a while,' Cookie begged. 'We see so little of you now. We never have time to talk.'

'You haven't seen my den,' said Joey. 'Come on, I'll show you my collection of little beauties. You'll love my oolites, Father Bosco, best of all. My oolites have got oomph, more oomph than Brother Jack.'

He led the way upstairs and unlocked the door. It was an airless room with a single unmade bed by a window that faced the moor and the road running east to town. There was a small writing table in one corner, two easy chairs, a bookcase and some open shelves displaying lumps of rock ranged in rows. On the walls were coloured posters showing the internal organs and reproductive systems of animals, insects and birds, many of them drawn by Joey himself. Above the writing table hung a square of cardboard with the following inscription in large Gothic letters:

To improve the knowledge of naturall things, and all useful Arts, Manufactures, Mechanick practises, Engynes and Inventions by Experiments — (not meddling with Divinity, Metaphysics, Moralls, Politicks, Grammar, Rhetorick, or Logick).

'I can see why you call it your den.' Father Bosco looked round at the clutter of the room.

'It's a den of science,' said Joey proudly.

'Science being the measure of all things,' Cookie smiled.

'We'll say nothing about that,' said Joey. 'At least not today.'

He went to a little cupboard by his bed and got out a bottle and three glasses.

'Is he sane or not? That's what I'd like to know,' he went on, as he poured the brandy. 'When he's at his most serious, he's usually at his most outrageous.'

'He's sane,' said Father Bosco.

'It's a difficult question,' Cookie said. 'He's got such a strong personality that everything he says commands assent while he's saying it. It's only when you go away and think about it that you realise the absurdity of it. Wherever he is, he creates his own world with its own laws and forces, and in his presence there's no escaping the pull of it. Isn't that why we always talk about him when his back is turned? In a way we ourselves are to blame. We talk about him as if he were a kind of god.'

'The Day of the Talents . . . Let me be your judge . . . To each according to his ability: it all adds up to a deity of sorts. What interests me is the size of our respective talents. If he's omniscient, what price-tag has he put on you, Bosco? Are you worth more than Cookie, for example?'

'It might be amusing to find out,' said Cookie. 'I'm willing to reveal mine, if you two promise to do the same.'

'Would you tell the truth? And would we?' Joey asked. 'We've all got an interest in deception. What I propose is this. Each of us will write down his sum on a slip of paper and put it in a box. There will be no names, just the amounts. When we open the box, each of us will know how much he got in relation to the other two. At the very least it will be a start.'

'Your backhand will give you away, Cookie,' Father Bosco said.

'Then we'll all type out the sum on identical slips of paper. Are you game, Bosco?'

'You know I never play games. You and Cookie play if you like.'

'Two isn't enough. For anonymity we need three. Come on, Bosco, where's your sense of humour?' Joey demanded.

'It's obvious, at least to me, that he must have given us all the same talent. It's only fair.'

'Isn't that what we're trying to establish? The nature of the beast.'

'I wouldn't doubt him for a moment,' said Father Bosco.

'Yet you won't put him to the test,' Joey said.

'To shame you both for being so suspicious, I'll play.'

One after the other they went to Joey's typewriter and placed their slips in an old shoe-box. Then Joey shook the box and opened it. When they examined the slips, they found the sum of £10,000 typed on each of them.

'You were right, Bosco,' said Joey. 'So he sees us all as equals in ability! What a travesty of the truth! Or is it just a cop-out?'

'He sees us as equal in his love,' Father Bosco reproved him.

'Ability was what he himself called it. He's a trickster, is Gulban. He was out to mislead us,' Cookie said.

'We're all in the race with an equal chance,' Joey smiled. 'The next question is: are we going to play his game?'

'I've told him already, I'm not in the running,' said Father Bosco.

'You are in the running, you accepted your talent,' Joey reminded him.

'Well, I'm not making the running. I leave that to you and Cookie.'

'Can we believe you?' Joey nudged Cookie.

'I must go now. That's enough idle talk for one day.'

As soon as Father Bosco had left, Joey poured another drink and, with his glass raised to the ceiling in both hands, walked round in a circle singing:

O and A and A and O
Cum cantibus in choro.
Let the merry organ go,
Benedicamus Domino.

'For a holy man, he is surprisingly unfree of pomposity,' Cookie remarked.

'If he were holy, we could believe him. It is not his pomposity that worries me but his lack of frankness.'

'He may be telling the truth. He's never had any interest in business. And what on earth would he do with a hotel? Turn it into a monastery or a nunnery?'

'You know what that means?'

'It's between you and me,' said Cookie.

'Question: Which of us will get it?'

'You could get the shop and I could get the hotel and farm. That arrangement would work.'

'No, Cookie, in the game of the talents winner takes all. To put it differently, you could lose.'

'So could you.'

'Which is why I've thought up a little proposition. We'll make a pact. Whichever of us inherits will share with the other. No need to take risks. There's world enough and time for both of us. What do you think?'

'I'm not sure.'

'It makes sense. Consider the alternatives. We'd both have to begin reading the financial pages of the newspapers; you'd have to neglect literature and I'd have to neglect science. If we make a pact, neither of us need run and we'll both win.'

'How will we share the estate?' Cookie asked.

'You will have the hotel and farm, and I'll have the shop. I love the shop, the clutter of little items in drawers, the things you seldom sell. Things you sell every day lose their novelty. The true pleasure of shopkeeping is when a customer once in a blue moon comes looking for something unusual and after a ten-minute search you find it.'

'The hotel wouldn't stand without the shop to prop it up.'

'Then we shall hold all things in common. Is it a deal?'

'Yes,' said Cookie, offering Joey his hand.

'Now nothing can go wrong.' Joey refilled Cookie's glass.

'Nothing can go wrong provided Bosco is out of the race.'

'Bosco disappoints me as a priest; his respect for the truth is less than total. You heard his address today, a litany of little untruths, all adding up to a great untruth that cried out to heaven for refutation.'

'What would you have said?'

'Something ferociously true,' said Joey. 'I'd mount the pulpit and look out over the heads of the people, waiting till every ear was cocked in expectation. Then I'd say: "Jack was first and last a hard man, utterly devoid of compassion for his kind. He was an egotist who was well on the way to becoming a monstrous egotist in middle age. So this funeral of ours is a lie from start to finish: Pauline playing the inconsolable widow in black, the gloomy undertaker, the sleek hearse. It's all a command performance, and the command was given by an even greater egotist than Jack. The only truth is that Jack is dead; at least that is not a performance. Surely the dead can be laid to rest without causing the living to bend double under the weight of self-aggrandisement and self-deception." '

'It wasn't a funeral,' said Cookie. 'It was a black wedding. Gulban walked up the nave with Pauline on his arm. In his own mind he was giving her away. Now he wants her to remain The Widow for evermore. He'd be horrified, for example, if she were to marry either of us.'

'She'll marry without marrying either you or me,' Joey smiled lopsidedly.

'For her only a man of steel will do.' Cookie placed his empty glass on the writing table. From the door he looked back and said, 'She may not have iron in the soul but she's got iron filings.'

'Now, if she were a hydrangea, they'd turn her hair the loveliest shade of blue.' Joey laughed and Cookie looked puzzled as he raised his hand in farewell.

Joey washed the glasses in the handbasin with the good side of his face towards the mirror, yet he could still see the red blotch burning under his left eye, which was small and yellowy with a puckered lid. He hated that side of his face. It was a scar on his consciousness that throbbed day and night. He spoke directly to his good eye, measuring the words:

'A man who suffers too much passes beyond the known boundaries of life. He becomes a ghost at a window looking in. Some pain is chronic, and some acute. Luckily for Pauline, an acute pain is soon forgotten. She'll forget Jack and go off and marry. Cookie and I have made a pact to share the spoils. We can't make a pact to share Pauline. There he stands the better chance. When she looks at me, she drops her gaze. Embarrassment? Guilt? A painful memory? She owes me more than she'll ever owe to any other man.'

He wondered if Cookie felt Jack's death in the way he himself did, not the pang of bereavement but a chilly sense of exposure. Jack, like Gulban, was solid. He was present even when he was absent, a windbreak that sheltered those he worked with. Cookie was the opposite, fluid and unstable, bookish and solitary, never himself unless alone. Today he looked shaky and unready. He'd never make a hotelier or anything requiring practical common sense. He'd become a lecturer, then a professor. He'd leave the running of the hotel to his partner and brother. He'd come back on holiday and draw an annual dividend, in every way a perfect arrangement for them both.

From the window he looked down on the flowing road and a red car gliding between the green clumps of rushes on either side. The driver was Alicia Bugler, an unwitting dispenser of constriction and pain.

'Perhaps I shouldn't have made a deal with Cookie,' he said. 'Perhaps I should try my hand at machination.'

Cookie sat above the slip, a crude concrete structure sheltered from the west by a sloping sea-wall and strewn with tangled nets, old lobster creels, broken oars and black lengths of plastic tubing. Alongside the slip were two split-level stages with rusty mooring rings set in concrete, and on the pebbled slope near by lay five white boats with green, blue and red gunwales. Two of the boats no longer in use were upturned and two schoolboys were sitting astride their keels, crouched forward in imitation of competing jockeys. Behind the sea-wall two punts lay at anchor with their outboard engines cocked and propellers glinting.

He often wandered down to the slip in the evening to watch the lobster fishermen returning and the seagulls soaring. It was a quiet and creative time of day. He would pick his way down the slip over the embedded skids, balance metal and plastic buoys in his hand, or stick his head into one of the black barrels to inhale the stinging smell of bait in pickle. It was the kind of aimless activity on which Jack would have poured scorn and ridicule, yet it gave Cookie a sense of communion with the world and himself that both soothed and surprised him.

This evening he did not go through his ritual of touching discarded objects. He thought of Jack driving off alone in his red sports car on Sundays, going from village to village, stopping at pubs, chatting up likely women — or so the gossips had it. How could Pauline delude herself into believing that she loved him? 'Sex is sport, and so are women' was his motto, though he had probably omitted to tell her.

One day, as Jack saw a girl bending down to draw water from a well, he had jumped two feet in the air, clicked his heels together, and shouted 'Hooh' like a madman, before finding the earth again. That for him was women. That for him was Pauline. He was a fraud who owed his success to the fact that no one really knew him. Would Gulban admire him if he had known that he seldom drank less than half a bottle of whiskey a day? Perhaps not even Pauline knew that.

He was cruel as well, contemptuous of anyone who showed hurt. Life wasn't life, it was a game. One summer evening he and Cookie and a young boy from the village were sitting above the beach watching two sisters bathing. The boy was in love with the younger sister and everyone in the village knew it.

'They must feel lonely, two women on their own,' Jack said. 'I wonder which of them I should try?'

'The older one,' said the boy. 'She's the prettiest.'

'Anyone could tumble her. I'll go for the virgin, she's more of a challenge.' Jack winked at Cookie.

'It's a bit early in the day for courting.' Cookie tried to deter him.

'Not early but a bit bright. The take is always better on a dull day with a light breeze.'

Jack walked down the beach to where the girls were

drying off. The following evening he told the boy that the younger sister was slow to begin and red hot once she warmed up.

'If you don't believe me, try her yourself and see.' He smiled as he turned the gully-knife in the wound.

When he had gone, Cookie told the boy that Jack had been making fun, that he had not been out with the girl at all.

'It wouldn't matter to him, even if he had,' the boy said. 'He never feels anything. Nothing does him any good.'

A seal broke water and swam round the store-box in which the fishermen kept live lobsters for market. Cookie watched the dark head bobbing and wondered if he had shown weakness in making a pact with Joey. It was an easy way out. What surprised him was that Joey, who was by nature competitive, should have suggested such a cautious arrangement.

He turned and saw a lightly built girl in a yellow dress and white sun-hat coming down the shore road. She was wearing dainty blue shoes with flat heels and was carrying a rolled towel in one hand. As she passed, Cookie waved to her and she waved back without smiling. Then he watched her making for the strand, a slight figure against a landscape of jagged rock and fenced fields where ewes and lambs were grazing.

'Alicia Bugler doesn't belong here,' he said. 'I wonder if she's fortunate enough not to know it.'

6

For Pauline the days passed slowly. The world was an affront to her every sense; seeing, hearing, tasting, touching and smelling were fraught with the pain of remembrance. There was no confluence, no ease, no comfort; nothing but distortion and jarring dissociation. Food was tasteless, and she could not drink. The thought of red wine or Scotch filled her with nausea and guilt. In the morning she'd wake up with a gripe in her stomach and no sense of having slept. Grief was the only reality, and she could not tell whether she was grieving for Jack's death or her own.

She felt imprisoned in her skull which had become a pressure chamber of heavy, swirling liquid. During the day she went about her work with overt efficiency, yet in the evening she could barely recall the morning. She was normally observant. She would note the movement of clouds, the changing light on the sea, the covert resentments that the waitresses betrayed in their gossip, and the quirks of elderly guests intent on ensuring their comfort. Today, all she could recall having experienced of the external world was the sight of a donkey rolling in the road.

She was lucky to have Gulban. He was a tower of strength and a source of comfort and unspoken sympathy. The day after the funeral he had asked her if she would like some memento from among Jack's things. There was no need to think. She said she'd like his new binoculars.

'Nothing more personal?' he asked.

'I gave them to him for his thirtieth birthday. I think he valued them more than anything else I ever bought him.'

Now she opened the drawer and took them out of their leather case. She went to the south window of her bedroom, holding them at waist level. She wanted to look through them, yet she hesitated. A knot of sheep on the hill scattered before a lolloping dog. A heavy man dismounted from his bike and spoke to another man driving a cow. A schoolboy with a hoop and rod came up the driveway. The sun was low over the sea. Rough tussocks cast spearlike shadows in a field where cattle were grazing. She trained the binoculars on the face of the heavy man, whose lips moved without smiling. His words were serious and soundless. The world had lost its voice.

South of the village Fort Knox gleamed blank and white, preserving a secret that Jack had not shared with her. If only she could talk to another woman. She had tried talking to Alicia Bugler when they'd met by accident on the road the day before. Alicia was intelligent. Her eyes sparkled with an inner life too intense for her body to communicate. Pauline wanted to sit with her above the sea and recall Jack's characteristic expressions. She looked at Alicia, not knowing how to begin. Then Alicia said, 'You miss Jack, I suppose', and Pauline knew that they would go no further. Alicia was either too young or too remote from life to know.

She sat on the edge of the bed with the binoculars in her lap. On the back of the door hung a light cotton dress which she had worn to the Atlantic Grill. Looking at it now, she experienced an immediate and powerful sense of her own body within it. To a casual observer it was a blue dress with a white collar, white cuffs and white pannier pockets. To Jack it was her 'sailor dress'. To her it was now a living object, and she could not imagine it as other than alive in her absence. It would enable her to be in two places at the same time. There would be two women rather than one to share the burden of grief.

Grief was not the only burden. There were also guilt and fear. The inquest was tomorrow. She felt guilt for having clothed herself in a lie, and fear that the coroner might strip her naked before Gulban and the rest.

From her seat in the village hall she waited to be called. The coroner was round-faced and pug-nosed with thin, white hair that failed to hide the pink scalp beneath. She gave evidence as briefly and as lucidly as she could, saying no more than the questions demanded. When she had finished, Forker, the landlord of the Spoke and Felly, described their brief visit to his pub on the evening in question. Jack had called with Pauline on their way to town. They talked about bridge and drank a nip of Scotch before leaving. Pauline relaxed. The other witnesses added little. Then the pathologist said that he had examined the body and found that it contained over three times the permitted amount of alcohol.

'The deceased', he said, 'would have been in no fit condition to drive.'

'Lies and slander,' Gulban shouted, as he strode out of the room.

Pauline and Forker were recalled to give further evidence. They both stuck to their stories. Then the coroner summed up. She wept as she heard the verdict of death by misadventure.

As soon as she got home, Gulban summoned her to his room.

'How much did he have to drink?' he asked.

'As far as I know, half a bottle of wine and two small whiskies.'

'That isn't three times the limit.'

'I know.'

'Was he a secret drinker, then? Did he have a drink on his own before you left?'

'He didn't look as if he'd been drinking.'

'I knew he took a drink from time to time but I never let on. I often got the smell of whiskey off his breath in the middle of the morning. Maybe he had a drink on the sly to screw up his courage before proposing.'

'We understood each other perfectly. There was no need for that.'

'You can tell the truth, I can take it. Was he a secret drinker?'

'He was fond of a drink but no one ever saw him drunk.'

'Maybe he had decided to blow a few fivers of his talent.'

'He was a serious man. That was not in his nature.'

'Pauline, you make me feel ashamed. I always had faith in him, I mustn't lose it now.'

That was the real inquest, she told herself as she returned to her room. Or was it just the first session of the real inquest?

The following morning Gulban didn't come down to breakfast. When she went to his room, she found him lying on top of the bedclothes, staring vacantly at the blank ceiling. There was a half-empty whiskey bottle on the table and a broken glass on the floor. She thought he was drunk, so she called Cookie. Cookie slapped his cheeks and smelt his breath. Then Joey came in. He lifted Gulban's right hand and let it drop. Then he did the same with the left.

'We must call the doctor,' he said. 'Gulban has had a stroke.'

7

They entered Gulban's office and drew their chairs round
the heavy mahogany table, Joey at one end, Cookie at the
other and Father Bosco facing Gulban's empty chair in
the middle. It was the first time they had met in his room
without being summoned. Father Bosco lit one of his
small cigars and Joey went to the bar for an ashtray and a
round of drinks.

'He's on the mend,' Father Bosco said, pushing aside
the drink that Joey had poured him. 'We must face facts,
however. Gulban will never be the same again. Now all we
can do is ensure that he ends his life with dignity and
in peace. He will never run the business again, the doctor
said as much.'

'He will want to run it,' Joey said. 'In his present state
he will be a greater nuisance than ever.'

'Then we must bear with him, if only for our own
internal peace. As man and priest, I know that there are
sins which no absolution can obliterate. The sin of dis-
loyalty is one of them. My first parish priest was an old
man called Father Tourish. He was so forgetful that he
used to leave out parts of the Mass on Sunday, which may
have suited some of his parishioners but not all. One of
them, a bank manager's wife, complained to the bishop,
and the bishop asked me as curate for my opinion. I
considered it my duty to tell the truth, and Father Tourish
was made to retire. He went into a home for old priests run
by nuns and never did a day's good afterwards. Now he's
ending his life in an indignity of *outré* sexual fantasy, and

for that I shall never forgive myself. God has forgiven me, I'm sure, but His forgiveness has only rubbed salt in the wound. In telling the truth I pronounced a sentence I can never unsay. So we must not be too self-righteous. We must create for our father an atmosphere of love and sympathy. We must shield him from the worst indignities of old age.'

'How do we do that?' Joey put on a face of extreme innocence.

'We must listen with respect to what he has to say. We must say "yes" even when our intelligence may prompt us to say "no".'

'Oh son, help your father in his old age . . . even if he is lacking in understanding show forbearance . . . for kindness to a father will not be forgotten . . . in the day of your affliction it will be remembered in your favour,' Cookie intoned.

'Are you asking us to deny the truth?' Joey turned to Father Bosco.

'Truth is eternal. Though you may put it in abeyance for an hour or two, the divine tide will still come in and wash all falsehood away.'

'I've never seen Gulban as a shorn lamb to whom we must temper the wind,' Cookie said. 'I doubt if he'd thank you for that kind of compassion.'

'I'll bet you're lenient in confession, Father. I must avail of your services some time,' Joey smiled.

'If there's any change in him, ring me. He isn't the only sick person on my list. I have arranged to visit four more before nightfall.'

From the window they watched him drive off in his trusted Fiat, the brim of his black hat resting on his ears.

'Professionalism is a great killer of spontaneity,' Joey said. 'Bosco is a professional. To him one sick man is as good as another. They all provide occasions for performing corporal works of mercy.'

'You noticed that none of us sat in Gulban's chair,' Cookie said.

'I noticed that Bosco faced it as if it were the seat of judgment.'

'It was an eerie feeling, sitting round his table drinking his whiskey and not censoring our speech. Now we have some idea of what it will be like when he's gone. We'll stretch our legs, breathe freely, and be ourselves.'

'We'll have to be serious in front of the staff, provide the centre of gravity, think of that! Aren't you just a little bit afraid, Cookie?'

'No, are you?'

'The only thing I'm afraid of is that Gulban may die intestate. He hadn't made a will on the Day of the Talents, and he hasn't made one since.'

'Will he ever again be in a fit condition to make a will?'

'If he dies intestate, the estate will be split three ways. The Holy Man will receive his share.'

'Bosco is right,' said Cookie. 'We must look after Gulban. Lying alone up there in his room, he could get all sorts of strange ideas in his head.'

Father Bosco drove quickly, as if trying to shake off a persistent pursuer. What pursued him, though, was irritation at the thought of Cookie and Joey drinking Gulban's whiskey in Gulban's room without a sign of filial respect — or respect for the priesthood, come to that.

Jack had been rooted in the ground and so was Gulban. Cookie and Joey were suckers on a rose bush, consumers not providers, fancy talkers rather than hard grafters. Joey was the younger but still he was the leader. In conversation he invented the ideas; he made the balls which Cookie then rolled for his brother's amusement rather than his own. Joey was a cynic without feeling for God or man. Cookie probably had some feelings, but in Joey's company he took care to conceal them. He was handicapped by his determination to consider one possibility as valid as the next. He probably had a literary phrase for it. All it meant was that though he'd got a first at university he'd get a third in life. Neither he nor Joey realised that the House of Heron had changed for ever. All they knew was the past which was Gulban's creation. They didn't truly believe in the present, their present, and they lacked the stomach to fashion the future. What would become of the shop, the farm and the hotel under their uneasy duumvirate was not for a charitable man to say.

He himself, he would admit, was not beyond censure. At one time he had imagined himself as staunch and as firm as Gulban and Jack. Now he wondered if he had both feet on the deck — or in the sanctuary, come to that. Today he had experienced a lack of solidity in his life that reminded him of his sense of shock when Benedict McBride left the seminary at short notice. Was it lack of solidity that had led him into the priesthood in the first place, the worry of skating over thin ice without a skater's light-footedness? But he must not question his vocation now, just because he'd had a momentary experience of insecurity and flux. 'Insecurity' and 'flux' were grand words — what Cookie would call euphemisms and Joey would translate as 'sexual distress', if he knew.

Yet it was all so innocent and accidental. He and Pauline had been sitting at Gulban's bedside and he had glimpsed the inside of her left knee. If he'd seen her bathing naked, as the elders had seen Susanna, he wouldn't have given the matter a second thought. What happened was that she uncrossed her legs, and in the moment of seeing he had looked away. It was preposterous to be over thirty and have your peace of mind shattered by the glimpse of a knee. What, after all, was a knee? A not-so-pretty bone which anatomists called the patella, with a little hollow on one side. It had the shape of a convex sea shell and its function presumably was to protect the knee-joint in front. Sadly, such scientific knowledge was mere thistledown before the wind of emotional compulsion. If he'd been moved by a look of sexual complicity in her eyes or by the bare nape of her neck as she bent forward, he would have understood. But a knee was only a knee. Or was it? In his heart he knew that it was not the convex bone but the concave hollow in the flesh beside it that caused him to look away. Yet nothing tangible had happened. There was no physical contact, no touch of hand or brush of arms. In that moment of shock not even their eyes had met. She had kept up a quietly intelligent flow of conversation, utterly unaware of the thunderstorm in his blood. 'Thunderstorm' was perhaps an exaggeration; it was more like a tumult that quickened the circulation, causing a disquiet that refused to subside.

After five minutes he left the room and ambled — or pretended to amble — down to the slip to watch the boats and the water. Again and again he counted the creosoted skids embedded in the firm concrete, as if he could not believe that there were twenty-nine, not thirty. He walked up and down the concrete, treading carefully, and he pulled on a heavy cable with the determination of a man who is convinced that pulling will break it. He walked back to the hotel, not quite weak but a trifle shaky, empty inside as if he'd fasted for twenty-four hours. He went to the kitchens and asked one of the girls to make him a salad sandwich.

'White or brown bread?' she asked.

He thought for a moment. It was an incomprehensible question which required careful consideration.

'The wholemeal is best, Father. It's fresh in this morning.'

'I'll have the white, then. If it's stale, it will serve as penance.'

He chewed slowly, trying to concentrate on the mushy tomato, crisp lettuce and cool cucumber between the slices. Then, in suppressed rage, he got up and dropped the half-eaten sandwich into the rubbish bin.

'I'll make you another with wholemeal bread,' the girl said.

'No, thank you.'

The solid world had become a gleety liquid. He was suffocating in a sea of floating garbage. He ran into Cookie and Joey in the lobby, and later when Joey poured him a whiskey, he declined for fear it might inflame his omnivorous imagination.

'It's nothing,' he told himself, swinging through the parochial house gates. 'What overwhelmed me was the immediacy of the experience, which made my life in the seminary and now as a curate seem like a kind of insentient stupor. It's the reality of the moment as opposed to the reality of eternity. I am as yet unable to think in eternities, I must learn at least to think in centuries. It is the way to spiritual serenity and freedom from personal necessity.'

Canon Sproule, his parish priest, was walking back and forth in the driveway, his hands joined behind his back through the slit-pockets of his cassock. The cassock was pulled backwards over the curve of his belly, and the toecaps of his shoes were turning up from years of kneeling and genuflecting. His high head was covered on top with a snowfall of sleek, thin hair that neither required nor received frequent combing. He was a happy, humorous man who loved his food, his pipe and genial conversation in the evening.

'And how is he today?' he asked.

'Same as yesterday.'

'I remembered him in the prayers for the living this morning. Are you free by any chance later on? I thought we might have a game of Scrabble.'

'First I have to make one or two sick calls. After that I was planning an evening of spiritual reading.'

'Who is it this time? St John of the Cross again?'

'I don't know yet. I have a little theological problem, Canon. Nothing serious. I thought an evening of contemplation might do the trick. I'm not an original thinker. I need St Augustine or St Jerome to point me in the right direction.'

'A theological problem? Do I know her?' The old priest threw back his head and laughed.

'Only too well. She's called the problem of original sin.'

'You should give up those short cigars, they're enough to make any man nervous. Get yourself a pipe and experience a change of culture, maybe a change of vision. As a man grows older, theological problems may provide exercise for the intellect but they fail to stir the cooling blood.'

They both laughed. Bosco went to his room to shave. He had a belief that shaving was an act of purification which, if performed with care and deliberation, could change the complexion of the mind itself. He liked exchanging pleasantries with the Canon. He loved him for his certainty and his humorous dismissal of all things that might threaten it. He was full of worldly wisdom, not all of it expressed in theological jargon.

'Priests are subject to the most subtle temptations,' he would say. 'The urges of the flesh they experience would hardly register with the more carnal of the laity. As an old archdeacon I once knew used to put it, "The devil finds work for idle cocks." Then he would laugh gleefully at his own joke. It was a daring joke for a clergyman. He had often made it before. He liked nothing better than making it again.

His psychoactive ablutions complete, Father Bosco knelt at his prie-dieu and spoke to the blank wall in front of him.

'I have achieved chastity of deed. What I have yet to find is chastity of thought. But nothing further will happen. That I guarantee. What occurred once in the past belongs in the life of a different man. What occurred today is humiliating because it is incomprehensible. It's an extra pain to be borne. It's a pain I could have done without. I shall go back to see my father tomorrow, and there I shall meet Pauline. I mustn't try to avoid her because that would only fire my imagination. I realise now that I am safest in her company, because she is rational, serious and matter-of-fact.'

8

Joey looked forward to Sunday mornings, especially in summer. The shop was less busy than on weekdays, so he could leave the two girls who worked for him to look after the odd customer who came in for sweets, newspapers or cigarettes, the only things that seemed to sell on Sundays.

The hotel bars opened from half-past twelve till two. It was now almost noon and he was enjoying a solitary drink in the lounge before the thirsty hordes came in. He had locked the doors against wandering guests. He was sitting by a window with his back to the sunlight and the unread Sunday papers strewn over the low table before him.

The lounge was spacious and airy with tall windows facing south. The brown tweed curtains had been chosen by Pauline to match the corded upholstery of the seats. The agricultural and household implements that hung from the walls and ceiling had been collected by Jack to provide a topic of conversation for bored tourists with a passing interest in rural folkways. There was an old scythe, a sickle, a pair of sheep shears, a sand-eel hook, a turf-spade, a churn-dash, a thraw-hook for twisting hay-ropes, a triangle of salmon net and an old-style lobster-pot. Needless to say, there were no such embellishments in the public bar where the locals drank. The locals came to the hotel to escape the very life that the lounge bar sought to celebrate.

Joey was thinking about how to invest his money, which was at present with a building society, earning little more than it would have done in a bank. He wondered what Cookie had done with his, because Cookie was hardly the kind of man who made regular killings on the stock exchange. He was incredibly ignorant of business, science, and the normal processes of rational thought. He once introduced Joey to a French professor of chemistry, who was staying at the hotel, as 'our resident stinks man', though Joey's true interest was geology, and the rock specimens he collected could scarcely be described as odoriferous.

'I have an advantage over both Bosco and Cookie,' he said to himself. 'What they fail to realise is that the world can be reduced to "Mechanick practises"; that God, if he existed, would be a scientist.'

He looked across at the fleeting shadows on the hill, irregular and dark, appearing for a moment and never reappearing in the same shape or place. It was a long, low hill with a dip in the middle that gave it the outline of a pair of human breasts. At its foot was a single stone-built cottage set in a fenced field with a double row of conifers providing shelter from the west. A narrow bog-road ran up past the cottage, ascending the hill in a double curve that looked like an S turned back to front. The road climbed between grey crags and patches of green ferns and purple heather until it vanished over the top in the valley between the great earth-breasts. The house, the field and the hill itself belonged to Old Gildea, whose younger son Slash ran the hotel farm and whose elder son Packie was the village butcher.

Joey sprang from his seat with a sense of purpose that came from sudden inspiration.

'Eureka!' he cried, then swallowed what was left of his whiskey. 'I have made a pact with Cookie but nothing must be left to chance. Gulban has a quirky and original mind. Even in his present state he will appreciate boldness and imagination. He will sit up in bed and say, "Only a scion of the Red Men could have thought of such a thing." '

He left his papers with the receptionist and set off in the direction of the stone-built cottage. He found Old Gildea at the back of an outbuilding, struggling with a flat stone which he had dug out of the foundations of a derelict byre. He straightened, as he saw Joey approach, and felt the small of his back with his hand. He looked down at the stone with his short bow-legs wide apart.

'Are you strong enough to lift her?' he asked. 'I'd lift her myself if the arthritis hadn't broken me grip, but what can you expect at seventy-eight and a bit?'

The breeze lifted a wisp of white hair over his bald forehead. He was lightly built, with a wizened face, narrow shoulders and big-jointed fingers.

'It would make a fine threshold stone,' Joey said.

'She'll make a backstone for the fire to see me out,' replied Gildea.

Joey carried the stone into the house and placed it on the pebble-paved hearth. The old backstone, which was standing behind a slow-burning fire, was cracked by heat in two places.

'It's tailor-made,' he said. 'All it needs is trimming.'

'Leave that to me,' said Gildea. 'Even with the arthritis, I can still hold a hammer and chisel.'

He laid his stick against the wall and lowered himself stiffly into an old armchair. Joey sat opposite, using the backstone-designate as a footstool.

'I've come to make you an offer,' he said.

'I'll do anything you say if you take fifty years off my age.'

'Will you sell the island? That's what I'm here to ask.'

'Sell it? Why?'

'For money.'

'You can have my island if you take my infirmities as well.'

He picked up his stick and shuffled painfully to the door. Joey followed, wondering what to say. The island rose out of the bright summer haze, low in the north and humped towards the south. From the house it looked like a half-submerged whale with a silvery spout where the white lighthouse stood on the higher ground.

'If you have a lifetime to live, you will wake up one morning and wish for a bare island with no house on it but your own. Every man longs for his own island some time during his life. Now, what can make you want an island so young?'

'I like the shape of it, long and narrow and high at one end. Some days it gleams like the blade of a knife in the sun.'

'It isn't long and narrow, it's almost round, but it looks long and narrow from whatever airt you view it.'

'You never built on it yourself?'

'There was no need. I go to the door first thing every morning and look out over the Sound. "That's my island and no one else's," I say before I put the kettle on the fire to boil. There's only one thing wrong with it: every Tom, Dick and Harry can see it. Now, I would like an island that could only be seen from a single spot on the mainland known to me alone. What I'm saying is that it is isn't perfect, so how much are you offering?'

Joey hesitated, thought of a price and halved it.

'Four thousand pounds.'

'What will you do with it?'

'I'll run sheep on it in the summer.'

'You'll have to get rid of the rabbits first.'

'I would hope to build a house on it.'

'How much did you say?'

'Four thousand.'

'I wouldn't part with it for forty thousand.'

'It would be a lot of money to refuse.'

'When you imagine this headland in the middle of the night, what do you see?'

'A long mound of a hill with a hollow in the middle and sheep grazing in flat fields below.'

'I see three things: my island, your father's hotel and

Fort Knox. A man who owned those three would be king of the headland. I may be seventy-eight but I'm not giving up my stake. How's your father?'

'Very low.'

'He's seventeen months younger than me. He shouldn't have given in so soon. He was a hard man in his time. When he was building the reservoir over there before the war, I spent a summer's day mixing his concrete and at dusk he gave me a shilling. I said nothing but I could have cried. He was a man more given to gathering than scattering. Are you?'

'I try not to gather where I haven't scattered, that's all.'

'I had one advantage over your father: a contented mind. I've always enjoyed good relationships with women, and I still do. Now, tell me what's different about me since you last saw me?'

Joey scrutinised the small round face, half-covered by a thin, grey beard. Gildea had lost his teeth. The collapsed lips puckered when he closed his mouth, which was the mouth of a makeshift purse pulled tight by a waxed drawstring.

'You've grown a beard,' Joey said.

'I'm growing a beard, my first at seventy-eight. I'm growing it for a young woman.'

Joey laughed. Gildea looked pale and wrinkled, the lobes of his ears white as flour.

'She came to me last month and asked if she could paint me. She's been painting me every day, and now she wants to paint my beard. She says she's going to start a summer school for young artists here. She'll bring students from every country and they'll all sit round in a circle painting Fergus Gildea from every angle. Why, I keep asking, would anyone want to paint Fergus Gildea? Your father is a more important man, and younger too.'

'You must have a more interesting face.'

'She didn't say "interesting", she said "full of character". I expected her to paint my hands because of the arthritis. Fair play to her, she was only interested in my face.'

'Who is she?'

'You know her well, Alicia Bugler, a lovely girl. Her mother is high and mighty. Alicia takes after her father. Now he was a gentleman of a man.'

'I didn't know she painted portraits.'

'She'd paint you if you asked her. She says she's searching for faces she can make unforgettable on canvas.'

Joey looked quickly away, then forced himself to meet the eye of the little man in front of him. Gildea's head was certainly unforgettable. In shape it resembled an up-turned bowl. Besides, it was a bowl that looked as if it had been shrunk by the pressures of physical labour and long endurance.

'I must be going,' Joey said.

'What did you learn from me today?'

'The island is not for sale.'

'No, no, no. You saw a table with three playing cards: my island, Fort Knox and the hotel. Knowing that is more valuable than owning one or even two of the three.'

'I shall think about it on the way home.'

'If you'd offered me four thousand for the island two months ago, I'd have taken it. An artist has changed my life, and a pretty young girl has given me a good reason for getting up in the morning. Yesterday she gave me a kiss on the cheek.'

'You're a lucky man.' Joey waved goodbye.

'I hope your father mends,' the old man called after him. 'No man deserves to suffer, not even a man who has caused suffering.'

On the road back to the hotel Joey leant on the stone bridge and looked down into the river which was over-hung by thick gorse bushes. The river was stony and the iron-laden water a murky brown. In a pool under the gorse he thought he could make out the quivering forms of four minnows facing upstream.

This was Cookie's river and Pauline's too. He could never cross it without thinking of them both, wading as children, searching for eels, lifting brown lumps of slippery stone. They were inseparable then. The river was a playground which they never shared with any other children from the neighbourhood. During the winter months she would romp with all four brothers in the empty bedrooms upstairs, but throughout the summer she was only Cookie's girl. The bond, whatever it was, had long been broken, and Pauline did not seem to care. It was Cookie who remembered and sought to re-create a lost intensity.

For Cookie and him the word 'Pauline' was a synonym for pain. Bosco had his surplice to protect him; he was the only one of them who was free.

'What would you like for Christmas?' he'd asked Joey last year.

'A thought-reading machine,' Joey replied. 'If I knew everyone's thoughts, I wouldn't ask to know more.'

'A thought-reading machine?' Bosco swept a straight-fingered hand across his forehead. 'It's like asking for the H-bomb! Only imperfect knowledge makes human relationships possible. The best of life is not knowing. Anything we can know isn't worth knowing.'

Bosco was protected by more than his surplice. His deadly seriousness was his deadly weapon. What went on in his head was as remote from ordinary life as what went on under the dome of St Peter's.

'I'd still like a thought-reading machine for Christmas. I'd train it first on Gulban, then on Bosco and Cookie. Finally, I'd enter Pauline's pretty head. She knows the business backwards. She's nurse to Gulban and secretary too. And his mind's no longer strong. Cookie said yesterday, "She could be king-maker, Joey, have you thought of that?" '

Joey, who had thought of it, was surprised that a man so innocent of guile as Cookie could have thought of it too.

A boy in short trousers came tearing down the hill on a bicycle. As he crossed the bridge, Joey never looked round. The minnows had vanished. The gorse had lost its gilt, and the water itself had become an ugly primeval soup in which only misshapen enormities could spawn. It was the present rather than childhood which was a dream.

He arrived back at the hotel with a sense of diminishment and defeat. He had a light lunch with Cookie and Pauline, neither of whom gave anything away. Half-way through the afternoon he found her reading the Sunday papers at one of the tables on the front lawn. There was an empty seat on either side of her. He chose the one that would enable her to avoid looking directly into his bad eye.

'I've been thinking about how to invest the money,' he said. 'Gulban knew what he was doing. He's given us a real teaser.'

'I'm sure he didn't mean it to be a headache.' She spoke as she read, without raising her eyes.

'It's more like a toothache.' He tried to make her laugh.

'You'll have to begin reading stories about bulls and bears to take your mind off the pain.'

'I'm going to put two-thirds of it in property, and I'd like to give the rest to you.'

'I don't think that's the way to maximize your income.'

She looked at him kindly, the sun on her lightly freckled face. She showed no surprise, only an amiable interest that caused him pain.

'Will you take it?'

'I couldn't. What made you think of such a thing?'

'It's only by taking that you'll be able to exercise your greatest gift, which is giving. You've given more to Gulban since he fell ill than Bosco, Cookie or myself could ever give. Without you, where would we be?'

He put his hand on her bare arm. His thumb sought the

ulnar nerve. She didn't move, yet he could sense the stiffening of arm and body as one.

'It's very good of you, Joey, but I couldn't take it. What would I do with it? I couldn't spend it and it isn't my job to invest it.'

She looked at him again, her eyes serious and bright, full of dispassionate assessment.

'You may be right,' he said. 'But I can't help thinking that you deserve it.'

He went to his room and lay on his side on the bed for an hour. He felt excited and at the same time despondent. In his breast was a kind of sobbing, dry and soundless, while his blood whispered sickeningly in his ear.

9

'What's hard to believe is how quickly it happened. One day I was healthy and robust, enjoying life. The next I was old, old. I went straight from summer into midwinter.'

It wasn't quite true, she thought. For six months before the stroke he'd been complaining of dizzy spells and, a few weeks before, he'd dropped a hammer on his foot and said that he couldn't understand how the grip had gone out of his hand.

'Now, don't fret, Gulban,' she said. 'It may take time but we'll have you on your feet again, wait and see.'

She helped him drag himself up from under the bed-clothes. Then she put two pillows to his back, before tucking in the coverlet. Lastly, she combed his wiry hair and poured him a cup of tea which he held self-consciously between his hands.

'Will you open the window, Pauline? I like to watch the curtains move in the breeze.'

He looked vacant and pale. His hands shook but the tea didn't spill because she knew by now not to fill the cup.

'What day is it?'

'Saturday. Father Bosco will be coming to lunch to-morrow.'

'And the date?'

'It's the 29th of September.'

'Nearly three months and no improvement.'

'Don't talk like that, you're getting stronger every day.'

'I've known a lot of old people in my time; not one of them died before he'd lost his grip on the truth. An old man is a man who wants to be swaddled in lies. He should have about him people who are strong enough to keep repeating the truth. He won't thank them for it, he may even come to hate them. But, if they respect him, they will take him seriously as a human being till the end. Are you strong enough, Pauline, to keep telling me the truth, even when I don't want to hear it?'

'I always tell you what I think, no more, no less.' She tried to look cheerful with no hint of uncertainty.

'I'm no longer sure. I've lost confidence in my eyes and ears, and, worst of all, I've lost confidence in my brainbox. For the first time in my life I've been wondering if I'm right.'

He spoke slowly, yet he slurred his words. The natural rhythm of his speech had gone.

'You've been lucky not to have to wonder till now.'

'Pauline, you'll have to be my eyes and ears. You must be strong, you must correct me when I don't think straight.'

'You're doing all right.'

'I gave them talents and a year to use them. And I appointed myself to pronounce judgment.'

'The year isn't over. There's another nine months to run.'

'Time may be shorter than you think. You must help me to winkle out the truth. We mustn't delay, we must give them tests.'

'Tests?'

'The talents won't tell all. We must surprise them into giving their true selves away. Bosco, Cookie and Joey, they won't suspect. Only you and me will know they're under the microspoke.'

'Microscope.'

'That's right, correct me when I'm wrong. The tests will be tests of character, I'm relying on you for help.'

'I'm afraid I don't know what you mean.'

'I'll tell you when I've worked the details out.'

She went to the wardrobe to give him an opportunity to drink from the cup. She knew that he had to cock his lips and that he didn't like being watched.

'If only I could sit outside. I'll lose my colour here. Maybe if I sat by the window, I'd catch a bit of sun.'

'The doctor said you must rest. You've already been out of bed today for as long as he allows.'

'I'm bored in bed. I'll sit by the window for twenty minutes and look across at my reservoir and at people passing in and out. Come here now and give me a hand.'

She pulled back the bedclothes and slowly swung his feet on to the floor. She put her arm round his waist as he tried to stand. She staggered under the unexpected weight and he sank back on to the bed.

'Hold on for a minute till I fetch Cookie.'

'Don't go bothering him. Ask Slash to come up. I want to have a word with him about the farmwork.'

She didn't like having to ask Slash, because he would make her feel that the favour was for her, not Gulban. He was in the vegetable garden doing something to the runner beans. He looked at her quizzically, as if he understood more than she did. It was not a look of insolence. It merely expressed a covert withholding of sympathy and assent. It said, 'I'll do so if you wish, but I'm my own man with my own mind, and I do things in my own good time.'

She waited for his reply, determined not to give him the satisfaction of making her repeat the question.

'Tell him I'll be up in a minute.' He spoke without moderating the pace of his work.

She kept an eye on him from the kitchen window for a minute or two. When she saw him leave the garden, she went up to tell Gulban that he was on his way.

He greeted Gulban with an easy-going smile. She could see that they had summed each other up a long time ago and that the assessment of each had been accepted without grudge by the other. She went to her room and lay on the bed, knowing that Gulban wouldn't need her, at least for half an hour.

It had been a morning of scattered rain and sharp sunlight reflected in wet roads and pools of water. The afternoon was mild and clear, the light on the bedroom walls gentle and soothing to the eye. She felt hollow and inert, devoid of the will to shape and control. She was coming out of one death and at the same time going into another. Nursing Gulban demanded all that she had to give. Now she wanted to sleep quietly and wake up on a bright morning full of happiness and hope, curious once again about the world outside and everything that breathed and moved in it.

'I should surround myself with life,' she heard herself say. 'I'm immersed in death and the fear of death.'

She entered a building she thought she recognised, small as a cowshed outside and spacious as a cathedral within. A geology lecture was in progress; the words on the blackboard were cirque, corrie, cuesta and arête, while emblazoned on a scroll across a stained-glass window was the text:

An intrusion is a body of igneous rock which has forced itself into fissures of pre-existing rocks.

The lecturer was wearing his mortar-board at a rakish angle and a white Arran pullover and no trousers. She sat down beside Gregory Bugler, who had put the lecturer on canvas as sheep above and man below, the spitting image of Slash Gildea.

She looked round the lecture hall. Everyone she'd ever known was present: girls from the convent whom she'd long forgotten, tourists from France and Germany, light-keepers who'd stayed at the hotel in the days before the lighthouse went nuclear. The lecturer was smoking compulsively, flicking ash all over his rock samples.

'Women are country rock,' he said. 'They predate men,

who are best described as younger intrusions. Will all country rocks present who have suffered invasion by a mass of plutonic igneous rock please raise their right hands?'

Mrs Bugler put up her hand in spite of Mr Bugler's attempt to pin it to her side.

'Isn't it wonderful that women share a history with the earth itself,' she shouted through his muffling palm.

Pauline tried to make sense of the scene. She was obviously at university reading a subject of someone else's choosing. She felt old and tired. Her intellect had abdicated its responsibility for finding harmony and order wherever she turned, and knowledge was cacophony and confusion. She had come to a place where the greatest pain was the memory of a better world forsaken, where punishment was not eternal fire but eternal anxiety — the consciousness of things gone wrong for ever.

Gregory Bugler was weeping over his canvas.

'There is no greater grief than to remember a happy time in misery and to remember it every day,' he moaned.

The lecturer put a record on an ancient gramophone which he wound laboriously with both hands, a shepherd hauling up a bucket from a cavernous mountain well.

'Now, take your partners for the next intrusion,' he shouted.

She woke in terror before the music boomed. She had slept for over an hour. She looked out across the sea, struggling to overcome the feelings of revulsion with which she had awoken. A cloud of sea fowl had descended on a dark patch of water. They were diving on sprat or mackerel, she could not say which. She got out her binoculars and scanned the scene of gluttonous havoc. Then, inexplicably, she found herself studying a young man and a girl on the edge of the cliff, in a spot she had known before.

He touched her breasts, first one, then the other, quite mechanically, and the girl never took her eyes off the carnage below. With a seagull swoop he touched her between the knees. She leant back, supporting herself with both hands, her face raised blankly to the sky. He kissed her on the mouth. His scorpion-hand crept up her thigh, a knot of active legs and fingers.

Pauline looked away. She felt hot and ashamed, which she blamed on the series of disconnected actions. In a nearby field young rabbits were playing among dog daisies. She returned to the cliff-edge, aware of white scuts flashing. The girl took his hand and placed it firmly on his knee. Then she got up and walked coolly away, flipping her long hair over both shoulders. His eyes followed her but he did not move. The girl was Alicia Bugler. The young man was staying at the hotel. He shared a room with another young man and they both drove about in an ancient car that never started without a push. They seemed to find fun in everything they did. That morning she'd overheard one say to the other, 'She's a real dish. If only her kissing didn't lack vibrato.'

She and Bosco had sat in that same spot on a June night before she'd ever thought of Jack. Now the memory of it was not so much painful as embarrassing. There had been no glint in the darkness to the north, and no glint in the west, except for the monotonous flashing of the lighthouse across the Sound. Below them the sea was far away. They waited for the dawn. It came shortly after three, and they walked back through the fields picking mushrooms, which were flat and cool and damp with dew. First they filled their pockets. Then he took off his shirt and they emptied the mushrooms into it in case they got crushed. They went straight to the kitchen and she cooked them in butter with a perspex plate over the frying-pan. They sat down to eat them with buttered toast. They were lovely mushrooms, full of the most delicious juice. He ate only one. With the second like a stinging nettle in his mouth, he got up and spat into the sink.

'Did you get a bad one?' she asked.

'I'm not hungry,' he said.

It was an odd way to behave. She realised then that he was not like other men. Jack used to say that there were two types of men: those who'd been disappointed in their first kiss and those who'd been overwhelmed by it. 'You recover from the second condition but there's no getting over the first,' he'd say with an ambiguous grin.

Alicia had walked out of sight. The young man had remained on the cliff-edge, gazing out over the sea to the north. In the field behind him a cow was standing with her hind legs apart, head down and back arched, her raised tail stiff and straight. She was urinating on the grass, making bright froth in the evening sun.

Pauline put down her binoculars. It seemed to her that there was nothing in the whole world she wished to see. She went into Gulban's room again. He was sitting by the open window, sleeping in his chair, and below in the driveway Cookie was trying to discourage an old tramp from coming in the gate. The tramp was a broad, heavy man with a white sack on his shoulder and a cudgel which he kept pointing at Cookie as if it were a finger. She had seen him before. He usually arrived during the winter and Gulban always gave him a bed for a week or two, when there were no other guests staying except one or two commercial travellers and the local schoolmaster. He wasn't quite as old as Gulban but he was just as headstrong. He neither washed nor shaved and his lumpy jacket was made up of patches of many shapes, colours and materials. He was known locally as Big Andy but Gulban always referred to him by his proper name, Andy Early.

She stole out of the room so as not to disturb Gulban and went down to lend Cookie some much-needed moral support.

'I must see Gulban,' the tramp was saying.

'I told you, he's had a stroke. He's very ill,' Cookie insisted.

'He's lost a son. I heard the news in town and I came straight away to sympathise. Gulban is a dear old friend.'

'He's sleeping now,' Pauline said. 'We mustn't disturb him, he isn't strong.'

'Gulban not strong! Like me, he's got the constitution of an ox and always had.'

Big Andy towered over Cookie, his slack, unshaven cheeks ruddy with broken veins. He was wearing a heavy pullover underneath the jacket which was making him sweat profusely. The uppers of his shoes were cracked, and his short-legged trousers revealed a right ankle with a yellow sock and a left ankle with no sock at all. Pauline could see that the combination of height and sartorial eccentricity was undermining Cookie's will to resist.

'If Gulban's asleep, I'll wait till he wakes up. I'll go into the bar and have a drink on the house. It's the custom whenever I call.'

'You usually call in winter when things are quiet here. We're full up now. Gulban would take a poor view of anyone disturbing the guests.'

'So there's no room for Early at the inn. I'd like to have that from Gulban himself.'

'He needs to be quiet,' Pauline intervened. 'The doctor said that he must not get excited. This evening I'll tell him you called. If he's well enough to see you tomorrow, he'll send for you.'

'And where am I to spend the night?' Big Andy glared at her with bloodshot eyes.

Cookie drew a rolled fiver from his wallet and held it out, as if he were offering a cigarette. Big Andy looked cynically at the note, giving a distinct impression that he was capable of refusing it.

'You'll get board and lodging in the village,' Cookie said.

Big Andy took the fiver between two fingers and slipped it into his breast-pocket.

'I'm not fit to walk to the village,' he said.

'It's downhill,' Cookie reminded him.

'And it's uphill back.'

'I'll give you a lift,' said Cookie. 'I'm about to go down to the shop.'

'I accept your offer but only because you're Gulban's son. He's always been a friend to me. If it wasn't for Gulban, I'd shake this house to its foundations. No one knows it but me and him. It's built on sinking sand.'

He climbed into the hotel Land-Rover beside Cookie, still muttering about the precarious condition of the building. As they drove off, he waved to Pauline.

'Give my regards to all and sundry,' he shouted. 'I was always a generous man.'

10

'How is he today?' Father Bosco enquired.

'Paler than yesterday,' Pauline replied.

'Did he have breakfast?'

'Only a bar of fruit and nut. He's beginning to take a fancy to things he's never looked at before.'

'I wonder if he'd like an orange. I brought him some juicy Jaffas from town.'

'He's upset about Big Andy. He called yesterday while Gulban was sleeping, and Cookie and I turned him away.'

'I can never figure out what he and Big Andy have in common. He was never an admirer of loafers, yet he treats Big Andy like a brother.'

Joey and Cookie joined them on the steps before the front entrance, where two or three guests were sitting on summer seats, gazing at the purple-patched hill to the south and across the luminous Sound to the island in the west. The bedroom windows were open, their white net-curtains making swag bellies in the breeze.

'My conscience is clear,' Joey announced. 'Cookie and Pauline must live in the odium, not of having discovered sodium, but of having refused bed and board to a drunken bum. For I was hungry and you gave me no cake, I was thirsty and you gave me no Scotch, I was a stranger and you refused me B and B. Forgive me, Father Bosco, if I misquote. We are not so much a generation of vipers as a generation of vulgarians. Even the Holy Book is not proof against our attentions. I wonder what Jerome up above makes of it all.'

Ignoring him, Father Bosco turned to Pauline.

'He's making slow progress. Perhaps we should get another doctor to give a second opinion.'

'I'll plant the idea in his mind. The only way he'll agree is if he thinks he thought of it himself first.'

'He needs a lawyer more urgently than a doctor,' Joey said. 'It would be tragic if he died intestate with the Year of the Talents still in the first quarter.'

'Perhaps you should remind him.' Father Bosco spoke without looking in Joey's direction.

'That kind of advice might appear more disinterested if it came from a priest,' suggested Cookie.

'The man who reminds him of death will be the loser,' Joey replied. 'Only those listed as non-runners can afford to confront him with even a milligram of that precious metal called the truth.'

After lunch the three brothers went up to his bedroom. They found him propped among pillows, stroking Balor, the hotel cat. Balor had only one eye. According to Gulban, the other had been scratched out by a rat while he was still a kitten, but Slash Gildea, who knew about animals, claimed that Balor had caught a chill out tom-catting one hard winter, that the eye closed with mucus and never reopened.

Gulban surveyed them individually as they trooped in. 'Why do you wear such roomy trousers, Cookie?' he demanded. 'There's enough surplus cloth in one leg to make a pair of togs for a lump of a boy. And you, Joey, why do you have such a long vent in your jacket?'

'What I want to know is why Father Bosco wears his collar back to front,' Joey replied. 'As a dresser, he's almost as snappy as Big Andy.'

The three of them pulled up their chairs and sat in a circle round the bed.

'Do you hear anything?' Gulban asked with a look of alarm.

'No,' said Father Bosco.

'There's an animal in the room,' said Gulban. 'And I don't mean Balor.'

'There's no animal here,' said Father Bosco.

'I can hear him breathing,' Gulban insisted.

'Where is he, then?' Father Bosco asked.

'He's hiding, I can hear him. Only a huge behemoth could breathe like that.'

'You must be imagining it,' said Father Bosco.

'It's heavy breathing with a rasping sound and now and again a rattle. I wonder if he's wounded and dying.'

Joey got another pillow and made him sit up straight in the bed.

'He's gone now,' Gulban said with what seemed like relief.

'He was never here,' Father Bosco assured him.

'It was frightening,' said Gulban. 'I don't want to hear him ever again.'

'Your ear was against the pillow, you were hearing your own heartbeats,' Joey said.

'You all think I'm potty,' Gulban shouted. 'Well, I'm not. I'm still warm, and I still pull the drawstring of the purse.'

'Don't get excited.' Father Bosco tried to calm him. 'Excitement is bad for a man in your condition.'

'Which of you turned away Andy Early?' Gulban assumed the severity of a Grand Inquisitor.

'I did,' said Cookie. 'Pauline said you were asleep and I didn't want him disturbing you.'

'Lies, lies. He didn't smell sweet enough to your fastidious sniffers.'

'If you mean he stinks, you're too right, so you are,' said Joey. 'If he had any respect for his hosts, he would have washed in a stream or polluted the sea itself before entering these pearly gates.'

'I didn't let him go empty-handed,' Cookie explained. 'I gave him a fiver of my own money.'

'How much would you have given?' Gulban asked.

'It depends on how highly he stank. Judging by the bouquet he brought to the village, I'd have given at least a tenner to see the back of him,' said Joey.

'What about you, Bosco?'

'You want me to outbid Joey, as Joey has outbidden Cookie. Well, I'm not playing.'

'Would you have given him a room at the parochial house?'

'No, my parish priest has a weak stomach. There's no excuse for not washing. I wouldn't inflict Big Andy's hogo on anyone except another hobo or a walking saint.'

'And you call yourself a Christian!' Gulban sneezed.

Joey got up with a great show of concern and closed the window.

'What I would like to know is how you got this obsession with Andy Early,' Father Bosco interjected. 'There are more deserving beggars who go out that gate as poor as they came in.'

'I don't advertise all my good works. I've got covenants you know nothing about.'

'Tax fiddles,' said Cookie.

'Covenants are cold collations,' said Joey. 'There will be more honour in heaven for the rich man who gives alms by hand, looks the beggar in the eye and meets his accusing stare.'

'I'm trying to find out which of you has the largest heart,' said Gulban. 'I had no idea what a task I'd set myself.'

'You haven't told us why Andy Early is special,' Father Bosco reminded him.

'You're all too young and too lacking in the heart that comes from suffering and observing suffering to understand. Now, where did Andy Early sleep last night?'

'He ended up in Old Gildea's barn after drinking my fiver in the village before closing time,' Cookie said.

'He'll be sleeping here tonight,' said Gulban.

'What will our guests think?' Cookie wondered.

'They don't have to see him,' Gulban replied.

'He drinks like a fish, he's bound to have to go to the toilet.'

'Then put him in a room with bathroom *en suite*.'

'We've only got two of those and they're both taken.'

'Put him in the best room that's vacant and leave him a po,' said Gulban. 'Have his meals brought up and give him half a bottle of whiskey so that he doesn't have to come down to the bar. A full bottle would be too much at his age.'

'This is ridiculous,' said Joey.

'It's bad for business,' said Cookie.

'I'm the businessman here,' said Gulban. 'I don't want any more discussion. You've all made me feel quite tired again with your niggardly moaning and groaning. I'm going to rest now. You'd better tell Pauline to come up and tuck me in.'

Big Andy turned up before nightfall. He was still carrying his hazel stick but he must have left his white sack in the last pub or in Old Gildea's barn. Cookie, who had been looking out for him, met him at the gate and suggested that he do up his flies before entering.

'Do up my flies in this weather!' he growled. 'I deliberately left them open to ventilate my bollocks.'

He was dishevelled and wide-eyed. He gazed down at Cookie with the self-possession of a hell-raiser who knows that his interlocutor would bend over backwards to avoid a scene.

'I've put you in a west-facing room. You'll be able to lie in bed and look out over the sea in the morning.' Cookie conducted him as quietly as possible through the back entrance.

'It's too early for bed. I must have a drink and a bite of supper before turning in.'

'Gulban said that you're to stay in your room. I'll have everything you want brought up. He's resting now, he'll see you first thing after breakfast.'

'Why all this whispering and secrecy? You're making me feel like a Russian spy.'

'I don't want you disturbing the other guests. They're mainly middle-aged couples who come here for a rest.'

'Middle-class bastards who need a good prod up the arse.'

He showed Early to a room which he had chosen because the bathroom and toilet were only two doors down the corridor.

'It's smaller than I'm used to,' Early complained. 'Gulban always gave me a double.'

'It's still the high season. It's all we've got left.'

'I'll need a pair of pyjamas and a dressing-gown. I don't think yours would fit me, you're too thin, but an old pair of Gulban's pyjamas would do, even if they are a bit short in the leg.'

'I'll see what I can find.' Cookie tried not to betray any hint of incredulousness.

'I'll have a drink while I'm waiting. If you bring me a bottle of Scotch, it will save you having to come up again. No need for a mixer. I'll have it as it comes. At my age a man can only taste the strongest flavours.'

'I'll do my best.'

'And don't forget supper.'

'I'll bring you a plate of cold beef salad. The sirloin is excellent. Do you like it rare or well done?'

'I don't like roast beef at all, and as for salad, I'm not a rabbit. If you bring me the Scotch, I'll have a look at the menu over the first couple of bumpers.'

Cookie met Joey on the way to the kitchen.

'The saucy bugger won't eat cold beef, he wants to look at the menu. I hope he orders something simple because the chef always leaves early on Sunday evenings.'

'Leave it to me,' Joey said. 'Just find out what he wants, I'll know precisely what to put in it.'

Cookie brought Big Andy half a bottle of Scotch and a bowl of roasted peanuts on a tray. He had taken off his shoes and trousers and was reclining on the bed with his open shirt revealing a hairy belly and hairier nether parts. Cookie left him to study the menu and went off to find a pair of pyjamas as a matter of urgency.

After prolonged comparative study, Early put down the menu and ordered lobster cardinal.

'The lobster cardinal is off,' Cookie said.

'I'll have the lobster Newburg, then.'

'There's no more lobster, I'm afraid. It's been very popular this evening and we never buy in more than we think we'll need.'

'Before I get excited over something else, you'd better tell me what's off and what's on.'

'Everything is on except the lobster.'

'I'll make things easy for the *chef de cuisine*. Can you do me a large T-bone steak, charcoal-grilled with mushrooms, tomatoes, broccoli and potatoes lyonnaise. I like my steak medium to well done and the broccoli underdone, rather than boiled out of its wits as it usually is.'

'You'd like an hors-d'oeuvre, of course?'

'I'm hungry, there's no need for an appetiser. Nothing but Scotch and the main course.'

'He's impossible,' Cookie told Joey, after giving the chef the order. 'What are we to do?'

'Throw him out, that's what.'

'You know what Gulban said.'

'If we can't use force, we'll have to use inducement.'

'Another fiver?'

'A fiver wouldn't wet his whistle. No, we'll have to make leaving worth his while.'

The following morning Cookie took him to Gulban's room after breakfast and waited outside on the landing in case he should escape. He emerged after an hour and Cookie lured him down the back stairs.

'Your father isn't near as chirpy as he used to be. Jack's death hit him hard, poor man.'

'He needs rest and quiet,' said Cookie.

'I won't disturb him, I'll only stay a fortnight.'

Joey was waiting for them both in the hallway.

'I know my father likes seeing you,' he said to Early, 'but the slightest excitement is bad for him these days. We can't put you up here in the height of the tourist season, so I'm going to give you a hundred pounds to keep you going till the winter. You can come back when things are quiet and we have the house to ourselves.'

He handed Early a long envelope which Early shook but refrained from opening. Cookie produced another long envelope addressed to Andrew Early, Esq., care of the post office in a certain seaside town fifty miles away.

'I'm posting this today. It contains another hundred pounds to be held for you *poste restante* and collected at your leisure.'

Early flung back his sun-tanned head and laughed.

'Last night you made me feel like a spy. Now you're making me feel like a remittance-man. What on earth do you yourself feel like, I wonder?'

'Call it a little inducement to travel,' Cookie smiled.

'Think of it this way,' Joey counselled. 'It will be one of those rare occasions when it is even better to arrive.'

'You're two clumsy gift-horses and I'm too old and too poor to look you in the mouth. I can be generous, too, though. I won't mention any of this to Gulban next time I see him. Even if I did, he's too much of a gentleman to understand.'

They watched him shuffle down the driveway, craggy and stiff-legged with a barely perceptible tremble of the hand that communicated itself to his hazel stick as he walked.

'He's an engaging old rogue,' said Cookie. 'Pity we had to show him the door.'

'He's not our real problem. Gulban's as daft as a brush. It was obvious yesterday that he was giving us some kind of test.'

'I wonder what it could have been,' said Cookie.

11

'The solicitor is coming at eleven,' Pauline said.

'What can he want?' Cookie wondered.

'It's what Gulban wants. He sent for him over a week ago, the day after he talked to Big Andy.'

'I'm sure he knows what he's doing.' Cookie went off to ring up Joey at the shop.

'There's something fishy about this,' Joey swore. 'Looby, Laxton and Phibbs were never bearers of good news.'

'You may be wrong. He may have decided to make his will at last.'

'Why now? We haven't accounted for our talents.'

'Perhaps he feels that time is getting short.'

'Don't let Looby go without pumping him. Find out as much as you can.'

Mr Looby came at eleven and stayed till one. On the way out he found Cookie in the lobby, immersed in a newspaper.

'Ah, we meet again.' Mr Looby extended a butter-fingered hand.

'How did you find him?'

'Find him?' Mr Looby tilted his head sideways, alert as a listening sparrow. He was light-boned and dainty, his mahogany-coloured briefcase disproportionately large and, to judge by his stance, disproportionately heavy.

'Is he looking better, do you think?'

'No, he's looking worse. Of course, I hadn't seen him since before the stroke.'

'He's rather forgetful, I'm afraid. He tends to ramble.'

'He addressed our agenda with exemplary acuity, I must say.'

'Agenda?'

'Our business.'

'Ah, business,' Cookie nodded.

'Always the perfectionist, your father. He wants to have Mr Laxton and Mr Phibbs present at our next meeting. They are the other partners.'

'And will they be coming?'

'Mr Laxton will, I'm sure. Mr Phibbs rarely leaves the office.'

'You pronounce his name "Pibbs"?'

'He himself prefers "Pibbs". When he became a partner, there was some talk that he might change his name by deed poll. Instead he elected to change the pronunciation. A man of the utmost integrity is Mr Phibbs.'

He smiled again and raised his car keys. For a moment he seemed to incense the air with a miniature thurible.

'When shall we be seeing you again?'

'That depends on Mr Laxton.'

'Goodbye.' Cookie held open the door.

His head was buzzing uncomfortably. He had spent most of the morning in the small back office with Pauline, going through the September accounts. She sat beside him, exhaling the fragrance of young chrysanthemums, undermining his concentration and self-confidence with the swiftness of her arithmetical calculations. She had a photographic memory for figures. She not only recalled the amounts but the numbers and dates of invoices she had passed the previous week. He kept looking at her thin Swiss watch and imagining the heavy black skids in the concrete of the slip. She knew the business inside out. In vain he tried to grasp the numerical imbrications she had set before him. He nodded his head though he failed to comprehend, and he winced at the precision of her mind which jabbed with the speed of a sewing-machine.

In the afternoon he decided to get away from Pauline, the hotel and everything that threatened dislodgement and annihilation. He crossed the river where they both used to catch eels and hide from Joey who was too young and too noisy to catch anything. She and he had shared the life of streams, heights and gullies. She would wade up and down the river in canvas shoes without socks, her dress tucked up above her knobbly knees. They were both the same age, but already she was wiser and more thoughtful.

'We catch the eels and you give them to Jack,' she'd said. 'Jack cuts them up for bait to catch pollack. Why don't we pinch a boat and go out and catch the pollack ourselves?'

'We're too young to go on the sea,' he'd replied.

'Will we ever grow up?'

'I think so. Maybe next year.'

'It's a long time to wait.' Wearily, she lifted another stone in the river bed.

Even then she was in a hurry. Already she wanted to be with Jack, just because he was four years older. At fourteen Cookie was packed off to boarding school and her mother sent Pauline to a convent to be educated by nuns. They both came home for the summer holidays. The river, the heights, the gullies hadn't changed, though they were now the haunts of other children. She wore a yellow dress and a white sun-hat. She seemed shot through with light, a summer's flower which was to the summer sweet. He met her in the road, and with a pang glimpsed the curve of her newly formed breasts. On the other side of the ditch was a field of yellow ragwort. He couldn't bear to look at her. She was a grown woman, she had sprinted out of reach. Instinctively, he knew that he would never catch her again.

It didn't matter now. Living had diminished her. She had become a prosaic, practical-minded woman whose days were filled with one narrow routine after another.

Her fair hair had grown dark. Instead of airy yellows and white, she wore strongly contrasting colours — red blouses with black skirts or green blouses with red skirts — and she often wore a shirt and tie like a man. She probably despised men like himself who followed no direction and no routine. Her own life at least had a focus now: Jack's empty chair in his still empty upstairs room.

He took the rising road past Gildea's stone cottage, winding through patches of close-cropped grass, between heather and reddening bracken. When he reached the top, he sat between the two breasts, looking down on the glassy surface of Gulban's reservoir below. To the north stood the hotel on a small rise above the sea, exposed to every wind that blew, solitary and gaunt, with white walls, blue slates and tall windows that seemed to be contemplating the pampered life within rather than the plain, hard-working life of the farms around. On the level below lay Fort Knox, squat and flat-roofed, a white cube in a square field, a doll's house in the middle of a miniature stockade. Beyond slept the hazy island, encircled by the sea which reached round behind him and stretched away to the south as far as his eye could see. His gaze returned to the hotel and Fort Knox, alien extrusions in the native landscape. In a sense their families were aliens too. Pauline and Alicia. Each would be seen more clearly if it weren't for the other. They hardly knew each other, yet their outlines merged.

He walked eastwards along the crest, up one side of the left breast and down the other, skirting the mound called the Nipple, which close up did not resemble a nipple at all. The October air was tangy and strong. The buzzing in his head had subsided. He trudged across a rolling plateau, with no houses, no roads, no farms, nothing but heather and sedge and small flocks of hardy sheep grazing. He had lost sight of the sea. His thin shadow flowed before him, while the evening light turned the brown sedge to red. He slackened his pace as the soft ground sucked at his heels.

After two hours he reached the road to town. He sat on a ditch and waited for a lift back home. He felt jaded and footweary, and immobilised by a paralysis of the will that caused him to let two cars pass without raising a hand. The cheque for £10,000 still lay accusingly in a desk drawer in his bedroom. Now and again he would look at it, as if it were a letter he could not bring himself to post. Gulban would expect him to consult his bank manager, a firm of stockbrokers, an investment analyst — all of them things he could not do without enduring the discomfort of self-ridicule. He had made a pact with Joey. That was enough. Neither of them would be seen to strive, and Gulban would sweat the more in choosing. Yet he must at least pay the cheque into his bank. He realised that he should have finished footnoting the doctoral thesis that lay open on his desk.

From time to time he would turn the pages and wonder how he had found the energy to write it. Increasingly, the true pleasure of life had become what he liked to call lucubration. It was a pleasure that started after midnight, when the hotel had finally gone to sleep. Then he would take down a book and read till three. Sometimes he would slip out for a walk along the cliffs to digest what he'd read and to drink the salty night wind off the sea. Once he embarrassed himself by declaiming to the mysteriously moving water:

> O well for the fisherman's boy,
> That he shouts with his sister at play!
> O well for the sailor lad,
> That he sings in his boat on the bay!

Afterwards he walked home wondering how much of his emotion came from lived experience and how much from off the bookshelf.

A red car rose over the crest of the hill on his right. He got up from the ditch and waited.

'We're all suffering from a deficiency disease, an essential element is missing from our spiritual diet,' he shouted at the approaching driver. 'We're all citizens of no city. Our heritage is in another country, never here, always there.'

The car showed no sign of slowing down. He placed one foot firmly on the road as he recognised Alicia Bugler Braking hard, she slid past him to a stop.

'What were you saying?' she asked.

'I was saying that I'm too tired to walk another step, that I want a lift. A lift to anywhere will do.'

'You should write it on a placard in large letters. You'll never be heard above the hum of any engine except one made by Rolls-Royce.'

He got in beside her. She drove off without turning to look at him. He waited for her to speak. When she didn't, he decided to break the silence.

'I walked up past Gildea's to the top of the hill and cut across the moor till I came to the road. It's a fair step. I was glad when I saw you coming.'

'If I hadn't come, someone else was bound to.'

He glanced at her dainty blue shoe on the accelerator. They were gathering speed on the hill. He felt an access of excitement, as if he were driving briskly in a post-chaise with a pretty woman. A sports car was not quite what the good doctor had in mind but it was the next best thing.

'You're a capable driver,' he said.

'I try to be capable while appearing to be reckless.'

'That's what I meant. You must never allow your passenger to get bored.'

Again he waited for her to say something, or to give something of her remote and mysterious self away.

'Do you remember my father?' she asked.

'Only vaguely. I remember him carrying his easel to the cliffs on good days.'

'Why good days? Surely he must have painted in all weathers.'

'I was a child then, I only remember the summers. I also remember himself and your mother driving to Mass in a trap with a tartan rug over his knees. He was well liked. I've often heard my father say that he never drank with the tourists in the lounge, always with the fishermen in the public bar. My father's got one of his paintings in his bedroom. Four fishermen in sea boots at the counter, two of them asleep and the other two with their heads in their enormous hands.'

'Do they look like local fishermen?'

'To me they look like Eskimos.'

'I'd like to see it some time. He sold all his paintings, we've got only a few unfinished sketches at home. They went all over the world. He used to sell them to the tourists at the hotel. My mother has no interest in them now that they've been sold. He died when I was four, and I can't remember his face . . . I hope I'm not boring you.'

'You're driving too fast for that.'

If Joey were listening now, Cookie thought, he would subject her every word to the dispassionate scrutiny of a scientist who both loved and hated the object of his investigations.

'I spied her going down to the slip this morning,' he had told Cookie the previous week. 'There wasn't a soul about but she was walking like a woman on parade before a regiment. Tossing her head though her hair was tied in a bun, adjusting the strap of her shoulder-bag, touching her neck and necklace with her fingertips. She couldn't have known I was watching, she was doing it entirely for her so, so conscious self. In that she's the opposite of Pauline. Now Pauline walks as if she were alone in a lonely world.'

'Pauline has been walking for longer. Compared with her, Alicia's only a child,' Cookie said.

'You can tell the difference in their ages by their skins.'

'It's only a difference of six years.'

'It's still there. Alicia's is soft and supple, and so pale that it's almost transparent. Pauline's is already going dry. Good skin is wasted on the young.'

They both laughed, and for both the laughter relieved pain.

'We can't allow Pauline to spend the rest of her life in mourning for a man who led her up the garden path,' Joey continued. 'You sit beside her in the back office flank to flank — or is it cheek to cheek? Why don't you pull her up short, tell her that Jack deflowered Alicia when she was only thirteen?'

'He didn't,' Cookie said.

'He boasted to me more than once. "I had her on the summer seat," he crowed. "Behind the rhododendrons in the garden while her mother was upstairs fucking Forker. I had to do it before someone else did. Sweet as young parsnips, she was. If you ever get a chance, don't pass it up. She's an even jouncier ride than her mother." Those were our brother's words. I think we owe Pauline a revelation.'

It was typical of Jack to try to drive Joey insane with sexual envy.

'Will you tell her?' Joey persisted.

'Why don't you?'

'It would come more convincingly from you, I think. As our literary man, you could quote her what Robbie Burns said about relentless promiscuity, and allow her to draw her own conclusions: "och; it hardens a' within, and petrifies the feeling".'

Last winter he and Joey had met Alicia out walking in the snow. The sun was sharp, the wind cold and keen. Alicia suddenly appeared in white: white coat, white beret, white scarf, white leg-warmers and white boots.

'She should have gone for Pauline's red and black today,' said Joey. 'Against the snow her coat looks a dirty cream, like one of Slash Gildea's sheep on the hill.'

Cookie didn't answer. All he saw was the sunlight making glinting pearls in the snow and Alicia's cheeks a delicate red in the leaping, overwhelming white.

She was driving quickly now, not briskly, taking out-rageous chances on hairpin bends. There was never much traffic on the road from town but you could conceivably meet another careless driver in the wrong place. They were coming down the hill towards the spot where Jack had had the accident. She gave no sign of slowing down and he refrained from warning her of the approaching bend. He knew that she knew that all he wanted for them both was to die. She never even tried to brake. The bonnet rose over the broken wall, they glided for a slow eternity, then gannet-dived through darkness towards a glowing green. They would land with a jolt. He turned to embrace her and found an empty seat.

Again they approached the bend, and again she gave no sign of slowing. At the last moment she hit the brake. As they slewed, he glimpsed the gap in the wall where Jack had gone off the road. Then she accelerated out of the bend and he breathed more freely, recalling a snowy day with a catch in the icy air.

'Were you frightened?' she asked.

'No, not frightened.'

'I thought I sensed you stiffen.'

'I may have been excited. I wanted it to go on for longer. The bend came up too quickly, that was all.'

She pulled up outside the hotel.

'You're home,' she said.

'Come in and I'll buy you a drink.'

'Not today, thanks. My mother is waiting for the car.'

'Why don't we have dinner in town one evening? I'll take you in the Land-Rover,' he promised.

'I thought you liked being driven by me!'

'Will you come?'

'It takes two hours to eat dinner. What on earth would we talk about all that time?'

A burly ram jumped out of a field on to the road. His black, insensitive face had the appearance of a Hallowe'en mummer's mask, crude and makeshift, concealing a smaller face beneath. He looked a bit like Jack. They're all the same, he seemed to say, who lift the tail and turn their fleecy backs to me.

'If you're worried, you could bring a book,' he said.

'Let me have a list of topics. I already know the menu in the Atlantic Grill. What I'd like to know is the agenda.'

'Thanks for the lift,' he said.

'You're welcome.'

She drove off without turning to acknowledge his good-bye.

12

About five in the afternoon one of the chambermaids came running into the lounge bar where Pauline was trying to pacify a querulous Englishman who was hugging his stomach, clearly regretting his lunch.

'Gulban's fallen out of bed and he's shouting his head off,' she managed to stammer.

Pauline, followed by one of the barmen, hurried upstairs to find him lying on the floor, slavering with unavailing effort.

'Now, relax,' she said. 'Just leave everything to us.'

They lifted him slowly and laid him on his back in the bed, while he angrily demanded to be put sitting by the window.

'Later, perhaps,' she told him. 'You must rest first. We'll get the doctor to examine you to make sure you haven't broken any bones.'

'Bugger the doctor, I want a glass of rum punch to warm me up.'

He looked pale and pinched about the gills. When she caught his hand, she could feel it shaking.

'How did it happen?' she asked.

'I fell asleep after lunch and the next thing I knew I was on the floor.'

'You're sure you weren't trying to get out of bed?'

'There's no need for an inquest, I'm not dead yet.'

She went downstairs to make the punch. Cookie had gone for a walk on the hill and, typically, had not said when he'd be back. She rang Joey who promised to come up as soon as he closed the shop for the night. She brought Gulban his drink and held the glass to his lips because his hands were still trembling.

'I feel warmer now,' he said at length.

'You must have rolled over in your sleep.' She thought he might relax if she could encourage him to talk.

'I had a dream about a dream,' he said. 'I thought I dreamt that I could hear harp music and that you sent for the doctor to make sure I wasn't dying. The doctor tested my hearing and told me that it was all an illusion, that at my age a man is further away from heavenly music than ever. Then he told me not to worry, that there was no after-life, and that even if there was my cards were stamped, and that I'd never given short measure. As soon as he left, a whirlwind came and whisked me up to heaven. Everyone was lolling about on Sleepeezee mattresses listening to piped music, drinking red wine and eating white wafers. They all looked childlike and happy. They were making small talk about cloud formations, and St Peter took me aside and explained that they had forgotten how to ask any of the big questions.

' "Where is God?" I enquired.

'He placed a cautionary finger over his lips and looked round, horrified, in case anyone had heard.

' "You've come to the wrong place," he said. "You should be down below. You're still asking big questions."

'Then another whirlwind came and I found myself stretched on my bad side on the floor.'

Pauline laughed and Gulban caught her hand.

'It was a lovely dream,' she said. 'Pity it made you fall out of bed.'

'Sometimes I could laugh myself. Mostly I'm too sad. I'm not dead, but my life, my work, is over. I listen to sounds downstairs, I look across at my reservoir, I count the cars coming in the gate. That's all there is left for me to do. Often I imagine I'm dead. Then I get a pain and realise that I'm still alive.'

His once ruddy face was now grey. He could barely move his right arm and leg. He kept falling asleep throughout the day and his eyelids kept drooping even when he was awake. He had lost his appetite, yet he hadn't lost weight. Joey, with customary brutishness, said that he was living on hot air; Cookie, that, like the capitalist system, he was quite worn out; and the doctor, that he showed so many symptoms that they couldn't conceivably represent one disease. They all sat in judgment, even Father Bosco who once offered the opinion over Sunday lunch that most men's lives are only an accumulation of bad habits, histories of self-seeking and self-justifying prejudice. He wasn't referring directly to his father, yet everyone present thought of Gulban in his bedroom, shorn of authority, hungering for sympathy and love.

'I always kept busy,' Gulban continued. 'I never spent much time alone with myself. Now I know why. Some days I think I'd be better off dead.'

'It's wrong to talk like that.'

'I'd never admit it to anyone but you.'

She stood by the window with her back to the bed. In a field of lush aftergrass beyond the road two of Slash Gildea's rams were building themselves up for the tupping season in a month's time. They advanced as they grazed, two old men with their heads down and their bottoms sticking out. The comparison took her aback. It was not a comparison that would have occurred to Slash, belonging as it did to a life of diminishment and non-participation. Out there was digging and sowing, reaping and gathering in season; cows and ewes giving birth; rain swelling clay and plants spreading themselves in the sun; roots stretching and gripping; men, animals and plants conjoining in a dance of concelebration.

'The wind is getting up,' she said. 'I like October because it's lively.'

'It's the completion of all that's good. After it the year can only go to the bad.'

She turned to him. He was propped against the pillows, his head back and his eyes closed. Now he needed her more and more. She was being drawn further into the family. At times she felt that she was being sucked towards a whirlpool which defied resistance, dragging all that entered it into unrelinquishing dark. He opened his eyes and closed them again.

'In middle age a man needs sons to take his mind off the dead-end ahead, to give him a sense of family history still to be written. In old age he needs a daughter, a good warm caring woman. I'm grateful to you, Pauline, for everything you do. Without you now . . . I can't bear to think.'

'Don't think, just rest. I'll bring you up a cup of tea in an hour.'

'Pauline.'

'Yes.'

'There's a nip in the air this evening. Time to light a fire in the public bar. I always liked the first fire of the dark season. It gave me a sense of comfort that made me remember women.'

'We've had a fire in the lounge bar for the last three weeks.'

'The lounge bar is for hothouse plants, it doesn't count. Now, don't forget to light a fire in the public bar this evening, and I'll lie here in the dark imagining the flames.'

'I won't forget.' She went quietly down the stairs.

When Joey returned from the shop, she recounted in detail all that had happened.

'He's a danger to himself,' he said. 'We'll have to make sure it doesn't occur again.'

Then he went up and told Gulban that they would have to put ropes round the bed to keep him from falling out.

'You'll be putting me in a straitjacket next,' Gulban said.

'If you don't like the idea of ropes, I'll have wooden

grids made. It wouldn't do to break an arm or a leg at your age.'

Joey asked Slash Gildea to get some timber from the shop and make two supports for Gulban's bed. Slash slowly rolled up his shirt-sleeves as he considered.

'No,' he said.

'Why?' Joey demanded, the good side of his face going pale.

'Because Gulban hasn't asked me.'

'I'm asking you.'

'I'll make grids for your bed if you like, but not for Gulban's.'

'It's Gulban who needs them.'

Pauline could see Joey stiffen from the effort of suppressing anger. Slash gazed down at him with the steadfast indifference she had thought he reserved for her alone.

'You want me to make his bed into a baby's cot. I've worked for him all my life. I'm not going to insult him now that he's past his best.'

'You'll regret this,' Joey said.

'Regret is nothing compared with guilt.' Slash walked away.

When Cookie came back from his walk, he and Joey went down to the village to see the carpenter. The carpenter came and measured the bed, and the following afternoon he returned with the grids.

'What do you make of these hurdles?' Gulban asked her.

'They're not my idea.'

'They're mine,' said Joey.

'They're only for your own good,' Cookie said.

'You're like two thrushes singing a duet. I suppose it must come from countersigning each other's cheques.'

'Try them for one night and see,' Cookie suggested. 'If you don't like them, we'll think of something else.'

'Should I try them?' he asked Pauline.

'Once will do no harm.'

That night they were woken in their beds by a hysterical shouting and thumping. Startled guests opened doors to see what was going on. Pauline rushed to Gulban's room to find Cookie and Joey standing speechless in a torrent of abuse from their father.

'Get me out of this coffin, get me out, I say.' He banged his fists against the heavy timber of the grids.

Cookie and Joey unhooked them and laid them against the wall.

'Take them away. Out of my sight. I never want to see them again. When I put out my hands in the dark, I could feel the sides of the coffin. Men have been buried alive before. It can easily happen to an old man who's barely warm.'

'You only imagined it,' Joey said.

'You dreamt it,' Cookie assured him.

'Get back to bed, both of you . . . Pauline, will you get me a hot drink?'

Cookie and Joey left the room with Pauline.

'They'll do for me yet,' Gulban told her when she returned with more rum punch.

'They mean well. They were afraid you might fall out of bed again.'

'It's a hard choice between them. Pauline, you must help me decide.'

'Don't talk now. Just sip your drink and then go back to sleep.'

'What do you think of Father Bosco?'

'He's a priest.'

'He doesn't have to remain a priest.'

'It would be sinful to tempt him with possessions.'

'He's no fool, he took his talent like the others. Possessions and responsibilities might make a man of him.'

'You mean the moral effort of rejecting them?'

'He's more capable than Cookie and Joey. He has chosen a different life, but he must be considered, especially now.'

'The life he's chosen is for good.'

'Ah, Pauline, the only man among them had to die.' He reached out and grasped her hand. 'We know he had his failings and we mustn't forget them. I must remember his secret drinking and you must remember his fornicating in every ditch, haystack and barn-loft in the county. Many's the time I told him to have nothing to do with that windbroken old nag Mrs Bugler, and every time I mentioned her name he pretended I was talking about bridge.'

'I know his faults as well as you.'

'On good days I recall the good things: his straightforward character, his firmness, his loyalty to me. When I listen to Cookie and Joey pretending to be businessmen, the heart inside me sinks. Those two never grew up, they're only playing games. They don't believe in what they're doing. At least schoolboys believe in their games. If Slash Gildea had had half their education, he'd be running the country by now.'

She took his mug from between his hands and tucked in the bedclothes round his feet.

'Pauline, will you do me a favour? Will you ring Father Bosco first thing in the morning and tell him I want to see him?'

13

Father Bosco arrived on Sunday morning. He pulled up in the driveway as Cookie was making for the gate.

'You'll find that Joey and I are *personae non gratae*. He's convinced we tried to bury him alive,' Cookie warned.

'He sent for me. I've brought my stole in case he wants confession.'

'Hardly. In his case the need of confession will be preceded by fear of the conflagration. That's a fear to come.'

'It's a pity you and Joey can't show him a little humanity.'

'In return for reason and justice?' Cookie smiled. 'Father, I must leave you. I shan't be in for lunch, I'm feasting at Fort Knox.'

'Taking up where Jack left off?'

'I never play cards, they're the Devil's prayer-book.' He waved an exaggerated farewell.

He had met Mrs Bugler in the village the previous evening. He observed her coming towards him, tall and strong, thick-waisted and thick-ankled, sure-footed in thick-soled shoes. Her Jack Russell paused to sniff the base of a telegraph pole. She turned to study the fascia of Heron's General Stores across the street, a sturdy figure in a white mac with a tightly drawn leather belt.

'What a coincidence!' she smiled at him. 'I was planning to ring you this evening. It's Alicia, you see. I'm so worried about her that I don't know where to turn. She should have gone back to university last week, she's taking her Second Med. next year, but she says she'll never open another medical book again. She's obsessed with her father's paintings. She wants to become an artist and paint like him.'

'Is there anything wrong with that?'

'Giving up her studies after three years! If she had a talent for the brush, I wouldn't mind. I thought that if you had a word with her you might make her see reason.'

'I don't know how I can help, I'm no admirer of the academic life.'

'But you're taking your doctorate very shortly.'

'I may not.'

'Alicia needs someone intelligent to talk to. She spends far too much time on her own. She stays in bed till noon and has breakfast for lunch. She paints in the afternoons and practises croquet alone. She's simply not with us half the time. At night she goes down to the sea to walk along the cliffs in the dark. She comes back after twelve and reads till three in the morning — light French novels, cookery books, fashion magazines, anything that won't stretch the mind. I thought that if you came to lunch on Sunday it might make a change for her. Owen Forker will be coming, and he's a sweetie. If it's mild, we'll eat *al fresco*. It could be fun.'

'I'd love to come.'

'It's a date, then.'

She smiled with in-turned teeth, all chin and nose, expressing extremes of self-will and self-command. From a doorway he watched her military walk, the measured strides contrasting oddly with the dainty trot of her long-bodied dog.

He had been contemplating the lunch with a mixture of curiosity and apprehension. He didn't know whether to sport an open collar or a tie, so in a spirit of uncertain compromise he settled for a silk cravat. He walked to the village and had a drink in the only pub before taking the south-running road through wire-fenced grazing fields to

Fort Knox. He had never been inside the gate before. He plucked a sprig of red Virginia creeper and put it in his breast-pocket for luck. On the other side was stillness, shelter, and a hint of geometrical exactitude reflecting in miniature the rectangularity of the fenced fields around. Here he felt a thousand miles from the gaunt and solitary hotel and a million miles from the drably huddling cottages of the village. Pock! On the lawn in front of him Alicia had hit a wooden ball with a mallet.

'You're early and lunch is late,' she called.

'I was invited for twelve.'

'You shouldn't have come.'

'Why?'

'Don't you have a sense of enchanted entrapment here?'

'No.'

'This is a place outside life. Over the wall the only house you can see is the hotel, which is equally remote from the things we seek to know. No fields, no farmers, no boats, no fishermen, no sheep, no cows. You can hear the sea in winter, though. And you can smell new-mown hay in summer. This is a place for reading rather than writing, for mixing colours rather than painting. I'm convinced that those who come forget what they've seen immediately they go out the gate. Hence the itch to come back. Again and again and again. So I'm telling you to leave before you fall into the silken toils that don't so much chafe as tease.'

She tossed her curling hair and laughed at him.

'Would you like a game?' Her eyes gleamed bright with mischief.

'No, I'm content to watch.'

'Yet another voyeur! You don't have to be an athlete to play croquet but it helps to be intelligent.'

Mrs Bugler bore down on them, stepping dauntingly and crushingly on close-trimmed grass with heels that were the more noticeable for not being fetlocks. She was wearing a darkly striped shirt with a stiff white collar and cuffs. Cookie had a distinct impression of chains and bracelets. He visualised the horse brasses on the chimney-brace in the lounge bar of the hotel. He glanced at her squarish forehead, half-expecting to see a blaze. She smiled in welcome. Then, to show who was mistress, she turned to Alicia with a challenging tilt of nose and chin. Beside her Alicia was a schoolgirl, dainty as a painted doll.

'Owen Forker has had to cry off. A flat battery, or was it a flat wheel? I can never understand impractical men.'

'It will be so flat without him,' said Alicia. 'Are you sure you don't want to go home?'

She turned from Cookie to her mother. By her very stance she seemed to emphasize that her mother had stopped being a woman, that she was now at an age when she was half-way to being a very practical man.

'We'll have to make do without him, just the three of us, I'm afraid,' said Mrs Bugler.

'Cookie will feel threatened, as the only male,' said Alicia. 'I suggest we flatter him by competing tooth, nail and tweezers for his favours. Or if you think competition unfair, Mother, we could go down to the crossroads and invite the first man in trousers to come along. The best luncheon parties are more than three and less than nine. More than the Graces and less than the Muses, isn't that what you always say?'

'Lunch won't be ready for half an hour. Would you like a drink, Cookie, while you're waiting?'

'He won't have a drink yet,' Alicia either decided or predicted. 'One thing at a time. He's about to try his hand at croquet.'

Mrs Bugler began walking towards the house, her high, wide bottom the very picture of unshakeable solidity.

'I've changed my mind,' he said. 'I'll try a shot or two.'

'It isn't as simple as it looks. The hoops are only one-eighth of an inch wider than the balls. There is little room for error.'

She handed him the mallet and stood beside him,

showing him the different grips. To demonstrate her skill, she played an oblique hoop-shot, hitting the far wire so that the forward spin of the ball carried it through.

She was wearing a light-blue, low-cut dress with a neat bow at the back which gave her the look of a Meissen figurine released into movement. As she explained the game and coached him in the swing and carry-through, he kept looking in the direction of two straight oaks at the other end of the lawn, silent twins who'd seen much yet reflected nothing more secret than the sturdiness of each other. She gripped his wrist as she showed him once again how to hold the mallet. The rhododendron sprawled between the oaks only thirty strides away, and her flat-bottomed mother was safely out of sight, immersed in *la grande cuisine*.

'Watch this!' She swung the mallet between her legs centre-style and hit the red ball off the black.

'I've made what could have been a roquet. Match it if you can.'

He hit the ball with fierce aggression, driving it wide of the hoop, straight between the oaks, in under the shapeless rhododendron. He ran to retrieve it, and sure enough behind the bush was Jack's wooden summer seat. He hadn't told a lie. It was here that he'd had her at thirteen while her mother was upstairs fucking Forker. A jet of anger did violence to the lining of his stomach. Blindly, he rolled the ball in her direction.

'I'll show you a rush stroke now,' she said.

'I'm going in for a drink. I know when I'm outclassed. As you say, it helps to be intelligent.'

'Perhaps you'd like to try the swing.' She pointed to the garden swing on the far side of the rhododendron.

'Not just now.'

'Would you like to see me swing? I can go higher than Mother and I'm more interesting to watch.'

'After lunch perhaps all three of us can have a go.'

'You mustn't feel bad, Cookie. Croquet is a truly

modern game. It's one of the few outdoor games I know in which a woman is not potentially at a disadvantage.'

He walked towards the cube that was the house — a plain, unpretentious building of white pebble-dash that bore the marks of eccentric, if not amateur, design.

'What do you think of the house and garden?' Mrs Bugler handed him a schooner of dry sherry.

'They make their own world. They have little to do with the world of harsh utility outside the walls.'

'The same could be said of your hotel.'

'The difference is that we are open to the public.'

She ignored his comment. He waited for her to speak again.

'Nothing binds a man and a woman together as closely as the building of a house,' she said. 'Most couples buy their houses already built; only the lucky few make a nest of their own. That's one of the reasons I've stayed on here: the house and garden are still warm with enlivening memories. I often recall the nights we sat up together arguing about the design. Gregory used to say that architecture was the queen of the arts, but, as you can see, he was no architect. The house he designed is as plain as it is solid; it has an uncompromising geometry that gives it a sullen presence. Then there was the garden. The site was a builder's yard once. We spent months digging up broken bricks, rusty paint-pots and ends of decaying timber. Then we spent as long again planning the layout, arguing about the flower-beds and which flowers to put in them. When it was all done, Gregory got the idea of enclosing it from the world. He built that six-foot wall with his own hands. He began down by the gate, you can see how the brickwork improved with experience as he approached the house.'

She laughed genially, her large breasts heaving within the tight bodice of her dress. Looking at her, he became aware of more than he could actually see. The handsome strength of her face seemed to spring from the structure of bone beneath. It came to him that she was one of those women who are plain at eighteen and grow more handsome every year until they reach their meridian on the far side of fifty. He began to understand something of what Jack must have seen in her, yet his eye dwelt obsessively on her lined neck, weathered as a portal dolmen.

He was about to ask her why her husband had built the wall when Alicia pranced in, having left a trail of mallets and balls behind her on the lawn.

'I'll bet Cookie is dying to know what's for lunch.' She flopped down carelessly on the sofa, and her feet lifted off the floor.

'Beef *à la mode*,' said her mother.

'It's all the rage up at the hotel, I'll bet.' She gave a kittenish grin and tucked her legs under her dress, causing Cookie to wonder if she were trying to tell him something about himself that he did not wish to know.

They ate inside with the french windows open, because it was a shade too cool to eat on the patio. The food and the wine were good, and Alicia's conversation bristled with cleverly prepared darts aimed by turns at Cookie and her unresponsive mother. Cookie tried to give an impression of worldly well-being, though a sense of unease in his stomach forecast for him an afternoon of querulous indigestion.

After the coffee and the brandy, Mrs Bugler asked Alicia to show Cookie her father's study. She led him into a small room at the back of the house that looked out on the two-breasted hill. There was a bare table, two chairs, and a book-lined recess on each side of the chimney-brace. The other walls were covered with line drawings, posters and lithographic prints.

'You've passed the test,' Alicia smiled. 'What's more, you've passed *magna cum laude*.'

'What test?'

'No one sees my father's study who hasn't passed the test. I remember the evening Jack qualified. To have passed at your age is an achievement. You are, in fact, what my mother calls a sweetie.'

'You speak in riddles, Alicia.'

'Life is a riddle, particularly as lived *chez* Bugler.'

She reached up to take down a book or possibly to show off her lace-edged slip.

'Father was interested in Arachnida. I came across this monograph on spiders the other day. Fascinating. I thought you might be amused.'

Cookie, looking nonplussed, waited for further enlightenment.

'Listen to this: "The male inseminates the female at arms' length . . . she's larger than he is, so he has to scale her while taking care to keep clear of her fangs. Sometimes his courtship includes tying her down with silk, just in case . . ." '

Her curls lifted and floated as she laughed. She had thin, spreading lips and her open mouth revealed two rows of tiny white teeth and clean, pink gums below.

'Kiss me, Cookie.'

She advanced and stood with her hands by her sides, her small round breasts touching him below the chest. He bent down and kissed her on the forehead.

'That was a chaste kind of kiss. Kisses are never chaste *chez* Bugler.'

He put his arms round her this time, while the monograph on spiders pressed against his groin. With a sense of being teased rather than desired, he kissed her slowly on the mouth and waited for her to draw away. She put her tongue between his teeth and drove the book edgeways between his thighs.

'Now you've seen the study,' she said. 'Like all good studies, it's full of dusty tomes.'

He followed her into the living-room, moving awkwardly and breathing quickly.

'I'm going for a walk now, Mother. I'll be back in about two hours.'

'If you're going up the hill, I'd like to come,' Cookie said.

'No, I'm going down to the slip to make some sketches for a painting.'

'Then I'll come along and sharpen the pencils.'

'Another time maybe. I'm working out an idea. It's something I need to do alone.'

'Surely Cookie can only help,' said Mrs Bugler.

'Ideas must come from me. Don't fret, Mother, I'll be back to show you the fruits of my genius. Like all artists, I'm just a teensy bit vain.'

'You see what I mean?' her mother said after she'd gone. 'There's no getting through to her. She lives in a world all her own.'

'I'm afraid I haven't had a chance to talk to her.'

'You did your best. Come, let me get you another brandy.'

With a smile that concealed reluctance, he handed her his empty glass.

14

Father Bosco, Joey and Pauline had lunch in the hotel restaurant. It was coming up to the end of the season, and there were only nine or ten guests staying. They chose a table by the window, looking out over the rising slope of the sea with darkly wrinkled patches in the green running before a fresh south-easterly breeze. The white lighthouse, white clouds and white seagulls gave Father Bosco a sense of self-indulgent self-discovery. He was dipping into the history of his childhood, which was a history of far-off things so remote and final that now it could never be blotted.

He liked returning to the hotel if only to enjoy a leisurely lunch served by young waitresses with genial country humour in their faces. They made a change from Canon Sproule's stiff-legged housekeeper, a dragon who knew no moderation in the kitchen. When she cooked, she over-cooked; and when Father Bosco gently reminded her that overcooking took longer than cooking and used up more electricity, she told him straight that the Canon liked his food well done. Dinner at the parochial house was as predictable as dinner in a boarding school, always either roast beef or roast lamb, except on Fridays when she served fried fish fingers or grilled mackerel and mustard.

'Much though I like coming back, it's sad to see the old order change,' he said. 'For a long time it seemed that nothing would ever alter. Gulban at seventy-five was the same as Gulban at fifty-five. Now suddenly we're full of uncertainty.'

'It's the uncertainty that must precede new certainty,' said Joey.

Father Bosco waited for Pauline to speak. When she didn't, he continued, 'The three of us have one thing in common. We come from families who never had a shanachie — a traditional story-teller in the chimney corner.'

'We didn't even have a chimney corner,' Joey pretended to lament.

'Though we were born and brought up here, our sustenance never came from the soil,' Father Bosco reminded them. 'Digging, scything, turf-cutting and lobster-fishing were always things that were done by other people. We had meat and gravy in this high-ceilinged room while our neighbours ate dry salted fish in their poky kitchens. We were tourists without ever leaving home.'

'Speak for yourself, Father,' said Joey. 'You have chosen the priesthood, you have made yourself a man apart. Whether you had meat or soused mackerel for dinner as a boy has little to do with your condition as a man. I can tell you that I feel fully part of all that goes on here, perhaps because I don't have your highly developed sense of guilt. I can watch a man trudging under the weight of a burden without wishing to share it.'

'It is surely a matter of personality,' Pauline said to Father Bosco. 'Jack had the same upbringing as you, yet I never once heard him express a word of doubt.'

'Jack was full of certainty because he saw no life but his own.'

'He saw the life of Fort Knox,' said Joey.

'If he did, he saw only his own reflection. Fort Knox is like the hotel, another enclave of unreality.'

'We'll ask Cookie when he gets back,' said Pauline. 'He's a man of feeling. He's bound to have something incisive to say.'

'He's feeling Alicia now — if he has any sense,' Joey said. 'And if he hasn't, he's feeling Mrs Bugler. He was invited to an *al fresco* lunch. Is it possible that he's engaged in a spot of *al fresco* troilism?'

Father Bosco glanced at Pauline. Neither joined in Joey's laughter.

'Why do you attach such importance to the shanachie?' Pauline turned two earnest eyes on Father Bosco.

'The shanachie was a folk historian,' he replied. 'By interpreting the communal past he gave resonance to an exiguous present. He peopled the landscape with larger-than-life characters. He created a world in which the landscape itself was a character. The three of us missed all that. While other children learnt why the hill has two breasts and why only one of them has a nipple, we were being taught to say "Bonjour, Monsieur" to Frenchmen and "Guten Morgen" to Germans coming down to breakfast. I can only say that I feel the poorer for it.'

'We had our own private folklore,' Joey reminded him. 'We had Gulban's stories about the Red Men. I remember you well, Bosco, jumping up and down in short trousers, singing:

> We are the Red Men,
> We are fly.
> No one makes fun
> Of us!

The Red Men were our Red Branch Knights and Robin Hood rolled into one.'

'The Red Men didn't bind us to the landscape, they set us apart. Other children ribbed us. They called us Shawnees and kept saying "Honest Injun" to annoy us. Some people still call us the Shawnees behind our backs. Fort Knox was another house without a shanachie. It's no coincidence that Cookie has gone there to lunch. Why, I ask myself, isn't he lunching with Old Gildea?'

'I wonder what he's doing now,' Joey cut in. 'Sits he, stands he, or is he holding forth?'

'Cookie is a scholar. He's probably fossicking in Mr Bugler's library,' Pauline laughed.

'Or in Mrs Bugler's bra. There's gold in them thar hills. Surely it must be the six-foot wall that attracts him. Little did Gregory Bugler realise that lust laughs at bailey builders.'

Father Bosco regretted the turn the conversation had taken. Joey had been maimed by negative experience. He saw the history of mankind as a practical demonstration of the Seven Deadly Sins, with the sin of lust forming the first and final chapters. In spite of him, Father Bosco had enjoyed his lunch. It was reassuring to sit opposite Pauline again without a sense of peril, to see her so calm in her bereavement, so cool in her judgments, so remote from the compulsions of envy and lust. Today she seemed to embody the virtues of prudence and fortitude, yet even she had drunk from the poisoned well of concupiscence. The ugliness of the thought brought a piercing sense of humiliation. It screamed at the white lighthouse and the white clouds; it darkened the surface of the cleansing sea. He smiled as he rose from the table.

'I'm going up to see Gulban now,' he said. 'Perhaps he'll be easier to talk to after he's eaten.'

Gulban was sleeping with his mouth open and one hairy arm across his chest. Father Bosco sat by the bed-side reading his office while he waited for him to wake up.

'Is it praying for me you are?'

'No, not just now, though I pray for you every morning in the Mass.'

'What good do you do apart from praying? Are you of any practical value to your flock?'

'I'm a healer, I suppose. A man comes to me with an overwhelming problem − a mountain he can't see across or beyond. I make him see the mountain against the landscape of eternity. The mountain shrinks, the man regains his hope.'

'You're a pedlar of dreams.'

'And you're a man who'd ask the number of steps in Jacob's ladder.'

'I've got an overwhelming problem: I'm dying between these sticky sheets. The mountain is only six inches from my nose. I'll give you the hotel if you blow the top off it.'

'God isn't on the fiddle.'

'Think of the good you could do if you owned it. You could abolish after-hours drinking and Saturday and Sunday night dancing in the ballroom, which, as you must know from the confessional, is only a prelude to promiscuous groping — what you call sins of impurity in your sermons.'

'Don't mock me, Gulban. I came here to comfort you.'

'They say priests are condemned to a lifetime of penance if they perform even one miracle. Would you do a lifetime's penance to make me well?'

'I would, if that were the case.'

Gulban closed his eyes. Father Bosco opened his breviary again and waited.

'What is the value of my life?' Gulban asked, as if from sleep.

'You worked hard. In worldly terms you achieved more than most.'

'The value of my life is that it happened to me. There's nothing else to it. No one else is interested. Life lacks body, shape, solidity. Life is a . . . fart. Prup, prup. Life stinks.'

'We all have moments of despair. Think of the good you've done, think of one good deed and build on it.'

'I failed you, Bosco. You would have been a businessman if I hadn't put you off. Was it something I said or something I did?'

'It was nothing like that, nothing to do with you.'

'You're the only man left, now that Jack is dead. You may have your head in the clouds but you're tall enough to keep your feet on the ground as well. Cookie and Joey have no head for business. Money isn't real to them, as a sheep is real to a shepherd. They don't think money, they get no pleasure from turning one pound into two. That's the test and there's no faking it. To a businessman money is what God is to a priest, it's in the forefront of his mind every hour of the day. Do you think of God every hour of the day?'

'I'm aware of His presence on good days and of His absence on bad.'

'You could think of money just as often. You were born with the right cast of mind.'

'Heaven forbid!'

'Surely you don't believe all that guff you preach? "If any would sue you and take your coat, let him have your cloak as well . . . If any one forces you to go one mile, go with him two miles." A businessman who did that would end up bankrupt. It's a recipe for profligacy and financial disaster.'

'It's a recipe for inner peace and true happiness.'

'So you think my life has been a waste of time?'

'You can still make amends.'

'If I left you the hotel, what would you do with it?'

'I'd turn it into a home for old priests, a place where they could end their days in prayerful thought, looking out serenely over the sea.'

Gulban gave a sarcastic croak of a laugh and closed his eyes. Father Bosco got up from his chair.

'Stay with us, for it is towards evening and the day is now far spent.'

'You don't know what you ask,' Father Bosco replied.

'You said you didn't want your talent, that you wouldn't be in the running. Let me tell you that you are. So sit down again and finish your office while I sleep.'

Father Bosco obeyed. He read as Gulban dozed and shadows inched unseen across the hill. On the level ground below, the windows of Fort Knox were sensual sheets of gold, while in the west the sky bore an intimation of austerity, of the chill purity of silver sunsets in the winter days to come.

As the evening darkened, Gulban's eyes seemed to sink in their sockets. He was retreating inwards, abandoning the outer extremities of his life. His body, now graceless and ungainly, was a territory which had become too extensive for his needs.

Cookie and Joey had put it differently.

'He's on his way,' Cookie had remarked. 'The light has gone out in his eyes.'

Joey smiled with half his mouth and said, 'The only question now is: will he linger or will he scoot?'

15

As Mrs Bugler refilled his glass and closed the french windows, Cookie knew that the familiar ritual of lunch was over and that an afternoon of unknown hazards had begun. It was now up to him to give form and content to the hour that must elapse before he could decently slip away. He suspected that he was sitting primly, so he stretched his legs and extended an arm along the back of the sofa in the attitude of a man who has fled disquiet and is pleased to have found relief and ease. She was telling him about Alicia, yet he could not think of Alicia. He could only give his mind to the mature and confident woman sitting opposite.

He had never before had an opportunity of studying her face. What he'd seen whenever he'd met her was a head of rich, brown hair that gave her strong, almost masculine, countenance a touch of bizarre luxuriance. Now he saw a thick, straight nose that led the eye downwards towards two full lips, the lower of which glistened with brandy. His eye travelled further to a small pouch of flesh to the right of her chin which caused him to look upwards in search of a corresponding pouch beneath the right eye. The eye was pouchless and so was the left side of her chin. Yet despite the obvious lack of symmetry, the face gave no sense of lopsidedness, rather the impression of a terrain of little rivulets whose courses had been cunningly concealed by the arts of conservation and landscape-gardening. His eye finally rested on her blue silk scarf which failed to conceal a little triangle of loose skin at the base of her throat bearing an etching of dendritic lines to form what his old geography master would have called a classic drainage pattern.

He felt shaken by what he'd seen or had forced himself to see, which was not what Jack had seen or what he himself might see tomorrow. She was smiling amiably at him, yet he could not enjoy his brandy. He would have felt more secure if Alicia had stayed, or if her exit had been less pointedly flamboyant.

'How is your father these days?' she asked.

'Going downhill slowly.'

'He was a hard-working, hard-headed man. Not an easy man to live with, I would say. I remember your mother. She was a gentle soul.'

'It's sad to see him now, gradually losing touch. Every day carries him further on the journey back into himself. One morning he'll wake up lost. Lost in his own double bed.'

'You don't mince words, Cookie.'

'We're all truth-tellers at the hotel — especially when we speak of each other.'

'In the early days Gregory and your father were friends. That's how I got to know him. He used to come down here for a pipe and a chat whenever the nights were long. Gregory, of course, spent a lot of time at the hotel. They fell out when Gregory painted your father looking like Andy Early — or so your father claimed. It was all rather silly. Gregory stopped going to the hotel for his drinks. He stopped drinking altogether. Then he became moody and introspective. The next thing he built that wall. I think the wall was his undoing. He had no natural gift for bricklaying. He found it difficult and it preyed on his mind.'

Cookie waited for her to continue. At length kindness constrained him to break the silence.

'My father always spoke highly of him to me.'

'He was an unusual man, was Gregory. He was widely travelled before I met him. He'd spent four years in India, and even twenty years later he still retained something of an oriental calm. He would steal up behind me like a big Persian cat and put his arms round me while I stood at the kitchen sink. It's what I miss most,' she sighed. 'He was very keen on Islamic art, especially ceramics. Let me show you an albarello, one of his favourite pieces.'

She opened a tall glass cabinet and took out a black, blue and turquoise drug-jar with concave sides decorated with floral and geometric motifs. He turned it over, examining the panels and friezes, marvelling at the delicacy of the underglaze painting, questioning the blankness of incomprehension in his mind. As he handed it back, their fingers touched.

'I feel heavy after the lunch,' she breathed.

'So do I.'

He thought the time had come to leave.

'Shall we go to bed for an hour?'

'I'd love a rest.' He tried to speak normally, though his tongue had gone thick and dry.

'It's the wine. One glass makes me forget my worries. Two makes me wish for a tumble.'

His wish for a tumble without commitment had been granted, though not in the circumstances he would have chosen. He studied the hard muscle of her calves on the stairs, wondering if he would achieve the required erection. It was by no means certain. The house, the garden, the lunch and the conversation had filled his mind with a sense of remoteness from the day. He wished to sit at Gregory Bugler's table and meditate for an hour. There was no time for meditation, however. They had already reached the bedroom door. Lines from a poem fell with a mechanical plink-plink-plink into the vacuum in his skull:

> I hid my love to my despite
> Till I could not bear to look at light:
> I dare not gaze upon her face
> But left her memory in each place;

Where'er I saw a wild flower lie
I kissed and bade my love goodbye.

'We can't draw the curtains,' she said. 'The window can be seen from the drive and Alicia could come back at any moment.'

She allowed her dress, a collapsing sail, to fall at her feet.

'I'm not worried about the light.' He made a kind of public declaration.

'There are men who are potent only in the dark.'

She was sitting on the edge of the bed, her spreading bottom giving her back the outline of a cello, an old-fashioned churn and a Florentine beaker, all at the same time.

'You're wearing black underpants,' she said. 'Are these the new fashion or are they meant to impress lady fetishists?'

'They're a pair I inherited. They're more serviceable than white ones, they need washing less often.'

'Have I seen them before?'

'Not since I've been wearing them.'

'They're Jack's, aren't they?'

'Yes, I thought it a pity to pension them off. Jack would hardly have approved.'

He kissed her on the lips to hide his embarrassment. He was struck by their unexpected softness and the faint odour of cardamom that leaked from the pores of her skin. It seemed to him that the upper lip tasted of port and the lower lip of brandy, so he kissed them both together, mixing one with the other, seeking the correct proportions.

What made her more attractive with her clothes off than on was her breasts, which in shape resembled those of the hill that overlooked her bedroom. Though she was at least fifty-five, they had not yet begun to sag. They were fully rounded above and below with strong, straight nipples as long as apple stems. Their curve seemed to begin just below her collar-bone and they rose and fell as she talked, close together, not touching, forming a hanging valley whose formation had nothing to do with the Ice Age. It was a valley for the drowning of the greatest sorrows and all mere irritation.

They lay under the turquoise sheet with the blankets rolled back for coolness. Her hair smelt of burnt leaves, reminding him of the Michaelmas term at university and fires smoking in suburban gardens.

'Your hair smells of autumn,' he said.

'Burnt grass, to be precise. I mowed the lawn and burnt the cuttings. Do you like it?'

'Very erotic. It could be the latest from the House of Chanel.'

Lying against him, so big in the bed, she traced with her forefinger the outline of a map on his lumbar region, which he took to be the map of Arcady, yet his member refused to wake and dispel the anxiety in his mind. For some reason he had imagined that her flesh would be firm. He was wrong. Her buttocks were flabby, the skin cold, smooth and dry, in its way not unpleasant to touch. He ran his fingers up her back, executing a perfect portamento, noting the gradual increase in warmth, while she clung closely, kissing him hungrily on the mouth, rubbing her legs hard against his thighs while her bristly mound rasped his groin. As he kissed her breasts and the floor of the dry valley between them, the light and sounds of the outside afternoon receded. He had been borne into a secret world of soothing warmth and silence. He forgot Jack's black underpants and the cold provocation of Alicia's kiss. What he had been trying to will into existence had arrived all shipshape entirely of its own accord.

'I'm ready,' she whispered with the resignation of a woman who has been cursed with a long succession of absent-minded lovers. 'Don't stop kissing my breasts. Keep kissing them even while you're inside me.'

He lay on top of her in the vice-grip of her legs and arms, surrounded by her, imprisoned in her, the acute consciousness of the eternal moment drilling an escape hole through his skull. He stopped kissing her breasts and buried his face in the pillow to obliterate all knowledge of the relentless drilling.

On the moor he had come upon a gypsy woman resting outside her tent late one evening. She was wearing a black skirt and a green blouse with a red plaid shawl round her shoulders. Her dry chestnut hair could have done with combing and her tanned face might have got its colour from hanging over fires of smoking green wood in the open.

'One of the O'Rourkes, a lecherous bunch,' his father would no doubt have said.

'Have you seen a man with a string of tin cans on your travels?' she asked.

'No.'

'If you meet him, tell him to hurry up. I'm famished with waiting. I've had nothing but a cold potato and a cup of spring water since morning.'

Her face was bony and hard. Bony faces are often long. Hers was bony and round or, more accurately, bony and wide with shadows in the hollows beneath the cheekbones. Her hair was parted on the crown and a crumpled ribbon tied it close against the skull behind. Hard arms and hard legs. A thin top lip and a pouting lower lip. Austerity. Sensuality. Cruelty. Tenderness. Bone and flesh. The flap of the tent behind her lay open. The sun had gone down. Night had begun its crawl across the moor from the east.

'Where do you live?' she asked.

'At the hotel.'

'You have a comfortable bed with a mattress, so. Have you ever lain on a blanket spread over rushes?'

'No.'

There was a red blotch on the side of her neck. Was it a

birthmark or had her husband branded her with his soldering-iron in a drunken rage?

'And you've never had a bag of hay for a pillow? Have you got a fag on you at all?'

He gave her a cigarette. She inhaled from the match flare, a hungry smoker.

The figure of a man appeared on the edge of the moor, dark against the afterglow.

'Goodbye,' he said. 'If I meet him, I'll tell him.'

'I'll bet you won't.' Her scornful laugh stuck pins and needles in his buttocks as he retreated.

Her husband was a violent man who got drunk at every fair, and again between fairs, in every village and between villages. Her name, he discovered afterwards, was Maeve, which was absurdly analogous to the naevus on her neck. For months he could not get her out of his mind. In bed at night he would see the moor all dark and mysterious with a straight grey road and rows of black turf stacks. Some evenings he would walk back to the circle in the heather where she'd lit a fire. In place of the tent there was a heap of musty straw and scraps of curled tin. She had small, brown feet. She was hard and lean, young and full of experience. He never saw her again. She had bequeathed him the word 'naevus' which was now for him a living word like 'mouth', 'flesh', 'nose', and 'breast'.

'My God, I needed that.'

It was Mrs Bugler calling him back, her breathing high from reckless exertion.

'It was a change to have it off in silence. Forker always talks, sometimes about the train coming through the Gap. And as you might expect, he likes to end with a whistle. He knows I collect books on narrow-gauge railways. He says that what he and I have in common is a happy confluence of complimentary fantasies. You're not in the least like him. You're younger and stronger, stronger in every way. You remind me of Gregory, you have the same strong hands. He had only one kink. He liked me to put my bottom in his groin, and then he'd put his arms round me and palpate my breasts and tummy. He used to do it for hours. Very soothing, it was. Sometimes he'd fall asleep doing it.'

'What does "palpate" mean?' Cookie strove to give the conversation a semantic turn. He could not imagine into what dark night her reminiscences might otherwise lead them.

'It means exploring by touch. Gregory liked to feel with his fingers and describe to me the movements of my inner organs.'

'Is that all? I thought it might be something more exotic — or erotic.'

As they talked, she gently moved his foreskin backwards and forwards with her thumb and finger till he was erect again.

'Lie on your back this time, Cookie, and leave the donkey-work to me.'

Obedient, though bewildered, he did her bidding, watching how she sat on him, her big knees on either side of him, her breasts with their reddish brown areolas flopping, and her swinging earrings glinting. She seemed to be pitching backwards and forwards, charging and tamping, plunging up and down. He closed his eyes against the sanity of light, surrounded by the scent of viburnum blossom. It seemed to rise out of their conjoining, or had it wafted through the open window? But there was no viburnum in the garden; and if there was, it could hardly have bloomed since lunchtime, right in the middle of October. He had strayed over the march into alien territory. He was a spare wheel lying flat with Mrs Bugler vigorously pumping. He opened his eyes to see if his belly was rising. Five pounds, ten, fifteen, twenty, twenty-five, thirty. The pressure was tremendous. If she didn't stop soon . . . Then the fury of the pumping relaxed. She had found renewed alleviation, her ache had been assuaged for at least another ten minutes.

'You're quite remarkable,' she said, dismounting. 'And to cap it all you're still upright.'

'Never mind, what goes up must come down!'

'I always need a double after wine, two in quick succession. Gregory could never manage more than one a day and even Forker isn't a hundred per cent reliable. You've got the advantage, the most precious of all commodities — unjaded youth. Jack had it too, and he was thirty. Maybe it's to do with being a Heron. I can tell you here and now that you're no disgrace to his underpants.'

'You can have a treble if you like.' He smiled to conceal a knowledge of what happens when love becomes labour.

'I know that, but I mustn't make a beast of myself. Besides, I promised Alicia to make a pie for tea. I wonder if you'd mind staying to help me peel the apples.'

'Not at all,' he replied, beginning to savour the power of his detachment, an almost inhuman remoteness from what he normally thought of as his life.

She kissed him playfully on the cheek.

'You were good in a different way from Jack. He used to start very softly and very slowly, and then come up hammer and tongs on the rails. You're steadier, you keep the same pace throughout. It's all a question of strategy. What matters is to bring the horse home with a couple of lengths to spare.'

He decided to get out of bed before the next race was announced, and when Alicia returned from her sketching she found him slicing Bramleys in the kitchen.

'Domesticated already?'

'Do you have a viburnum in your garden?' he asked. 'I thought I recognised one on the way in.'

'You're so naive, dear Cookie. What you recognised was my new perfume. No matter how often I hide it, Mother keeps finding it.'

He left before the pie went in the oven and walked down to the slip in the gentling quiet of the evening. It was no quieter than any other Sunday evening, he supposed; it was merely so in relation to the howling inside his head, which had started as soon as he came out the gate. He sat on a bank above the slip watching gannets and seagulls, trying to make sense of their plummeting and swooping. A fishing boat with an outboard shot round the point, two men trolling and one standing in the stern with a hand on the tiller. He listened in vain for the puttering of the engine above the screaming of the gulls. The bow scraped on the end of the slip and one of the men in yellow waders jumped out to hold the boat steady for the other two. Then the three of them hauled until the stern was clear of the water, splashed the floor with brine, and let the bilge flow out though the spile-hole. The tallest and strongest took the end of the rope which was attached to the bow and began hauling hand over hand while the other two shoved, one from each side. It was heavy work pulling over the wooden skids up the whole length of the slip, but it was done with as little apparent effort as the counting and sharing of the catch which followed.

'Do you feel better now?'

Joey sat down beside him, the mockery in his tone unmistakable.

'If I say no, you won't believe me; and if I say yes, you'll jump to conclusions.'

'There is always "perhaps".'

'Now you're putting words in my mouth.'

'I'll put it another way: did you get your end away, and if so, how many times and in which of the canonical positions?'

'I've been watching the three Harleys hauling.'

'I know what that's code for.'

'There is an extraordinary spiritual value in work rituals: tying knots, mending nets, mooring boats, unloading fish. They are activities that enrich both the doer and the observer.'

'It's easy to romanticise plain living after six hours in

the flesh-pots of Fort Knox. Don't give me humbug and hypocrisy, Cookie. I've had enough of both from brother Bosco over lunch.'

'Is he still above?'

'He's been closeted with Gulban all afternoon. What do you make of that?'

'I'll think about it on the way home and give you my considered opinion in the morning.' He refused to acknowledge Joey's quizzical smile.

'I'm thinking of enriching you, Cookie.'

'A share of your talent?'

'I'm going to buy a boat so that you can watch me tying reef-knots and carrick bends, and making fast with a slinky clove-hitch. Will you come down with me to inspect the object of my dreams?'

'You're not being serious?'

'Not all of us are called to scale the Mount of Venus. For some, true pleasure can only be vicarious.'

Pauline was watering her plants in the hall when he got back. She was peering without touching, pouring the water gently around their stems. He coughed, as if he'd surprised her in a little act of intimacy he was not meant to see.

'One thing is obvious,' he said. 'You know that they know that you know when to water them.'

'How was lunch?'

'The beef was delicious but the vegetables were slightly overcooked.'

'Were both of them there?'

'Oh, yes. Safety in numbers, I suppose.'

'What did you talk about?'

'Islamic ceramics, spiders, croquet, narrow-gauge railways.'

'An educational afternoon?'

'The curriculum lacked diversity. The interest, I found, was largely scientific.'

'And Fort Knox itself?'

'It's an academy that makes you quite oblivious of the extramural. When you leave, you're surprised to find the world outside the walls still there.'

'It sounds like a kind of paradise. Did they mention Jack?'

'Mrs Bugler did, once or twice. She said that he was steadier than me.'

'That's true.'

'And that he could sit a horse.'

'Utter nonsense. What, I wonder, could he have seen in such a place?'

'I think he went there to forget. In spite of appearances, he was not a contented man.'

She turned her back to him. He watched her examine the leaf of a Swiss cheese plant that showed distinct symptoms of gigantism.

'Have you seen Bosco?' he asked.

'He's still with Gulban. I expect they're both asleep.'

He went into the lounge and ordered a whiskey and water at the bar. A few waistcoated worthies from the village and four or five tourists were sitting by the windows absorbing the deepening shadows on the hill. The wife of one of the tourists came to the bar for cigarettes. Her skin was dry as a mummy's, her hair dyed the colour of barley straw. He knocked back his drink and went round to the public bar where he ordered a pint of stout to be in the fashion. Two youths were playing darts and three fishermen were taking their ease at one of the tables. It was still early. The empty evening lay ahead. It would be pleasant to talk to Pauline over a drink but she was talking to her plants. He sat by the window overlooking the eastward-rolling moor bounded by a blue paling of low hills in the distance. Gradually, the landscape darkened, heights and hollows melted away. Finally, all became featureless and the reflection of the blazing turf fire took shape in the panes. He thought of his father slipping between waking and sleeping and hardly knowing which was which. He wished for the company of noisy students with a gift for impromptu ribaldry; beer flowing and spilling; and quick-witted barmaids good for a jape, a joke, and nothing more serious than a squeeze.

Four sheep farmers entered and nodded to him without speaking. The barman had gone down to the cellar to change a barrel, so he got up and served them the tot of whiskey they invariably drank as an appetiser before the soup of the day, as Joey called the draught stout. He gave them their change without attempting to interrupt their discussion of the merits and demerits of Slash Gildea's new ram.

He came out of the bar and found Father Bosco and Joey locked in conversation on the stairs. Father Bosco, who seemed excited, beckoned to him.

'Now that the three of us are together, I have a little announcement to make,' he said.

'You're going to give us all unconditional absolution,' Joey predicted.

'I must be absolutely frank with you both. I'm not a dark horse, I don't believe in surprises. I've entered the race, you see. I'd like you both to know.'

'Which race?' Cookie, after his recent experience of the turf, showed confusion.

'I'm not making the running but I'm in the running. I've discussed with Gulban the possibility that I may inherit. Nothing has been settled, I hasten to say. If I'm offered it, I shall take it, that's all.'

'The hotel?' Cookie looked incredulously at Joey.

'The hotel, the farm and the shop. I'll turn the hotel into a home for elderly priests, I'll get lay brothers to run the other two.'

Joey laughed and Cookie hiccuped.

'God and Mammon in harness. You simply can't lose,' Joey said.

'I'll become a lay brother if you agree to give me a job,' Cookie promised.

'I have no wish to inspire bad feeling. I thought I should tell you, so that everything is open and above board.'

Cookie and Joey watched him hurry out through the lobby.

'He's a twit,' said Joey.

'A twit, a twat and a gom,' said Cookie.

'Can a man so lacking in stratagem go any distance in the Church?'

'At this rate he'll never be Pope and neither of us will get to be camerlingo.'

Cookie turned and climbed the stairs. He had decided to spend the evening alone.

'You're pooped and ready for bed,' Joey shouted after him.

Cookie did not reply.

'I've got the perfect exam question for you,' Joey called again. ' "A middle-aged woman is a ruined abbey — food for romantic thought. Discuss." '

'She's a city much like Babylon,' Cookie declaimed from above.

'And you, Cookie, were a king in Babylon for an hour. But were you every inch a king?'

Cookie waited outside his bedroom door until the laughter of ribaldry below had ended.

'I give you a mid-year resolution,' he shouted. 'Acquire a self to which you can be true.'

'Too late, too late,' Joey called up the stairs. *'L'esprit de l'escalier*, it simply will not do.'

16

On the way home Father Bosco stopped above Undercliff beach to breathe air that was pure and salty. Below was an old graveyard, a dark spit of land, pale grey sand, and an arm of water alive with pinpoints of the moon's reflection. A lorry and van passed on the way to town. He waited for silence, then listened hard for the murmur of moving water. He thought he heard it, yet he could not be sure. He listened again, aware that somehow in not hearing he was failing in his priestly function.

He got out of the car and descended the shadowy steps to the beach, clutching the thick wooden handrail all the way down. The lees of excitement still stirred his blood. He felt grateful for the cooling touch of the night breeze on his neck and cheeks. He had acted correctly in telling Cookie and Joey of his talk with Gulban. Now all was in the open, and neither could say that he had been dishonest or disingenuous.

The more he thought about it the more convinced he became that he must and should inherit, if only to ensure the exercise of compassion and reparation. Father Tourish would have a new home in which to end his days in the company of other elderly priests. The home would be run by even-tempered men with one foot in the outside world, chosen for their amiable and open-hearted nature. There would be no bossy nuns to anger and irritate with emotional compulsions that had no place in the spiritual life which was essentially sweet in its detachment. There would be no strict regimen of spiritual exercises. The priests would lead the normal lives of the old — reading, watching television, listening to music, going for walks on the moor, sitting in the sun gazing out across the Sound. Gradually, they would shed the loneliness that had come from a lifetime's knowledge of being special. Prayer would no longer be a ritualised, introspective and world-denying activity. It would recede into the very fabric of their waking and sleeping, and they would become spiritually the richer for it. They would shed the habits and habiliments of self-enclosure and go to their Maker for judgment as would any ordinary man. They would acquire the fullness of experience that comes with double vision, and they would realise that if they had their lives to spend again they would be less obsessed with their own salvation. They would risk all to save all, not surround themselves with the mote and bailey that denies the soul the nourishment it must possess if it is to communicate glory.

He walked between the driftline and the edge of the water, the sand soft and damp underfoot. He climbed the slope under the graveyard wall and stood above the moonlit waves. He could hear a murmur now but still he was not satisfied. The murmur he heard was the loudest and crudest. What he craved were the thousand gentle exhalations it concealed, to be followed by the roaring of a thousand angry seas all in unison. His ear was not attuned. Life was a symphony of sounds he would never hear.

His years as a clerical student and priest had begun as a retreat from life, at least ordinary life, and now at thirty-three he was aware every day that he was still retreating. The first such act had been involuntary, a shudder of horror he could still neither comprehend nor forget. It had begun with Pauline, when she was fifteen. She had come home from the convent for the summer holidays, a grown woman with the innocence of a child. He stopped to speak to her outside her mother's cottage, where she was plucking roses from the trellis by the door. It seemed to him then that he had never looked at her before. He had just taken his degree exams at university. He had studied hard, he was full of academic self-confidence, and he was planning a summer of outdoor relaxation. It was the 23rd of June, St John's Eve, and it was the local custom to light bonfires on the hill after sunset. Young men and women gathered to make light-hearted fun, and he and Pauline were among them. After midnight, when the last of the fires had died down, he walked back with her across the river to the road. Her mother had gone to Dublin for a few days. She offered him coffee, and he said that it would be a pity to go indoors on such a lovely night.

They walked down the lane and sat on the edge of the cliff. For a long time they talked. He told her about the university and she told him about the convent and the nuns. Beneath them the sea spilled and murmured. The water was luminous, and the air sweet with the smell of cut grass and heavy with salt at the same time. The sky bristled with starlight. To the left of them the lighthouse cast lonely beams down the bay. He put his arm round her waist and kissed her. It was his first kiss, and the thought that it might have been her second or third was torment. If he kissed her a hundred times, she would still be two kisses ahead. Yet what were two kisses compared with a hundred? Though the breeze turned cool, they never moved from the cliff edge. At dawn they came back through fields full of mushrooms under a reddening sky.

That morning as he bent down to kiss the altar at Mass, he felt the short grass of the sea cliff under his hands. He paused before the Consecration to expunge the insistent memory of the bonfire and the smoke in her clothes and hair. As he prayed for a prelapsarian purity of heart and mind, his knowledge of carnal desire was a cold, wet alb that clung to his chest and legs.

He could not understand the force of his feelings, or the terror they inspired in him. Nothing shameful or unnatural had happened, yet he could think only of the *osculum infame*, the kiss of perverted worship that witches at their sabbaths bestowed on the Devil in one of his animal forms. It was a gangrened foot that suffocated him daily with its odour of sweet putrefaction. It was a grey wolf that skulked in the shadows of the foreconscious, growing leaner and more ravenous with every year that passed. He read St Augustine, grateful for his 'cauldron of unholy loves'. Was he a man who had to struggle nightly with the demon or was he an old fraud, exaggerating his sins to humiliate himself in the eyes of God while surrounding himself with a personal mythology that would illuminate his name for ever in the errant hearts of men? Sometimes he'd wake up from a dream and wonder if, like Father Tourish, he would end his days among nuns, making ribald jokes and mocking God for creating women.

He never kissed her again. He left university and entered the seminary, turning his back on the secular life because in three short hours his experience had grown into a monster that had to be slain. He knew that he was taking on a lifelong struggle that would require fortitude, humility and God's daily grace and mercy. He combed the writings of the ascetics for every weapon and word of comfort he could find, yet it was a sentence from Leonardo da Vinci that in those early years awakened the sharpest echo of recognition in his soul:

> The act of coitus and the parts employed therein are so repulsive that were it not for the beauty of the faces and the adornments of the actors and the frenetic state of mind, nature would lose the human species.

It was a sentence and a sentiment that he kept to himself, and the secret knowledge of it surrounded him with a wall that gave him an appearance of high purpose in the eyes of the other young seminarians. They respected his intelligence and diligence, his objectivity in discussion and his courtesy in personal relationships, and perhaps half-jokingly they began to forecast a distinguished future for him. Their respect and overtures of friendship restored his self-confidence and muted the self-scrutiny and self-criticism that had begun to weary his mind and body. In his fourth year he relaxed a little. He developed a sense of humour and became friendly with Benedict McBride, a fellow-seminarian with a reputation for intellectual high jinks and high spirits. McBride had a habit of quoting Ecclesiastes and laughing as he did so. 'All the rivers run into the sea, but the sea is not full,' he would say. And Bosco, who read Ecclesiastes too, would reply, 'In the place where the tree falls, there it will lie.' It was a harmless game which neither of them took seriously, and it served as the foundation of a congenial friendship. During the summer holidays he visited McBride, whose parents lived in a seaside town on the south coast.

'This week we'll try to look like everyone else,' Benedict said. 'We'll wear jeans and polo-necked tee-shirts. When we're ordained, we'll be different. I once heard an old curate say that there's nothing more enfeebling for a priest than the feeling of being special.'

'Why polo-necks?' Bosco asked.

'They conceal chest hair. We don't want to arouse the passions of young women.'

Laughing at the absurdity of it, they went down to the sea-front and lay on the grass above the beach, quoting Ecclesiastes and making good-natured jokes about the professor of moral theology. A young girl in a black bikini passed by without looking at them. Benedict raised himself on one elbow and studied her swaying figure.

'There's a world of hell there, Bosco,' he said. 'We're lucky to have settled for the purifying fires of Purgatory.'

Bosco pretended he had not heard.

Ten minutes later the girl returned, licking soft ice-cream from a cone. Concord passed into discord. The sun danced promiscuously on the supine sea.

'Heaven and earth shall pass away, but the

trigonometry of girls' bottoms in bikinis shall not pass away,' Benedict laughed delightedly, his pale skin slightly yellow in the sharp sea-light, his already thin hair matted and dry.

'I wish you wouldn't say these things,' Bosco chided.

'They must be said for sanity's sake and you are the only person I know who can hear them without taking scandal. Women have such a luxury of hip and bottom. Who said that?'

'St Augustine?' Bosco ventured.

'Henry James, believe it or not.'

'I don't believe it.'

'He said something very similar in a letter to a sculptor friend.'

'That doesn't give the thought theological sanction.'

'We mustn't fight shy of life. We must put ourselves in the way of ordinary human experience. Only then can we fulfil our mission among sinners.'

'Benedict, do you really mean the things you say? Answer me truthfully.'

'Do you think I do?'

'No.'

'In that case there's no harm in it.'

'There could be scandal. I could go back to my room and dwell on it. You just can't assume anything at all about another human being.'

'Bosco, you're as solid as the Rock of Gibraltar. Neither death, nor life, nor angels, nor principalities . . . You know the rest.'

Bosco had come to see Benedict as a rock on which he himself had a foothold. Benedict's aphorisms gave him a sense of the essential health and sanity of the religious life. They proclaimed that to be good you didn't have to be a solemn ape who wiped the smile off his face every time he entered a church vestibule. Above all, Benedict possessed a magnanimity that enabled him to note another man's weaknesses without any loss of compassion or sympathy.

Bosco thought he had found in his friend the innocence and simplicity which he himself had forfeited. He was shattered when Benedict upped and left the seminary only a month before he was due to take Holy Orders. His first reaction was one of anger. The pious plodders would be ordained. Jackasses would bray from pulpits, and the faithful would bow and listen uncritically in their humility. Did it mean that in Christ's Church there was no mansion for individuals as opposed to stock characters? After anger came self-accusation. His own judgment had been at fault. He had been taken in by the sparkle of appearances, he had preferred Benedict's intellectual spoofing to the conventional conversation of his teachers and colleagues. He sought God's forgiveness and tried to pray for Benedict in his new vocation. Throughout the ordination ceremony he kept thinking of him. What should have been a day of glorious light had become overcast with regrets about the past and fears for the future. It was an unfortunate start to his ministry, it left him with an abiding and humiliating sense of imperfection.

Parish work helped to assuage the pain. Gradually, he came to see the experience as a belated entry into manhood. Things had taken a serious and final turn. Laughter was frivolous, enjoyment an intoxication as insidious as brandy and port mixed in equal proportions. Life was for evermore under suspicion, not the life of the spirit but the life of the senses, which was what ninety-nine point nine per cent of the faithful meant by 'life'. In the company of Benedict he had learnt ebullience and light-heartedness. Now he was slower and more cautious in making connections. A kind of depression had settled over his mind which he assumed to be a condition of maturity.

He was leaning against the roughcast wall of the graveyard. Below him the sea lay flat and docile, constrained and impotent under the dull face of the moon. Waves splashed and spilled, but only half-heartedly. The night held no surprises.

'All the rivers run into the sea, but the sea is not full,' he whispered. 'Better to remember, "He who digs a pit will fall into it." '

He would have to bear that in mind in his dealings with Pauline. Yet it was necessary to keep her friendship and enlist her help. Nothing would be gained by running away.

He walked back to the car thinking of the directness and simplicity of Jack's mind and character. He had given all his strength to getting things done. If he had become a priest, he would have built churches and kept his parish accounts in order. He would have been talked about by other priests at chapter, he would have been a bishop before he was forty.

When he got home, Canon Sproule invited Father Bosco into his study for a mug of cocoa to end the day. They sat in silence on either side of the fire, the Canon smoking his big cream-coloured meerschaum without moving a muscle.

'Even the best pipes go sour — if you smoke them long enough,' he said at length.

Bosco lit a cheroot and the Canon put the pipe back in its rack.

'Have you ever had a sense of being tainted by sin but by no sin in particular?' Bosco asked.

'Tainted by people and events, you mean?'

'I suppose so.'

'Even for a priest the enemies of the spiritual life are still the World, the Flesh and the Devil. Temptation is our daily companion, and we must meet it fully prepared — with a body that has suffered mortification. The tradition of flagellation in the early Church is frowned upon today, yet flagellation is an essential weapon in the armoury of anyone who takes Satan seriously. The greatest saints never flinched from physical suffering. St Francis of Assisi flung himself into a rose-bush to escape temptation, and Padre Pio was beaten regularly by the Devil. I had it from a priest who lived with him that he often came down to breakfast looking the worse for wear. We can only assume that the Devil had given him a bad time in the night.'

The Canon was a priest of the old school and Father Bosco loved him for it. Sadly, his armour was for another century; the Devil had changed his tactics since he was a boy.

Father Bosco went to his room, said his prayers and got into bed. Some time in the small hours he woke up in a sweat. He had been dreaming about Pauline and he could not remember the end of his dream. She had just married Slash Gildea and he had been killed in a car accident on the way back from the church. She came to Father Bosco in a black fur coat and sat on his knee for comfort in her second bereavement. Then he realised that she was wearing her coat back to front, that it was open, and that she had no clothes on underneath it.

He got out of bed and ran the cold tap till the bath was almost full. He stood in the near-freezing water and immersed himself gradually till it covered his shoulders.

The body was the enemy of the spirit and must be chastened. Now he saw the way ahead with clarity. He *must* inherit. The hotel as a home for elderly priests would be his gift to God, and it would be God's gift to them for a lifetime of selfless service. He would pray, of course, and in addition he would take certain practical steps of his own. He would visit the hotel more regularly and talk to Gulban who was probably lonely in his room. He would make Pauline understand his purpose. She was intelligent and loyal by nature. She was bound to feel sympathy, she would intercede with Gulban on his behalf.

He towelled himself vigorously and returned to bed. Before he fell asleep, he thought he heard Benedict McBride shouting after a girl in a black bikini:

'The Virgin Birth isn't a myth, it's a necessity.'

17

The man on the hill moved back and forth with slow strides, standing now and again to observe a sheep at close range. The pattern of to-ing and fro-ing seemed aimless from where she watched. It was as if he'd lost his way and was trying out this direction and that, then doubling back with his eyes on the ground searching for a concealed pathway. He stooped over a ewe, one leg on each side of her, and buried his hands in the thick fleece. Slash Gildea was one of those men who excel at whatever they take up. He was good with sheep, good with cattle, and good in a boat, and he was an efficient manager of the hotel farm. He was open and fair in his dealings with other people, yet no one knew his thoughts. Two summers ago he'd asked her to put her hand on a ram's horn to feel how warm it was. He spoke as if he were letting her in on a secret, and she expected him to explain. Then he walked away and she realised that he considered further explanation unnecessary.

She trained her binoculars on the field next to the road, where his new ram was grazing with six less burly ewes. The ram followed one of the ewes up the slope, while the other five raised their heads and watched. The ram rubbed his head against the ewe's neck. She didn't seem to notice, she continued with her grazing. Then he nibbled her ear. He must have annoyed her, because she took off down the slope towards the other ewes that had already resumed their grazing. He didn't follow. He walked away with stiff-legged indifference and scratched his neck against a rock at the other end of the field.

A blurt of wind scattered hailstones as big as pebbles against the windows. The weather had finally broken. Towards the end of October it had rained continually for four days. Snow had been forecast for the 1st of November. Instead came three dry days with a black east wind that beat against the windows and nipped her ears and hands whenever she went outside the door. The very landscape seemed to have contracted. Men and animals moved stiffly, and the exposed houses stood starkly on the hard, bare ground. It was now the first week of November and it was already cold enough for snow. All but two of the guests had left. Hardly anyone came to the hotel, apart from the locals who drank in the public bar. The chambermaids and waitresses had gone back to their homes till spring. She wandered from one silent room to another, thinking that the soul is an empty hotel in winter when the last of the guests has departed.

Sometimes she thought of going away and starting afresh, but the draughty hotel held her prisoner. It had always been at the centre of her imagination. As a girl, she had been outside the windows looking in. Now, as a woman, she was inside looking out. She would sit in her bedroom observing the movements of men and animals in the landscape, while her thoughts hovered over Jack, returning again and again to the Spoke and Felly, the beach, the graveyard and the Atlantic Grill.

Sometimes she would see him as a good, simple, roughcast man whose only fault was a lack of sensitivity to other lives. At other times she would envisage him as a heartless monster who used everyone he knew for his pleasure. There was no knowing. He had been so many things to so many people.

She turned her binoculars on Fort Knox, now bare and windswept without a sign of human movement. It, too, had taken on the aspect of a life frozen for ever into immobility.

She was grateful for Gulban; he kept her busy with a score of pains and bedsores. At times she felt that he was the only living thing in her life. He was becoming more forgetful, though. Now it was impossible to tell when he was attending and when he wasn't. Sometimes he could not recall the events of the previous day, while at other times he would surprise her by referring to a conversation that she could have sworn had taken place in his room when he was asleep. Mostly he was pessimistic.

'Life is a wild-goose chase, a hunt that yields nothing,' he would say. 'You fail to catch the wild-goose, so you think you'll catch the fox. You run him to earth, you start to dig him out, and then you find he's gone to another den on the other side of the hill.'

Father Bosco came to see him three times a week, and he often went out of his way to talk to her. He would come into her office and sit by her desk, looking as if he had an unknowable sorrow he could not share. After half an hour he would say, 'Duty calls. I'll see you the day after tomorrow.' He was caring and good-natured, as a priest should be. He showed more warmth towards his father than did Cookie and Joey, who had more opportunity since they were living in.

Cookie tried to take an interest in the business but his mind was on other things. He was a dreamer who imagined himself in love with Alicia or Amaryllis, while all the time he was sporting with the image of Narcissus in the shade. He was an irresolute and unworldly man who was now and again goaded by Joey into a show of strength.

Joey was harder, more aggressive and more excitable, yet equally remote from the common experience. He had bought a punt from one of the local fishermen and he now spent his leisure time going out to the island whenever the sea was calm. He never seemed to catch any fish and he never said what he'd been up to. He'd come back at nightfall and go straight to his room, unlike Cookie who spent his evenings reading in the lounge bar or wool-gathering over crosswords.

Whatever the tensions that existed between the two brothers, the reappearance of Andy Early united them as against a common enemy. Early had turned up again the previous week looking shaggier, craggier and more aggressive. He had spent the money that Cookie and Joey had given him, and he'd obviously come back expecting another incentive to leave immediately. Instead, on Gulban's instructions, they gave him a small room on the east side of the building which he described as 'cold, cramped and architecturally undistinguished'. For that reason, perhaps, he spent most of the day in the public bar, snorting, farting, shouting and blowing his nose between his thumb and forefinger. As he neither washed nor shaved, he had all the more time to devote to the practice of these sounds, as well as to eating, drinking, swearing and making rude sexual gestures when the barmaids' backs were turned. He was a thorough-going nuisance, dirty and smelly with all the arrogance and pretensions of a man who had studied theology in his youth and had spent the rest of his life playing visiting professor in whatever bar he happened to be drinking.

Pauline went to the kitchen to get Gulban his glass of rum punch before settling down in front of the television for the evening. The sound of raised voices drew her to the lounge bar, where she found Cookie pleading with Andy Early.

'I've already told you, I don't want you in the lounge,' Cookie was saying.

'The seats in the lounge are softer and the fire here throws out more heat. The lounge bar is first and foremost for guests, and that's what I am — a guest,' Early boomed.

'You're not a paying guest.'

'I've never heard such impertinence!'

'If it's a drink you want, you'll get served in the public. You won't get one here.'

'I'm no second-class citizen, I'm a registered voter.'

'Then, drink where you vote and vote with your feet,' Cookie advised.

'So you fancy yourself as a wit! Let me tell you something: you'll never be half the man your father was.'

'For the last time I'm asking you to leave this bar. We've got two guests staying, and I don't want you disturbing them when they come in for a drink before dinner.'

'And if I don't leave?'

'It's no good, you won't get served.'

'I'll make a sound you've never heard before.'

He towered over Cookie, leaning forward on his toes, a ton of bricks threatening to come down. He looked wild-eyed and fanatical, and he smelt of stale beer and vomit.

'I've been making allowances for you because of my father, but my patience is running out.'

Early opened his mouth wide and guffawed.

'You should have a little hour-glass on your lapel, me boyo, so that we all can see the level of patience left to run.'

Pauline motioned Cookie to follow her into the lobby.

'It's no good pleading with him,' she whispered. 'He'd never behave like this if Gulban were on his feet.'

'I'll get Slash to lean on him. A look from Slash, and he'll know we mean business.'

'If I know Slash, he'll tell you to lean on him yourself.'

'I can't call the police. If I did, Gulban would have a fit.'

'We've had him a week already, and he's getting more obstreperous every day. If we don't do something quickly, he'll be here for the winter.'

'I'll have to make him see reason,' Cookie said. 'It's all a matter of quiet persuasion.'

'What's the problem?' Joey asked, as he joined them.

'It's Big Andy. He won't leave the lounge bar till he gets a drink.'

'Won't is a declaration of war,' said Joey.

They both followed him into the lounge. Early was

relaxing before the fire, which he had replenished liberally with black peat from the basket.

'I believe you'd like a drink,' Joey said.

'A large whiskey. I'll have it neat. It's been one of those days.'

'Enough of your lip. If you're not off these premises within three minutes, I'll ring the police.'

'I'll see your father first.'

'It's got nothing to do with Father. You've got two minutes and forty seconds left.'

'You can't chuck me out on an evening like this. The east wind would skewer bog-snipe.'

'Two minutes,' Joey said.

'I'll make a bargain. Let me spend the rest of the evening in my room and I'll go first thing in the morning.'

'Then go to your room at once. Don't expect any more drink and don't disturb Father. If you do, I'll turf you out bag and baggage with every mongrel dog in the townland at your heels.'

Early got up and went to the door.

'I could shake this house to its foundations,' he shouted. 'The trouble with you young pups is that you don't know how to get your way without bringing the roof down round your ears. It's a question of politics. Playing the game. Your father always knew how to play the game.'

Early slammed the door and climbed the stairs.

'Set a beggar on horseback,' Joey laughed. 'I must see that he doesn't disturb Gulban. I'll go up straight away and lock him in his room.'

About ten the following morning Pauline brought Big Andy his breakfast. She knocked on his door but there was no response. She got her keys from the kitchen, wondering if he'd skedaddled in the night. She found him lying over the bedclothes with nothing on but a vest that failed to cover his distended belly. The air in the room was warm and stale. His eyes and mouth were gaping. An empty whiskey bottle lay on the floor. With a sense of queasiness, rather than shock, she opened the window. She could tell by the look of him that he'd been dead several hours.

'How did he get the whiskey?' she asked Joey when she rang him at the shop.

'He must have had it in his room all the time.'

'You didn't give it to him?'

'Of course not.'

'It makes an odd story.'

'We'd better not say that I locked him in,' Joey advised. 'It might give rise to the wrong kind of speculation.'

When she brought Gulban his coffee, she told him the news. He closed his eyes and let the corners of his mouth droop in an arch of pain.

'He died some time between dinner and breakfast,' she continued.

'I'm not surprised in a way. The last time he came in, I could see that he was going downhill fast. He was short of breath, and what breath he had stank of sour whiskey.'

'We'll have to tell the sergeant, the doctor and the priest. Between them, they should know what to do with the body.'

'Before you tell anyone, I want to speak to Bosco, Cookie and Joey. Will you ring Bosco and ask him to come at once?'

Father Bosco arrived just before lunch. The three brothers trooped into Gulban's room as she was making his bed. When she had finished, Gulban asked her to stay, because he wished to speak to all four of them. They sat round the bed and waited. For a long time he just stared at his feet.

'We'll have to give him a proper send-off,' he said at last. 'It must be a big funeral, the offerings must be the biggest ever collected on the headland. They must set a new record and put even the richest families to shame. His name must go down in the history of the parish and in the parish accounts.'

'Who'll pay these record offerings?' Joey asked.

'I'll kick off with five hundred pounds,' Gulban said. 'And I'll expect the rest of you to contribute your share.'

'We'll be the laughing-stock of the neighbourhood. It will give offerings over the dead a bad name,' Cookie said.

'The sad news must be announced in the local paper, and you, Cookie, will write a little verse for the death column. You know the kind of thing I mean: "Will those who think of him today, a little prayer to Jesus say?" '

'You're thinking of the *in memoriam* column,' Cookie reminded him. 'That isn't for another year.'

'We'll have all the trimmings — an undertaker and a hearse. And you, Bosco, will officiate at what the papers call "the obsequies". It will have to be a High Mass with seven concelebrating priests, one for every decade of his life. As a beggar, he was well known in parochial houses. You should have no difficulty rounding up enough clergy.'

'You're making a mockery of priests and religion. Take care you don't mock God Himself,' said Father Bosco.

'Will you do what I say?'

'No,' Bosco answered. 'It would be perverting the true purpose of religious ceremonial.'

'What have you got to say, Cookie?'

'I agree with Father Bosco, though I'd put it differently. I'd say it makes no sense at all.'

'Joey?'

'Before I answer, I'd like to know why Andy Early deserves to be wheeled out of here on a red carpet.'

'Because I want to shake my fist at every small-minded, self-righteous bugger on this headland. And I want to shake my fist, too, at all those who think they've got a hot line to heaven.'

'He said last night that he could shake this house to its foundations. What did he mean?'

'Shake this house? He never said that to me. How much whiskey did he have in his belly when he said it?'

'No more than his daily bottle.'

'He was always rash but he was a friend. He respected

me and I respected him. Your mother was fond of him too. She once told me that she saw him as another Elisha. Do you know what that means, Bosco?'

'Of course I've heard of Elisha. Second Book of Kings.'

'Your mother was a holy woman, and she saw him as a holy man who'd lost his way. She said that there should always be a bed for him here, as there was for Elisha at Shunem. Does that answer your question, Joey?'

'It doesn't explain why you continued to give him bed and board long after Mother died.'

'I loved your mother, she was a good woman. Now, will you carry out my instructions?'

'No,' Joey said.

'Why?'

'Because your instructions don't accord with my sense of reality.'

'Reality, my foot. None of the three of you is a son of mine. I could only have got you when I wasn't thinking. Now, for God's sake, will you go and leave me in peace with Pauline?'

When they were both alone again, he said, 'What do you think of that?'

'Do you want me to speak the truth?' she asked.

'The truth, yes, the truth. I want nothing but the truth.'

'I think they don't understand.'

'Do you?'

'I'm afraid not.'

'Then I'm on my own. Do you think I went over the top?'

'I think you did.'

'I once asked you to be my eyes and ears. You're a level-headed girl. You know, as I do, that none of this would have happened if Jack were alive. Would he still be alive if I hadn't named the Day of the Talents?'

'We'll never know.'

'What should I do?'

'Call them back. Tell them you've changed your mind.'

He caught her sleeve and tried to smile.

'Okay. I'll tell them I was testing them and that they all came through with flying colours. Honour on both sides must be satisfied.'

When they returned, Gulban shook hands with all three of them.

'I'm pleased you've passed the test,' he said. 'You may have realised that I was only joking, but I like to think that you stood up to me because you felt I was off the beam. Congratulations, all of you. Now I know you're incorruptible.'

'We still haven't solved the problem,' Joey said.

'Which problem? There is no problem. Now you don't have to worry about the cost of shipping saulies in from Scotland to weep at the graveside.'

'The problem is what to do with the body,' Joey reminded him.

'Buy a plain wooden coffin and give him a decent burial. Nothing flash. You can save the fireworks for me.'

They left him dozing against the pillows and quietly closed the bedroom door.

'Why did he change his mind?' Joey asked Pauline.

'He didn't, he was playing games,' she replied.

'It's a shocking thought that the will he finally makes may depend on such trifling,' Joey said.

'None of you need worry this time. He said you all came through with flying colours.'

'He's daft, and gaga with it,' Cookie said.

'Don't kid yourself,' warned Father Bosco. 'There are no flies on Gulban, at least not yet.'

'He enjoys the occasional lucid interval,' Joey conceded. 'The question is: can he be trusted to make a sensible will?'

'We have no cause to doubt his competence,' Father Bosco replied.

'The old are at a disadvantage, they look old,' said Pauline.

They buried Early in the headland cemetery two days later. It was bright and cold with an aggressive east wind that kept lifting dust and twigs and blowing them in their faces. Cookie, Joey and Pauline, and six or seven elderly villagers who could remember Early in his youth, drew round the grave in a tight, protective knot, as Father Bosco read the final prayers. An eddying gust blew the surplice out over his head. He staggered on the brink of the grave with one hand raised to maintain his balance, then slid down the side on top of the coffin. Another gust shook Pauline, blinding her with sand. For a moment she swayed, trying not to follow Father Bosco. Joey caught her arm and she clung to him. When she managed to open her eyes again, she saw Cookie pulling Father Bosco out of the shallow hole that contained the coffin.

It was an unnerving experience for reasons she could not understand. After the funeral she went to her room to be alone. The closed windows rattled. The empty hotel shuddered to its foundations in the wind. She kept thinking of Early — of his tall, broad frame, booming voice, blue eyes, and red, pockmarked nose. In spite of loneliness and poverty, he had remained fully alive till the day he died. She got into bed and curled up under the clothes with her back to the windows. Gradually, her body warmed the bedclothes and she fell asleep.

18

Mr Looby and Mr Laxton of Looby, Laxton and Phibbs came twice the following week and on each occasion spent two hours with Gulban.

'What does it mean?' Joey kept asking Cookie.

'He must be making his will, giving judgment at last on our use of the talents,' Cookie replied.

'He hasn't asked us what we've done with them, so how can he know?'

'I'd rather he made his will now than later. If he puts it off much longer, he may be in no fit condition to make it.'

'Was he in his right mind last week when he wanted to import saulies from Scotland to weep over Andy Early?'

'He has a mischievous sense of humour, he likes to keep us guessing.'

'Maybe he keeps changing his mind, or is there some obscure legal tangle to be unravelled?'

'That's what you're meant to think.'

'He's playing God, a dying god with an ego that won't lie down. It's always been both his weapon and armour. It's consumed everything and everybody round him. Now all that's left for it to consume is his own shrinking body.'

They waited for Mr Looby and Mr Laxton while pretending to be busy sorting typewritten sheets in the lobby. At last the two solicitors came down the stairs, first Mr Laxton, the senior partner, tall, hoop-legged, with an arching back and a head that probably appeared heavier than it felt. Mr Looby followed light-footedly with a bulging briefcase.

'I trust you've managed to finish your business,' Cookie smiled. 'I know it must be difficult, he gets tired so quickly now.'

'The great thing about business is that it's never finished.' Mr Looby returned his smile.

'My partner means that we're off now to see another client,' Mr Laxton explained.

'Perhaps you'd like a coffee,' Joey said.

'Or a drink?' Cookie suggested.

'I'm sure Mr Looby would like a coffee and I myself would love a sherry, but unfortunately we've got time for neither.'

'He isn't as strong as when you came two months ago.' Cookie introduced a note of serious concern.

'He's failing fast,' said Joey.

'He's full of the most ingenious ideas,' Mr Laxton assured them.

'You have a most extraordinary man for a father,' said Mr Looby. 'I'm sure you must all be extremely proud of him.'

'He's been complaining a lot about the weather recently,' Joey said.

'I don't blame him.' Mr Laxton made for the door.

'Who would?' Mr Looby tugged at the front of his double-breasted suit and flashed a complacent smile.

'Leeches,' hissed Joey when they'd gone. 'They'll bleed him dry before they've done.'

'And we still haven't seen Mr Phibbs!' said Cookie.

'I keep thinking of the bastards coming and going and not giving anything away.'

'It would be nice to escape for a week or two from all this madness.'

'We could both escape this afternoon. I'll take you out in the boat. You've never been on the island, I'll bet. We'll stand on the highest point and observe the House of Heron from a distance. With luck we'll see things as they really are.'

'I'd love to come but I can't this afternoon. I'm supposed to be lunching at Fort Knox.'

'Again! Surely you could cry off. It's late in the year, we may not get as mild a day again.'

'It's awkward. I don't get invited all that often.'

Joey laughed at Cookie's uneasiness.

'Was it Mrs Bugler who invited you?'

'No, Alicia. Mrs Bugler's in Dublin for a day or two.'

'You know what that means?'

'It means that lunch won't be up to much. Alicia hates cooking.'

'It means shafting, my dear Cookie. I hope you're in form, that you haven't been bashing your bishop overmuch lately.'

Cookie tried to escape up the stairs.

'Alicia is the prettiest thing around. Surely she must have some effect on you.' Joey followed him.

'I like her,' said Cookie.

'Do you love her?'

'I could love her.'

'That would mean not loving Pauline. Have you thought of that?'

'I don't need to think. You're doing my thinking for me.'

'Come to my room for a minute. I've got something to give you.'

Joey's room was a mess. The wash-basin was full of unwashed mugs he'd brought up from the kitchen and omitted to return, and the floor was strewn with books and folders. He got down on his knees to rummage in a drawer at the bottom of the wardrobe, then handed Cookie a squarish packet wrapped in strong brown paper.

'It's a gross of French letters,' he explained. 'I took them from Jack's room in case Pauline came across them. He used to get them from a rep from the North.'

'You have great ambitions for me,' Cookie said.

'You don't need to carry the lot around with you. Keep

the box in your room and put one or two in your wallet from time to time.'

'Don't you want some yourself?'

'I've got another gross. Jack was a businessman, he knew all about economies of scale and bulk buying.'

Cookie went to his room and splashed some aftershave on his neck and cheeks. He'd had a bath before breakfast and had powdered himself below the waist with talc. Now he felt clean, fragrant, smooth-skinned and a little excited. He broke open the packet and took out two of the French letters which he put in the innermost pocket of his wallet.

Joey had once said that the most beautiful thing about Alicia was her mouth, which looked redder than red because of her pale skin. For Cookie it was her slender shoulders. He had actually been able to feel the bones individually through the light dress that day in the library. He opened his wallet and put the two French letters back in the packet.

Alicia came to the door as soon as he knocked. He breathed a sigh of relief, as he'd had visions of Mrs Bugler coming back a day early. Alicia was wearing a white silk shirt and black dicky bow with a flared skirt that ended above the knee and gave her the look of a precocious schoolgirl.

'You're punctual,' she said. 'I was late getting up, I still haven't decided what to do about lunch.'

'There's no hurry. I had a late breakfast too.'

'I'll show you the house first. You didn't really see it last time. Then we'll have a glass of wine, or would you prefer what my mother calls sherry wine?'

She hooked her arm in his and led him straight up the stairs while he tried to make coherent conversation to conceal his state of unreadiness. He arrived breathless on the landing, wishing that they'd started with a little aperitif.

'That was Daddy's room,' she said, opening a door.

The room was almost bare, the air cold inside. There

was no carpet, the narrow floorboards creaked. She sat in her father's rocking-chair while he looked out of the window across the Sound to the stark island and thought of her all in white against a landscape of whiter snow.

'It's a shame we haven't got even one of his pictures,' she said. 'All we've got here is a folder of pencil and crayon sketches, none of them finished.'

'It's a measure of his success. Everything he painted sold.'

'My mother wasn't interested. The nearest she gets to art is cooking.'

She led him to her mother's room which faced the river and the hill beyond.

'Note the two double beds,' she said. 'I see you're not surprised.'

'I prefer double beds to single. I hated the single beds at school.'

'The one by the window is for cooling off, when things get too hot in the seedbed.'

'That *is* a luxury,' Cookie said seriously.

'Do you fancy a swing?' She pointed to a tubular frame at the end of the room with heavy wooden blocks for feet and a metal seat suspended on two chains.

'Is it a permanent fixture?' He tried to be matter-of-fact.

'No, it's movable. It was mine when I was little. I had it stored in Father's room till Mother took a fancy to it.'

He helped her to drag it out from the wall into the middle of the room. She eased herself into the seat and allowed herself to swing gently to and fro. He waited for her dress to lift, but she wasn't going high enough for that.

'It's very relaxing. Do you know why Mother's got it in her bedroom?'

'I can't imagine.'

'Neither can I. Now tell me what comes to mind as you watch me.'

She gave a push with one foot so that she rose a little higher, but still her dress did not lift.

'When I look at you, I think of opening the window.'

'Why?'

'To create a gentle breeze that would lift your curls as you swing.'

'That's the wrong answer. You were meant to say "The Swing" by Fragonard. Very erotic. Cookie, you've let me down!'

They returned the swing to its place against the wall, after which she hooked through his arm again and took him to the third upstairs room. It was smaller than Mrs Bugler's and more striking too. As soon as he entered, he felt bombarded by a score of rival blues that leapt from every wall, from the spaces between a dozen drawings and posters. On the single bed was a coverlet with bright red and green stripes, and above it a single shelf of French and Italian paperbacks. He felt slightly dizzy. In his chest was a sensation of fullness, as if his heart and lungs had swollen. The window hung open, the air was light with perfumes of tantalising subtlety.

'Of the three rooms, which do you prefer?'

'This one.'

'I thought you didn't like single beds.'

'It's small and cosy and beautifully untidy, and you can see the hotel from the window. From the other two you can only see the island or the hill.'

'If you had a pair of binoculars, you might be able to spot Pauline.'

'No, I think she's probably working in the back office.'

He turned from the window. She was lying on the bed, one leg fully stretched and the other raised with layer upon layer of flimsy slip showing.

'Are you in love with her?' she asked.

'Who?'

'Pauline, silly.'

'No.'

'It's hard to believe. You live under the same roof, you must see each other a score of times a day.'

'Perhaps seeing is deceiving.'

'I think about her a lot. She's the only person I know who is good-looking in a way that makes me envious.'

Feeling foolish and exposed, he crossed the room and sat on the edge of the bed. She was smiling up at him, her curls a piece of delicate filigree on the white pillow. He bent down and kissed her, and with the first taste of her lips he felt that he'd been kissing her passionately for at least half an hour. She pulled his shirt out of his trousers and began caressing the small of his back with her fingers. He was kissing her slowly, almost secretly. He could hardly believe what was happening to him, or the speed with which it was happening. It was as if he'd never kissed a girl before, as if all the other girls he'd kissed had been nothing but imposters in women's clothing. Her body was so short and light and her face so small and round that she seemed to have been reduced from twice the size, making every inch of her twice as precious. He felt enveloped and enfolded. He had lost all sense of himself as separate and distinct from her.

Suddenly she pulled away.

'You're not very original, Cookie, are you? What would you say if I drove my hand up the leg-hole of your trousers?'

She laughed impishly and tweaked his nose. He tried to kiss her again, his body drugged, his movements uncoordinated.

'No, don't, Cookie. The stars aren't favourable today.'

She got up off the bed. Ignoring the heavy hopelessness in his legs and arms, he tried to catch her from behind.

'I'm sorry,' she said. 'You're so excitable, and all I wanted was a cuddle.'

He gazed out of the window, while she went to the bathroom. The hotel was perched on top of the rise, gaunt, gabled and exposed. There were no other houses near. It stood alone between moorland and fenced fields, the very picture of uncompromising solidity. Yet the lives within wilted under a pervasive sense of dissociation. All were passing guests except Gulban; only he was not a lodger. He was confined to bed, and the bed belonged to him. He was, and always had been, one of life's owner-occupiers.

Fort Knox was built on the level. The ground around was firm, yet the footing was still uncertain and there was no reliable purchase. Alicia was erotically elusive. Her preoccupation with 'The Swing' said it all. She flushed the toilet with a high, hissing noise that turned into an aggressive rumble at the end.

She came up behind him and put an arm round his waist.

'Why did my father build that wall?' she asked.

'He was an artist, he may have wanted solitude to paint.'

'I like to think that it was to keep your father out.'

'My father and yours were friends.'

'Until they had a row about Mother. We must never fall out, Cookie. In fact, I'm sure we won't.'

She gave him a little hug to which he did not overtly respond.

'Would you like a drink while I'm getting lunch?'

'I'll have a large whiskey with no water.'

She laughed indulgently.

'There's only wine today. It was given to Mother, it's rather special.'

She poured him a glass of burgundy and left him the bottle while she busied herself in the kitchen. He sat by the fire wondering why he felt such pain close to where his heart was beating in his chest.

She brought in bread, cheese and apples, and asked him to follow her into her father's study with the wine.

'I'd like to sketch you as you eat,' she said.

'What about you? Aren't you having lunch?'

'I don't feel like anything just yet. I hope you don't mind eating on your own.'

'I'd enjoy lunch better if we shared it.'

'Then we'll share the wine.'

She smiled sweetly and put him sitting at the end of a bare table by the window with a shelf of books behind him. He didn't quite know what to say, didn't even know what he felt. She got a large pad and sat down with pencils and crayons at the other end of the table. The food looked attractive. He broke a piece of the bread and took a sip from his glass, carefully and shyly, as if he were lunching in public with ecclesiastical dignitaries.

'I'm going to make one or two sketches of you today. Later, I'll do a painting. I'm convinced that I can do something good.'

She went to the bookcase and took down a leather-bound copy of *The Rubáiyát of Omar Khayyám*.

'I'd like you to read that as you eat. Open it anywhere. It's one of those poems that can be read with advantage by taking a series of lucky dips.'

'Aren't you overdoing it, Alicia? Or are you trying to make me poke fun at myself?'

'No, this is just right. We'll laugh at it later, it will bring us closer.'

'I hate Fitzgerald. I'd much rather read Hardy or Blake.'

'Don't make excuses. Just keep eating, drinking and reading. It's all in my head.'

'I suppose this is what is called a working lunch.'

'Take another sip of the wine to moisten your lips, and do let them pout a little. I want you to look like Rupert Brooke. All young poets should look like R. Brooke and all old poets should look like R. Bridges.'

She got up and changed the parting in his hair. He continued munching, pretending to ignore the mockery. The bread was fresh but the cheese was dry. The wine, as she had promised, was rather special. Gradually, he relaxed. The tension left his chest. His heart and lungs resumed their normal proportions. He ate one of the apples and picked up the last few crumbs of cheese.

'I'm quite pleased with them.' She closed her pad.

'May I see?'

'Not yet. You'll see the finished painting.'

'I'll come again tomorrow for another sitting, if you like.'

'There's no need. All I wanted was a few characteristic features. The rest will come from my head.'

She poured the last of the wine and came and sat on his knee.

'How long is your mother away?'

'Another two days. She's up in Dublin. Up to no good. Still trying to put pressure on me to go back to university.'

'She means well, I'm sure.'

'She has no feeling for any of the finer things. She doesn't want an artist about the house, but she'd love a doctor. I hate medicine. I don't mind learning about the body but the thought of practising fills me with disgust. I've been trying to get her to pay for art school, just for one year. She's rotten rich, thanks to Father, and she refuses to spend another penny on my education.'

Listening to her voice while her thighs pressed on his knees filled him with an extraordinary surge of happiness. He touched her hair and she began nibbling at his lips. It was different now. He wasn't too excited. He just knew that he had never experienced such quietly enduring pleasure before.

'The afternoon we played croquet, did you go to bed with her?'

He began kissing her neck inside the collar of her shirt.

'Tell me the truth, Cookie.'

'Yes, I did. It seemed at the time that there was nothing else to do.'

'Did she sit facing the engine?'

'Sorry!'

'Did she sit with her back to it, then?'

'The engine?'

'She's got a different metaphor for every man. For Forker it's trains. For Jack it was horse-racing. What is it for you?'

'Horse-racing.'

'It must run in the family.'

'You say these things to tease me.'

'I like to think that going to bed with her killed off whole areas of your experience, just as drinking to excess can kill sizeable areas of the brain. Am I right?'

'I'm not aware of it.'

'I'm trying to establish whether certain zones of your body have been desensitized.'

She put down her hand and gripped him tightly on the knee.

'You're still alive in parts,' she pronounced.

'I've told you about your mother. Now tell me about Jack.'

'Why Jack?'

'Did he ever make love to you?'

'Not love.'

'Did he ever . . . ?'

'Yes, he did. I was hardly thirteen. Some people would have called it rape.'

'You should have told on him.'

'Told Mother? She'd have been jealous.'

'Alicia, you mustn't allow yourself to feel like that. I want you to be happy and whole. I don't want you to feel pain ever again.'

She began kissing him on the lips. His mind lost its sense of shape and its desire to shape. He longed to lie on his back with arms and legs outstretched and die to ensure her happiness.

'Alicia.'

'Yes.'

'How much money do you need for a year at art school?'

'I asked my mother for five thousand pounds, expecting to get three.'

'I'll give you five thousand.'

'I didn't know you were flush. I'm very grateful but I couldn't take it, Cookie. I might be tempted to spend it recklessly.'

'I want you to have it. The thought of you spending it would give me enormous pleasure.'

'Why would you want to do such a thing?'

'I love you, Alicia.'

'For myself, or as a substitute for Pauline?'

'How can you say these things? I'd do anything for you. I'd give my life if I knew it would ensure your happiness.'

'Then, you do love me. There can be no question of it now.'

She smiled with her nose touching his. He became very excited. The idea of her spending his talent recklessly made him giddy with delight.

'Will you take it? I'll not stop asking till you do.'

'What would you get in return?'

'The pleasure of seeing you soar. I want you to be a great artist. I'd like you to feel the warmth of life, I want you to blossom in the sun.'

It was true. He could give and give and give. Take nothing and still have everything. No sacrifice was too great. He had been born for one triumphant purpose.

'I'll accept on one condition. You must allow me to pay you back one day.'

She kissed him sweetly, running her fingers up and down his neck and through his hair. Quietly and dreamily, he had a nocturnal emission though it was less than two hours since noon.

19

He went out the gate, treading softly on balmy air. He looked back over his shoulder at the house. She appeared in the doorway and waved.

'I'm going over to see Old Gildea now,' she had said.

'What's he got that I haven't?' he asked.

'He's older. When I give him a peck on the cheek, he doesn't get excited. He's a first-class subject, he can sit for hours and put on any expression you ask for. He reminds me of a tree growing out of the ground or a rock that's lodged deep in the earth. Compared with him, the rest of us are slithering on quicksilver in the moonlight.'

'Let me give you a foothold,' he smiled.

'For you and me there is no foothold here. House of Heron, Fort Knox: they make me laugh. We don't belong. What I'd like to know is whether we'd feel as remote from life in London, Paris or New York. I often wonder if Pauline feels as I do. I'd like to know.'

At the crossroads he met Joey who was making for the slip with a heavy pullover draped over his shoulders.

'You didn't dally?'

'It was a working lunch.'

'Then you must need a rest, you tired old shaft-horse. I'm going out to the island for a run. Will you come?'

'It's a bit late, it's nearly two.'

'It's still light at half-past four. I want to show you my little secret.'

They walked down the lane to the slip. Joey readied the boat, a small, white punt with a blue gunwale and thwarts that were smooth in the centre.

'Isn't it a bit choppy?' Cookie said.

'It's the best kind of day, it's neither rough nor calm. When you look across the Sound before launching, you wonder if the water will hold its skin till you get back. If you have spunk, you won't hesitate. You'll know that it could be a life-or-death run with no prize for winning. A wild day is no fun, just plain suicide.' Joey laughed.

'It isn't my idea of a joke,' Cookie said.

'Relax, man, you're in safe hands. Never turn your back on an experience.'

When they were afloat, Joey pulled the stuttering outboard into life. They nosed out through the channel between black rocks and grey rocks with slanting seams rising into serrated pinnacles. The wind caught the bow and in the same moment Joey gave challenge with open throttle. Cookie sat facing him on the centre thwart with one leg stretched and one hand gripping a thole-pin. The wind had an edge that caused him to envy Joey his pullover. He glanced at his brother's face, a corner shop with the shutters up. He looked back at the receding rocks, now a series of dark, irregular gables.

'What was it like with Alicia?' Joey asked as soon as they reached the open Sound.

'The lunch was simple: bread, cheese, wine and an apple for dessert.'

'It's the apple that interests me. Was it sweet?'

'It wasn't a crab.'

'Was it rosy-cheeked?'

'It was green.'

'Did she make you eat the core?'

'She'd cored it already. It was baked, you see.'

As it happened, the apple wasn't baked. He lied to conceal his sense of vulnerability.

'Served with cream?' Joey spoke without taking his eye off the island on the bow.

'With cloves, sultanas *and* cream.'

'What did you talk about?'

'Fort Knox, the hotel, her father, Old Gildea.'

'Old Gildea dotes on her. She paints him and gives him a wee kiss once in a while to keep his circulation going. Has she ever kissed you?'

Cookie didn't answer straight out. He could sense Joey's mounting excitement. A young gun-dog with his snout to the breeze.

'Oh, yes.' He decided to tease him a little.

'Today?'

'Yes, today.'

They were half-way over. The sea was choppier now. Ugly waves curled unpredictably. A south wind was blowing across the rising and falling bows. Cookie looked over his shoulder at the approaching island. It was higher, and also darker, in spite of the sharpish sun.

'Do you love her?' Joey asked casually.

'No.'

To port, a wave rose and rolled: a grinding-wheel with sparks of spume flying. Joey gave a sudden turn to the tiller and Cookie gripped both thwart and gunwale. A splash came in under his arm, soaking his left trouser-leg. The wave rolled right in under the keel. An invisible hand lifted the boat out of the water. For a moment they lingered above the sea, then dropped without warning into a rising valley.

'Look what you're doing, you madman,' Cookie shouted. 'You deliberately let the wave come at us broadside, we could both have ended up in the water.'

'Answer me straight,' Joey said. 'Do you love Alicia?'

'Head out north-west with half the wind behind you, then turn and come up again with the bow cutting the waves. It's the only way we'll ever get across dry.'

'Don't panic. Just answer my question. Do you love Alicia?'

Cookie considered the question as if his life depended on his answer. The fanatical look in Joey's good eye gave no clue to the answer he sought.

'I could love her if she'd let me.'

'Not good enough. Too ambiguous.'

Joey gave another turn to the tiller. The engine smothered and roared. Cookie braced himself without knowing why. Then the port side rose. They soared, sliding sideways, and rose again. They came down with a sudden slap that shook the hard thwart beneath his buttocks.

'Say it firmly and resolutely. Say, "I love her." '

'I love her,' said Cookie. 'Now will you steer like a Christian?'

Joey laughed with mad excitement.

'Stretch your legs and relax. I'll give you a smooth ride now, there's no need to give you a rough one.'

'You've been drinking,' Cookie accused him.

'Not a drop. As you must know, a man in love has no need of liquor. I just want Alicia to be happy. And you too.'

His sharp, bony face was set hard against the wind, which had drawn a tear from the corner of his eye. He shook his head impatiently so that the tear fell without running down his cheek. Ignoring the pitching of the boat, he stood up straight in the stern. Cookie said nothing. He knew that this was no time to show either undue interest or undue anxiety.

They had come into the shadow of the island. They entered a small cove which seemed airless after the hurly-burly of the Sound. The keel grazed the concrete of the slip. Cookie jumped out and made fast the painter to one of the mooring rings. He felt such relief to stand on a surface that did not move. He picked up a turnip-sized stone and flung it at the tilting water.

He felt angry with Joey and irritated with himself. They walked up the slope and paused on top for breath. The small island, a mere sixty acres, was rocky and bare with coarse, patchy grass that had been cropped by rabbits.

The wind whistled with an occasional whirroo round the lighthouse lantern. The lighthouse itself was no longer the sparkling white tower he had often observed from the mainland. Its paint was peeling and the locked doors with their rusty ironmongery gave it the look of a disused belfry. The last of the lightkeepers had left over ten years ago. Now it was nuclear-powered, and no one climbed its winding stairs except the maintenance man who came once a month for a few hours.

'It must be a cold stand on a winter's day,' Cookie said.

'Let me take you to my little haven where no wind will lift your Casanovesque forelock.'

Joey took him to a hollow between two upright slabs, from which four wailing seagulls rose into the wind.

'These two rocks were one a long time ago. You can tell by the seams that it must have split down the middle. It's a lovely spot on a warm day. The sun shines on the south-facing slab. You can feel the reflected heat, and now and again a little eddy of cool sea air mingling with it. I'll bring you and Alicia out here in the spring and leave you alone for the day. You'll get to know her, you'll have the island all to yourselves.'

Cookie placed a hand on the face of the slab and did not answer.

'I'll take Pauline out another day. We'll picnic here. I've planned it all.'

They left the hollow and walked back to the landward shore with the low sun behind them.

'Something has been settled between us two,' said Joey. 'You're in love with Alicia, you've given up your claim to Pauline. Now I see the open road before me. Nothing and no one stands in the way. Are you happy with that?'

'Do I have to be happy?'

'I want you to be happy. I thought we'd agreed to be partners.'

'I'm happy, then,' said Cookie.

Joey jumped and clicked his heels together like Jack.

'Have you ever noticed Pauline's face? It looks quite perfect, yet it's full of flaws. One cheek is more rounded than the other. Her forehead is higher on the right side because of the higher hairline, and the right eyebrow is fractionally higher to match it. The whole effect is one of fullness and roundness. Her nostrils are round and so are her eyes. When she looks you in the eye, you know in the marrow of your bones that you're being scrutinised. It's what I call full-frontal communication. All lost on obtuse old Jack, of course.'

'You're a specialist, Joey, and Pauline is your special subject.'

'One thing I forgot to mention is her mouth. The upper lip is longer than the lower. How can that be?'

'I hadn't noticed.'

'Of course you hadn't. It may be a kind of illusion created by the wanton fullness of the lower lip in relation to the straight and narrow upper.'

'One thing is certain: you haven't been neglecting your studies.'

'You have no idea what it's like being obsessed with a woman. Your mind is in hock, it's no longer your own. Once I'm sure of her, there will be no stopping me. I'll devote myself a hundred per cent to business.'

'I can see it all,' said Cookie. 'I shall marry Alicia, you'll marry Pauline, and we'll share the estate. It's so simple that it must come true.'

'It must, it must, it must. And if it doesn't, there will be hell to pay.'

They were standing above the shingle with the white boat on its side among the grey beach stones.

'Why did you buy the boat?' Cookie thought they might talk about something less emotionally demanding.

'I didn't buy a boat, I bought a coign of vantage. Now I can come out here and view the hotel, the village and Fort Knox from a long way off. I seek a god's eye view, and I have it here. If I ever manage to buy this island off Old

Gildea, I shall be adding more lustre to the history of the House of Heron than Gulban ever did.'

'It doesn't look much from where we stand: sixty acres of rocky ground with grass that's been burnt by blown salt-water.'

'I wouldn't buy it for the grass but for its place in the imagination of everyone on this headland. Something Gulban will be the first to appreciate.'

Cookie said nothing. It occurred to him that his brother had gone cuckoo. They picked their way down to the boat in silence. Light would be failing in forty minutes. He was keen to get back and determined not to give Joey further cause for erratic steering. He tried to give the appearance of imperturbable serenity as he watched the island recede with the setting sun behind it.

'Pauline isn't perfect,' Joey said when they were out in the Sound. 'She's so introspective now. I sometimes think her whole life is Gulban, her pot plants and the hotel accounts. The shock of Jack's death put her into reverse. It will take another shock to force her back into forward gear. Will Gulban's death achieve it?'

'You expect great things from Gulban's death. I hope you're not disappointed.'

'I'll be satisfied if it's not an end but a beginning. We must be honest with each other and with Gulban too. He's lived too long. It's a thought you must not shirk. You can love and honour your father and still welcome his death as a necessary rebirth.'

'You may be right.'

'In many ways he's already dead. Pauline lives and remains unknown. She's a queen bee that must be overtaken and boarded in flight. What worries me is that the man she finally marries will only be a substitute for Jack.'

The sun had already set by the time they reached the slip. They hauled in the boat and put an oilskin cover over the outboard. When they had finished, Joey offered Cookie his hand.

'You were my only rival. Now I have the field to myself. You were her first love, when she was only twelve. You lost her to Jack-in-the-Orchard, and she never looked my way. I've thought about this. The hotel has always been her pivot. As a girl, she played with us, never with the other children from around. She won't look outside now, she'll turn to me. Is that how you see it, Cookie?'

'You could be right.'

'Don't say "could be". Are you rooting for me or are you not?' He squeezed Cookie's hand till it hurt.

There were no guests for dinner that evening. Cookie, Joey and Pauline dined alone in the kitchen.

'It's almost winter,' Cookie sighed. 'Nothing will happen now till Easter.'

'You forget Christmas,' Joey said. 'There's always something new at Christmas.'

'Winter is a weird time here,' Pauline said.

'It's a long, sleepless night,' Cookie agreed.

'When the hotel is empty, it's difficult not to feel that your life is empty too,' she said. 'We all thrive on other people's movements and demands: guests coming and going, complaining about pot-holes in the car park, the chef's sauce Béarnaise, or the lack of a telephone and television in the bedrooms. All these things irritate and stimulate at the same time.'

'Let's celebrate the end of the season,' said Joey, when they'd had their coffee. 'Let's have a drink in the lounge. Pauline, do you fancy a brandy?'

'Why not?'

'Cookie?'

'I had wine at lunchtime. I think I'll go straight to my room and read a book.'

They both went into the empty lounge bar and took their drinks to a table by the fire. Pauline sat on a low stool with her elbows on her knees and her face cupped in her hands. The dancing firelight shone on her legs and forehead.

'The wind is rising, it's getting colder,' she said.

'Then, you mustn't allow the cold to get inside you, Pauline,' Joey advised.

She kept staring at the heart of the fire, as if he had not spoken.

'Life, it's hard. Jack's death was a blow, and Gulban's illness is another. You must live and continue to love, in spite of the cold. I know I'm not as sensitive as you, but even I often wonder what keeps me going. It's easy to get into the habit of doing the same things, and then, before you know where you are, you've built a railway with a runaway train you can't get off. I try to keep fresh by changing my leisure interests. You haven't seen my new boat? You'll fall in love with her when you do. I've just had a thought. Why don't you come out to the island one day for a run?'

'In this weather?'

'Cookie and I went out this afternoon.'

'I'd like to see the island. I'll come when it gets warm again.'

'You'll be surprised by what you see. The hotel, Fort Knox, the Hill. All else shrinks into the landscape. Nothing else exists, except sky and water.'

'That's how I've always seen it, even from here. It's wrong, you know. There are other lives and other ways of life.'

'We're cocooned, they don't impinge on us.'

'Isn't that our weakness, being inside looking out? We see a landscape with men and animals moving. Men digging and mowing, cattle and sheep grazing. We see figures, not faces. We see a life and know it only through reported speech.'

Joey laughed excitedly.

'You were born half-way between Fort Knox and the hotel. You could have turned to either. I'm glad you turned to the hotel.'

'There was no choice for me. The hotel, I thought,

represented the life of effort — the serious, strenuous life — while Fort Knox was only appetite and desire.'

'Poor Cookie, he had lunch there today. I hope he knows what he's doing, I hope he doesn't get eaten.'

Pauline laughed unexpectedly.

'Does he go for Alicia or Mrs Bugler?' she asked.

'Oh, Alicia.'

'Perhaps he'd like to be eaten, then.'

'Don't mention it to Gulban, he mightn't approve. Better not mention it to Bosco either.'

'Is it a great secret?'

'I'm thinking of Cookie. He'll mention it himself when he feels he must.'

'I don't like secrets, they make for edgy relationships.'

'How is Bosco? He seems to visit Gulban every day.' Joey decided to seek a foothold on firmer ground.

'Every other day.'

'I'm usually at the shop when he comes. Is he keeping well?'

'I'll tell him you were asking after him,' she smiled. 'If you like, I shall ask him to call in at the shop tomorrow.'

'He can't be overburdened with parish work.'

'The corporal works of mercy, like charity, begin at home.'

He wanted to ask her about Gulban, if he found Bosco's visits tedious and if he realised what Bosco was up to. The fire blazed. She turned an inscrutable face to him.

'I must wash my hair before turning in,' she said.

She got up and placed the stool under the table.

'I'll have one more drink in the public bar,' he told her. 'Who knows, I may learn something from the reported speech there.'

She smiled at the fire and left him nursing his empty brandy glass.

He did not seek out the company of the locals in the public bar. He hung over the dying fire alone, until a smock of yellow ash had covered the shrinking coals. He felt puzzled — confused by a sense of guilty exposure. He had been talking to her through a closed window. He could discern passing moods reflected in her features. He could observe the movement of her lips forming words. Yet her voice remained muffled and impersonal.

She was a woman of many windows, as the hotel was a building of many windows, and what you saw of her depended on the window she chose to present to you. The Pauline that Jack had seen was not the Pauline that he himself saw, nor was she the Pauline that Cookie, Bosco and Gulban saw. She remained unknown and unknowable, perhaps because she lacked the sense of fellowship that must precede the desire to be known. Everything had appeared so simple from the island with the bare, unyielding rock underfoot. Here was the quivering quagmire of life itself, full of perilous holes and gullies, emitting phosphorescent gases that beguiled the eye with a treacherous semblance of light.

He climbed the stairs and paused outside Cookie's room. The light was on inside. He listened for a sound and heard the rising wind charging the gables and whistling over the roof. With an urgent desire for secrecy, solitude and unhurried recollection, he turned down the corridor to his room.

Cookie was in the bath, immersed to the neck. He had come back from the island with his skin atingle from the wind and sharp salt-water, and after dinner he had felt uncomfortably alert, too critical to make amiable conversation over brandy.

He had left Fort Knox in a state of excitement, which had bestowed on him a sense of rightness and strength. By the time they'd reached the island he was numb. Joey had lost all awareness of life and modes of life that were not his to command. Years of unshared suffering, of living passionately within himself, had brought him to the threshold of compulsive action. Now nothing mattered but a personal vision that had been nurtured in secrecy and in pain. He had cut life to the measure of his needs. He had lost sight of the cutting edge of the external world; his actions were no longer those of a man who takes account of the ebb and flow of human relationships and the indifference of other lives to his own.

Before the water had time to go cold, he got out of the bath and dried himself with a warm towel, then lay on the bed in his pyjamas and drank two whiskies as he waited for the flutterings in his chest to subside. His thesis lay open on the writing table. It was good enough to earn him a doctorate, yet the sight of it filled him with self-loathing. The argument was scrupulous and intelligent, the structure conventionally sound. To the examiners it would appear solid and well researched. Only he himself was aware of the alternative thesis, the one in his mind's eye as he began. What he now saw was shapeless by comparison, and he had lost the will to reshape.

He fell asleep and woke in the small hours. He had dreamt of a spinnaker run across the Sound, before a lively wind with Alicia at the helm. The taut sail did not flap. Not a drop came over the gunwales. He sat in his pyjamas on the centre thwart, facing her in the stern as she rose and fell on an invisible swing, advancing and retreating with legs extended. Joey came down the island slip to greet them, and drew Alicia's attention to Cookie's erect penis which had pushed its head through the front of his pyjamas.

'Look at those two ugly blue veins, Alicia. They're the living replica of a well-known river system.'

'It can't be the Amazon because the pyjamas are unstained,' she said.

'I beg your pardon.' The words sounded pompous, not his own.

'The Amazon stains the sea yellow for two hundred miles. Mud, not semen, no offence.'

'Try again, Alicia,' Joey smiled.

'There's the Vistula, the Irrawaddy, the Guadalquivir and the Murrumbidgee.'

'It's the Tigris and Euphrates, don't you see. Birthplace of great civilisations.' Joey stooped and blew fiercely into the eye of his organ.

'The Tigris is of greater volume than the Euphrates,' Alicia declared. 'On its banks stood some of the great cities of ancient Mesopotamia, including Nineveh.'

Joey side-stepped and the sun shone warmly again on his penis. He got back into the boat and headed straight out to sea against the evening light, while Joey and Alicia sang 'Yo, heave ho!', unaware of his departure. Reluctantly, he kept going, waiting for them to call him back. When at last he looked round, both the island and the headland had vanished. He was at the centre of a glum and featureless sea, and a yellowy stain was spreading from beneath the keel of the boat.

He did not regret his rapture of generosity. He would go to the bank tomorrow and pay £5,000 into his current account before writing a cheque for her. Yet he could not conceal from himself a sense of loss that had nothing to do with bank balances.

20

When Cookie returned from the bank the following afternoon, Pauline, who was taking down the lounge bar curtains for washing, told him that Alicia had telephoned while he was out.

'She seemed disappointed that you weren't here. She sounded as if she had expected you to be waiting by the phone with one hand hovering.'

He went straight to the back office for privacy. Listening to the burp-burp of the Fort Knox telephone, he felt flurried and anxious, as if he'd let himself down. Alicia gave a trilling little laugh when she heard his voice.

'Are you doing anything this evening?' She spoke with a hint of breathlessness.

'Nothing that I'm looking forward to.'

'Mother has just come back — I feel like an evening out.'

'We could have dinner at the Atlantic Grill.' His voice had caught a nuance of her excitement.

'It's too far to drive in cold weather. Why don't we eat at the hotel?'

'The chef is having his winter break, there's no one here to cook except Pauline.' It had occurred to him that Pauline might have no wish to cook for his guest.

'You're making excuses. Let me be chef just for this evening.'

'No, that's too ridiculous.'

'And you, Cookie, are too conservative. I must insist on eating with you at your hotel.'

'Have you ever eaten here before?'

'No.'

'Then that may explain your enthusiasm.'

'I'll not be put off. I'll see you at seven, and if you like, I'll cook something and bring it with me, just enough for the two of us. All you need supply is the china, cutlery, table and chairs.'

'Too bizarre, even for the House of Heron. Don't worry, I'm sure we'll find something to eat, since you insist.'

She came at six, not seven, and they had drinks in the lounge bar which looked bare without curtains. Pauline smiled sweetly at Alicia and said that if she had known she was coming she'd have cooked something less conventional than roast lamb and roast potatoes. Alicia told her that she loved being conventional once in a while, that she had come to sample the hotel cuisine for that very reason. Pauline and Joey ate in the kitchen, while Cookie and Alicia ate alone in the dining-room. At first it was cold and somewhat cheerless, so Cookie got two electric fires and placed one on each side of their table. After the soup Alicia turned off all lights except one, so that the absence of other guests would be less conspicuous.

'Now all we need is a candle and an empty brandy bottle, or a fiasco if you can find one,' she suggested.

He couldn't lay hands on a fiasco, but he found a blessed candle in Gulban's room which he put standing in a brandy bottle in the centre of the table.

'Isn't this romantic, Cookie?' She touched his sleeve. 'Don't you just love it? Mother would be jealous if she knew.'

She was wearing a light blue shirt with a white wing collar and black dicky bow, which made her look even younger than her years. She was in a flippant mood, slightly scatter-brained; she kept jumping from one topic to another without exhausting any of them. From time to time she teased him, but he did not mind. He was so happy that he wanted dinner to go on for ever.

'As you sit here in this empty room, don't you feel gloriously remote from the life outside the hotel gates? Think of Old Gildea in his cottage, sitting before the fire with both hands on his stick. Is this headland his or is it yours?'

'I wouldn't like to say. He's rich in imagination, is Old Gildea.'

'Almost every penny earned here finds its way into one of your tills. You sit on this rise looking down on the farmers in their fields and the fishermen on the sea making the money that will enable you to remain remote.'

'I also look down on Fort Knox which draws its sustenance from neither farmer nor fisherman, and I tell myself that you are more remote than remote.'

'I know we have the edge on you there. It's our six-foot wall that does it, as Joey will tell you if he's honest. It obviously excites his imagination. Last summer I found him skulking in our garden early one morning.'

'Perhaps he came to brush up his croquet.'

'He was sitting on the summer seat behind the rhododendrons, looking at my swing like a man transfixed. Then he got up and set the swing in motion. He sat down on the seat again and watched it till it stopped.'

'What was he up to?'

'Perhaps he saw my swing as a kind of pendulum. He may have been trying to find out if it swung with a constant period.'

'His interest was more personal than scientific, I imagine.'

'He never saw me. After twenty minutes he shinned up the wall and was gone. Somehow I felt excited. I couldn't account for it. It was the kind of excitement you feel standing still and observing a fox close up.'

'He's still obsessed with Jack. He always envied him and now his envy has been preserved in a glass jar for all of us to look at. He told me once that he'd give ten years of his life to play Jack for a day.'

'I never thought Jack was to be envied. How could a girl like Pauline have loved him? Do you think she was just making the best of a wrong, wrong world?'

'She still hasn't recovered from his death.'

'Mother has, you will be pleased to hear. She's very resilient, is Mother.'

She gave a ringing laugh to which Cookie did not respond. It reminded him of her mother's gaudy ormolu table.

'I detect in Mother a nascent obsession with you and Joey, and possibly with Father Bosco too. She said this morning: "One redhead in any family is enough. Two is excessive and three is extravagant." I took care to remind her that you're not all equally red. "No," she said. "Joey is redder than red. He's so red that he shrieks at you." I think she may be planning to invite the three of you to Fort Knox for one of her tests. I suspect she's out to prove that reddest is hottest. Would you be willing to put your finer feelings on one side and undergo a controlled experiment?'

She smiled at him with coldly dancing eyes, and he wondered what on earth she expected him to say.

'Joey, as you know, is our resident scientist. In anything to do with the laboratory he's bound to have the edge on me.'

After dinner he took her up to Gulban's room to show her one of her father's paintings. The room was quiet. The night light was on above the bed.

'Father, are you awake? I'd like you to meet Alicia.'

His father did not move. The colourless face was turned away, the mouth slack, and the once bulbous nose a naked bone with a tuft of moss at its tip.

'Can that have been done by my father?'

She gazed up at a painting of four fishermen in the public bar sprawled about like odd articles of clothing that had been discarded by real fishermen before putting to sea.

'They're supposed to be drunk,' he explained.

'Those heavy browns and crude slashes of black and yellow. It was Father who was drunk, I imagine.'

'You must come back tomorrow and view it in proper light.'

'There's no need, I can see it all.'

Nonplussed, he followed her to the door.

'Who's that?' his father asked.

'It's Cookie. I'd like you to meet Alicia.'

'Alicia who?'

'Alicia Bugler. I invited her up to see her father's painting.'

'Bring me my nose, Cookie. I must have left it on the chair. I can't see anything without my nose.'

'You mean your specs. They don't seem to be here.'

'Don't worry now. Come back tomorrow and I'll view you both in proper light.'

'He's lost.' She clung to him when they were alone in the corridor. 'Seeing him like that makes me anxious and afraid.'

'Come to my room, I've got something to give you before you go.'

He wrote her a cheque for £5,000 while she sat on the bed protesting that she would never be able to repay him.

'You must have it, I insist. I want you to be independent for a year. I want you to take off alone into the wind.'

'Don't you want me to come back to you?' She gave him a sly little smile.

'You must feel free. It's a gift. I've never had such pleasure in writing a cheque before.'

She kissed his signature without blotting it and put the cheque in a little red purse which she carried in her handbag.

'Now,' she said, 'I want you to make love to me.'

'I couldn't do that, not now.'

'Do you mean not yet?'

'The cheque is a gift, there's no obligation.'

'It is you who is under obligation. No gentleman ever refused a lady in need.'

'It's too deliberate, not spontaneous.'

'I'll tell you what we'll do: we'll go to bed. That in itself is innocent enough. Nothing may happen, or next to nothing. All we can do is find out.'

She switched off the light. He heard the rustle of her falling clothes in the dark. He sat on the edge of the bed and unlaced his shoes. The mattress heaved beneath him as she got in.

'Your bed is damp. No wonder you don't attract guests in winter.'

He stripped to his vest and underpants, wondering if it was all a practical joke, half-expecting to find her fully clothed between the sheets.

'Hurry up and make me warm. My teeth are beginning to chatter.'

He got in beside her. She clung to him naked with her head under his chin. She was shivering, so he held her close and ran his hand down her back, feeling the jutting vertebrae under the smooth skin.

'Why are you all buttoned up, swaddled like a piece of porcelain packed for transport?'

She pulled off his underpants and put her left leg between his thighs, because, she said, it was a better conductor of heat than her right.

'You talk too much,' he complained.

'Far be it from me to distract you. I'll say no more.'

They lay quietly waiting for the bedclothes to warm. He kissed her and stroked the back of her neck. She pulled the coverlet over her shoulders and he thought of her as a wary child in a strange place who'd been hurt once and could easily be hurt again. The thought of Jack and the gross of French letters at the bottom of the wardrobe kept pestering him. The wardrobe was at the other end of the room. The packet was at the back of the bottom drawer. It would be a long journey across the square of carpet in the cold. She kissed him warmly and sweetly. She removed her leg from between his thighs.

There was nothing aggressive in his love-making; there was a tenderness verging on self-effacement that came from his sense of trespassing in a secret garden. She was open and soft, and more feminine than any girl he'd known. She left him slack-limbed and full of heavenly ease, aware of the hush in the night when a high wind has just fallen.

'We'll sleep now,' she said. 'Put your arms round me and keep my shoulders covered. They always get cold in the small hours.'

She turned her back to him, and he buried his face in her hair and held her close.

'Tell me about Pauline,' she said after a while.

'What is there to tell? She's efficient and practical. Her passion for pot plants is her only indulgence. She treats them as little children, bending over them, talking to them and feeding them liquid from a bottle. She is so caring that she will not take a leaf between her fingers; she will only touch the edge with the palm of her hand. I once asked her what she sees in them. "They're so relaxing," she said, "like the sound of water falling or waves breaking over pebbles. I can be myself with plants, they never make demands I can't satisfy." '

'I didn't mean Pauline and plants, I meant Pauline and you.'

'We hit it off well enough. She feels I'm not cut out for business, though. To me it's drudgery; to her it's meat, drink and emotional fulfilment.'

'Have you ever been in love with her?'

'Only as a boy. She was more precocious than I was, she lost interest in me at fourteen.'

He hugged her more closely. She felt so small in his arms, a child that needed sheltering from everything that pierced and stung. He began stroking her belly with his hand.

'What are you doing to me?'

'I'm palpating your tummy, feeling the movements of your inner organs.'

'You're a romantic with a difference.'

'I thought that as an ex-med you might know all about palpation.'

'I've heard the word before, not in the medical faculty but at Fort Knox.'

Her shoulders began to heave.

'What's wrong?'

He realised that she was sobbing and trying hard to stop.

'I read something yesterday I wasn't meant to see.'

He waited for her to regain her breath.

'I found a bundle of letters in the loft, in an old suitcase belonging to my mother. They were all to a man she called Grizzly Bear, they were written in her hand and signed "Your Darling Kittykins". There were several references to a little time bomb ticking and kicking in Kittykins's belly. You know what that means. I'm not my father's daughter.'

'Your father was often away from home. Your mother may have written the letters to him.'

'He always called her Katy, she told me so herself. And she used to call him El Grego. He was a lightly built man, to judge by his photos. It would have been absurd to call him Grizzly Bear.'

'Think of Robin Hood's Little John.'

'I loved my father — I mean Gregory Bugler. The only thing I remember about him now is that he wore a white suit. I was too young to understand when he was taken away. He died in a mental hospital and never knew how much I cared.'

'I think you may be jumping to conclusions.'

'My mother's a slut, and I have lost a father. My real father could have been any one of a dozen men.'

'Have you spoken to your mother?'

'There's no point. She's been to bed with so many men that she lost count long ago. Poor Gregory Bugler should have been a damsel-fly. As Joey will tell you, the male has a special kind of penis that sucks out any sperm left in the female by a previous male before he inserts his own. Now, if dear old El Grego had been equipped with one of those, I might have been his daughter.'

'Alicia, how can you say such a thing?'

'I'm a stranger to life. No matter where I go I'm in the wrong place.'

'You must talk to your mother. It's for your own good. You mustn't allow yourself to think such thoughts. At your age you should be celebrating everything that grows under the sun.'

'You don't know what it's like to have a father taken away from you. I'd give anything for a father, even an old dotard who needs mothering and asks you to bring him his nose. If you have a father, you're never lost. You can sleep and forget, you can accept yourself as you are.'

She turned towards him in the bed and put her leg over his thigh.

'You can have me again, any way you like. Mother is always saying that she can satisfy any man. Put me to the test. I'm not my father's daughter. Prove to me that I am my mother's.'

'No.'

'Why not? Give me one good reason.'

'I'm not ready . . . and I think you're trying to defile what we've found together. I know you're spoofing, you're not really like this at all.'

'I know why you refuse. You're half-afraid I may be your half-sister. Gulban was a bulky man, he could easily have been Grizzly Bear.'

'Nonsense.'

'Take me, then. Prove to me that I'm not your father's daughter.'

'You say these things to provoke me.'

'I've been wasting my time. I'd planned a night till morning, ending in revulsion and exhaustion. I mustn't keep you from your beauty sleep any longer.'

She got out of bed and began dressing in the dark. He found the light switch and embraced her in her slip.

'Please don't go, stay till morning. I'll set the alarm and you can leave before any of the others get up.'

'You're too conventional to make a happy-go-lucky hippy. You'll never write a line of poetry. You'll end up rich and in middle age you'll play tennis in braces.'

He followed her into the raw night full of needles from sadistic stars.

'Shall I see you tomorrow?' he asked as she unlocked the car door.

'Not tomorrow, but don't let it worry you. Think of it this way: you've had the most expensive ride in the history of the headland, and you refused a second because you didn't want to halve the unit cost. You may not be a businessman but you're a record-breaker.'

She handed him a flat parcel from the back of the car.

'I'm a rule-breaker, as you will see from my painting of you. I hope you'll like it.'

She gave him an unbalancing hug and kissed him warmly on the mouth. Then she got into the car and started the engine. He followed her down the driveway. At the gate she hardly slowed to see if the road was clear. She turned left, not right, and accelerated up the hill.

'Alicia, where are you going?' he called. 'Alicia, that isn't the road home.'

'I've had enough. I need time to think,' she shouted back.

He returned to his bedroom and put the oil painting standing on the writing table. It showed a tall, awkward-looking tree holding a book in one of its branches. Beneath it was a table with a loaf of bread, a jug of wine and a little bird singing. The upper branches were cleverly arranged to make a face which clearly resembled his own. He laughed at the absurdity of it, but when he studied it more carefully he felt pained by its cold, unfeeling precision. She had reduced him, not to a tree but to a not-very-difficult crossword puzzle.

In bed he kept thinking of her. He could not sleep. He told himself that she was capricious and excitable, demanding and unpredictable. The man she married would have to devote himself twenty-four hours a day to making her happy. It would be a do-or-die occupation, there was no middle course. Life with her would be impossible, but an impossible life was better than a dormant life, than half a life or no life at all.

He had meant to say to her: 'Let's go away, just the two of us. We'll find a place with no hotel, no Fort Knox, no island and no hill — a private place with no associations where we'll live simply, drawing sustenance only from each other.'

'You want to make me into an ordinary woman.' He could hear her dismissive laugh. 'I'll bet you've got grandiose plans for yourself. How do you see my painting? Is it as tedious to you as your Richardson and Fielding are to me? Do you see it as you see Pauline's pot plants, another crutch to be thrown away when the patient takes up his bed and walks?'

'I want you to be a great artist,' he would assure her. 'I want you to burgeon and blossom, to feel joy and warmth, not just misery and cold. I want you to glorify life — paint the sky with larks so lively that their singing will put real larks to shame.'

Before he fell asleep, he resolved to telephone her first thing in the morning.

21

Cookie got up early and had a bath before breakfast. The day was bright and cold. The wind had fallen. The landscape looked sullen and still. As he sat at the kitchen table finishing his fruit juice, he suddenly felt a tingle of excitement. He would suggest to her that they both go to Dublin for a week. They would stay at a good hotel, see plays, films, exhibitions, and eat well. They would go to art galleries and make plans. A bright morning was a wonderful fillip, and even the most difficult things seemed possible after a hearty breakfast.

He took his newspaper into the lounge bar and sat by the east window with the sharp November sun over the moor behind him. She wasn't an early riser. He would wait till ten before giving her a ring.

'So this is where you come to do your skiving!' Pauline looked in the door.

'I'm resting for five minutes before the fray.'

'Gulban would like to see you now. When you've finished talking, perhaps you could bring down his breakfast tray.'

His father was staring at his knuckles, opening and closing his fist.

'You've been seeing Alicia Bugler, I hear?'

'We meet from time to time.'

'Give her up.'

'Why?'

'She's no good.'

'She's talented and charming, and I'm very fond of her.'

'Would you marry her?'

'The thought had crossed my mind.'

'Mrs Bugler's a bad egg and Alicia is her daughter. She may be rosy-cheeked now and sweet to look at, but, take it from me, she's got a grub in her. Some fruit rot before they ripen.'

'I've never heard such nonsense. You're running her down because of her mother.'

'Do you expect to inherit the hotel and shop?'

'That's my ambition.'

'If you do, you'll need eyes in the back of your head. It's a round-the-clock job, I can tell you. How can you run a business if you have a flibbertigibbet for a wife?'

'I think you misread her, she's serious and sincere.'

'She'll do to you what her mother did to Gregory Bugler. You'll be her husband on paper and the butt of her jokes with other men in bed. She's only twenty but already she'd buy and sell you ten times over.'

Cookie flushed with the effort of concealing anger. He decided to appeal to his father's greed for property.

'Marrying her would make good business sense. If I were to inherit the hotel and the shop and Alicia inherited Fort Knox, between us we'd own everything worth owning on the headland. She's friendly with Old Gildea. If he sold her the island, we'd own everything in sight.'

'What would you do with Fort Knox? Turn it into a knocking shop? Officially, that is.'

'I have plans but it would be premature to reveal them.'

'And the island? It would make a lovely holiday resort, if this were Polynesia. Even that would have its disadvantages. It might take business away from the hotel.'

'All this is hypothetical, Alicia might say "no".'

'If you ask her to marry you, she'll say "yes", as her mother said "yes" to Gregory Bugler. And if you marry her, you may say goodbye to your chance of inheriting. Do you want to inherit or not?'

'Of course I do, but I won't be bullied.'

'Say no more, you've said it all.'

He left Gulban comparing his fists and carried the breakfast tray downstairs. Slash Gildea was in the lobby talking to Pauline, who gave Cookie an anxious glance.

'Bad news, I'm afraid,' he said to Cookie. 'Alicia has had an accident.'

'Is she badly hurt?'

'It's worse than that, she's dead.'

'She must have crashed the car.' The effort of saying six words left him drained of feeling.

'She went out over the Gravelly Shoulder, straight through the railings and down into the sea. The car's a wreck. They had to wrap her in sheets before hauling her up.'

'I'm sorry, Cookie.' Pauline grasped his hand.

'I'd like to see how it happened,' he said vaguely.

Slash accompanied him to the Land-Rover. The butcher's van went by, and Slash told him that the body was in the back. They watched the van turn left at the crossroads and drive over the narrow lane to Fort Knox. Cookie felt that he was going to be sick. He turned his back to Slash for a moment, then climbed into the passenger seat of the Land-Rover and asked Slash to drive.

Four or five men were gathered on the Gravelly Shoulder looking down the slope to the rocks and sea below. The road ran along the edge of the cliff, bending sharply midway. She would have driven downhill into the bend. There were no tyre marks on the road. It looked as if she had not braked. The only evidence of mischance was the broken railing and a wooden post on the slope underneath. The small car was a broken box crushed between the jaws of two serrated rocks.

'She must have known this road like the back of her hand,' one of the men said.

'She was a demon driving,' his friend replied.

'There's no sign that she even tried to take the turn,' said another.

Cookie moved away from the group. The angular edge of the land bristled with pointed rocks, ugly black monsters with white-breasted seagulls on their backs. The shore gleamed with the clarity of nightmare. The gabled rocks with their sabrelike apexes became a shower of arrows flying into his face. His eye travelled over the rising slope of the sea towards the horizon where the offshore blue faded into white light that merged with the softer hue of the sky. It was there he wished to dwell, cradled and suspended above all that pierced, encroached and diminished. His eye returned to harsh solidity. A car was a toy that bounced and dented. Flesh was made to bleed and bones were made to be broken. The fire-tested rock remained. She had spent her life in the haze between sky and sea. The rock that broke her had yet to find its way into a geologist's handbook.

When he got back to the hotel, he found Pauline repotting a delicate fern in the porch.

'It's a great shock,' she said. 'I know how you must feel.'

'She had everything ahead of her, she'd barely begun to live.'

'Was it an accident?' She looked pointedly at his chin.

'It was a waste of talent and of life. She knew the road from childhood. I can't imagine what came over her. Even rash drivers go slow over the Gravelly Shoulder.'

He left her because he could not bear her quickening curiosity. He went into the bar, he could not think. The headlines in the newspaper referred to remote, incomprehensible things. His mind was a pool of thin liquid on which nothing could be etched or written.

After a while Joey came in and sat on the stool beside him.

'You loved her, Cookie. The next six months won't be easy.'

'She was very special, not an ordinary girl.'

'I remember thinking once that she would never grow old. Though she was twenty, she hardly looked sixteen.'

'She lived in a different world from you and me,' Cookie said. 'She lived in a different world from Pauline. There was a charge of poetry in everything she said and did. Today there isn't even prose.'

'You are bound to suffer at first. You must allow yourself to suffer because suffering heals the wound.'

'Don't give me the bedside manner, Joey. All I ask is that you respect my feelings. Silence is best. We must never talk about Alicia again.'

'I was only trying to help.'

'I don't want to hear her talked about. I don't want to lose her, I want to preserve her as she was. I shan't be going to the funeral; I couldn't bear to listen to the address.'

He rang Mrs Bugler. She could hardly speak, she sounded miles away.

'I'll call down in half an hour,' he said.

'Wait till the afternoon. Everything's in a muddle now. I don't know where I am.'

Just before lunchtime Father Bosco arrived.

'It was Pauline who told me,' he said. 'I didn't know.'

'What did she tell you?' Cookie asked.

'That you loved her. I mean Alicia. I am sorry. I'll remember you in the Mass and in my prayers.'

'I'd prefer you didn't. I don't wish for help, either visible or invisible.'

'Then I'll pray for Alicia.'

'She's dead, poor girl. She can't stop you now, but if she were alive she'd laugh at you. She lived in her own world, which was neither this world nor the next. She was determined to have no truck with either.'

'Try not to lose your sweetness, Cookie. Sourness in an old man is understandable. In a young man it's intolerable.'

'You should put on your biretta before you talk to me like that.'

'I'm trying to help.'

'Then you must never mention Alicia to me again. There is so much else to talk about — Gulban, Gulban's will, Gulban's loss of memory, your Fiat, your parish priest, Pauline's pot plants. We shall never be short of subjects, and provided the subjects are not important to either of us, we'll never quarrel.'

'You're determined not to be comforted.' Father Bosco turned on his heel and went.

Cookie remained in his room till lunchtime. He ate with Pauline, Joey and the Comforter in the dining-room and listened while they talked about Gulban's confusions — how he would expect breakfast at supper time and complain of the 'noisy' guest in the empty room next to his own. No one mentioned Alicia. He knew that she was uppermost in their minds and he wondered why he was not moved to tears.

He went down to Fort Knox in the afternoon. A distracted Mrs Bugler embraced him and led him into the study, where one of Alicia's unfinished paintings stood against a bookcase. They both sat at the table. She offered him a drink which he declined without speaking.

'She was with you yesterday evening,' she said.

'She came to dinner. Afterwards we talked, and she gave me the painting she'd done of me. She left just before one and drove off in the direction of the Gravelly Shoulder. I was surprised when she didn't make straight for home at that hour.'

'Did she have much to drink?'

'Two whiskies and half a bottle of wine.'

'What did she talk about?'

'You, her father, her paintings. She was in a strange mood, edgy and rather splenetic.'

'Was it an accident, do you think?'

'I don't know.'

Mrs Bugler dabbed her eyes and neither of them spoke for a while.

'She was always difficult to know. She never showed her

true feelings. No one got close to her, not even the students she went round with in Dublin. She lived within herself. She didn't expect anything from anyone and she seemed to feel that no one had a right to expect anything from her. She never sent Christmas cards or birthday cards and she rarely wrote to me when she was away. Though she made jokes, you could tell that they came more from unhappiness than a sense of fun. She was like that even as a child. She never played with other children, she was always unresponsive and remote. When she grew up, she blamed her lack of feeling on her father's early death. She was fond of him, I know, but losing him didn't bring her closer to me. Things got worse between us when she decided to give up medicine. I tried to make her see sense. She became more aggressive, she did her best to irritate me in every way. When she began taking an interest in you, I thought she might soften. She liked you, I know. She was jollier when you were around.'

'Can I see her?' he asked.

'I'd rather you didn't. She's unrecognisable. Better to remember her as she was.'

He gazed through the window at the bare hill, not wishing to give way to nausea and grief.

'Wait here for a moment, I've got something to give you.'

She left the room and returned with a piece of paper. He stared at a crumpled cheque for £5,000.

'It was in her handbag.'

'I gave it to her last night. She didn't want to take it until I insisted. I felt that she should have a chance to make something of her talent. It was meant to enable her to go to art school for a year.'

'Oh, Cookie, it was very generous of you. I know how you must have cared for her.'

He was unable to speak, so he got up and went to the door.

'There may be an inquest. Better to say as little as

possible. No one knows about the cheque except the two of us. I think it should stay that way.'

'If I don't go to the funeral, I hope you'll understand,' he said. 'It's just that such a public act seems a kind of desecration.'

She went with him to the door and grasped his hand.

'It might be easier for me if I could see her.'

'I think you'd only regret it. She was almost too good-looking. She took after her father and she knew it. He was small and light-boned and very handsome as a young man. If you saw her now, you'd never forgive me for allowing it.'

He hurried home in the coldly stinging air. Autumn was over. The fields, like the hill, were bare. Beside each house was a turfstack and a haystack to see the winter through. Cattle were being stall-fed, and the sheep had come down from the hill seeking what little shelter there was on the lower ground. A stiff-legged old man was driving two black cows to the river for their evening drink. On the coping of a ditch a single bachelor's button shook its withered head in the breeze. It seemed to him that all existence had contracted into a hard dry hazelnut which no spring rain would bring to life. He ran up the steps, glad to escape into the relative warmth of the hotel. His father had asked to see him. Slowly, he climbed the stairs to the sick-room.

'I just heard about Alicia,' Gulban said. 'You must be grief-stricken.'

'It's a blow I didn't expect.'

'Maybe what I said about her this morning was harsh. I could not think of her without thinking of her bitch of a mother. Before she came between us, Gregory Bugler and I were friends. He used to spend a lot of time up here and I used to go down to Fort Knox when the nights were long. She began flirting with me, pretending that I had my eye on her, and poor old Gregory believed her. I had a certain reputation but there was nothing in it. She was trying to cover up for another man. Gregory stopped coming to the hotel. He grew odd in his ways and built his six-foot wall. He gave up painting; brickbuilding took over his life. It's a sad, sad story. Alicia was the apple of his eye.'

'She was fond of him too.'

'You mustn't take it badly. Don't let it prey on your mind.'

'Do you want anything? I'll bring you up a drink if you like.'

'Can you mix me an elixir? I'd give anything to feel the pains of youth again. In old age pain deserts the flesh for the brittle bones beneath.'

Cookie went to the door. He wished to escape from the dryness and the prying of a mind that had built round itself a stouter wall than Gregory Bugler's.

'You're back in the race, me bucko,' Gulban called after him. 'I'd struck you off the list. Now you're reinstated.'

He sat by the window in his bedroom staring vacantly at the moor and the road running east to the Gravelly Shoulder. He could go to the funeral and pay £5,000 in funeral offerings. She would break all records. The parish priest wouldn't believe his luck and Gulban would strike him off his list once more. For a moment it seemed the only thing to do. Random images slid back and forth through his mind. He felt exhausted, on the verge of sleep. Light had faded from the sky. Night was falling over the moor, levelling heights and hollows, beating the dark tussocks of melic grass into the darker ground.

He drew the curtains and lay on the bed. Now there was nothing but winter. Frost and blown salt-water would burn the grass, the moor would turn a reddish-brown. The sea would rear up on the land. Wind would tear the seaweed from the rocks and paste wet strips of it on the window panes. Pauline would wander through the empty bedrooms, because the hotel accounts would be quickly done. She would devote more time to her pot plants, and he would sit in the public bar listening to conversations

that had first been made a thousand years ago. Alicia . . .
Alicia . . . she had escaped from one eternity to another,
and it seemed to him that in some unfathomable sense he
had joined her.

22

Spring came unexpectedly. One morning he woke up to find sunshine steaming warmly on the rain-bleached moor. He opened the window and the breeze that came through was gentle and pure. The moor ran down to a black enceinte of pointed rocks and an upward-sloping sea. He washed and shaved, and descended the creaking stairs to the lobby where he stood by the south-facing window, a stranger among Pauline's pot plants.

A newly married man was digging a vegetable patch near a cottage, bending and straightening, levering up spadefuls of black earth, slicing them expertly with the side of the blade. At the far end of the lawn Pauline's young daffodils peeped darkly green against the lighter green of the grass. They were just in bud, weird water fowl with long necks and bent heads, gazing down sternly at their cold feet.

The winter had been long, grey and miserable, or so he believed. He had listened more frequently than he had spoken; he accepted the word of those who cared about such things. Most mornings he got up at eight and went for a walk before breakfast to clear his head. He had given up drinking and smoking; even chilli eggs, his favourite dish, had lost their flavour. In his chest was a vacuum that neither human companionship nor intellectual endeavour could fill. He lived behind a sheet of ripple glass through which he glimpsed vague forms or heard far-off noises, and nothing he saw or heard seemed to relieve the measured monotony of his thoughts.

Once or twice he went down to Fort Knox to visit Mrs Bugler. He strolled between the trees and sat in an overcoat on the summer seat behind the old rhododendron. Mrs Bugler looked dispirited and distrait. She and Alicia had lived together as strangers. Without her she was friendless. She gave him tea and queen-cakes in the sitting-room and made polite conversation to which neither of them attended. She told him that she was planning to move to Dublin, and in February she put Fort Knox up for sale. Everyone said that it would fetch well over £50,000, provided a well-heeled buyer could be found. Cookie felt sad at the thought of Fort Knox in the hands of a stranger. He tried to persuade Gulban to buy it for renting during the summer.

'Are you mad?' Gulban huffed. 'Who wants to spend a holiday behind a six-foot wall?'

'You could pull down the wall,' Cookie suggested.

'She'll never get its price. I'm the only local man with the money to buy it. It's too big for an outsider looking for a holiday home or even for a quiet place for retirement.'

'If I had the money, I'd buy it,' Cookie said.

'You're too young to shut yourself away. Fort Knox is for someone who wants to escape from life, like the man who built it. Sadly, after he'd locked the gate and bolted all the doors, life scaled his high wall and took him by the scruff of the neck when he thought he was impregnable.'

He told Joey what Gulban had said, and Joey thought carefully before replying.

'Gulban is wrong. Fort Knox would remake you. There's enough experience behind those walls to keep a man warm for a lifetime. You should count yourself lucky, Cookie. At least you had her to yourself for a day.'

He could tell that Joey was thinking of his own lack of success with Pauline. She glided from room to room. She watered her plants and carried trays upstairs to Gulban. She taught Cookie how to do the monthly accounts. She never seemed to consider Joey except when she wanted something from the shop.

As he looked out of the window, a sturdy, black donkey came down the road, sniffing the tarred surface, testing it with pouted lips. He lay down on his left side and tried to roll over. He failed and tried again. For a moment his four legs hovered in the air, while he balanced precariously on his backbone, which had become the keel of a boat out of water. Then he rolled on to his right side and lay exhausted with expense of effort. He struggled to his feet and shook himself, sending a cloud of dust into the bright air. With a look of boredom he walked out of the cloud and began cropping the selvage of the road.

For Cookie it was a moment of unsought magic. It was the first time since Alicia's death that he had found himself reaching out for common experience with another moving, breathing body.

March was mild. On St Patrick's Day she opened the windows in Gulban's bedroom to let in the gentle air of spring. The green of young buds blurred the dark outline of the hedge at the end of the driveway. Corkscrews of blue smoke rose from chimneys on the other side of the river. Larks sang over the moor. People were booking for Easter, which was falling later this year than she would have liked.

She took down the curtains in Gulban's room and washed them. She thought she might repaint the walls, then it occurred to her that a wallpaper with a puzzling design might beguile his eye and take his thoughts off his bedsores.

'Wallpaper?' He sounded doubtful.

'We have some lovely patterns below in the shop.'

'The wall at the far end has got a crack above the window. Have you noticed how it's getting longer?'

'That crack's been there since I can remember. The wallpaper will cover it. You won't have to look at it any more.'

'If you paper over it, we won't know if it's getting worse. Before you do anything, I'd like to have a word with Cookie and Joey.'

She got them to come up after lunch, having warned them about his latest obsession.

'What are you going to do about that crack?' he asked.

'It's only a plaster crack,' Joey said. 'Nothing serious.'

'It could be the start of something serious.'

'If you like, I'll fill it.' Cookie tried to show willing.

'Filling's no good. It's like patching old trousers.'

'That crack has nothing to do with shrinkage or settlement,' Joey assured him. 'Cookie is right. Filling will cure it.'

'Has it occurred to you that this hotel may be built on sand?'

'You're beginning to sound like Andy Early.' Joey sniggered.

'I want you to get a building surveyor to inspect the house from top to bottom.'

'Why?' Joey asked.

'You think I'm cuckoo? You think that when I ask for my nose I mean it?'

'When you ask for a surveyor's report, do you mean it?'

'The trouble with you two is that you have no imagination. You only see with your eyes, and even then you're scared in case you see too much.'

'You could be right.' Cookie winked at Joey.

'Which surveyor did you have in mind?' Joey asked.

'There's only one in town. If you look hard, you may find him.'

'I'll ring him this afternoon,' Joey promised.

'I want a written structural report, remember, typed in double spacing so that I can read it without squinting.'

'Whatever next?' Cookie said when the three of them had left the room.

'It's one of his silly tests again,' Joey remarked. 'He

wants to find out if we're prepared to waste his money just to humour him.'

'I think he's being serious,' said Cookie. 'What do you think, Pauline?'

'I'm afraid I don't know. You and Joey must do what you feel is best.'

They discussed their dilemma with Father Bosco at lunch the following day. He passed his hand over his ecclesiastical dome. His lips moved as if he were praying for divine guidance.

'He is confusing the eternal with the merely temporal,' he pronounced. 'When he says that the hotel may be built on sand, he is speaking metaphorically, yet he expects to be taken literally. For the first time in his life his thoughts are turning to the eschatological. With one foot here and another there, he simply wants to make certain that the foot still here is resting on solid foundations. My advice to you is to ring the surveyor.'

'And pour three hundred pounds down the drain?'

'He's our father. We must take him seriously till the end. It's no more than the fourth commandment enjoins.' Father Bosco spoke solemnly with just a hint of pulpit elocution.

'I know what I'll do,' said Joey. 'I'll write the report myself.'

'You're not a surveyor, your opinion on building construction is as worthless as Cookie's or mine.'

'Not correct. I have a scientific cast of mind. I'll carry out an inspection and put my findings on paper. No building surveyor could do more.'

'If Gulban finds out, you'll be up a gum tree,' Father Bosco advised.

'Has it occurred to you that he won't find out unless you tell him?'

Pauline said nothing. It was obvious to her that none of the three had any idea how to talk to Gulban. Not one of them had the courage to insist that the crack was in the imagination rather than the wall.

Joey took his self-given commission seriously. He spent a morning going from room to room with jotter and pencil, and within three days he had written a 4,000-word report on the state of the building, including the roof, walls, foundations, plumbing, electrics and drainage. It was a workmanlike report, though somewhat deficient in technical jargon. Cookie said that it was too uncritical to deceive Gulban's critical eye and he suggested that Joey find a few unimportant faults, 'just for the sake of verisimilitude'. Within the hour Joey returned with one or two additional paragraphs which he read to Pauline and Cookie.

'How about this?' he laughed. ' "The hotel is built on shallow, sloping ground which necessitates a flight of steps as access to the front entrance. This has occasioned the one structural fault in the building. The lounge bar and dining-room floors have apparently large depths of hardcore under the concrete floor slab, and these have settled, causing a gap of approximately six to eight millimetres to appear under the skirting. At present the movement is not significant, but if settlement should continue over a long period, some remedial work may have to be undertaken." '

'Excellent,' said Cookie. 'Now, that has the ring of truth.'

'For good measure I have also included a reference to the creaking stairs: "Most of the joints have loosened and several of the treads have split. Furthermore, the joints between the newel posts and the strings are weak, and will weaken further with constant use. Little can be done to rejuvenate this structure short of complete replacement, which would be costly, so what I would recommend is that you employ a carpenter to brace up a number of the treads and newel posts as a temporary measure." '

'No, no, no. That's too realistic,' said Cookie. 'The first paragraph about floor settlement is all we need.'

When Joey asked Pauline to type out the report, she said that she did not wish to be party to the deception. Then Cookie volunteered his help, promising to introduce a sufficient number of misspellings, *non sequiturs* and dubious grammatical constructions to enhance the professional appearance of the document.

She was making Gulban's bed the following morning when Joey and Cookie entered. Cookie smiled breezily at the patient and Joey waved a large brown envelope above his head.

'It's come at last, the surveyor's report which will set all doubt at rest for ever.'

'I didn't see any surveyor,' Gulban said.

'He came one afternoon over a week ago when you were sleeping,' Cookie explained.

'Resting, not sleeping. I only sleep at night. Now, what does it say?'

'I've only glanced at it. I haven't had time to digest it fully,' Joey said.

'It looks quite comprehensive to me,' Cookie commented.

'Let me be the judge of that.' Gulban reached for the document.

With a little glint of mischief in his eye he asked for his nose, and Cookie dutifully handed him his specs, which he put on with difficulty. There was silence while he leafed through the eight-page report, until Joey could bear the silence no longer.

'As you will see, he says specifically that the crack in this room is no deeper than the plaster.'

'Who says?' Gulban let his spectacles slide down his nose so that he could glare at Joey over the rims.

'The surveyor Bernard Shovelin.'

'He didn't write this report, it isn't typed on his headed notepaper.'

'He was out of headed notepaper,' Cookie explained. 'As we needed the report urgently, and to save time, we agreed that he might type it on ordinary A4 bond. If you want it typed on his headed paper, we can always ask him to do it again.'

'I don't want it retyped, I can read it as it stands. What I do want is to go through it with him point by point and ask him certain questions. You see, he's said nothing about the warped joist in the ceiling above the back office. Either he doesn't know his job or he's skimped it. Ring him up and tell him I want to see him. Ask him to come tomorrow, and if not tomorrow, before the weekend.'

'It's rather difficult, you see. He's on holiday at the moment, we'll have to wait till he comes back.'

'Excuses, excuses, all I get is excuses!' Gulban shouted.

'Surveyors need a break like everyone else,' Cookie said.

'I'm not interested in surveyor's breaks. What I want to know is which of you wrote this report.'

He looked from Cookie to Joey, both of whom looked non-committally at each other, and at Pauline. Gulban opened his mouth to speak but no word came. His cheeks flushed and the report shook in his hand. Pauline went to the bedside. He was seized by a fit of coughing that seemed to steal the breath from his lungs. He hunched his shoulders and gasped desperately for air. She put an arm round him, she was certain he would choke. Then came a wheeze and a rattle. He turned his perspiring face towards her. She relaxed as he found his breath again.

'I happened to swallow, and my spittle went down my windpipe,' he said.

He stared at Cookie and Joey, as she put another pillow to his back.

'Which of you wrote the report?' He spoke deliberately, with a moment's pause after each word.

'Joey wrote it and I typed it,' Cookie replied.

'It was meant as a joke,' Joey explained.

'It was meant to deceive me.' Gulban raised his voice.

'Now, don't get yourself all worked up again,' Pauline advised him.

'It was only a jape,' said Cookie. 'It's the 1st of April today.'

'April Fool's Day! Get it?' Joey tried to laugh it off.

'No one makes a fool of me. Now, get out of here, the two of you, and don't come back unless I send for you.'

'You shouldn't allow yourself to get excited,' she told him when they'd gone. 'Try to relax while I go down and make you a nice cup of coffee.'

'I don't want coffee, I'll have a glass of rum punch.'

'It's hardly ten, it's too early for rum punch.'

'I'm my own doctor. I only prescribe what's good for me.'

She found Joey and Cookie arguing in the kitchen.

'He's a sick old man,' she said. 'He deserves better from both of you.'

'It was Cookie who blew the gaff. What a stupid thing to do.'

'It was hopeless denying it. He was going to send for the surveyor,' Cookie objected.

'The surveyor knows the score. He'd have kept up the fiction if we'd asked him to. Now it's a right shambles. You've queered the pitch for us both.'

'Leave it for a day or two,' Pauline said. 'When he cools down, I'll make him see the funny side.'

23

She gave Gulban his rum punch and went to her room while he drank it. A breeze from the moor was blowing through the curtains. She stood by the side of the window, looking through her binoculars at the random movements of sheep on the hill.

Some of the ewes were lying down placidly with their lambs. Those that had not yet given birth were grazing with their backs to the breeze, their bellies close to the ground and the teats of their swollen udders sticking out on either side. Next to a rock lay a torn piece of rag. It occurred to her that it could be a young lamb that had been killed by a mink or fox. As she refocused the binoculars for a clearer view, the rag shook itself into life on four thin legs and ran straight to its bedraggled mother. Pauline laughed with unexpected delight. The hill was alive with soft, white bodies, black faces and black legs with thick knee-joints.

The new-born lambs had hollow flanks, spindly legs and ears that looked too long for their narrow faces. In three or four weeks their bodies would fill out, their legs would look thicker and shorter. They would bleat and frisk from morning till night, jumping straight up into the air as if on springs and mounting each other in play while their mothers looked on uncomprehendingly.

Two young lambs came running after a solitary ewe. She gave a quick kick with her hind leg and off they ran in alarm. Another ewe came trotting and gave them her udder. They suckled with tails wriggling, but not for long.

The mother lifted a hind leg in warning and slowly walked away. They followed her until she lay down, her udder now protected against their hard noses.

Slash had put all the twin lambs with their mothers together in one field. She took a keener interest in the ewes with twins because they looked more motherly than the others, and at the same time she pitied them. The lambs were the opposite of meek. They would butt their mother's udder with their snouts till her hindquarters shook as they suckled. Both lambs and ewes inhabited a world of necessity which seemed both mechanical and unalterable.

With a sense of ineradicable imperfection, she remembered coming home early from school one afternoon and finding her mother in the garden asleep in the sun. She grasped her mother's hand and waited. A hen that had just laid began to cackle under the trees. It was warm in the garden, there were beads of perspiration on her mother's upper lip. She shook her mother's hand and her mother opened her eyes. She smiled from under the wide brim of her sun-hat and said, 'Is it that time already? I was far, far away.'

That evening her mother took her bicycle from the shed and said that she was going shopping. When she got back, the house was an upward-running river of flame, and then they were even poorer than before.

While still a young girl, she often went over that scene in her mind: her mother asleep in the airless garden, the heavy scent of woodbine and hawthorn mingling; the silence broken by the cackling hen. She had experienced a moment of anxiety as she waited for her mother to open her eyes, yet in retrospect that day had come to represent a life of never-to-be-recovered perfection. Had memory invested it with its peculiar density of atmosphere and emotional coherence? Or did it now seem perfect because the fire that broke out a few hours later had altered her life for ever?

Increasingly, the best of her waking life lay in childhood

remembrance, which awakened in her a desire to recover a lost intimacy with the physical world around her — with stones, streams, tree-stumps. At one time these were more than inanimate objects, they were living things invested with a personal magic that enriched and illumined her young, unexamined life. Growing up was a gradual withdrawal from the warmth of a world in which stones had hearts and in which there was no exterior that did not express an interior. Now all she saw were surfaces. She was cursed with the apprehension of relationships in which she herself had no part to play.

The winter that had gone was a time of further withdrawal into a world of disinterested observation. She noted Cookie's silent trudge through each dark, short day; she could only guess at the pain of the endless nights that followed. He never once mentioned Alicia. He spoke drily of impersonal things, and in speaking of them made clear that nothing he said or did had any value. In his stoicism he had taken on an unsought dignity that placed him beyond the reach of Father Bosco and Joey and of Gulban, too.

Through her binoculars she watched a young man ploughing a north-facing slope. He was going back and forth on the tractor with his young wife perched on the mudguard behind him, both glancing over their shoulders at the brittle sod turning and the thin furrows glistening as they lengthened. She found herself weeping. She put down her binoculars and sat on the bed. She could not say what had caused her breasts to heave.

When she looked again, a man was moving among the sheep on the hill. The ewes came to him. He walked to and fro, standing now and again to look about him. He picked up a lamb by the hind legs and slapped it on the shoulder. The mother came running, and he put the lamb down again.

Slash had a brother called Packie who ran a butcher's shop in the village. He bought wethers from Slash and hung their carcasses from hooks in the window. He looked every inch a butcher. While Slash was lanky and wiry, his brother was short and stocky with the set of a man who lived entirely on meat and soup. His interest in his work was passionate. Last week she asked him for three pounds of middle neck, and he spent twenty minutes trimming the meat, so great was his delight in his butchering.

'It's lovely to watch your own meat being cut. It's like having a suit made to measure,' he told her as he rubbed two greasy hands on his blood-speckled apron.

She ordered two chump chops, one for herself and one for Gulban. He took the hindquarters of a lamb off a hook and severed the legs with a single stroke of his cleaver. Then he cut a chop off the top end of each leg with his saw, and she recoiled from the thought that the fat man in the shop diminished the lanky man on the hill.

Just before noon Slash came back carrying a lamb with a broken leg. He put a splint to the leg and tied it neatly with a piece of string.

'Will he be all right?' she asked.

'It usually works, given time.' He spoke without turning to look at her.

'It is a he, isn't it?'

'He could be a ram but my own feeling is that he will grow into a wether.'

'I'd like to look after him till he's well,' she said.

'No need. I'll bring down his mother this evening. She's a great lady, she'll give him every care.'

'I could keep an eye on him, it's no trouble.'

'It isn't good to get too fond of a lamb. They grow up quickly. Now a bullock is different. He takes longer. There is time and plenty to get to know a bullock. If I ever have a sick one, I'll let you nurse him.'

He looked up and laughed. His lean face was weathered and he had a chipped tooth in front which he'd got as a young man trying to lift a hundredweight bag of flour with his mouth for a bet.

She went back to the kitchen to prepare lunch and recalled a summer afternoon while she was still a school-girl. Cookie and she had been playing in the river and on the way home they came upon Slash trimming castrated lambs in a pen. Some months earlier he had put an elastic band up over the scrotum of each male lamb that wasn't designated for tupping. The scrotums withered and turned black, as Cookie never ceased to tell her. Slash bent over a kicking lamb, the thick haft of the knife in his hand. A hard, black clod rolled on the ground. He pocketed the rubber band for future use, and she and Cookie pretended that they hadn't been looking. He kicked the heap of black, round clods with his wellington boot and scattered them all over the sheep pen.

'Roasted chestnuts, roasted chestnuts!' he called after Cookie and Pauline. 'Five for sixpence, twelve for a shilling. Get your roasted chestnuts here.'

If Cookie had been on his own, Slash wouldn't have said anything. The roasted chestnuts had been entirely for her benefit. Fifteen years later his attitude towards her was still the same.

When she brought Gulban his lunch, she found him slumped on the bed, slavering at the mouth with one hand hanging over the edge. His face was grey, he looked barely warm. She fetched Cookie and Joey and called a doctor. She felt cold herself. She could not help wondering if this was the beginning of the final struggle.

The doctor said that he'd had another stroke and he recommended that they get a nurse to sit with him day and night until his condition became stable.

'Stable?' she heard Joey say to Cookie. 'It could become stable either way.'

Father Bosco came before dinner and gave him extreme unction. They all stood round the bed. Gulban lay on his back with his eyes closed and a pair of rosary beads that were not his own wound round his fingers. His rigid lips were dry and his breath came from between them in slow, high rasps. All that remained unchanged was the wiry hair that stood out in tufts above his ears.

Father Bosco took her into the back office and pressed his thumb into the flesh of her forearm. She stood close to him, breathing the musty smell of his cassock, resisting her desire to move away.

'This is more serious than the first,' he said. 'Only toughness and determination will pull him through this time.'

She waited impassively for him to release his grip.

'It must have come suddenly,' he continued. 'He was chirpy enough when I saw him yesterday.'

'You can never tell with strokes,' she replied, not wishing to mention the surveyor's report.

'Anything could happen now. I must ring Canon Sproule and tell him that I'll be staying the night.'

'I'll put you in the room next to him. I'll air the sheets and get everything ready — '

He released his grip and transferred his hand to her shoulder.

'Thank you, Pauline. Without you, what would become of us?'

She escaped from the office, pleased to have something practical to do. As she climbed the stairs, she realised that she had never before thought about life without Gulban.

'Where are we now?' Joey asked.

'Exactly where we were yesterday,' Cookie replied.

Joey had invited him to his room for a review of strategy and in the hope that under the threat of Gulban's death they might find common ground.

'Where were we yesterday?' Joey pursued.

'What I mean is that nothing has changed. He was cross with us this morning but he hasn't yet had time to disinherit us.'

'If he recovers, we could be the worse for it.'

'I want him to recover,' said Cookie, picking up a book

on the Jurassic system which lay on Joey's bed.

'Is that true?'

'It is true.'

'You can never know the truth about yourself. Your aim must be to define the false and in defining it edge an inch closer to the truth.'

'I want him to recover,' Cookie repeated.

'So do I — up to a point. If I knew he would disinherit me on recovery tomorrow, I'm afraid I should vote for a quiet and easeful exit today. I'm being frank because I abhor humbug, my dear Cookie. Humbug is a means of ensuring that other people think well of us. Unfortunately, we must also contrive to think well of ourselves.'

'I'm not as obsessed with inheriting as you are. Over the winter I'm afraid I lost some of my enthusiasm.'

'Is that why you split on me?'

'I didn't split on you. I said that it was a prank and that we were both responsible.'

'It was a careless thing to say.'

'We see things differently,' said Cookie.

'As you say, you've lost your appetite for property. Is that why you haven't made an offer for Fort Knox?'

'Where would I get fifty thousand pounds?'

'I've made an offer of ten thousand. Being in the running, even as an outsider, gives me a pleasure which I can only describe as erotic.'

Cookie's incredulous laughter had the force of a gunshot.

'If I had fifty thousand to spare, I'd gladly pay it. Fort Knox is a palace of dreams and a hall of mirrors, worth every penny. If it's worth fifty grand to me, what must it be worth to you?'

'It hadn't occurred to me to put a price tag on it.'

'So little has occurred to you lately, Cookie, that I wonder if such innocence can be genuine. Has it occurred to you that soon we may have to deal with Pauline. She's headstrong and self-assertive. Will there be a place for her here after Gulban goes, I ask myself?'

'She's intelligent and industrious. She's a capable manageress.'

'She could be difficult to work with. Would she take orders from you or me?'

Cookie got up and placed the book on Joey's pillow.

'Why do you read about rocks?' he asked.

'They're more durable than plants. I like the Jurassic because I care to think that it contains the ancestors of Pauline's ferns, beautifully fossilised for ever and ever and ever. Now, wouldn't you like to be beautifully fossilised? Come on, admit it.'

'I must dash.'

'Sit down and let me pour you a drink.'

'You know I've given up.'

'A martyr for love's sake!'

'You must tell me more about the Jurassic at dinner.' Cookie went to the door.

'Take care how you go,' Joey called after him. 'Don't fall into the fronds of one of Pauline's ferns. Don't be taken in by her lovely maidenhair, it conceals an adder's-tongue. And don't, whatever you do, lose your sense of humour. It's precious and irreplaceable. It's what distinguishes us from apes, baboons, stockbrokers, solicitors, politicians and other solemn primates.'

Joey went to the shelf and took down two of his rock samples, then sat on the edge of the bed with one in each hand. He had wanted to talk amiably to Cookie, but Cookie had the knack of awakening in him a kind of irritation which was akin to self-hatred. He stared at the sharp-edged rocks in his hands, not knowing what was to be done.

'I'll never make a scientist now,' he said aloud. 'I was born three hundred years too late. Locke said: "Take a frog and strip it. You may see the circulation of the blood if you hold him up against the sun." To me that is real science. To make discoveries in those days you didn't need a laboratory and a government grant. All that was necessary was to be observant.'

Ever since he could remember he had wanted to be a scientist, preferably an earth scientist with the breadth of intellect to take geology, geography, geophysics, geochemistry and geodetics in his stride. He was good at science at school. He was the best in his class at physics and chemistry, and he never got less than full marks in mathematics.

'What makes a great scientist?' one of the plodders asked the maths master in order to waste time one afternoon.

'Having a creative mind, a mind that oozes ideas. A great scientist is as creative as a great artist.'

'Do we have any creative minds here, sir?' the time-waster asked.

'No.'

'What about me?' Joey enquired. 'I always get a hundred per cent in maths.'

'Your strongest suit is certainly maths. You solve every problem I set you, but I suspect you'll never discover for yourself a new mathematical problem. Creativity is only the formulation of problems.'

The class laughed delightedly. One of the dunces said, 'Poor Joey, you'll never win the Nobel.'

Joey laughed too. He laughed with such effort that he nearly choked. He loathed the sight of his own face but he had had faith in his intellect. Now the maths master had pronounced a sentence of death. He did no work in the study hall that evening, and he couldn't sleep that night. At three he got up and made his way to the maids' dormitory in the far wing of the building. He listened for young breathing and leapt in beside the sleeper in the first cubicle. Pulling up her nightdress, he pinned her down. He lay on top of her and prised her thighs open with his fist, making no effort to stifle her horrified screams. The lights came on and he was pulled by the legs off the struggling girl who turned out to be the matron, grey-haired and in curlers. The following morning he was expelled before breakfast. When he arrived home, he told Gulban that he couldn't help it, that he had been overwhelmed by desire for a virgin in the middle of the night. To his surprise, Gulban kept his cool.

'You have a lot to learn,' he said. 'Next time make sure it's a virgin who is overwhelmed by desire for you.'

After that nothing much mattered. He was serving not one sentence but two. He had a face that no woman cared to look at and a mind that could solve only other men's problems. Pauline owed him so much that she wouldn't admit to owing him anything. Not that he considered himself a hero. He had never been aware of having made a heroic choice. If he'd deserted her and let her die, no one would have blamed him. He was only a boy at the time, yet he was old enough to have been capable of blaming himself. His act of courage changed the shape of his life. He had sacrificed sexual and emotional fulfilment so that Pauline could look cool, elegant and grandly superior.

At first she used to mother him because he was two years younger than she. On his first day at school she held his hand going in the gate, and when he had to go to the toilet in the middle of the morning, he asked her to take him. She waited outside and talked to him through the door while Cookie looked on and made fun of them both.

She spent the afternoons playing with Cookie in the river. He knew that they wished to escape from him, but now and again he caught up with them and joined in their games. Cookie favoured tig because he wanted to be touched by her. He himself favoured hide and seek because he wanted her to find him. He loved hiding from her with his heart beating, and it was such relief when she stole up behind and pounced on him. It was a moment for just the two of them that not even Cookie could share.

She was at her best then. No girl, not even Alicia, could have held a candle to her. At sixteen she was still beautiful, her face plump and soft, though her body had begun to thicken. It had lost the suppleness of a sappy sally rod. She had begun to fill her dress. Something had gone wrong, and it was spiritual rather than physical. Now at twenty-six the metamorphosis was complete. Her skin had gone dry and no decortication would cure it. Her throat had become stringy from too much slimming, and her hair had begun to lose its lustre. Strangers who came to the hotel thought her stunning because they had not seen her as a girl. Her gifts had come from a cynical and misogynistic god who conferred on her an elegance to inspire love while denying her the warmth that would satisfy it.

How she must have envied Alicia as she saw in her face the bloom and beauty which she herself had enjoyed so briefly. He had once seen her walking round Alicia, viewing the backward flowing lines of her hair-style, trying to invent a nuance of imperfection that wasn't there. He should have said to Pauline that afternoon, 'The curious thing about Alicia is that the back of her head is no less interesting than her face.'

He would have loved to see the ease with which she would conceal the pain of the affront.

The wrongness of his feelings tormented him, because the wrongness was invincible and inescapable. He went to bed with it and woke up with it, a too-tight skin that could never be shed. Yet there was a time when he and Cookie had shared her and when neither envied the other. Bosco and Jack were older; they couldn't and didn't join in the laughter he and Cookie found with her. Then she left both Cookie and himself standing. She took up with Jack and became like any ordinary girl. They pretended not to miss her, concealing the loss of magic from each other. Cookie's scar was internal; his own was an ugly blaze on a vandalized tree. Jack did nothing, felt nothing, and took everything. His advantage was that he was older, and the games he played were more banal. Only Bosco escaped unscathed.

'If he'd felt even a tenth of what I've felt, the chastity of the priesthood would have been an impossible price to pay.' He returned the two pieces of oolite to the shelf.

Yesterday he'd seen a girl of sixteen in the butcher's standing on one leg waiting meekly for her pound of mince. Her skin was clear as Alicia's but her short, black hair was coarse. Alicia's hair was long, sometimes curly and sometimes straight. It was light brown, almost fair in front, and when she combed it back, it formed streaks of different shades above her ears and a tight dark bun at the back, whelklike in its involutions. By comparison the hair over her forehead looked bleached, as if she'd spent her young life facing the sun. If the sky remained clear tonight, there would be a moon after eleven. He would go down to Fort Knox and scale the wall. He would sit for an hour on the summer seat behind the rhododendrons, which was more than Cookie would do for her now.

24

Before going to bed she looked in on Gulban. The nurse was reading and he was asleep, breathing softly with his lips pressed tightly together. It seemed to her that he might expire at any moment without the slightest accompanying movement or sound. She went back to her room thinking that he would never see the morning.

The three sons, though not in absolute accord, were sleeping tonight under one roof. She had prepared Father Bosco's room herself. He came up as she was putting a hot-water bottle in his bed and he stood by the window with his back to her.

'I have a vivid memory of this room as a boy,' he said. 'I came in here one morning early and looked out over the moor at three or four sheep grazing. The dawn was creeping up the sky behind them. Their bodies were still dark but there was a glowing line of light all along their backs. It was extraordinary, a kind of revelation. I had a sense of timelessness. I felt very close to . . . the Bible.'

'If you wake up early, you may see sheep in back-light again tomorrow.'

He turned to her with a little laugh that she found predictable and patronising. He always talked loudly and volubly whenever they were alone together, yet behind the words she could hear a terrifying silence. He seemed to be standing on a beach with a ground-sea breaking round him. He was shouting to make himself heard between waves, while she stood alone on another beach from which the sea had ebbed before she was born. In spite of that, she was never aware of unease in his presence, only when she rehearsed their conversation later with a disorientating sense of having been talking to a stranger.

Joey was also a stranger, and in a way which she found more abrasive and disturbing. He came up behind her in the porch one day and told her that the most interesting thing about her plants was their red and blue colouring matter.

'The chemical structure of anthocyanins', he said, 'is a thing of endless fascination.'

Another day he'd asked her if a bat was a bird.

'No,' she said firmly.

'It flies.' He smiled omnisciently.

'So does a daddy-long-legs.'

'It's a bird in so far as it flies and a mammal in so far as it is viviparous and suckles its young. Consider yourself lucky that you don't have to classify it.'

Then he told her that, joking aside, he greatly admired her plants, that if humanity had their gift of photo-synthesis, the world would be more efficient, more orderly and more humane.

There was no ignoring him. Even when she was in the back office with Cookie, she was aware of Joey below in the shop and of a quirky, unconventional commentary that could only have come from him. The good side of his face reminded her of Alicia's, because both faces expressed a conscious containment that seemed to hint at a passionate and tortured life within.

She switched off the light and got into bed, knowing that she would not sleep. Impulsive yearning was what gave her emotional life its character. The yearnings came and went in a hundred different guises. Last summer she'd heard an American girl telling her boyfriend about three white leopards sitting under a juniper tree. The phrase had an extraordinary effect on her. She kept imagining them white and feline in the dark shade of the tree, and she told herself that she must flee the hotel and the headland because she would never find them here. She stayed put because she knew that no matter where she went there would be loss. The life of the headland and the hotel was the only life she knew. Even if she should find the white leopards in another place, she would lose the afternoon light coming into her bedroom in summer, all brightness and reflection, as if the sea below had become the sky above. She would lose the September sunsets, too, the western sky full of golden clouds, far off and smooth, brushed into haunting forms that threatened to turn into spotless leopards.

Going away now would mean deserting Gulban, and that she could not do. Once she had feared him. Since his illness she had come to feel affection for him. On his sick-bed he had made her respond to the passionate life still left in him.

She dozed and woke again, wondering if the nurse had called her. The hotel was quiet. Her pillow was wet with perspiration and her back felt stiff and cold. In her dream she'd been naked, and no matter how she dressed, her clothes always melted away. In the distance she heard the clip-clop of hooves in a gallop. She looked round. There was no horse. She was walking briskly along a dusty road with a tussocky moor on each side. The hooves were ringing behind her again. She turned and saw sparks but still no horse. She began to run, her body naked and her loose hair flying. She ran faster and faster with the clip-clop-clip-clop still behind her. She was out of breath and weak at the knees. She saw a stakelike rock by the roadside which she embraced with both arms to keep herself from falling. Then she felt a forefoot on each shoulder and a pulsing warmth against her back. She looked round again, and all she saw was the straight white road laid ribbonlike over the ugly moor. After a while her strength of will and limb returned. She crossed the road to a still pond in order to wash the hot slime from her back before day finally yielded to night. Kneeling, she cupped her hands and again felt the weight of the forefeet on her shoulders. Afraid to look round, she groped with her right hand and found a slack and wrinkled belly pressing against her buttocks. Further down her hand encountered a moist and loamy morass, palpitating and hotly protruding. She retched twice in revulsion. The invisible horse that had been pursuing her was a mare.

For a long time she lay with the bedclothes over her head trying not to think of her dream. She pictured white leopards, whiter than newly shorn sheep, and she thought it would be amusing to make them jump over a stile one after another until . . . Then Cookie was stretched in the bed behind her, embracing her closely, holding her breasts and kissing the nape of her neck. She had no idea how he had come to her bed. He did not speak, and she turned and kissed him warmly on the mouth. It was a kind of miracle, a celebration of wholeness and rightness after the unspeakable horror of her dream. The bed was warm and sweet, and their lips made no sound as they moved. She became aware of far-away music, the sound of a river flowing and frothing between worn stones with summer breezes in the gorse above. All sense of withholding left her. She lay open to sunlight, a landscape on a day in summer. The day passed without her knowing and she became a still water full of still reflections, all of them whole and perfect.

He went without word or sound. The door closed behind him. She listened for receding footsteps and heard none. A sweet languor had spread thickly through her limbs, yet she felt neither weakness nor weariness, only an intoxicating sense of rightness and ripeness. A dry, hard capsule had split open and discharged its toxic contents. For a moment loss was forgotten. All was gain. She fell asleep on her back remembering the uncompromising firmness of his body in the bed and his hesitant presence in the back office during the day. She dreamt that she had confessed their sin to Father Bosco, who, before giving her a light penance with a wink, diagnosed her spiritual malaise.

'You've spent all your life possessed by only one devil. Now at last you know what it's like to be possessed by seven, one for every day of the week. What you needed all along was a man with the two cardinal virtues, energy and lunacy.'

'I love my devils, Father Bosco. You must never attempt to cast them out.'

'Of course I shall cast them out,' he reprimanded. 'And when I do, seventy times seven devils will take their place and your state will be seventy times better than before.'

'Oh, Father Bosco, Father Bosco, in heaven you'll set the Lord's table on a roar.' She thrust her hands deep into the slit-pockets of his soutane and hugged his buttocks with innocent gratitude.

'Now, you must tell me who put the seven devils in you, so that I may go and shrive him right away. It was Cookie, wasn't it? Tell the truth.'

'Not Cookie.' She tried not to blush. 'It was Slash Gildea.'

'I should have known,' said Father Bosco gravely. 'All the others see love as a game that's been played before. They sit down at the table only to find that the cards they've been dealt bear the thumb-marks of more skilful and daring players. Slash alone had not heard of Paolo and Francesca, Tristan and Isolde, and Héloïse and Abelard.'

'It made no difference.' She laughed brashly in his face. 'He knew all about Adam and Eve.'

She woke again, certain that she'd heard the click of a door closing. She pulled on her dressing-gown and crossed the landing to Gulban's room. Gulban was still slumbering and the nurse was dozing in her chair.

'No change,' she said sleepily. 'He hasn't moved since you looked in before.'

On the way back to her room, a strip of light under Father Bosco's door caught her eye. She returned and asked the nurse if she would like a cup of coffee. The nurse pointed to a thermos flask on the night table and said that she'd just had a cup of tea.

'Has Father Bosco been in to see Gulban since bedtime?'

'No,' said the nurse.

'He's in the next room. If there's any change in the patient, let him know at once.'

She went back to her own room and stood by the window in the dark with the curtain pulled round her hips. The flat ground below and the hill beyond were enmeshed in shadow that glimmered with little pointed patches of light. Fort Knox had become a white box in a cardboard enclosure, and, where the river banks were low, the water flashed intermittently in the moonlight. The scene was an oil painting that showed a bulging seine of silver herring, dreamlike and unreal. Her midnight visitor had come out of that mysterious landscape. He had come and gone, leaving behind no visible sign of his visit.

Father Bosco was kneeling beside his bed with his head in his hands. He had heard footsteps on the landing. It was after three. The night was endless and the fire which Pauline had lit in the grate had gone out.

'Please, God, keep my mind sweet,' he prayed. 'Through middle age and old keep my thoughts pure.'

After arriving at the hotel that afternoon, he had seen her going up the stairs. She was wearing a light green dress with buttons up the back, and the stress on the fabric seemed so great as she climbed that the buttons looked in danger of coming undone. Slightly breathless, he had turned away and peered out between her cheese plants at the calm, solid hill beyond. The world was a sane and orderly place. A place of objects and of people as objects.

All the chaos in the universe seemed to be concentrated inside his head.

After she'd wished him good night, he could not sleep. The hotel fell silent, and he saw himself stealing naked to her room where she lay on her back on a cold slab that did not in the least resemble a bed. With his thurible he walked clockwise round the slab, going chink-chink-chink as he incensed her naked body. He disliked incensing. He was over six feet tall, and it made him feel slightly ridiculous. He bent down to kiss the little lappet of flesh below her navel and found that what met his lips was the smooth, cold slab itself, which had shrunk to the size of an altar stone. He raised his eyes, expecting to see her enshrouded in the fading cloud of incense smoke above his head. Then he found himself lying face downward on the slab, his body rigid, his legs and arms outstretched. He levitated until he seemed to balance on the top of an upright spindle that pressed painfully into his belly. An invisible hand gave his feet a shove. He began to revolve, slowly at first and then with increasing speed. He became a spinning top, yet strangely his head remained clear. The spindle penetrated his intestines. He came to rest on the slab with the spindle deep inside him. Pauline appeared by his side, and with a ceremonial stoop kissed the nape of his neck in the V of his priest's collar.

'I've been revolving on my own axle,' he explained.

'Not axle, but axis, Father Bosco. An axis, as Joey will tell you, is an imaginary line about which a body rotates. Don't feel ashamed. No one will ever see your axis.'

He woke up hot and disconcerted, questioning the subtle deceptions of the spirit at the mercy of hungering flesh. He tried to pray in bed. Then he knelt beside the bed with the window open so that the austere night air might purify his thumping heart.

'If only I were open to sweetness,' he said. 'A man who is open to sweetness is open to grace. A man who is not can only know self-loathing and defilement.'

He got into bed again. The sheets were cold and stiff with starch. He lay rigidly on his back, forcing himself to make an inventory of things that had no seed of carnality in them: jagged rocks, iron filings, missals, monstrances, knives and forks. When he ran out of items, he thought of Joey as a boy torturing small creatures. He would build miniature dams beside rivers and watch them burst their banks and carry kicking beetles away. As he grew older, he became more sophisticated in his cruelty. He would play on his victims' greed, and sometimes in a spirit of generosity he would arrange his 'catastrophes' so that his prisoners might escape by using their intelligence. Though he no longer contrived natural disasters, he hadn't changed. He was blind to beauty and spirituality, and he was a bad influence on Cookie. It was impossible to envisage a role for either of them once the hotel became a home for old priests. Pauline, on the other hand, was industrious, level-headed and loyal. Her management would ensure that the accounts showed a credit balance. There were dangers, of course. Spiritual dangers. Yet they must and would be overcome. He would not flee temptation, he would face it.

Before falling asleep, he made a kind of declaration. 'I am a soldier of Christ,' he said. 'My ideal of conduct must always be perfect steadiness under fire.'

25

In the moment of waking she heard the cuckoo calling from across the river. The clear-sounding notes gave no sense of repetition but rather of a gloriously antiphonal celebration. Her awakening was a reawakening to the beauty of sound, shape and movement, to the mystery of the familiar made unfamiliar, to a landscape that had been moulded by dreams.

When she went downstairs, she found Cookie making toast in the kitchen. He smiled a casual good morning and, with his back to her, ground a handful of coffee beans from the big glass jar on the shelf above the work top.

'You look tired,' she said.

'I woke at four. I couldn't get back to sleep.'

'I had a look at Gulban around three. The nurse says that he's had a peaceful night.'

There was silence as Cookie buttered his toast. He was the most handsome of the brothers. His sandy hair and thinly freckled nose, and the light, golden fuzz on the back of his hands, communicated a sense of luminosity that made her think of a cornfield by the sea. She waited self-consciously and self-critically, determined to make him speak.

'The last nine months haven't been easy for you,' he said at length. 'It's time you had a break from the sick-room.'

She felt a stab of puzzlement. She thought of touching the hair on his arm to see if it would dispel the fog of non-communication in the room.

'I wouldn't mind an evening out,' she admitted. 'Why don't we eat in town for a change? We've eaten here every evening since Christmas.'

'We could go to the Atlantic Grill this evening.'

'I've eaten there before. Let's try somewhere different. What about one of the hotels?'

He drove her to town in the Land-Rover and they ate in a hotel overlooking the sea. There was a patch of beach, a low cliff and a stone breakwater from which two boys were fishing. They sat by a window watching the light of evening on the broken water. The conventional menu required little study and the main course came with an abundance of insipid vegetables from the hotel freezer. She sipped her wine abstemiously and tried to forget the excesses of her last evening out with Jack. Cookie was relaxed and detached. Unlike Jack, he did not chaff the waitresses. When he'd finished the entrée, he commented wrily on the absence of *haute* in the *cuisine*.

'Have you finished your thesis?' she asked.

'I've finished the writing. I've still got to check the footnotes.'

'You haven't finished it, then.'

'I may never finish it. When I look through it now, I feel that I've outgrown it. I began with great enthusiasm, I felt my insights were original and true. Now I know that all I've been doing is coating the crumbling old edifice with a different shade of emulsion. It could well get me a doctorate, but even if it did, I wouldn't feel inclined to call myself "Doctor". The word has been devalued somewhat since Samuel Johnson's day.'

'A doctorate might get you a lectureship.'

'That sounds like putting out to sea. I'd prefer to wait for a better tide. In a sense we're all in the same boat. Gulban is slumped in the stern and he hasn't released his grip on the tiller.'

'You should be making plans, none the less.'

'I may stay here or I may go away. If I go away, I shall

go so far that coming back will be out of the question. Gulban can't have long to live. I'd like to stay on for what little time he has left.'

'I know you're fond of him, though you don't show it.'

'Neither does Joey. Father Bosco is the only one of us who performs his filial duties with a flourish.'

His ironic laugh dispelled all possibility of ambiguity.

'It's a pity he gets such short shrift from Joey. He means well, he never does less than his best,' she remarked.

'Joey sees Bosco as a cunning hunter, a man of the field. He sees himself as a plain man, dwelling in tents.'

'Where does that leave you?'

'Neither in the field nor in the tent, which is where I wish to be.'

'All three of you have been wounded in different ways.'

'You and I have been wounded in the same way,' he said. 'We have both experienced possession and suffered loss.' His alert brown eyes registered neither hope nor regret.

'After loss should come retrieval.'

'Not always. Life can be loss, loss, loss. It can also be loss, search, search with no possibility of retrieval.'

'You're a cheerful soul,' she smiled.

'The great thing, Pauline, is that we're not as old as Gulban. There's a grain of hope in every year that's still to come.'

He drove home carefully. At Undercliff the moon formed jagged fragments that gleamed on the wrinkled water, and the graveyard wall cast a deep shadow on the slope above the sand. It seemed to her that Cookie himself was surrounded by another such shadow. Over dinner he had been affable and amusing in a way that Jack could never have been, yet he had left her with the feeling that she was still the little girl who came up to the hotel to play and went home thinking about the marvellous things that went on behind the tall, bland windows. He was not the man who had come to her room while she slept and had stolen away again soundlessly in the dark.

He pulled up in front of the hotel and switched off the headlights.

'The dinner was no good but I enjoyed the conversation.' He gave her a playful peck on the cheek.

'I enjoyed the evening, too.'

'We'll do it again, then, and do it differently.'

As she climbed the stairs, the evening seemed to fade away. She went into the bedroom next to Gulban's and locked the door behind her. The empty hot-water bottle lay on the night table. The bed had been made, the previous day's newspaper formed a funnel in the waste paper basket. She lay on the bed while a moth circled the light above. It went round and round the lampshade, a big, heavy moth rising and falling, going out wide and coming back in without any discernible pattern. Her mind whirled, too, climbing and swooping, as if she'd had too much wine.

Twelve years ago Bosco took her to the swing-boats. He was only a student then. They sat face to face in the narrow boat and he pulled her higher and higher till she could see the upturned faces below from above the crossbar. He nodded without speaking, and she tucked in her billowing dress between her knees. Cookie and Joey were still in short trousers then. Joey had a chemistry set in his room. He spent the afternoons playing with little pillboxes of sulphur, charcoal, iron filings and lycopodium powder, and he was saving up his pocket money to buy a Bunsen burner. Cookie spent his time reading; he knew *Palgrave's Golden Treasury* by heart, not to mention *Lyrical Ballads*. At that time the world was one. Now it had been broken up into cantles, and the cantles would never come together again. Now there was rivalry, discord and denigration. Only a week ago Joey, the plain man who dwelt in tents, had spoken to her all too plainly.

'He's a role player, is our Cookie. All he wants is to make himself interesting — not just to you and me and

Father Bosco but to his own dear shimmering self above all. He longs for the obsessive personality. He longs to be obsessed by Alicia. He'll never forgive her for having taken her life while he still only fancied her.'

Now there were two moths circling the lampshade. She closed her eyes, not wishing to see, feel or think. The evening in retrospect filled her with despondency. The mare that pursued her in her dream and the man who came to her room were more real to her than anything she'd ever experienced. They seemed to be one and the same. They had grown out of her mind and body, and the thought of them filled her with self-loathing.

Luckily, there were things to be done. She would go to Gulban's room and the nurse would speak unambiguously about Gulban's condition. She could not say whether he would live or die, yet she would give no indication of doubt. She would confine her observations to things that could confidently be observed and known.

The following morning Cookie had a telephone call from Mrs Bugler, inviting him to Fort Knox for coffee. He was taken aback. He stammered in hesitation before accepting. He did not want to go and at the same time the thought of going filled him with curiosity.

'She must be lonely,' Joey said. 'Did she say she felt lonely?'

'No, she just invited me for coffee.'

'Cookie, you're a romantic or an innocent, which is the same thing. Her coffee-house is the most popular in the country. It's a club from which no member has ever been blackballed.'

Joey's hysterical laughter propelled him out the door. He walked slowly downhill with one eye on the road and the other on the red-brick wall and the white-walled house behind it. The gate was open. The daffodils and the narcissi were out, and the rhododendron was coming into bud. Someone had been digging the flower-beds. A garden fork leant against the summer seat. He felt weak and slightly queasy. He wished he had not come.

She came to the door and offered him her cheek. She had put on weight. Her face was formless and her body looked broader because of the heavy, loose skirt that hung in tucks round her hips. Over coffee she told him about her work in the garden. He listened sympathetically in the knowledge that she had weightier matters on her mind.

'I still haven't found a buyer,' she said at length. 'Two or three people have expressed an interest but it's obvious that they don't have the money.'

'It will be difficult to find someone here who has.'

'I thought you might like to make me an offer.'

'I would if I could afford it.'

'I no longer expect to get the asking price. Your Joey has offered me ten thousand. Would you be willing to offer as much?'

'It's worth five times that.'

'I'd let you have it for ten on condition that I could have it back for a month every summer and that you left my bedroom as it is. The house and garden are very dear to me. Sadly, I just can't live here any more, it's so depressing when it rains. I'd like to sell it to someone who'd know its sentimental value. I can't think of a more suitable buyer than yourself.'

'I may not be staying on here, I'm thinking of going away.'

'Shall I sell it to Joey, then? I know he's keen.'

'No, I think I have a better claim. I would like to own it. It's just that I feel embarrassed, you're practically giving it away.'

'We've got a deal, then.'

They drank a glass of dry sherry and discussed the conveyancing. She had bought a small cottage in the Wicklow mountains not far from the town in which she was born and close to a few remaining childhood friends. She did not speak of Alicia or Jack or Forker. He could see that in every sense that mattered she had already gone away.

He left her at noon in a mood of exhilaration. The garden would be his, the summer seat and the swing; also the house with its book-lined study and the single bedroom upstairs. He was going down to the village to break the news to Joey. At the crossroads he hesitated and walked up the incline to the hotel. He had stolen a march on his brother. He had brought off a coup. Though it was really a *coup de chance*, it might still impress Gulban, if he should ever get his strength back.

A week later Gulban showed the first sign of recovery. He called for rum punch and, as he sipped it, he complained that he could not taste the Angostura bitters. He was still weak. His mind wandered more frequently, his words came slowly and from far away. Cookie, Joey and Father Bosco went up to see him. He talked for five minutes, then closed his eyes and emitted a loud, drawn-out snore. He had said nothing about the talents, and Cookie wondered if he'd finally forgotten them.

'Not a bit of it,' said Joey. 'He's still trying to call the shots, he'll keep us guessing while there's a puff left in him.'

Gradually, the weather turned warm. Farmers with spades emerged from their barns and blackened the fields as they dug. Ewes and their lambs climbed higher on the hill. In the evenings Cookie began going for walks with Pauline. Once or twice they drove up into the mountains in the east and she sat with him on the edge of a cliff watching sea birds through her binoculars, while he feigned an interest in shags, gannets and guillemots. His thoughts began turning to the university: the smell of ancient calf leather in the library on damp mornings, the stiff-legged walk of an English professor in a crumpled raincoat, his own sense of suffocation, of being buried under a scrap-heap of useless learning and dead culture. That sense of aridity had returned to him on his walks with Pauline. He would observe trees coming into bud and fresh green leaves unfurling in ditches, yet in his mind and heart he had a sense of winter. He was still in hibernation, with a low body temperature, low respiratory rate and slow metabolism, living off the stored fat of a warmer season. All vigour and enthusiasm seemed to have ebbed away.

He could not account for it. He liked Pauline. She was intelligent, witty and good-looking. Perhaps, he told himself, he was jealous without knowing it — jealous of her unremitting obsession with Joey and Father Bosco. She talked about them endlessly. Her imagination did not seem to range beyond the grinding routines of the hotel.

'Joey has more than a streak of cruelty in him,' she said one evening. 'When he sits beside me now, he always turns the bad side of his face to me. He keeps staring through me, torturing me with the knowledge that my own face is without a scar. Does he ever say anything about his face to you?'

'No, and even if he did, it would not be a straightforward statement. He is interested mainly in propositions that are neither true nor false. I'm sure he means no harm. I think he only wants you to be aware of him.'

'I am aware of him. How could I be otherwise?'

'He thinks the world of you.'

'I'd feel more comfortable if he didn't.'

That evening he kissed her on the lips for the first time. They were alone in the Land-Rover on the grey mountain road. He kept kissing her for twenty minutes with a deliberation that appalled him, and all the time he kept thinking that Alicia had killed all sexual impulse in him for ever. At last Pauline broke his embrace and asked, 'Is Father Bosco happy?'

'He's the sort of man who doesn't expect to be happy till he's dead. Even when he was growing up, he never communicated happiness. He was always secretive and withdrawn. When he decided to enter the seminary, no one was surprised. We all said, "Now at last we know his secret." '

'He still has secrets. Sometimes, as he talks, you feel that the words bear no relation to what's really on his mind.'

'The about-to-be-demised estate? He's become very attentive to Gulban lately. For a priest who should know better, he has no fear of Mammon, or of the hotel and shop which are the haunts of Mammon. I know he wants to turn the hotel into a home for superannuated clergymen. What he doesn't realise is that some poor servant of Mammon will have to make a whacking great profit below in the shop to keep the servants of God in luxury on the hill. It's the sort of parasitic economy that a scrupulous priest would shun. Or has he so much faith in God that he has lost all fear of the Devil?'

'He never mentioned that to me.'

'Perhaps he sees you as the manageress who will make his heavenly dream come true.'

'That's something else he's never raised.'

'You must wait and see which way the cat jumps — once she's out of the bag.'

'You're a strange family, you never speak well of one another. Jack was hard on Bosco, and so are you and Joey. Isn't it possible that he means well?'

'So does Gulban, so do most of us.'

'You always call him Gulban. Are you afraid to call him Father?'

'He likes being called Gulban. It's the kind of name that doesn't need a double-barrelled surname to lend it singularity.'

They drove home in silence. At the hotel gate she said, 'You've been pulling my leg. You're quite sensitive, really. You just want to make me think that you're cold like Joey.'

A few days later Joey pounced on him in the back office while Pauline was upstairs with Gulban.

'You've got something to tell me,' he said.

'Nothing, I suspect, you don't already know.'

'Perhaps you thought it best for me not to know.'

'What are you talking about?'

'I'll give you a clue. She plays a musical instrument. Surely you can't have forgotten how well she played yours?'

'Mrs Bugler's told you I'm buying Fort Knox? I had meant to tell you myself.'

'But it slipped your mind?'

'It wasn't on my mind.'

'Now it's on mine. I rang Mrs Bugler yesterday to raise my offer to twelve thousand. You can imagine my chagrin when she told me that you'd bought it for ten, the price I offered before you took a hand. What's wrong with my money? Answer me that! Or should I have said, "What's wrong with my dong?"'

'I have no idea.'

'Oh, you're a sly one. I had thought of you as greater than a brother. I had seen you as a friend.'

'For sentimental reasons Mrs Bugler wanted me to have it. She invited me to make her an offer.'

'Just as she invited you to fuck her. How very cosy! And how enjoyable for you, too. You were born lucky. You're even luckier than Jack. And to beat the band you're still alive and fucking.'

'This is ridiculous. I refuse to quarrel.'

'You made a pact with me, remember, and the pact said, "Hands off Pauline". Unfortunately, you made it while you had a comely mare between your knees. Your mare jumped out over the Gravelly Shoulder, so you jumped on mine instead.'

'That's surely a matter for Pauline. As for Fort Knox — '

'Forget about Fort Knox. We'll deal first with the means of transport — the mare, the mare, the mare.'

'You're quite mad.'

'No, no, no. First she was yours, then she was Jack's. For a time she was nobody's, and you surrendered right of turbary to me. Now you've got out your spade and you're digging turf on my mountain.'

'I can hardly keep up with the metaphors.'

'I'm mixing them because it's the only language you understand. There are humbuggers, silly buggers, and literary buggers, and the greatest of these is the literary.'

'I'm not talking to you in this mood.'

'Then we must part as enemies. Our pact is annulled. If I get the estate, I'll give you neither quarter nor lenity. You'll be out of here on your ear before Gulban is cold in his coffin.'

'Goodbye.'

Cookie hurried out of the back office and up the stairs to his bedroom. Though he felt that he should do something, he had no idea what it might be.

26

Joey remained in the back office playing with Pauline's calculator while trying to recall from his schooldays a mnemonic for trigonometrical ratios. He was full of heady excitement, which led him to think that life would be more enjoyable if it provided more occasions for self-assertion. It was a pity that Cookie had made no attempt to explain away his double-dealing. He had been aware, no doubt, that if you present your opponent with an open goal, he will soon get tired of scoring.

Pauline came in with the post and told him that bookings for Easter were up on last year.

'I'm impressed with your calculator. Mine can only add, subtract, multiply and divide. Yours has got all sorts of funny buttons: sines, cosines, cosecants and cotangents. It must be a godsend for calculating small profit margins.'

'I didn't choose it.' She sliced open a banker's envelope with her keen little guillotine. 'It was given me last year by a commercial traveller who said, "Punch that and think of me." Sadly, he changed jobs and I haven't seen him since.'

'Life is full of little tragedies, and the sad thing is that no amount of them will ever add up to a great one. My little tragedy is that I must leave you to your guillotine now. I'm going over the way to cheer up Old Gildea.'

She opened another envelope and never looked up as he said goodbye. Crossing the river, he gave a sustained whistle in response to an invisible lark somewhere in the vacant sky above. The torrent of song pursued him to the bottom of the hill where Gildea's lane led off the paved road, lasting all of six minutes without a break. It lent impetus to his sense of mission, of knowing what he was about, of being totally and indubitably in control. He laughed as he remembered the mnemonic: 'Snails of high class are horrible to one another.' He would tell it to Pauline when he got back, if only to complicate her hitherto innocent relationship with her calculator.

He found Gildea on his knees in the garden, weaving a creel from sally rods, his wrinkled neck noticeably pale after the sunless winter. As Joey approached, he straightened and lit a stump of a pipe in which nothing but the dottle remained. He did not turn to Joey. He stood staring at the green wigwam of rods in front of him.

'So you've come to offer me a hand?'

'How did you guess?'

'Get weaving then and let us see how handy you are.'

'I've come to make a bargain, not a creel. I'm here to offer you four thousand pounds for the island.'

'Again?'

'I'm a fair-minded man, I wouldn't offer you three.'

'What would an old man like me do with four thousand pounds?'

'You're not too old yet, you'll soon find someone young enough to help you spend it.'

'I need so little these days. Slash bought me an ounce of expensive pipe tobacco yesterday. I told him I'd prefer cheap plug, not because it's cheap but because it's stronger. I have two new pipes that poor Alicia gave me. I never smoke them now, I just look at them.'

'You could travel. You've never seen the city. It's a marvellous and sinful place.'

'What's the good in watching other people sinning?'

'I'll make it four and a half thousand. That's my final offer.'

'Would you take me to the city for a week and show me the good by day and the bad at night?'

'I'll do better: I'll show you the bad and the good both day and night.'

Old Gildea fished the heel of a plug from his pocket and slowly charged his pipe. Joey looked out at the distant island and waited. Smoke rose from Gildea's pipe, and still no word broke the tension.

'I'll take four and a half thousand clear. The money we spend in the city must come out of your own pocket.'

'It's a bargain,' said Joey. 'We'll get our solicitors working on it right away.'

'I said four and a half clear. You'll have to pay my solicitor as well as your own.'

'You're a hard man.'

'So is your father, though he has a likeable side to him as well. When he married your mother, he went out and bought himself a swanky hat. The first Sunday he wore it, a gust of wind blew it off his head into the sea. His head was the wrong shape for a hat. I've worn a hat all my life and never lost one yet. The Herons always had money but they never had luck. If I knew you'd bring bad luck to my island, I wouldn't let you have it.'

'Do you have to clear the deal with Slash?'

'No, the island is mine to sell or not sell. Now it will be yours and the money will be mine, but the sight of the island will still be mine.'

Joey couldn't wait to get home. He went straight to Gulban's room and shook him by the shoulder. Gulban woke, then seemed to drop off immediately. Joey sat by the bed and waited.

'Are you awake?' he asked.

'There's something on your mind. That's why you're here.'

'I've got news for you. I've bought the island off Old Gildea.'

'You could breed rabbits on it, big white ones that will look like lambs from the mainland.'

'This is a red-letter day for us Herons. At last we'll own

the island. We'll be on the headland and off it.'

'You'll have to pay rates on it.'

'Of course.'

'I'll make a bargain with you. If the income from your island in the first year is enough to pay the rates, I'll give you a fiver.'

'It will be greater than the income from Fort Knox. Now that's a white elephant if ever there was one.'

'I see two white elephants, two big, lumbering behemoths so white that I can't tell which is which.'

'You'll see the island differently when you've had time to think about it.'

'Time . . . I haven't got much of that left. Now I'm trying to get up my strength for one last meeting. I want the three of you here in this room a week today. I have things to say that can't be left unsaid any longer. It will be a formal meeting. Pauline will take the minutes. There must be a record of the proceedings in case you need to refer to them when I'm gone. And we'll have a proper typewritten agenda so that you can all doodle on it and pretend to be thinking. Is that clear?'

'Yes.'

'You'd better warn Bosco and Cookie now. Saturday morning in this room at eleven. Dark lounge suits for you and Cookie. Bosco can come in his cassock.'

Father Bosco was washing his underpants when the telephone rang. He always gave them a rinse before turning them over to the Canon's housekeeper who was in the habit of inspecting what she washed and commenting on it. From experience he knew that she expected a priest's underwear to emit nothing less than the odour of sanctity, and, as a man who took his mission seriously, he felt it his duty not to give cause for scandal. The odour of sanctity, she had told him, was something pure and austere like the odour of wild honey and locusts. That, he knew, was an ideal of pristine Christianity. The best a twentieth-century country priest could aspire to was the keen and haunting odour of Sunlight soap.

He allowed the telephone to give seven rings before answering.

'Sorry to have kept you waiting, I was in the middle of a lengthy prayer.'

'How right you are to pray,' said Joey. 'The Day of Reckoning is here at last. Gulban wants to see the three of us on Saturday at eleven hundred hours for a final meeting. It's all hush-hush. Top secret. No one knows the agenda. Aren't you excited?'

'I can only do my best to share your enthusiasm.'

'You're worse than Cookie. He's affecting total indifference, the pietistical hypocrite. Just think! This is it.'

Father Bosco was in fact excited. He had merely thought it proper in a priest to keep excitement under a bushel. He rang Pauline in the afternoon, who was even less informative than Joey. Then he rang Cookie, who said that he was pleased to see Gulban getting his strength back. The following day he visited Gulban himself, whom he found sitting up in bed saying his rosary. It was such a remarkable sight that he was filled with the conviction that his own prayers were about to be answered. He spent a week of mounting excitement which reached its acme when he received in the post from Pauline a typewritten agenda which told him nothing. It simply said:

House of Heron
Board Meeting
Saturday, April 20th at 11 a.m.

AGENDA
1 Apologies for Absence
2 Minutes of Last Meeting
3 Matters Arising
4 Chairman's Report
5 Any Other Business

He took the first item on the agenda so seriously that he allowed two hours for the one-hour journey, in case he should get a puncture. He arrived at the hotel to find Cookie and Joey enjoying a drink in the lounge bar and showing no sign of the strained relations he had detected between them on his last visit. They were both in their Sunday best, and Joey had rather ostentatiously brought along a clipboard for his agenda.

'There's no table in the board room,' he explained. 'You'll need something to write on, Father Bosco. Now, if you were a bishop, you could use your folded mitre.'

At five to eleven Pauline came down to tell them that the Chairman was ready. He had discarded his pyjama top and was wearing a new white shirt with an open collar and red cravat. He was sitting up in bed, the agenda resting on a tea tray in front of him, his spectacles already in position on the tip of his nose. Three high-backed chairs from his office had been placed in a row at the end of the bed, with another chair for Pauline by the bedside table.

The Chairman welcomed them one by one, shuffled his papers, and asked them to be seated. As he peered at them over the rim of his glasses, Father Bosco felt certain that he detected a twinkle of approbation in Gulban's watery eyes.

'Have you ever taken minutes before?' He directed the twinkle towards Pauline.

'Not of a board meeting.'

'I was chairman of the parish council once, so let me tell you how it's done. First you write down the names of all present, one underneath the other:

      Anthony ("Gulban") Heron (Chairman)
      Father Bosco Heron, C.C.
      Thomas ("Cookie") Heron
      Joseph Heron
      Pauline Harrison (in attendance)

Have you got that? Good. Now we can make a start. Item two: as we don't have any minutes of the last meeting, the secretary can't read them, and it follows that I as Chairman can't sign them. Item three: matters arising. As there are no minutes, there are no matters which could conceivably arise. Is all clear so far?'

Joey, who was sitting next to Father Bosco, sighed audibly and ticked off items two and three on his clipboard.

'Now we come to item four, the Chairman's report and therefore the meat of the agenda. I should like to begin by saying that this is the last formal meeting I shall call. From now on I may see you individually but never again together. This is an extraordinary meeting, because the subject I wish to address is not business but death. In a word I have decided to die.'

'You can't just decide to die!' Father Bosco remonstrated.

'Unless you propose to commit suicide,' Joey added.

'All my life I have decided everything at the House of Heron, and I'm not going to change my tune in the last few bars. I've lain here long enough. Soon I'll turn my back to the window and the sunlight, and I'll close my eyes. I've made my will, all is in order. Nothing remains to be done except snuff it.'

The Chairman closed his eyes and wrinkled his forehead in an act of extreme concentration. Pauline waited with head down and pencil tilted in readiness. She looked so serene that it seemed to Father Bosco that nothing Gulban could say would now surprise her. Joey had drawn the front elevation of the House of Heron on the back of his agenda, to which he'd added a frieze of matchstick figures that spelt the legend: 'Abandon hope, all ye who were born here.' Somewhere in the fields, a donkey brayed mournfully. The Chairman smiled patiently as he waited for the braying to stop.

'Now we come to the purpose of this meeting, which is

to finalise the arrangements for my funeral.'

Joey groaned and drew a picture of a donkey in spectacles sitting up in bed with a little girl in a pretty hood beside him.

'Listen carefully, because these are my last wishes. I don't want to moulder away slowly in a graveyard. I want to be buried at sea and my bones picked clean within three days. I want my thigh-bone to be washed ashore in the north and my collar-bone in the south. I want to be everywhere when I'm dead, not imprisoned in a narrow graveyard waiting for the next funeral to bring down the next man with the next instalment of news from above. On the morning after I die, you will take my coffin eastwards by road to Undercliff, then westwards by boat along the coast. You will bury me out behind the island at a point where the north chimney of the hotel sits on the lantern of the lighthouse, and you, Father Bosco, will say a final prayer — one Our Father and no more. There will be no requiem, no singing, no sermon, no funeral offerings, and no tide to carry me back.'

'I'm not sure I can agree to that,' said Father Bosco. 'The funeral service must accord with liturgical practice. I shall have to consult the appropriate canon to see if it contains a loophole.'

'What do you say, Joey?'

'It's all a great waste of petrol. First you go east only to go west.'

'I'm fulfilling the old saying: "The short-cut to the wedding, the roundabout to the graveyard." '

'There are difficulties,' said Father Bosco. 'The parish priest won't like being robbed of the funeral offerings, which, in your case, are bound to be substantial.'

'Give him a thousand pounds for his consent. I'd rather that than have people paying half-crowns over my remains and saying afterwards that the offerings fell well short of the record.'

'What if the sea is rough?' Joey wondered. 'Sometimes

in winter no boat can get out for weeks on end.'

'I'll die in the summer, then. Any further comments?'

Father Bosco counted the buttons down the front of his cassock. He had decided that strenuous objection would be impolitic. His present duty was to ensure that he inherited. When the estate was his, he would make whatever funeral arrangements suited best, taking due account of the requirements of canon law.

'Any further comments?' the Chairman repeated.

'No,' said Cookie.

'Father Bosco? Have you nothing more to say?'

'One Our Father is on the scant side. I'd like to be able to sing *In paradisum* to lend the occasion a touch of dignity. *In paradisum deducant te angeli.* May the angels lead thee into paradise. It will sound lovely on the open sea.'

'No need to sing it yet. You can sing it on the day if you think it will do any good. But no *Dies Irae*, please. It's far too long. I want a quick service without falderals, and no one looking furtively at his watch half-way through.'

'Understood,' said Father Bosco.

'We've dealt with the funeral arrangements. Now we must deal with what comes after. For most of my life I've been so busy that I had little time to think of anything except business. As Pauline will tell you, the hotel accounts are in order, but there are one or two irregularities that might not escape an auditor with more than numerical accuracy on his mind. In the early days things were hard. Revenue was uncertain, every penny counted. In the shop I could have overcharged. Instead I gave short measure. Since then I've tried to make amends. I've given alms to the poor, and bed and board to Andy Early. Over the years I've confessed my sin to six priests and one bishop, but the knowledge of short measure given won't go away. It's a tumour inside my skull, pressing down on the surface of my brain. What good is God's forgiveness if knowledge of sin returns to torture the sinner? I'd give every penny I own to the man who would show me the act that would rid me of the memory of scales bouncing too quickly.'

'Some sins are deciduous and some are evergreen,' said Father Bosco. 'Evergreen sins give no rest to the sinner. They sprout needles that coalesce to form a hump on his back. The hump grows bigger and heavier with every day that passes, while the man beneath grows smaller and weaker from the weight of the unequal burden, and finally only the hump remains. It is a condition which can be arrested by an act of extraordinary goodness, and fortunately you have it in your power to perform such an act. You must dispose of your property in a way that will turn it to spiritual account.'

'Crap,' Joey shouted. 'Father Bosco is playing on your fear of the hereafter. Let me give you the good news here and now: there is no hereafter. The wages of life is a dreamless sleep at the end. Complete oblivion. It's the only thing that makes this disgusting pantomime bearable.'

'I'm not looking for comfort,' said the Chairman. 'I want the truth.'

'You crave the comfort of religion and you jib at the price,' Joey said. 'If it's the truth you want, you won't get it from Father Bosco — he's got vested interests. So listen to the voice of common sense inside you. There's nothing after life but nothingness. Turn your back on Bosco's after-life and your guilt will melt away.'

'I refuse to argue,' said Father Bosco. 'Truth, like charity, is not puffed up. All I shall say is that the word "after-life" is a misnomer. What we call the after-life is really the true life. What we are experiencing now, what Joey calls "this disgusting pantomime", is only a protracted birth.'

'What I need is certainty,' said the Chairman. 'Have you got anything to say, Cookie?'

'I don't have the answer, I doubt if there is one.'

'There is no certainty, only pedlars of false certainties,'

said Father Bosco. 'Now, in a case of uncertainty, what does a prudent man do?'

'He takes out an insurance policy!' Joey shrieked.

'Silence! Let me think,' the Chairman shouted.

He put his right hand over his eyes and supported the elbow with his left. Father Bosco found himself looking at Pauline's mouth and thinking of Jack's sexual gluttony. Then he, too, closed his eyes. Joey continued doodling and Cookie wrote on the agenda beneath 'Chairman's Report': 'Call no man rich till he's dead.'

'I've got it,' the Chairman announced. 'The short measure I gave was in weighing flour, tea and sugar. I'll give every family on the headland a free hundredweight bag of flour and enough tea and sugar to last a month. I'll sit here by the window and watch the lorry going from house to house with deliveries. That way I'll see the reparation being made with my own two eyes. There will be no doubt ever again, my sin will fall away like fur from a moulting pelt.'

'You'll make yourself look ridiculous,' Joey protested. 'People will want to know why, and those who are proud will refuse what they're bound to see as charity. Besides, no one buys hundredweight bags of flour any more. That was when times were hard and people baked their own bread. Now they eat gâteau from the supermarket; it sounds posher than cake.'

'The best charity goes to the most deserving,' Father Bosco advised. 'If you like, I'll make a list of suitable recipients, the very, very poor. I'll organise everything. It must be anonymous giving, though, the giving blessed by Christ Himself.'

'That's settled, then,' said the Chairman. 'Over the next few days I'll calculate the sum to be spent. I won't be niggardly. To guard against error, I'll use a factor of three in marking up. Now we come to Any Other Business.'

The Chairman looked at each of them in turn. There was silence till Joey spoke.

'Nearly a year ago you announced the Day of the Talents. Isn't it time that their use was assessed? Some of us haven't been idle. We now look forward to the Day of Judgment.'

'Judgment will come but not yet. It's beyond the scope of this extraordinary meeting. As it is our last meeting, there is no need to fix a date for the next. The secretary will type out the minutes and each of you will receive a copy within a week. Thank you for coming. I declare the meeting closed.'

Gulban sank back against the pillows. Pauline mopped his forehead with a handkerchief as the three sons filed out of the room.

'You'll stay for lunch?' Cookie suggested in the lobby.

'Impossible, I'm afraid. Canon Sproule is down with flu, I must get back.'

'At least have a pre-luncheon drink.'

'I'd rather not.'

'A glass of Perrier water perhaps?' Joey enticed him.

'We have Évian as well, fresh in yesterday,' said Cookie.

'Thank you both.'

They followed him out into the driveway. He hurried to his Fiat, pretending they weren't behind him.

'You have it in the bag.' Cookie leant against the car door.

'I thought your psychology too transparent, Father. Gulban might have appreciated the subtlety of serpents more.' Joey gave his split-level smile.

'The wisdom of serpents,' Father Bosco corrected.

'To play on an old man's fear of hell-fire is hardly Christian. Or am I deficient in my knowledge of liberal theology?' Joey pursued.

Father Bosco looked across the river at the hill.

'The landscape is at its best now,' he said. 'Washed clean by rain, burnt down by months of frost. Though you can't see it, you can sense the pure green, the new growth, underneath the reddish bracken.

'The meeting achieved nothing,' Cookie sighed.

'Poor old Gulban did his best to discuss the eternal trivialities, while the three of us were immersed in temporalities. The world is too much with us, we sing *In paradisum* out of tune.' Joey shook his head in mock-sadness.

'You must deal with the world as best you can,' Father Bosco tried a word of encouragement. 'Even if you don't, it will still melt away like the flesh-seeking flesh itself.'

'And nothing but the Devil will remain,' Cookie intoned.

'Wasn't it He who said, "Lo, I am with you always"? He's the only constant. In more homely language, He's your only man.' With a sweeping bow, Joey opened the car door.

'I must leave you,' said Father Bosco. 'I can see I'm only an occasion of sin for you both.'

As he drove out the gate, he found himself looking forward to the afternoon and the confession of simple sins. Sins that lost all particularity in the telling. 'Father, I've committed fornication. Father, I've entertained impure thoughts.' No prurient detail, no painterly images, none of the sensuous density of passionate living. He was not an inquisitor, grand or otherwise. He would not demand depiction. He would forgive without interrogation. The penitent spoke in a formula and so did the confessor. Perhaps that's what had chained Gulban to his sin. He had said, 'Father, I gave short measure', and to him *Ego te absolvo* was not enough. He had expected to be cross-examined, humiliated, stewed slowly in the juice of his own avarice and hauled out painfully to dry in the sun. He wished to relive his transgression fully and searingly till the merest residue of guilt had been burnt away. Perhaps there was a case for inquisitorial interrogation, for the prurient particulars, after all. A dangerous thought. The confessor also had a soul that needed saving. The penitent must remain a mere sinner, not an occasion of sin for the invisible man behind the grille.

As he passed the Gravelly Shoulder, he breathed a prayer for Alicia and another for himself. Then he said aloud, 'The meeting was pure ceremonial, a diabolical exercise in worldly enticement. Cookie says I have it in the bag and I think that he has. Only God and Gulban know.'

27

With Easter came the first guests of the year: four middle-aged middle-class couples and two spare bachelors who sat in the lounge bar reading their papers before dinner, each observing the other while pretending that the other wasn't there. The weather had turned mild and dry. The hedges and fields again looked green. Only the hill and moor bore the reddish-brown marks of winter. Below on the slip fishermen sat on empty fish-boxes mending nets and lobster creels as they waited for a calmer sea.

Cookie had begun to sense that he himself had waited too long. He knew that soon he must retackle his thesis and give some thought to finding a job. In the meantime he went for walks on the hill with Pauline or for drives down the coast in the direction of Undercliff. He tried to seek out new places, yet wherever he took her he could not help feeling that both he and she had been there before.

Mrs Bugler had moved to Wicklow. Fort Knox, a cold and lonely station, was now his own. Most days he went down and lit a fire in the living-room. Then he would wander round the other rooms for an hour, upstairs and down, or sit on the summer seat in the garden and watch blue turf-smoke uncoiling over the blackened chimney. One evening he and Pauline sat silently before the fire, drinking tea and looking into the flames.

'This place gives me the creeps,' she said. 'Not a breath stirring inside or out. It's difficult to imagine a normal life here. How on earth did they keep sane? Up at the hotel at least you can see sane people in the distance.'

Before sunset they placed the fender in front of the fire and locked up. As they went out the gate, she said, 'You must have been crazy to buy it. I shall never come here again.'

On the way back to the hotel she stopped to listen to a cuckoo calling from the holms. He stood beside her, waiting for her to speak because he himself had nothing he wanted to say.

He went up to Gulban's room and sat by the bed until he could no longer make out shapes in the twilight. His father now slept for most of the day. Sometimes he woke and enquired about business, but his thoughts soon returned to the room, the bed, the ceiling, and what he could see out of the window. His mind slipped and wobbled, unable to retain its grasp on any single thought for long. The doctor came twice a week and went away without saying anything new. Towards the end of May, as the weather grew warmer, he seemed to recover a little of his zest and acuity. That morning he had demanded bacon rashers for breakfast and he had read the newspaper before lunch. Now he opened his eyes and asked Cookie if he could lose his temper.

'I don't like shouting and I don't like bluster,' Cookie replied.

'A good hotel manager must be able to lose his temper. Otherwise how can he control a bone-idle staff?'

'He could talk quietly and carry a big cudgel.'

'You must be *seen* to lose your temper. I've been seen to lose mine more often than I've actually lost it. The knack is to lose your temper only when all about you are keeping theirs.'

Cookie laughed. He had heard this cynical incisiveness before.

'Life is a game of hide and seek,' Gulban continued after a pause. 'Some men are good at hiding and some are good at seeking. Are you a hider or a seeker?'

'A seeker.'

'And what are you seeking?'

'What the hiders have hidden.'

'You won't get elected on that ticket.'

'If I don't get this hotel, I'm going to be a professor.'

'A professor! Go into politics. Live in the power-house. I always said that if Grandad had stayed in America, we'd have had a Heron in the White House by now. We're every bit as lecherous as the Kennedys, and besides, we know when to be lecherous — and where. Are you lecherous, Cookie?'

'Very.'

'I like a man to be specific. How do you spend your evenings?'

'Mostly reading.'

'A lechery of the mind! What did you do yesterday evening?'

'I took Pauline to town for a meal.'

'Have you taken her out before?'

'Oh, yes.'

'Regularly?'

'We do go out together fairly regularly.'

'I didn't know. Growing old is knowing less and being sure of less. And not just because no one tells you anything. I'm surprised that Pauline never mentioned it.'

'Perhaps she didn't realise that you were absolute for lechery.'

'You have the makings of a professor, I can see that. Remember this, remember it when I've gone: keep your grip on common things — you're descended from practical men who never drew the dole.'

Cookie crossed the landing with a sense of imminent disablement. He took down his suitcase from the top of the wardrobe and stared into it. He could pack in twenty minutes. If he left in the morning, he could be in Dublin by lunchtime. He would find a flat and finish footnoting his thesis before taking the Golden Road to Samarkand. He gave a laugh of derision and closed the suitcase. He thought it wise to talk to Pauline before Gulban sent for her.

She was in the back office typing a business letter which began: 'I am sorry to have to tell you that there is no substitute for . . . ' Yet we are all hell-bent on the quest for substitutes, he thought. Gulban seeks a new Jack. If Joey is right, Alicia was just a paler Pauline. And now Pauline herself? Perhaps only childhood is central: perhaps all else is a search for surrogates.

'I've been up to see Gulban. He asked me more questions than a policeman.'

'He must be on the mend.'

'When I told him we had dinner in town last night, he wanted to know if we go out together often. I got the impression that he was surprised you hadn't told him.'

She looked up from the typewriter with a patient smile.

'Then he's really on the mend,' she said.

She sat staring at the letter in the typewriter. It ended in mid-sentence with the word 'because'. She felt weary and stale, and it occurred to her that the weariness and staleness were an infection she had caught from Cookie. It was not like her to sit paralysed before an unfinished letter, as if the burden of work, indeed of all existence, had become too heavy for her shoulders.

Yesterday he had said to her, 'The foremost thing to be avoided in life is doing the same thing for too long. We are restless souls. We must have change, even change for the worse. On his sick-bed Gulban continues to maim us all. As we wait for him to die, we ourselves die instead, and by our dying we give him strength for yet another day. We should cut free, you and I. As long as we stay here, we're only symbols in a dying man's cosmology. What do you think?'

'We have different responsibilities,' she had replied. 'You have to finish your thesis and think of your career.'

'I wasn't thinking of either. I was thinking of young life,

and spring all round us in the fields.'

'I've thought about that already, I shall stay.'

She wondered if her paralysis had come from her sense of wrongness in the order and shape of things. She kept remembering the mare in her dream and the visitor who came and went and now did not bear thinking about. She lived in a dark, damp basement in which the air was thick with the spores of puffed fungi. She plucked the unfinished letter from the typewriter and said loudly and clearly, 'I shall never, can never, fall in love with anyone again.'

At ten she climbed the stairs with Gulban's rum punch on a tray. He was lying on his back, his hands locked and his tufted nose venting above the covers. His eyes were closed, his features set in a grainy mask of suffering. She placed the tray on the night table, closed the window, and quietly drew the curtains. Now the fresh-scented night had been locked out. The room had become an enclosed retreat where time was viscous treacle through which thoughts and words swam slowly and in no predictable order.

'What do you think of Cookie?' His eyes remained closed as he spoke.

'We get on reasonably well as a rule.'

'At our extraordinary meeting he was the only one who didn't try to influence me. Is that a good thing or a bad thing?'

'It shows detachment.'

'Or apathy. You like Cookie, I can tell.'

He opened his watery eyes and peered through a twilight haze without seeming to focus. She sat down beside the bed, her face now close to his.

'Will you drink your rum punch?'

'You must stop going out with him.'

'Why?'

'Because you're brother and sister. You share the same flesh and blood.'

His hands unlocked. One of them twitched on the bed,

which caused him to place the other on top of it. His wiry hair had become a cap of matted bristles. She knew that he could not see her. Though his eyes stared, what they really saw was the frantic succession of images inside his head.

'You mustn't say such things. You've been sleeping and dreaming, now you're awake again.'

'You're his half-sister and I'm your father. Your mother never told you, she didn't wish you to know.'

He closed his eyes and seemed to drop off. Though she wanted to shake him, she sat frozen on her chair.

'If I'm Cookie's half-sister, then I'm Bosco's as well.' The words were alien but horrifyingly real.

'Your mother and I fell in love. After you were born, we had a row and even after her husband died she never relented.'

'Can't you see it's all a dream?' she whispered. 'You never had a daughter and you want one. Well, I'm willing to be your daughter.'

'It isn't wishful thinking, it's the truth.'

'Then it's worse than wishful thinking. You've made it up to drive a wedge between me and Cookie.'

'I've lived my life without speaking. Your mother died without speaking. If I died and took the secret with me, I might suffer for the evil I'd left behind.'

'It can't be true. I was engaged to Jack and you said nothing. I know you wanted Jack and me to marry.'

'Jack and you weren't related, Jack was not my son.'

'He was your favourite son. You were going to leave him everything, you told me so yourself.'

'He was Andy Early's son. Ellen confessed to me on her death-bed, she wouldn't have told a lie. After that I watched him growing up from a distance. By the time he was sixteen, I'd realised that he'd become my son. From the start he modelled himself on me, he was the only one among them that grew into a man. When he took up with you, I was delighted. You're a Heron. The hotel would be run by a Heron and your family and his would have the blood of the Red Men in their veins.'

'Is Bosco your son?'

'Yes.'

'And Joey?'

'Yes, and if I say he's God's vengeance on me for sinning with your mother, will you believe me?'

His voice was barely audible. He spoke with such effort that he seemed to be making up the story as he went along. She thought for a moment and pounced on the glaring fault.

'Andy Early was a tramp, and you've said yourself that your wife was a holy woman. She'd never have been unfaithful to you with Andy Early.'

'She was a religious woman, at least from the neck up. She never read a book without a *nihil obstat* and an imprimatur signed by a bishop. When Bosco was born, I told her I wanted a daughter next. Two years passed and nothing happened. One night she dreamt that she would never conceive again. Andy Early was a good-looking young man then. He was a spoilt priest, he'd been expelled from the seminary, and whenever he passed this way he would talk to her about the lives of the saints. She saw him as Elisha; and herself as the wealthy woman of Shunem in the Bible. She asked me to give him free bed and board, and I saw no reason to refuse, because he and I got on well and he used to do odd jobs for me from time to time. She told him that she was praying for a daughter, and, having read the Bible himself, he took the hint and gave her a son.'

Gulban gave a long, hacking laugh that ended in a wheezing cough. When he got his breath back, there were tears in his eyes and on his cheeks.

'He opened the floodgates with his prophetic you-know-what. After Jack, she had Cookie and Joey. She'd have had more if she hadn't died.'

'It's all lies,' she told him fiercely. 'With each new twist

you give the story, you make it more impossible to believe.'

'If you're not my daughter, why did I pay for your
convent education?'

'My mother told me why. You wanted to bribe her into
going to bed with you but she refused.'

'I told you that after you were born she turned against
me. She thought I was going to bed with Mrs Bugler
because it suited Mrs Bugler to give that impression.'

'You're wicked, wicked, wicked. You couldn't be my
father. I have a father already, and you're jealous. You
know you haven't long to live and you refuse to leave
without wreaking as much havoc as you can.'

'Ask yourself why you got the job of manageress here.'

'I've got business brains, that's why.'

'You weren't qualified. I took you on because you were
my daughter. Your business brains come from me.'

'Lies, lies, lies.' The words became stones that did not
thud as she hurled.

Incensed by her own impotence, she took him by the
shoulders and plunged him up and down on the springing
mattress. His body became a wet sheet, and the head-
board a corrugated washboard on washday.

'I had a father and he's dead,' she insisted. 'He was a
kindly man, a doctor and a gentleman who wouldn't hurt
a fly. If he'd lived, he'd have sent me to a good school and
he wouldn't have taken me away before I'd done my
exams. I'd have gone to university and got a good degree.
I'd have read medicine and . . .'

He struggled to raise his arms. He seemed to cough. A
rattle of phlegm and a loud, rasping KR-A-A-H came up
out of his open gullet. She stopped plunging and his bristly
head fell sideways on the pillow with its slack mouth open.

She waited for a movement, an exhalation, the merest
sign of life. She stood over him, paralysed by panic and a
kind of physical revulsion that made it impossible for her
to feel his pulse. At length she dragged herself to her room

and sat by the empty bed staring at a threadbare rug between her feet. A moth came in the window and started circling distractedly about the cylindrical lampshade. It rose and dropped, it grazed the ceiling with its wings, while through the transparent base of the lampshade loomed the blurred forms of other moths that had been attracted by brightness on other summer nights.

She sat for a long time, aware of nothing but emptiness and exhaustion that turned her thoughts into random involutions, unfocused and unfelt. She could not move, she could not instigate. She could only sit impassively and wait for the frantic moth to join the other dead moths inside the lampshade. After a while she struggled to find a hard, dry oat of truth among the fluffy chaff of falsehood that threatened to smother her, but all she could see was an ugly gash, a malodorous wound from which no poultice could draw the paralysing poison.

She would say nothing to Bosco, Cookie and Joey. What Gulban had told her was meant to hurt them too. She would do her best with the funeral arrangements and endure the funeral itself. She would escape from the disgusting nightmare to a place without a history that warped and thwarted. Would she escape from the memory of the pursuing mare and the midnight visitor whom she thought had come to cleanse and had left her smeared and filthy?

The moth had entered the lampshade. It was circling mesmerically in the heat, seeking urgent escape from the burning bulb. She struggled to her feet and switched off the light. For a time she stood by the west window staring out through the darkness at the beam of the lighthouse sweeping the Sound and the wider bay.

At midnight she went back to Gulban's room. He hadn't moved. She made as if to touch his cheek, then quickly withdrew her hand. She roused Cookie and Joey, who came in their pyjamas and after a brief consultation pronounced him dead. She telephoned Father Bosco, who murmured *In paradisum deducant te angeli* and promised to come immediately. Other people were hurrying, talking, planning. Things were happening round her, conveying an impression that perhaps somewhere, though not here, was a world of sanity, order and light.

28

At Father Bosco's suggestion the brothers met in Gulban's office immediately after breakfast. They looked pinched for lack of sleep. Father Bosco had nicked himself shaving. On the rim of his shiny white collar was a tiny speck of blood. They sat round the desk, facing a vacant high-backed chair.

'It's the end of an era.' Father Bosco gave an impression of stubborn deliberation.

'We must try not to blame God for that,' Joey said.

'As the eldest, Father Bosco, you should take the chair,' Cookie suggested.

'If you are both agreeable, we'll do him the courtesy of leaving it vacant till after the funeral.'

'Till after the will is read,' Joey said firmly.

'I thought we should meet to consider the funeral arrangements,' Father Bosco began. 'He has expressed his wishes. Quite simply, we must decide whether to carry them out.'

'You will be officiating,' said Cookie. 'You know what is proper. I'm content to leave the decision to you.'

'Ditto here,' said Joey.

'In that event I suggest a quiet funeral on land rather than water. I'll say a Requiem Mass with two other priests concelebrating. We'll have a choir, the local choir, but no undertaker and no hearse.'

'Will there be funeral offerings?' Joey asked.

'Of course. Are there any other questions?'

'No,' said Cookie.

'In that event I'll get on with the arrangements.'
Father Bosco rose ceremoniously.

'It must be one of the shortest meetings ever held in this room,' Joey said. 'Try to be a bit less laconic in your funeral tribute, Father. People might get the wrong impression.'

Soon the hotel, upstairs and down, flowed with visitors — neighbours and customers who hadn't seen Gulban for nearly a year and who wished to take the opportunity of satisfying themselves that the news of his death was not just another rumour. Father Bosco had appointed himself master of ceremonies; he had taken charge of all arrangements except the catering, which he left to Pauline. Already she had become a mere observer on the forgotten periphery of things.

She drove to the funeral with Cookie and Joey, sunk between them on the back seat of the car while they stared out of opposite windows. None of them spoke. All three walked quietly up the nave and sat in the same pew, while Father Bosco intoned the Requiem Mass in a special high-pitched voice she had not heard before, and which changed down an octave for the address. He spoke slowly and softly without modulation or embellishment, so that no phrase or sentence seemed more memorable than any other. She strained to catch each fleeting syllable, while remembering the heart-rending histrionics of his last sentence over Jack less than a year before.

At the graveside she stood beside Cookie, who put an arm round her as the coffin vanished from view. Joey, who stood opposite, covered his face with his hand. She had become a secret member of the family, yet she could feel neither grief nor bereavement, only a kind of numb constriction that made breathing difficult. She sensed that she had been reborn; she knew less of herself today than she had ever known before.

She tried to grasp what was happening. The sun struck

blindingly through the overhanging ash. The air was mild and still. An ordinary summer morning with no wind to blow either sand or dust. Nothing to make extraordinary this most extraordinary of days. When Joey removed his hand from his face, she saw his good eye red from weeping and the trace of a tear on his cheek. As they drove back to the hotel, he spoke to Cookie of the sense of nothingness, of empty eternities, that Bosco had unwittingly conveyed in his unadorned address.

After lunch Mr Looby arrived with his mahogany-coloured briefcase to read the will.

'You, too, are to join us, Miss Harrison,' he smiled. 'Those are my instructions. I am here to carry them out.'

In the office they sat opposite Mr Looby who, without a blink of hesitation, had taken Gulban's chair. Bosco folded his arms and inclined his polished forehead to the light. Cookie passed a hand over his silken hair and waited with expressionless resignation. Of the three Joey alone seemed alert. He was a fiery ember that could only be described in terms of pain, though in any summation of his volatile personality it had to be acknowledged that the pain he gave was less intense than the pain he so obviously endured. Now all three looked at Looby, a man for all occasions who could assume any shape he pleased without an accompanying word or gesture of self-revelation. He drew a small tape-recorder from his briefcase and placed it in the centre of the table. He pressed a button, and she heard Gulban's voice, more grainy than gravelly, coming out of the vacuum she sensed in the room.

'*I am dead now,*' he began. '*No apologies for absence. The Day of the Talents is past; now is the Day of Judgment. Listen carefully, I am about to be brief. To Pauline I leave the hotel, shop and farm. To Father Bosco, Cookie and Joey I have already given talents to the value of ten thousand pounds each. That, my sons, is your patrimony. I trust that you have invested it wisely. Even if you haven't, you will each receive in addition a share of Jack's unused talent: £3,333.33 to Cookie, £3,333.33 to Joey, and £3,333.34 to*

Father Bosco, who, as the eldest, receives the largest share.

'Now for a look at some skeletons from the family cupboard, or at least those skeletons with a bearing on the distribution of my estate. Pauline is my daughter. Mr Looby has in his possession several letters signed by her mother which put the matter beyond dispute. For the record, and to scotch unsavoury speculation, I should also reveal that Jack was Andy Early's son, not mine. You may speak openly of these things now or you may keep them quiet among yourselves. As for Pauline, I have named her as my beneficiary, not merely because she is my daughter but because she has inherited my business imagination to a degree which renders even me uncritical. She is neither too rash nor too cautious; she has the businessman's instinctive understanding of when to be bold without jeopardising what has already been achieved. I have no wish to pre-empt decisions that now belong to her, but here on this distant cloud I like to think that there will always be bed and board — room at the inn — for each of you at Christmas time, as there was for Andy Early. You know my thoughts, you've had my example. These are your true inheritance.'

'So the old bugger had a sense of humour after all!' With a raucous laugh, Joey banged the table.

Father Bosco leant towards Pauline and whispered, 'Congratulations!' Cookie offered her his hand and Joey got up from his seat and kissed her cheek.

'You're my sister at last,' he said. 'What's a little kiss between siblings?'

Pauline struggled to speak. The dry detachment of Gulban's recorded speech made her wonder if it were all a cruel and outlandish joke. She expected the brothers to start jeering and mocking at any moment.

'We came in to hear you read the will,' she said to Mr Looby.

'It's in my briefcase, all in order. I shall read it if you wish. I must warn you that it's more formal than the recording.'

'I think that after what we've just heard we can take it as read,' said Father Bosco.

'Your father was a perfectionist, a most extraordinary man. The recording you've just heard represented hours of his time and mine. He went over it again and again till every pause and inflexion was beyond improvement.'

He smiled and turned to her.

'Now I have a few things to discuss with you alone.'

The brothers looked at one another as the solicitor and Pauline left the room. Joey took down a dusty old ledger and turned the crackling pages.

'The history of the firm is here,' he said. ' "One crate of HP Sauce . . . fifteen shillings." The kitchen has come on since then. Those were the days before Pauline became chief accountant. Why did she get it? How did she best us all?'

'She's an able manager and she's got a talent for sincerity,' Father Bosco said.

'Sincerity is in the eye of the beholder,' Joey reminded him. 'No humour, no irreverence. Gulban wished for a baker of unleavened bread.'

'We've gained a sister,' Cookie said half to himself.

'Then we must learn to love her as a sister.' Joey laughed with forced gusto. 'We must get to know that darling face afresh. Till today she wore a near-transparent veil. Does the veil that Gulban whisked away conceal yet another veil beneath? It all makes for excitement and the expectation of new surprises. It makes you want to be daring and think outrageous thoughts.'

'Could Gulban have invented all this just to turn us arsy-versy?' Cookie wondered. 'A final *coup de foudre* to singe and blast us all. The irony of lives lived on false premises being suddenly up-ended by an even greater falsehood would surely have appealed to him.'

'No, Cookie, that simply will not do,' Joey reproved. 'You must confront the grisly truth, reinvent your childhood and all those dreamy afternoons with Pauline in the river. You'll have to reinvent the past six months as well.'

'Childhood's no problem, we keep reshaping it all the time. As for the last six months, I shall deal with them as best I can.'

'I'm sure you'll discover some consolatory literary precedent. Father Bosco and I can only try to comfort each other.'

Pallid and preoccupied, Father Bosco got up from his chair. He was in no mood for banter.

'What are we to do?' Joey asked him.

'Accept. Simply that. Accept without question.'

'Total submission to the stern and uncaring clout of providence?'

'I must be off. I've neglected my parish work long enough.'

'Have you no other word to say?' Joey pursued. 'Surely the Good Book must offer a little light: "It was sweet as honey in my mouth but when I had eaten it my stomach was made bitter." '

When Father Bosco had left, Joey returned the ledger to its shelf.

'Our priest is nonplussed. He prayed for a hotel and was given a sister. Surely there must be some mistake, O Lord?' Joey cackled and Cookie, ignoring him, went to the door.

'Before you vanish to your room, let me give you a quote for the day, one you've often aired in all innocence yourself:

For lust of knowing what should not be known,
We take the Golden Road to Samarkand.'

Cookie closed the door and Joey's gloating laugh seemed to precede him into the lobby.

After talking to Mr Looby, Pauline went to her room to be alone. Now she had three brothers instead of none, and she must steel herself to meet them as brothers without allowing the past to tip the balance of the present. She herself might feel doubt and disquiet; she must not be the cause of doubt and disquiet in them. She must concentrate entirely on things to be done. What mattered now was continuity. She felt grateful for a new strength of will which could only have come from urgent necessity, yet she was troubled by a threatening sense of shapelessness, of familiar appearances made strange by distortion.

That night she woke up in panic. There was no sound inside or out. The darkness round her bed was thicker than the darkness outside her window. She knew that she must have been dreaming. No image came to dispel the featureless gloom in her mind.

'I am a Heron, not a Harrison.'

The thought filled her with horror, as if she alone had been responsible for all the mean contrivances of an unloving life — the penny-pinching, the short measure, the tinkle of the insatiable till — for the ugliness of the village, for all the ugliness of the world. The Herons lacked innocence and joy. They were too full of care, containment and misery, and therefore too full of themselves. Jack was not a Heron, which must have been why she had taken to him. For all his lack of feeling and imagination, he had stood for the order of day-thoughts as opposed to the dream-demons of the night.

'People keep wounding one another wittingly and unwittingly. Bosco's scarred soul shows in Joey's broken face. The wounds Jack gave were clean, they did not fester.'

With morning came a kind of reasoned serenity which seemed hard won. The inner life, the craving to ponder and understand must remain, for the time being, unsatisfied. In common with all who seek to convince, she must be seen to think only thoughts with the stamp of certainty. She had an early bath and dressed carefully. She put on a little make-up and tied a ribbon in her hair. After breakfast she had a word with Joey in the back office; she had already decided to redecorate Gulban's office before making it her own.

'I want you to know that for the moment everything will continue as before. There will be changes in time, but they need not affect you at the shop.'

'You want me to run the shop?' He gave an uneasy smile with his parted lips askew.

'Of course I do. You run it very well. We'll talk about your salary later. That's important. Gulban, being Gulban, saw work as its own reward.'

'He was a kind of mountain, always there, there, there. We made jokes about him in order to communicate. What shall we find to say to each other now?'

'We'll miss him for a long time to come.'

'I suppose he had already warned you about the will.'

'No, it came as a surprise and shock to me as well. However, he did tell me that I was his daughter shortly before he died.'

'Now, that's a definitive surprise. It makes you feel that there will never be a surprise again.'

He smiled at her as she left. She felt pleased. She had chosen to speak to him first because he was more touchy than Cookie, and less predictable. She would talk to Cookie before lunch. Father Bosco was different. She would give him time. He would come to her when he had found the words to lay new stepping-stones. The old ones were treacherous. They must never be trodden again.

29

Not just a life but a world had ended. Gulban had lived in a castle with its own laws and internal economy. It was built of certainties, and those who lived within its moat had learnt to accept a life of one theme without variations. There was only one season. The year had been arrested in late autumn, and anyone who wished for winter in the hope spring might follow was condemned to dream in vain.

In dying he had pulled down the castle walls. Now it was possible to see beyond the drawbridge a landscape full of beckoning roads leading off in all directions. Suddenly it was summer. A shimmer of excitement enlivened the surface of the sea.

To Cookie it seemed as if he had spent his whole life in a keep. He had been through a succession of dark days and darker nights where dreams took the place of action. He had been going about with a quernstone pressing down on his head. Now the quernstone had been toppled. He was left with a sense of lightness and the memory of an unbearable weight which had crushed each new thought at birth.

Pauline looked up as he entered the back office, pert and lively with a light blue ribbon in her hair. She was bright as a butterfly in a summer meadow, and as delicate. He had never laid eyes on her before.

'I was looking for you earlier,' she smiled.

'You should have looked in Fort Knox.'

'I'd like you to know that you are free to stay on here as long as you wish.'

'I've already made up my mind. I'm leaving for Dublin tomorrow. I shall finish footnoting my thesis and then clear off to America — if they'll have me. I shall start from scratch. I've put my life as a Heron behind me. I've decided to change my name.'

'You'll still have Heron blood in you, there's no changing that. If you go to America, go as a Heron. Who knows, it may be the start of something.'

'For me the Red Men are dead. They're a fibre in the ganglion of lies that died with Gulban.'

'That's a bit harsh.'

'We all see him differently. For me he was a dark, heavy cloud that blotted out the light.'

'He was extreme and extraordinary. The world of the hotel and shop was too narrow to allow him elbow room.'

'While he was in robust health, I never thought of questioning him. Once he began to die, I couldn't but be aware of how he dithered. He made me realise that the only way to die is quickly.'

'In time you'll see him differently. He was an actor with a superb sense of ceremony. He could easily have prepared us for the will, but he found the desire to shock irresistible.'

'The will showed him at his best. I think you got no more than you deserved. And he did you and me a great, if belated service. In the surprise he sprang we must acknowledge a sense of rightness revealed.'

He waited for her to respond. She picked up a pencil and sharpened it with remote efficiency.

'You've had a hard winter, you must feel tired.' He broke the silence.

'Tired or not, I must carry on. First, I'll live from day to day, then perhaps from week to week. I don't believe in digging up roots and shredding them.'

'That's how I feel too. I'll content myself with looking at the surface glitter of the sea.'

'What about Fort Knox? Is that surface glitter?'

'Mrs Bugler sold it to me on condition that she could come back to stay for a month every summer. I'll talk to her when I'm in Dublin. If she has no objection, I may invite you to make me an offer.'

'Has it got nothing for you any more?'

'I spent the morning going from room to room. It's . . . empty.'

'And Alicia? Was she mere surface glitter?'

'She was special. She pretended to see only the rolling wave but her mind ran on sea caves and sea monsters. If she had lived, she would have found things to paint that no one had seen before. As I look back on the last year, I have a feeling that it's all been Gulban's creation. He, too, was an artist in his way. Without him there would have been no Fort Knox and possibly no Alicia.'

'We ourselves aren't giftless,' she smiled. 'Between us we created our idea of Gulban, which is why we feel so diminished. Joey, I'm glad to say, now seems more human. When I spoke to him this morning, there were no acid drops in evidence.'

'He always says more than he means and he always means less than you think.'

'If that is true, he said very little this morning.'

She picked up her pencil and began ticking off a column of figures on a statement. After each tick, she turned over one of the invoices, seemingly unaware of his presence.

'Time to start packing,' he said from the door.

Canon Sproule had gone to a whist drive and given his demon housekeeper the evening off. Father Bosco had the presbytery to himself. He was resting on his bed, leg-weary after a day of corporal works of mercy, yet not sufficiently quiet in spirit to put his head down.

Sitting in the darkness of the confessional the previous evening, he had observed through the curtain an approaching penitent with a bulbous nose that gave his face the look of an old swede, mottled and coarse-skinned with one or two whitish scars. He listened to the predictable sins of intemperance and, as he gave absolution, he had a vision of a lake on a still summer day. There was no ripple and no sense of surface, only the incorporeal reflections of airy sky and cloud. He had felt on the brink of heavenly enlightenment, leading to something fine, distinguished and good. Then the man shuffled off and another middle-aged penitent took his place.

After going home, he went to bed early and dreamt that he was in a dark room searching for the light switch, with moving figures just discernible against the faint sky outside the window. The figures looked stooped and predatory, and they seemed to be searching too. In panic, he realised that they were searching for him. He ran from the house to ring the police, and at last found a call-box in the external dark. He dialled 99 and hesitated as he strove to recall the third digit. He could not remember, so he dialled the operator who said: 'At the third stroke it will be nine sins past the hour precisely. A man who believes in sin can do nothing but — ' A crackle on the line drowned the final word. He waited in the dark booth for a life-transforming perception that refused to come. The line went dead. All possibility of enlightenment had gone. On a square of cardboard above the telephone he scrawled in luminous chalk: DARKNESS RULES OK.

He recalled being with Benedict McBride in the seminary library, going through a pile of books, listing recent accessions. Benedict opened a book on biblical iconography with a reproduction of a painting called 'Christ and the Woman of Samaria'. The woman was standing beside the well, her left elbow resting on the rim of a water jug, her left breast covered and her right breast exposed, while Christ on the far side of the well, looking light-boned and serene, emphasised a point with the forefinger of his left hand.

Benedict's laughter was spontaneous and reckless.

'The Old Testament is full of prurience,' he said. 'By comparison the N.T. is a vicarage tea party, yet painters keep putting prurience in.'

'It's just a rotten painting,' Bosco said. 'It's the least truthful painting I've ever seen.'

He left Benedict to the study of biblical iconography and went for a walk round the football field. It was a sleepy June afternoon, somehow remote and unreal like the woman in the painting, and he felt troubled and uncertain about the cause of his distress.

Now he sprang off the bed and opened the New Testament at random. As usual he found Matthew 7:22:

On that day many will say to me, 'Lord, Lord, did we not prophesy in your name, and cast out demons in your name, and do many mighty works in your name?' And then I will declare to them, 'I never knew you; depart from me, you evildoers.'

He must have pondered that text a hundred times, yet only now did he realise fully the burden of doubt and loneliness it imposed. There was no need to go to Matthew, Isaiah had said it all before: 'Truly thou art a God who hidest thyself, O God of Israel . . .' Cookie had put it differently: 'The Elusive Presence keeps religion alive as surely as Inexhaustible Meaning keeps art alive.' And Joey, not to be outdone, added his own mite of mean-mindedness: 'Father Bosco, never despair. As long as you have the Elusive Presence, you have a spiritual pork barrel.' Even Gulban had wished for certainty, in his case absolute certainty. The most certain of men could not bear even the thought of either . . . or.

He went down to the hallway to ring Pauline. He picked up the receiver and looked at it, not for the first time that week. Then he replaced it on its hook and climbed the stairs again.

30

June brought three weeks of sunshine without a shower of rain. The hotel was busy. She no longer teetered on the edge of necessity; she had begun to feel that some time in the future she could go to her room and enjoy an hour of unhurried reflection now and again. The staff, too, seemed more relaxed and amiable. Even Slash Gildea, who in Gulban's time pretended to have difficulty understanding her, now answered her questions as if she were almost his equal. Cookie wrote once or twice from Dublin and after a lengthy silence Father Bosco telephoned to say that he would be looking in the following week. She saw Joey every day, of course. Sometimes they had dinner together, and two or three times a week she paid a visit to the shop. Though melancholy and preoccupied, he never allowed his moods to interfere with his desire to please a customer.

He had been pestering her to come out to the island — now his island and his alone. It had become for him a kind of retreat. On weekdays he would take the boat out in the evenings and not come back till dusk, and on Sundays he would leave after breakfast with enough food and drink to last the day. His reticence kindled her curiosity. She promised to accompany him one Sunday. She told him that she would prefer the morning but he was adamant that the evening was the best time. They would stand, he said, on the high ground at the south end and look back with the sun behind them in the west.

'You'll see things you've never seen before,' he promised. 'It's like looking from a great height at someone else living your unlived life.'

As they made their way down to the slip, seagulls were dozing on the rocks or perhaps watching through half-closed eyes a shiny-backed seal further out. She climbed gingerly into the boat and waited while he fiddled with the outboard. They cleared the sea-wall. The seal went under and did not appear again. She sat facing him, looking past his shoulder at the changing shape of the receding inlet. The soporific plup-plap of the water, not the boat itself, bore her away from the land, lulling her with the rhythms of prehistoric millennia, obliterating all that was commonplace and plain.

'Pity it's so calm,' he said. 'You need waves rising, coming at you right and left. I took Cookie out on a breezy day. It was lovely and choppy. I think he was glad to get back.'

'I'm not surprised.'

'He's been called to higher things. Is he really bound for a professorial chair and a funny hat?'

She was aware of his nonchalant scrutiny and of her own desire to avoid a serious conversation, to be at once circumspect and inconsequential.

'He may feel he'd look funny in a funny hat. I think he'll go to America and get a job in advertising.'

'I read his thesis thinking I'd learn something about seduction. Nothing but dates and references and extracts from other theses. He himself is absent except on the title page where he gives his name as Thomas John Heron. It made me laugh.'

'It sounds like a well-judged thesis.'

'He's too reticent. I once said to him in this very boat, just for the cod, that the sight of a rising wave gives me a yearning beyond earthly things towards something powerful and undisclosed. He didn't say a word, just looked embarrassed. He lacks the courage of his finer feelings. Maybe his ambition is not to stand at a lectern and wear a funny hat but to be another Jack.'

'If he's lucky, he'll achieve both.'

'Anyhow he's upped and left. Fort Knox is closed and padlocked. Maybe it was all a game. Maybe he was only interested in the name or the two words that make up the name. He was once saved by a word, you know. Told me so himself. After Alicia's death he went down to the cliffs and stood on the edge with the water straight below. He was thinking of taking the leap when he remembered some lines from his school anthology:

Farewell, ye opening heavens!
Look not on me thus reproachfully —
You were not meant for me — Earth! take these
    atoms!

It was the word "Earth" that saved him. If it had been "Ocean", he'd have gone over.'

Joey laughed and she looked at him uneasily. Did Cookie want to be Jack or did Joey want to be Cookie? She felt relieved when they entered the cool shadow of the island. It was the end of an uneasy journey. Joey tied up and ran excitedly to the top.

'Now look back at the headland and tell me what you see,' he said breathlessly.

'I see what I know to be there: the hill, the village, Fort Knox and the hotel. They've shrunk in size.'

'I want you to look at them as if you were seeing them for the last time. It's the only way you'll ever see them as they are — or have become.'

'There's no movement anywhere. The sheep on the hill are still.'

'When you look at the hotel, what do you think of?'

'Gulban, who else? It's solid, solitary and gloomy just like him.'

'I always think of the winter months when we were children playing tag and hide and seek in the empty bedrooms. Do you still remember that?'

'I'm afraid I don't.'

'It's over, it will never happen again.'

'It may to other children.'

'Isn't that what's so unbearably sad?'

'I'd like to walk round the island. Pity to come out here just to look back.'

'There isn't much else to see. Rabbits, rocks, birds, the lighthouse winch. The lighthouse itself is padlocked like Fort Knox. The paintwork is flaking. I can never understand how it gleams so white from the land.'

'I've brought my binoculars. I hope to spot one or two birds I've never seen before.'

'I'm going down to the boat, I'll come back for you later. There's no way we can miss each other here.'

She crossed to the seaward side and sat on the edge of a bank with noisy sea birds coming and going below, self-important messengers who seemed not to realise that they'd forgotten their messages. The low sun hurt her eyes. She lay on her back with one arm over her forehead, aware of release from long imprisonment and the promise of excitement that comes from the governance of possibilities. She lost touch with earth, sky and water. She woke with a start as Joey spoke. The ground seemed to yield beneath her. She reached out a hand to assure herself of its solidity.

'I have something to show you, a rare and haunting place.'

He led her to a hollow between two upright slabs of rock, a kind of bowl with grassy sides that could have been formed with a single scoop of an enormous ladle.

'It's lovely, isn't it? Not a blade stirs here, even on a windy day.'

'It looks man-made.'

'What does it remind you of?'

'A punchbowl.' She smiled as if to humour him.

'Remember the little hollow by the river? You and

Cookie imagined it was a post office. You used to leave letters for each other under a flat stone. I got to know about it, though I wasn't meant to . . . Sometimes I used to read them and forge messages of my own.'

'I don't remember.'

'I'm not making it up.'

'People recall different things.'

'What do you remember?'

'Getting tar on my first communion dress and a roasting from my mother when I went home. I think it was all your fault,' she smiled.

'Even then there were traumas.'

'There was certainly pain.'

'We could have survived pain, ordinary pain. We were blighted, all of us, including you. There's a curse on us, and Gulban knew it. He thought it started with short measure in the shop.'

'He was imagining things towards the end.'

'At least he had imagination. An hour ago you looked across the Sound at the hotel. You must have seen a mound of dust.'

'We have to carry on. It was Gulban's wish. He knew that in the bombardment of life new pains drive out the old.'

'How can you go on? Don't you want to say, "I've had enough. Fini. Kaput. I'm baling out." '

He was shaking with emotion, the pale side of his face almost as red as the other. She tried to move away from him, then realised that they were together in the narrow hollow.

'We've all got responsibilities and we mustn't shirk them,' she said.

'Have we got imagination? Cookie can't see beyond his dry-as-dust thesis, and the most profound question Bosco's ever asked himself is: "Has the Recording Angel stamped my cards?" No one sees the nightmare. You all think it's morning again with a day of sanity and sunlight to come. Don't kid yourself. You can't put the horrors of the night behind you by burying your head in work. You'll never look in the mirror again without seeing another face beneath the skin. Look at my face! Two faces in one. The only difference between mine and yours is that in mine half the real face has been exposed. And the nightmare continues. Nightmares, I should say. Yours and mine, interlocking circles closed to the outer world. And no morning. No sanity. No confidence. No light.'

'You've been under strain for the best part of a year. You need a holiday — peace and quiet to readjust.'

'A holiday! Surely, you're not as simple-minded as that. Don't you realise? It was I who came to your bed in the night. The night of the 1st of April, to be precise. As if you didn't know! And if you didn't, who did you think it was? Slash Gildea?'

'I remember it as a kind of dream, or a continuation of a dream. I certainly don't blame you, and neither do I blame myself. We couldn't conceivably have known.'

'Dream, my eyeball. I once thought that lack of feeling was the best armour for life. Now I know nothing compares with self-delusion. Just think, from now on you'll have to struggle against your experience every day, as if it were an enemy to be overcome.'

'For me there's nothing new in that.'

'Then all I can say is that you are invulnerable.'

'I think you exaggerate my capacity for what you call self-delusion.'

'I always liked to think that you and I were close to each other in a different way from the others. Not just because of the fire, though that was how it began. When I asked you out here today, I thought that neither of us would be going back. I drafted a will for you to sign, leaving the hotel, shop and farm to our beskirted brother Father Chrome-Dome, and I made another will myself leaving this island to Professor Cookie. There was to be no coercion, no attempt at persuasion; I had hoped that you'd feel exactly as I do. I had imagined us getting into the boat together just before sunset, having first pinned our wills on the lighthouse door. We'd face out behind the island, and as light failed we'd go down as brother and sister in the spot that Gulban had chosen for himself. Well, I've said enough, I must leave you now. You won't be joining me. I'll make what's left of the journey on my own.'

'You can't do it. It's madness, madness, don't you see?'

'We see things differently. For me there is a problem, for you there is none. I've listened to the weather forecast, it will be a dry night. You'll be safe here till morning. They're bound to miss us by bedtime, and they'll be out to look for you with first light.'

'Don't do it, Joey, please. Can't you see it sets nothing right.'

'I can see there's no need to set you right. You're as certain as Gulban was in his prime.' His lower jaw trembled compulsively as he laughed.

'Don't just think of yourself. Think of Father Bosco and Cookie, and think of me. You mustn't imagine you're alone.'

She followed him down the slip, tugging at his sleeve and talking wildly to take his mind off his obsession. He did not listen, he did not seem to hear. He stripped and heaped his pullover, shirt and trousers on a rock.

'You may need those after the sun goes down. I'm keeping on my underpants out of brotherly delicacy — a trifle late. There's my will. The island and my gross of French letters will be Cookie's. What I have, I don't desire; what I desire, I cannot have.'

'Joey,' she implored. 'Put on your clothes. We'll go back to the hotel and neither of us will speak of this again.'

'Isn't that why I'm doing a bunk? Because no word is ever spoken. Find something to quest for that can't be found. Only that will keep you going. There's nothing else. And next time you see Father Chrome-Dome ask him which of his two Gods has done this to us — the Old Bugger of the Old Testament or the Young Bugger of the New. I'm sure he's already worked out the answer and offered Mass in thanksgiving.'

He got into the boat. She stood on the sloping concrete, no longer trying to restrain him.

'I'll head due west. When the petrol gives out, I'll go for a swim.'

The engine stuttered and wheezed. She prayed for it not to start.

'You'll never know how much I envy you,' he shouted. 'I've always wanted to spend a night to morning here. You were born lucky. You'll see the great beam sweeping the bay and never notice the darkness at the foot of the lighthouse.'

The engine caught. Inexplicably, he took off with a bound for the mainland. She held both hands to her mouth and called. She felt like crying. She could not believe that this was his idea of a joke. The engine seemed to smother. The stern skidded sideways with the port gunwale low over the water. The engine roared again as he faced the bows out to sea.

Breathlessly, she ran up the slope and across the island to the spot where earlier she had slept. He was already there below her, heading straight into the setting sun, his furrowed wake quickly unfolding as if smoothed by an invisible harrow. He stood in the stern in his blue underpants with one hand shielding his eyes, and never once looked back.

Further out the water was a gilded pond. As he entered the pond, the boat became a gilded tub with a flagless flagpole in the centre. She found it difficult to look directly into the glare. The tub seemed to lose its form. Within minutes the sun itself had lost half its light. It had become a dimly glowing ball behind a haze of cloud which thickened into an opaque, blue rack below. The precise edge of the ball melted into the haze. It slipped and slipped. She scanned the darkening water for a sign of the vanished boat. Black spots danced before her eyes. Her gaze returned to the sun, now a tiny arc which was soon to become a shapeless blob above the bank of cloud. Again she sought the boat. The sun had finally vanished. All that was left of it in the west was a feint red line which slowly faded into the overwhelming blue. The sea below was a flat and empty plain.

She remembered her binoculars. She focused with the left eye, then with the right. She swept the blankness in front of her. All was melting shadow. She could not be sure what, if anything, there was to see.

After a while she turned and made her way down to the slip to fetch his clothes. She stood on the high ground waving his pullover in the air at the houses across the Sound whose windows faced the sea. Darkness gathered in from the east. Shapes grew blurred, houses merged with rocks, and finally the solid hotel itself seemed to steal back off the rise into the shadowy moor behind. The lighthouse lantern had already begun to cast its beam against the advancing night.

She thought she might spend the night in the shelter of the lighthouse wall, then it occurred to her that the grassy punchbowl would be less exposed. The air had already cooled, a steady breeze came off the land with an edge that made her hunch her bare shoulders. She put on Joey's pullover over her dress and curled up under the standing slab whose surface now felt warmer than the grass. After a while she sat with her back against the slab, counting single stars advancing and retreating, piercing and fading, in the gloom above. It wasn't quite eleven; morning and light were still five hours away. The beam of the lighthouse swept the blankness above. One, two, three . . . she counted slowly until it came round again.

She closed her eyes, her ears now open to the faintest sound. She could hear rustling and nibbling, and the lisping of water over round stones. She kept thinking of

Joey, of his thin, pale legs and flat belly, of his triangular shoulder-blades protruding through hairless skin. He had said that she and he were close. 'Deep' would have been a better word. They stirred each other in their secret selves. Each knew how to wound and be wounded, yet show no knowledge of a wound given or received. The feelings one evoked in the other had nothing to do with affection or love. She could never look at his face without a sense of physical withdrawal, a shirking from something in herself as well as in him, and he never looked at her squarely, but always furtively as if looking were taboo. He was not a half-brother. He was a twin-brother who sensed her every change of mood and feeling, and that was something she could only resent. Now that he had gone, she had become aware of an alarming lightness in her head.

The short June night was endless. She kept dozing and dreaming and waking again. Her mother had gone shopping, and she and Joey were playing hide and seek in the house on their own. He had locked the front and back doors to keep Cookie out and to ensure that she could not escape. She knelt in the darkness of the cupboard under the stairs, holding her breath as a loose tread creaked above her. She heard a crackle, and, as she peeped through the cupboard door, she saw the curtains and the sofa in flames. Smoke was pouring across the room. Terrified, she called to Joey to open the front door. He had left the key in the kitchen, and the kitchen was now cut off. She panicked. She began to cry. He led her upstairs while behind them the fire was spreading from another room to the hall. The bedroom floor was already hot. Joey pulled her on to the bed and opened the window at the top. Through the smoke below, she could see neighbours gathering and Slash Gildea running with a ladder. Suddenly, his face was on the other side of the pane. Joey pushed her through and Slash handed her down to one of the men below. As she looked back up the ladder, Joey's frightened face vanished from the window.

'He's fallen through,' someone shouted.

Slash smashed the downstairs window with two blows of a spade. He clambered in through the thickening smoke while the other men kept pouring water from buckets through the broken panes. Slash seemed to be gone a week. Then she saw his blackened face and Joey unconscious in his arms. Smoke was rising from Joey's clothes and his face was a raw and shapeless layer of burns. She did not see him again for over a month. He was rushed to hospital, and when he came back one side of his face was red as newly killed beef.

She opened her eyes and looked up at the rim of the hollow. A small animal with a cunning head and cocked ears peered down at her. She felt stiff in her legs and arms. The lighthouse beam came round again, revealing an untidy clump of couch-grass. Her teeth began to chatter. She pulled on Joey's trousers and lay down at the foot of the slab again with her knees touching her chin. The cottage spewed flame and acrid smoke and Slash was calling to her to hurry up. She got a light aluminium ladder and climbed in through the dormer window. He was choking and coughing. She lifted him in her arms and carried him to safety as if he were only a teddy bear. He was lighter than Cookie and Joey and not much heavier than Bosco and Jack.

She climbed out of the hollow and wondered if she could discern a thinning of the darkness in the east. She waited in a state of indecision, not quite certain if what she saw contained a hint of blue. Gradually, the horizon rose into view. The hotel came forward out of shadow, the headland took shape before her eyes. Soon she could make out the white of other houses and remnants of the east-running road over the moor. She thought she had seen a movement on the slip. She looked through her binoculars but could see even less than with the naked eye. It was hard to be certain. The movement might have been a trick of the dawn light.

The sun came up, a half-hidden cutting wheel with an orange rim. It was morning, and a white boat had already cleared the sea-wall. The dark figure in the stern was not one of the lobster fishermen, because they rarely fished alone. He was making straight for the island, the high bows now obscuring the lower half of his torso.

She got out of Joey's trousers and stood on the high ground waving. The crossing took ages. Sometimes she felt that the boat, far from making progress, was being driven back by a hostile wind and tide. At last it entered the inlet. She recognised Slash, his face narrow and lean under his cap. With Joey's trousers over her arm, she ran down the slope to the slip below.

'Where's the boat?' he called.

It was typical of Slash. Anyone else would have asked where Joey had gone and if she herself were all right. She felt foolish and ridiculous. She hesitated before offering a reply.

'Joey took it out yesterday evening. I haven't seen him since. He left his clothes on that rock and said that he was going round the other side of the island for a swim.'

'Hop in. We'd better go and look for him.'

They puttered slowly round the island, weaving to avoid submerged rocks at which she peered over the gunwale with almost morbid fascination. Slash sat silently in the stern, confident, efficient, and perhaps somewhat critical of the inexplicable antics that had made such early demands on his day. As she glanced at him, she could understand why Gulban used to say, 'While Slash is in charge, nothing ever goes wrong except by act of God.'

'There's not a sign of either himself or the boat,' he said when they had come full circle.

'What do you think's happened to him?'

'Did he have a pair of oars?'

'I don't think so.'

'He may have run out of petrol. He could still be drifting. Last night the breeze was from the land.'

'We'll have to keep looking.'

'I'm nearly out of petrol myself. We'll go back and get help, it's the sensible thing to do.'

'I hope he's all right.'

He looked at her searchingly.

'It might teach him a lesson. Only fools don't respect the sea.'

She didn't reply. Now a full-scale search would begin. They might find the boat and possibly the body. There would be nodding and winking and shaking of heads. It seemed to her best if no trace of him were found. No boat. No body. A clean and absolute exit. And she would remain the repository of a truth which neither Bosco nor Cookie should be required to confront.

31

The search went on for two days. Local fishermen aided by an army helicopter and divers from Undercliff Sub-Aqua Club combed the seas to the north, south and west of the island. It was only the third week of the lobster season and the local fishermen could ill afford the time, but nevertheless she could not bring herself to intervene. On the first day a French trawler reported a drifting boat due west of the island with an outboard engine and an empty fuel tank. An intensive search of the area followed. No body was found.

The following week a funeral service was held. Cookie came down from Dublin and Father Bosco, clearly over-wrought, gave an emotional address which was embarrassing in its incoherence. His voice failed twice. He ended abruptly as if words had finally lost their function. A heavy silence bound the still air in the crowded church until one of the Mass servers coughed. At least there was no body for burial. It was a blessing to be spared the pathos of Father Bosco's graveside prayers.

The next four weeks submerged her in a sea of compulsions. She could not bring herself to think about anything except work in progress. She spent the mornings in the shop with one of Joey's assistants whom she had promoted to manager. In the afternoons she came back to the hotel to cram ten hours' work into five. She might have been wearing a bridle and blinkers; she could see only whatever was set before her nose. Though industrious and painstaking in all she did, she had lost joy and satisfaction in little things. Life was work, sleep, work, and she was a stolid beast of burden.

One morning towards the beginning of July she looked out of her bedroom window after breakfast, as a builders' merchant was unloading some posts and wire fencing under the supervision of Slash Gildea. The sight came as a revelation. She remembered saying to Slash a month before that the fence by the river needed mending, and he said at the time that mending would not be enough, that both posts and wire needed replacing. She had thought that this was his way of wriggling out of a job he did not relish. Now the sight of the heavy posts and wire bales made her realise that necessary work could get done without any act of will on her part. Life seemed possible once again. A mantle of depression had lifted from her mind.

She remembered that Father Bosco was coming to lunch. He came once a fortnight – with a thudding regularity that reminded her of a pile-driver.

'Just looking in,' he would announce on arrival. 'The days when I came and stayed *ad multam noctem*, as we say, are gone for ever.'

His visits had become a test of courage for them both. As he talked, he would sit sideways looking out of the window at an invisible interlocutor, and from time to time he would turn abruptly and look her straight in the eye for a split second before addressing again the other presence. He seemed to consider it his duty to talk to her. He was determined to show that nothing had changed, and the greater his determination, the more obvious it became that they could never again talk as one human being to another. The waters of innocence had been muddied long ago. Now, in addition, they had been poisoned for ever.

He came at noon in a black polo-neck sweater with his beribboned breviary under his arm. Normally, he wore a long soutane reaching to his shoes, which lent him dignity and detachment in equal proportions.

'You've changed into something more comfortable,' she said, as she greeted him.

'Less formal, I agree. I'm a new man today. I'm going out foreign. I've decided to become what the faithful call "a missionary father".'

'I've always felt that you would do something different.'

'I'm very excited. It's like getting a new vocation. And I owe it all to an old friend of Canon Sproule's who came to stay last week. He'd spent thirty-five years in Africa, serving a parish of fifty square miles on his own. He was full of stories; we could only listen. Stories about faith and privation and always being on the move with no luggage but a blanket for sleeping on. The people would give him food, whatever was available — bananas, elephant meat, monkey meat, sometimes a rat. Often the meat had been hanging from a tree in the heat for a month. When offered food which he knew to be tainted, he would bless it and eat it without a moment's hesitation. He was never ill. As he says himself, "The Lord looks after His own, and so He should." He worked himself to a shadow. He never experienced — never had time to experience — a single doubt. He overcame all sorts of obstacles, not least of them an obscure language with over a hundred irregular verbs and thirty-six tenses. Now he's old and a little frail. He's been sent back here to collect money for the missions, it's the only work he's fit for at his age. I've made up my mind to take his place in the field. I know I can never be tested here, not in the way I should like to be.'

'You're sure it's yourself you're testing? It isn't God?'

'Joey is speaking through you there,' he said with a sad shaking of the head.

'I hope you'll be happy in Africa. It's a long way away.'

He turned to the window to consider, then addressed his invisible interlocutor, 'Now you'll be left here alone. Perhaps that's how it should be. Perhaps that's how you would wish it to be.'

In the afternoon she went for a stroll along the river, where Slash was working at the new fence. He had already placed the heavy straining posts in position at each end and had anchored them with strut posts and stays. He was now digging holes for the intermediate posts which lay in a pile beside some bales of mesh and barbed wire. The mesh wire would keep sheep in without damaging their wool and two strands of barbed wire above it would make taller animals keep their distance.

'Will you do it yourself?' she asked.

'Most of it. I'll need the help of another man when I come to strain the wire.'

Lean and weathered, he kept digging without turning to look at her, his long arms and springy back expressing a resilient stoicism.

'You enjoy putting up fences?' She thought she might tease him a little.

He straightened his back and stood facing her with one foot on the lug of the spade. He was solid and independent; their relationship would always show wariness. As Cookie used to say, 'There is a pleasure in the pathless woods only because they're pathless.'

'Fences are two-sided,' he said without a smile. 'Good fences make good neighbours.'

She left him scraping wet clay off his spade with a stone. She walked back along the river bank, past the hollow where she and Cookie used to post letters to each other, never realising that Joey knew their secret. She had lost one world and gained another. What had been lost was murky, cramped and distorted. Could she fashion what she now held into something lucid, commodious and true?

On the bridge she paused to look down at a boulder with brown water swirling round it. The water clarified before her eyes until she could discern the clean, coarse gravel of the bottom. Father Bosco would go to Africa, Cookie to America. She would live here alone in a large house on a hill. The afternoon emptied. No cuckoo called from the holms. It was a time of silence after rasping noises.

In the lobby of the hotel she plucked a dead leaf off her only spider plant. Lovingly, she turned the pot to admire the sunlight on the green and white stems. She went into the lounge bar and got herself a glass of Perrier water with one cube of ice and a slice of lemon. She sat by a window and gazed up at the tweed curtains which had been chosen by her, and the old agricultural implements which had been collected by Jack. In the fields the warm afternoon stood still. The sheep that had been grazing upwards on the hill since morning in search of cooling breezes had become white stones set deep in ferns and heather. Slash was resting on his spade, concealed below the waist by river reeds. In the west the island had become a fading mirage that refused to vanish.

She sank into her chair, ensconced in an awareness of both changelessness and change. A new order had been established; *l'ancien régime* had found its end. *Le régime nouveau*, she had come to realise, would be no less a regime — an invisible chain that would bind her as surely as it would Slash Gildea and all those who would see her as the smith who forged it.

Now the twelvemonth that had gone seemed like a prolonged contemplation of death. Gulban had been a tyrant in life, and death had not overthrown his tyranny. He was present in everything she did — in getting up and going to bed, in plans made and decisions taken — and his presence seemed as enduring as the unspectacular progress of the seasons. Summer. Autumn. Winter. Gulban. Gulban. Gulban. A narrowing road that lost itself in the middle of nowhere. She must traverse that road with something like Slash Gildea's resilient stoicism. Perhaps the best that was open to her was to live her life so that no one could say:

'The truth is in abeyance because of Pauline.'